SING

For Tom

3

SING

1

It was morning. In the cul-de-sac of detached houses, at the top of the lane, Alistair and Helen dozed lying back to back, each aware of the other's proximity and trying not to touch. Alistair groaned inwardly and turned over.

'What's the matter?' asked Helen. His groan had not been silent at all.

'Nothing.' He reached down and scratched himself. She got up and went across the room to select a pair of big knickers from her drawer. He groaned again and closed his eyes. Once he would have watched her putting on pretty lingerie, well aware of his eyes on her, and pretending not to notice. He listened to the ritual sounds of morning. The loo flushing, the shower humming, taps running, Helen came back into the bedroom. He pretended to be asleep again until he heard her footsteps going down the stairs.

In the kitchen, guiltily eating a second piece of toast, Helen decided she may as well finish off the coffee as well. Alistair seldom wanted anything first thing.

She could hear that he had come down and gone to the piano. He tried to fit in some practice every day. She pictured his long fingers moving over the keys, remembering how sensuous she had found that in those early years before the chemistry between them had faded.

Nowadays she got more satisfaction from lining up a row of jars of freshly made bramble jelly or strawberry jam. She smiled to herself recalling the intense pleasure she always got from stirring the enormous amount of sparkling white sugar required into a pan of simmering crimson fruit – the colours merging and melting together. Did that make her an earth mother in tune with the rhythm of the seasons, or a sad, boring housewife?

This could be a year of new beginnings. Yes, they'd grown apart a bit. But at least they were standing shoulder to shoulder in their respective ruts. They would grow old together, replacing passion with contentment. Passion was over-rated anyway, Sex had become just another household chore. There were plenty of women at school and in his dratted choir to tell him how wonderful he was and keep his ego boosted. She tied an apron round her still slim waist and began to wash up the things she didn't trust to the dishwasher.

Now, where had she hidden her new toy? Alistair would have a fit if he knew how much it had cost. How clever to be able to measure the level of bacteria on your work surfaces. She wiped over the worktops with her cleaning spray and passed the little device over them until it beeped and gave her an acceptable reading. That'll do. Satisfied, she returned it to its hiding place.

Thanks Mum and Dad; without your money, we'd never have been able to sell that awful damp flat in Bristol and buy this lovely, new house. No spiders, no mice, no dust or cracks spreading across the ceiling. No damp penetrating the old walls, softening the plaster and giving off that horrid fungal aroma.

She was glad now they hadn't been able to have children. That nightmare attempt at fertility treatment was long ago. The advice was to wait and hope, against the odds. Now that they were well into their forties she could accept the fact there would never be a family. Anyway, she'd never been one to peer into prams, cluck and coo over babies or, heaven forbid, ask to feel somebody's pregnant stomach. People had suggested she got a dog or a cat instead, but cats had fleas and she had no intention of running round after a dog, collecting turds in a plastic bag.

Maybe she was smug but, with Alistair settled at South Heath School, life was sweet enough.

The washing up completed, work surfaces rendered pristine and germ-free, and with expensive hand cream smoothed into her hands, she took out her feather duster to do a whole-house sweep for any cobwebs that might have had the temerity to appear overnight.

2

Diana stood in the doorway of the church hall. Faces turned towards her. The overhead lights were bright and harsh and she felt the judgement of sixty pairs of eyes.

Suddenly that cookery class felt like a more attractive proposition. She scanned the rows of chairs. Where should she sit?

A balding man in a blue jumper rose to his feet and approached her. He had a nice face.

'New soprano? Hi, come this way. I'll find you a seat.'

'Thank you.'

He led her past the altos and stopped by a woman in her fifties with wayward hair. There was an empty seat beside her.

'This is Victoria. She'll look after you.'

Diana sat down and looked around. People were laughing and chatting and fiddling with sheets of music. A tall man peeled himself away from a group at the front. He approached her with his hand out.

'Hello, I'm Alistair. I'm glad you could make it. Caroline said you sounded a bit unsure. I wondered if you'd turn up.'

His hand was firm and dry and held onto hers a little longer than strictly necessary. He looked directly into her eyes and smiled. It was infectious - she felt herself blushing as she smiled back up at him.

'Victoria will sort you out some music. If you'll excuse me…'

Her eyes followed him as he went over to the young pianist, while shrugging off the brown leather flying jacket than had seen better days. Reacting to something the pianist said, he smiled broadly, pushing back his slightly over-long, curly black hair.

He laughed with his eyes, she liked that. Perhaps she had made the right decision. She crossed her legs and relaxed a little.

Victoria stood up and went to a table heaped with music, then returned to her side with her hands full. Her slightly bohemian clothes set her apart from the others and Diana admired the look. It suited her. There was a suggestion of Guerlain's Mitsouko in the air.

'Here's enough to be going on with. If there's any missing, you can share mine.'

Diana tried to smile. What was she doing here? She looked around to see if there was anyone else who looked as though they might be in their early thirties like her. She didn't want to be in a choir full of oldies. There were quite a few youngish women she could see and she settled back in her chair reassured.

She'd seen the poster for the choir's next concert in the newsagent's window and had asked the assistant inside if she'd ever heard them sing. She hadn't, but she'd heard they were quite good. Pointing across the shop, she'd said,

'You should talk to Caroline, over there by the magazines. She sings with them.'

A small woman in an expensive coat, hearing her name, had come across. 'Hello. Were you asking about the choir?'

When she heard that Diana was new to the area, the woman suggested she came along to the next practice.

'Tuesday nights at the Church Hall, 7.30. Have a couple of taster sessions and see how you go. No auditions. We're very informal. Have you done any singing before?'

Diana had shaken her head. She had, but she wasn't about to tell this woman about it.

'Our next concert is only a few weeks away. If you decide to join us, I'll get you a practice CD so that you'll be able to catch up.'

'That's very kind of you.'

Alistair stood before them, waiting for the buzz of conversation to die down, and looked over the sea of faces. Well aware of those who watched and listened and tried to please, the easy ones; he frowned in mock disapproval at the few who chattered and giggled like school children in the back row of the class.

He entertained them with anecdotes whilst also expecting their undivided attention and effort. Mostly, he felt, he got it. There was always the occasional complainer or one who felt obliged to put him right on his interpretation of the score, but, generally, they were a good crowd and he was as fond of them as they were of him.

'Quiet everyone please. Jonathan – a C major chord, if you would be so kind.'

That new girl sitting next to Victoria is quite a looker. He caught Jonathan's eye. He grinned at Alistair and smoothly gave them the notes to begin the warm up of arpeggios and scales to prepare their voices for two hours hard work.

'I can tell you're not feeling confident, but we've still got three weeks till the Christmas concerts. I've had to include these new carols to make sure the programme is balanced. I know a couple of them are extremely challenging with some dissonant harmonies and tricky timings. Tonight we're going to tighten up on entrances and word endings. We'll start with the Rutter.'

Whether it was the beauteous creature sitting right in front of him or simply the moon being in the seventh house, Alistair's eyes flashed mischievously as he called, 'Stop, stop! That's not right. The tenors are grovelling in the altos' passages. You need to assert yourselves, gentlemen. The last thing they want is to be exposed. Isn't that right, altos?'

The altos giggled obediently. He saw that Victoria was trying to hide a smile and hoped the innuendo would slip unnoticed past those of his more strait-laced singers. That new soprano has a strong voice as well as beauty. Good. A bit of eye candy will help with the task ahead.

3

It was the night of the concert. Victoria sat at her dressing table, brushing her hair and pinning it up. She'd heard that the tickets had not been selling well. Reflected in the mirror behind her, the dreaded black dress was hanging ready and she recalled a conversation she'd had with her brother, James. He'd joined a choir in Salisbury after his wife died, and had brought Victoria's two nephews up to South Heath to one of her concerts. Nathan and Luke had fidgeted throughout, but politely said they'd enjoyed it.

James had laughed at the formality of the black dresses and told her his choir dressed in white tops and denims for performances. Now, that was amusing; the thought of the good ladies of South Heath in denim.

It was times like this, when she needed reassurance and moral support, that she really missed Robin. Her husband had become adept at calming her worries.

She heard his voice. 'Don't whittle, darling, just look after number one. Have a good sing and forget about the politics.'

Too young to be a widow in her mid-fifties, she had, in her darkest moments, wished she'd been with him in that car crash that had taken him away from her. She glanced across at his photo on her bedside table. Would she ever get used to living alone? It was more than two years ago and she still talked to him in her head, missed him sitting opposite her at the table and longed to feel him pulling her close in bed. But it could have been worse. At least she had plenty of things to keep her busy – fingers in lots of pies as he would have said. Not least this choir. It had been a godsend in so many ways.

Then the flashback came. Insidiously it pushed aside all thought of the imminent concert. It occurred less frequently these days but she had learnt from experience that she should just go with the flow, let the scenario play through the horror of that night, acknowledge her loss, then focus on the present.

It was almost midnight. The rain was making so much noise on the windows that Victoria could barely hear the radio. She reached over and turned it off. She sat for a minute twisting her fingers together. The air was hot and humid. Perhaps she should open a window. No, she didn't want flying things to come in, or spiders. She could sit under the porch outside the back door for a bit, cool off, but then the midges would find her.

Where on earth was he? He'd never been so late before, certainly not without phoning. The monthly meeting of classic car enthusiasts never went on after the landlord had called time. Should she call the Red Lion, see if he was still there? No, he'd be the butt of their jokes for weeks if they thought his wife was checking up on him. Surely he'd have rung if there was a problem? She should go to bed. He'd be home soon enough.

She got to her feet and began the nightly rituals; turning off the lamps, checking that the back door was locked, and taking the milk bottles out. Should she cancel the milkman? She could buy her milk much cheaper at the supermarket, but he was a nice man and it was one less thing to think about. The appearance of milk bottles on her step was something to be relied on and, besides, she quite liked hearing the sound of his lorry at four in the morning, the hurry of footsteps and the clinking of bottles as she lay unsleeping but warm and cosy in her bed. She left the hall lamp, which Robin would need when he came in.

She was at the foot of the stairs when the knock came on the front door.

She froze. Robin wouldn't knock. Who was it? She forced her unwilling feet to take her to the door.

Two figures, illuminated by the orange light of the street lamp, stood awkwardly on her doorstep.

'Victoria Dunn?'

She nodded, fear flooding through her. The police. They stood, stiff in their uniforms. A man and a woman.

'Can we come in?' She moved aside. They turned off the radios attached to their lapels.

The young man ducked his head as he came through the door. He was very tall. The woman was short and chubby. Didn't police have to be able to chase after criminals? This woman didn't look as if she could run far. Victoria was conscious of her thoughts, putting off the moment when they would have to say why they had come.

The policeman looked awkward. Did he really need all that stuff strapped round his waist? This was like something off the television. She held her breath, waiting for them to say something. Don't be silly. It could be just something small, a minor accident perhaps?

He spoke. 'Mrs Victoria Dunn?'

She nodded.

'I'm Constable Moore and this is WPC Porter. Is there somewhere we can go to sit down?'

Victoria turned and led the way into the sitting room, switching the lights back on, and gestured to the sofa while she sank down onto her armchair. Aware her breath was coming in short sharp gasps, she gripped the arms of the chair and swallowed hard.

'I'm sorry to have to bring you some bad news Mrs Dunn. Your husband, Robin, has been involved in a road accident. He died while paramedics were trying to revive him.'

The world stopped turning.

'What? No, no, no...'

There was silence.

The WPC got up and came over to her. She knelt with some difficulty down on the carpet and took Victoria's hand. There were tears in her eyes. Victoria thought she should be the one who was crying. She looked down at the policewoman's hand.

The nails were bitten down to the quick.

The woman apologised. 'I'm sorry. This is the first time I've had to do this. Can I make you some tea?'

'No, thank you.' But the woman got up and went into the kitchen anyway. Victoria followed her and stood in the door way. 'The tea bags are in that cupboard.'

'It's ok. You go back and sit down. I'll find what I need. Do you take sugar?'

Victoria shook her head and went back into the sitting room.

He asked if they could call someone for her. She cast round in her mind.

'I suppose you could call Rachel, but she's probably in bed by now.' She pictured Rachel, lying next to Marcus, asleep with her mouth open. She probably wouldn't hear the phone ringing anyway.

'There's James, my brother, but he lives in Salisbury....'

'We'll call them both.'

'What happened? He's such a careful driver...'

The constable, who'd looked as though he would rather be anywhere in the world rather than her sitting room at this moment, stumbled over the details of the crash, mindful maybe how much was appropriate to tell her at this juncture.

'The paramedics said death was relatively instant. He didn't suffer. It's too early to be sure but it looks as if the lorry may have been on the wrong side of the road.'

Rigid in her chair, Victoria pitied him both for being the bearer of such tragic news and for the terrible acne which covered his face. Couldn't it be treated with antibiotics nowadays? Why was she thinking about acne? Robin was dead. Dead? She looked wildly about her. He couldn't be dead – there was his photo on the piano. She could hear the WPC talking on her phone in the hall. Then she came in with a mug of tea.

'Your friend is on her way. We'll stay until she gets here.'

The next day, when James arrived, the police suggested he

went to identify the body.

'It's not necessary for you to go Madam,' they said. But she insisted. I want to say goodbye, she'd said.

It was every bit as dreadful as she'd feared. The cold body on the metal table wasn't the man she'd adored, his spirit had flown, but it was irrefutable proof she would never see him again.

Robin had been the only man to say that he loved her. He was kind and funny, wise and imaginative. He'd kept her safe and indulged her attempts to be different. Now he was gone.

Her over- strict, controlling parents had barely tolerated their arty, flamboyant daughter, making it clear she was not the son they had hoped for.

On the day she married Robin, her mother had written in her diary,

'Now I lay my burden down.'

Victoria had found it after her mother's death. She hadn't been surprised. It was true.

But Robin had understood her little idiosyncrasies and loved her for them.

The clock chimed seven. It broke the memory. She swallowed and realised she should get a move on. She looked down at her hand. She was holding a lipstick. Oh yes. The bright red one or the deep rose pink? Robin would have known. Or would he have taken the easy way out and told her she looked lovely in either? She was going to be late. She'd need an umbrella and a voluminous mac. The rain poured down as she hurried along to the hall. Where was everyone? The streets were deserted.

She joined the rest of the choir, waiting in a back room, all clutching music folders and bottles of water. The men, gathered at one end, were trussed up in dinner jackets and bow ties, and she joined the ladies at the other, looking around to see who had splashed out on something new. There was a lot of black lace this year, some beaded jackets and several chiffon sleeved blouses – all the better to cover ageing arms. Her own pièce de resistance was a glittering paste diamond necklace and long dangling earrings she had spotted on a market stall in the summer.

Admiring a brave attempt to show individuality with a pair of racy pink four inch heels, she went over to congratulate their wearer. There too was Diana. Glowing in a classic, figure hugging gown, the girl smiled at her.

'Hi Victoria. So this is it - my first concert. I'm really nervous. I'm so glad I'm sitting next to you.'

'You'll be fine. I wish I could wear a dress like that.' She looked at Diana's breasts, firm and lightly tanned and she wished she were young again.

Diana looked down at her cleavage.

'You don't think it's a bit too low cut? I got it from that second hand dress shop in the village. Your necklace is wonderful.'

'I know. It was a real find.'

Diana shivered. 'Why is it so cold in here? My arms are covered with goose bumps.'

'Antiquated heating system that doesn't work. It'll be hot out there though, under the lights.'

Victoria stifled a grin at one brave soul striding round in baggy black trousers and a black jacket, which made her look like a chimney sweep searching for her brushes. She turned to another friend standing beside her. 'I love those purple streaks, your hair looks amazing.'

Where were her throat sweets? She passed them around just as Alistair called them to get into their lines, ready to run through a few vocal exercises to warm up their voices. He didn't seem nervous, straightening his bow tie, pulling on his cuffs and dishing out encouraging smiles.

What was the worst that could happen? They could fail to come in together at the beginning of a song; they could lose the timing so that all four parts clashed horribly against each other; the sopranos might screech on a high note.....she decided to think about something else, reminding herself that, as often as not, no-one noticed when mistakes were made. The signal came to file out into the big hall and take their seats.

She relaxed. The place was full. It was going to be alright.

While Alistair, now in full performance mode, welcomed the audience with his usual suave bonhomie and charm, Victoria searched the faces in the audience to spot friends and neighbours. There were two small children on the front row, waving at their mother in the altos. She hoped they would manage to stay awake for the duration. No sign of Alistair's wife – as usual.

Alistair smiled confidently at them and raised his arms. They began with Ding Dong Merrily on High, sung with gusto. Gusto was something the choir knew they did well. Victoria experienced the adrenaline surge as she sang out, the sound of sixty voices resounding around the hall, thrilling her as always.

The next carol, Elgar's subdued piece, The Snow, although sweetly sung, highlighted her most frequent, but unvoiced, criticism of their abilities. Controlled, soft singing, far more difficult to do, was, as yet, completely beyond them. As one of the tenors had muttered to his neighbour, 'Never mind bel canto, our motto should be can belto!'

They acquitted themselves admirably, however, on the fiendishly difficult, 'A Babe is Born' by William Mathias with its clashing harmonies, a challenge, Alistair had assured them, for any amateur choir.

Solos were sung, poems were read and the audience joined in enthusiastically with the singing of O Come All Ye Faithful and Hark the Herald Angels Sing. All too soon, it was over. The hall emptied in a flurry of scarves, gloves and woolly hats, together with cries of Happy Christmas, into the cold, wet December night.

'Are you coming to the pub, Victoria?'

'No. I don't think so. Not tonight.'

She walked home alone. It was still raining. The euphoria evaporated and weariness crept into her bones. She thought about the conversations she'd overheard in the interval. Someone was complaining about one of the soloists and another thought that the programme had been predictable and unimaginative. Was it worth the petty irritations, the interminable politics and the conflict of egos? Perhaps it was time she called it a day and let the Facebookers and the control freaks get on with it.

When she got in she made herself a bedtime cocoa in her Elvis mug and changed out of her concert clothes into a comfortable dressing gown. Towelling her hair dry, she hummed the tune of Rutter's Angel Carol, one of her favourites. Her cat wound its way around her legs and she cursed it. Go away. Evil feline.

Tonight, as she climbed the stairs, cocoa in hand, she thought she might commiserate with Alistair on the sopranos' increasing tendency to sing flat? He was clearly aware of it, but didn't seem to be doing anything about it. Perhaps if others voiced their concerns he might do something. Quite what he could do, she didn't know; that was his problem, that's what they paid him for.

She was very fond of Alistair. He'd been so kind in so many practical ways since Robin's death. It was Alistair who knocked on her door one rainy night holding a bedraggled ball of mewing fluff. 'Can you give this little creature a home?'

And a couple of months later when the kitten disappeared, he designed and printed some posters with an appealing photograph of it under the word MISSING, and helped her tie them on lampposts around the village. Of course, she was to curse his kindness when the kitten was returned to her and grew up to be a killing machine, but the blame for that could hardly be laid at his door.

The downside of being in the choir was that on singing nights, sleep was a long time coming. Her head rang with music; earworms insinuated their tunes and lyrics into her unwillingly receptive brain. Most choir members went on to the local pub after practices and concerts, but often Victoria just wanted to get back to her fireside. Should she have invited Diana back for a glass of wine and a post mortem? She had seemed to be a lonely soul and, oddly familiar somehow.

Lying sleepless, she suddenly gasped, remembering a darkened room, some months ago, heavy with the scent of candles and the sound of singing whales. She had indeed met Diana before.

The occasion stuck in her mind because while treating herself to a relaxing, hot stones massage after a particularly difficult term, she had found herself weeping silently, lying face down on the bed. Was it because she was paying someone to touch her? The sadness was replaced by the thought that it was really not dissimilar to men visiting prostitutes, and she recognised her reliance on self-justification. In the end, deciding that a good massage was like glorious sex but without the bodily fluids, she tipped the pretty girl generously before she left.

Oh, the embarrassment. Diana had massaged her naked body.

The grandfather clock in the hall struck midnight. She sniffed, thinking it kept her awake at night more than the past lover she'd bought it from ever did. Initially it stood resplendent in her sitting room. But when the relationship soured and died, the clock seemed to be watching her, so she dragged it out into the hall.

After two hours and not yet a wink of sleep, she got up and went downstairs to make a cup of tea, taking care to scan the kitchen floor first for little corpses – trophies of the murderous cat's night out hunting. To tread on the latest gift of a headless blue tit or a half-eaten field mouse in her bare feet was a nightly dread.

Tea, coupled with a chapter or two of her current library book, was often enough to still the chatter in her head and carry her off into the arms of Morpheus.

4

The telephone rang. Alistair, shaving in front of the bathroom mirror, waited for Helen to answer it.

'It's for you. Sam - from the Cathedral.'

'Coming.' The foam on his face transferred itself onto the receiver.

'Ah, Alistair. How are you, young man? Is that little choir of yours still in business?'

Supercilious git.

'Yes, indeed it is Sam.'

'Would you like to come and do a short lunchtime concert here in the cathedral in a couple of months' time? You won't have much of an audience, although it being a free concert should bring in a few ne'er-do-wells off the street.'

Alistair fought to remain civil.

Great. Thanks Sam, we'd love to. It'll be good experience for them.'

The following week Alistair walked with his long, easy stride down to the church hall, quietly confident that the new music he had chosen for the Easter concert would meet with everyone's approval. OK - maybe not everyone's. There was always someone who declared they hated the new stuff. Sometimes the odd rebel would leave for the duration of that programme. Their loss, he always felt.

He'd found a solo that would suit that pretty new soprano down to the ground, if her voice was up to it. He looked forward to finding out. He reached his destination, put the new music on his stand and looked around.

There was Keith moving towards his usual place in the back row of the bass section, his pink cashmere jumper clashing with his ruddy cheeks. Initially, he had confided in Alistair his concern as to whether it was quite fitting, as the Head of South Heath School, to sing in the village choir. Alistair suspected that Keith's wish to join was partly because he enjoyed hearing the sound of his fine bass voice, and partly because it afforded him an uninterrupted view of forty or so personable women. He watched as Keith exchanged kisses around the room, ostensibly to celebrate the New Year, and then settled in his seat, winking at his favourites across the hall.

It was warm in there and Alistair, removed his jumper, and drew the attention of various female members of the choir. Aware of their appreciation of his tall, rangy figure, he smiled.

'Welcome back, everyone. I trust you are all rested and ready to go again. We have the spring concert coming up next, and I'm looking at the possibility of arranging a choir trip in the summer. I've also been asked if we could do a short concert in the cathedral. I'll tell you more about that when I've had a chat with the committee. So, lots to do. Let's have a look at this new music.'

Only two bars into the first song, he waved them to stop. The usual suspects, their heads buried in their music rather than watching him, sang on - oblivious to the fact everyone else was silent.

'Basses, you came in bang on time and your dynamics were just right - pity about the notes.'

He saw the basses looked embarrassed and felt sorry for them. Three of their strongest singers were missing tonight, no wonder they were struggling.

'Don't worry. Some of these new pieces are tricky. You need to watch me. We've got plenty of time to get them right.'

He tried not to show his irritation. They didn't come to be chastised.

After forty minutes of note bashing, he decided to be kind to them.

'You all know this one. It's a bit corny but a real crowd pleaser.'

'You Raise Me Up' hit the spot as predicted. The smiles

around him proved that.

'There's a wonderful key change coming up. I like a key change.'

Energised, he strode up and down, stopping them all every so often to go over a few bars that were less than accurate. He aimed at perfection, but all too often had to content himself with good enough.

Back at home after the practice, the rain now lashing at the windows outside, Victoria settled herself down in front of the still warm ashes of the fire. She was marking her music with scrawled messages to herself, such as 'breathe' and 'watch', and drawing circles round the forte and pianissimo marks, when the doorbell rang.

Victoria tutted and said to the cat, who lifted her head with interest, 'Who's that at this time of night?'

She opened the door to a woman standing on the doorstep, red eyed and visibly shaking, her hair plastered to her skull and mascara running down her cheeks in sooty rivulets.

'Rachel! Quick, come in out of the rain. Here, give me your coat.'

Rachel took off her mac and wiped her face dry with the back of her sleeve.

'I'll get you a towel for your hair.'

What on earth could have brought Rachel to her door so late at night and in such filthy weather?

Victoria hadn't seen her for several years. She always felt guilty that after Rachel and Marcus moved away from South Heath, the relationship had dwindled to Christmas and birthday cards and suggestions that they meet up for lunch which somehow never came to fruition.

'Oh God, I'm so glad you're in. I've just left Marcus. I've been driving around in the rain wondering where to go.'

'You're shaking. Come into the warm.' Victoria mentally reviewed the state of the spare bedroom; she had a feeling it might be needed. She watched as Rachel vigorously rubbed her hair dry and dragged a comb through it.

She said, 'That's better. You don't look so much like a sea lion now. I wish I had straight hair like yours. Rain and curls don't create a good look at all.'

Rachel pulled a face. 'I hate my hair. I always wanted hair like yours, don't you remember?'

'Yes. Your Mum told me that all people with straight hair wanted curls and vice versa, and I should stop wanting something I couldn't have'

Rachel smiled. 'She would do. It's bizarre, I really wish she was here right now.'

Victoria nodded. She knew that it didn't matter how old you were; whether you had a good relationship with your mother or not, every woman, at some point in her life, finds herself remembering a mother's arms around her, keeping her safe and promising to make everything better. She guided Rachel to a chair and, placing a box of tissues on her lap, observed mildly, 'I hate to sour the imagined moment of maternal tenderness, but you know that your mother would have briskly told you to pull yourself together, go back to your husband and do whatever it took to keep your marriage together.'

Rachel gave a watery smile. She took a tissue from the box and blew her nose. 'You're so right. That's exactly what she'd have said. I'm sorry you've drawn the short straw.'

She accepted Victoria's offer of a drink, and, sitting on the edge of her chair, took gulps from her glass with trembling hands.

'It all started months ago. Marcus was in the bath and I picked up his phone to find the photos he took when we went to London. I thought if I sent them to my phone I'd be able to show them to friends. There was a photo of a woman I didn't recognise. As I scrolled through there were more. Then there were selfies of them, their arms round each other.' She drained her glass.

'God, I wish still smoked. I didn't know what to do. I didn't dare say anything – you know what he can be like when he's angry.'

Victoria nodded, remembering only too well. Marcus was a big man with a big temper.

'So I started to keep tabs on him. If he said he was going to a police 'do', I checked that there really was one. I know one or two WPCs, so I'd ask if he'd been there. That sort of thing. At home the atmosphere was frosty to say the least, but he never said anything. Our sex life was almost non-existent – but I was grateful for that.' She looked anxiously at Victoria whose face was unreadable.

'Then he said he thought we should split up. He said there wasn't anyone else, he just didn't want to be married to me any longer, and that he'd had felt like that for a long time.'

Victoria had to ask. 'Did you believe him about there not being anyone else?'

'No.'

Victoria got up and poked the fire vigorously. Did she want to hear anymore? But Rachel clearly hadn't finished.

'I begged him to come to Relate with me. I thought our marriage was worth saving. The therapist we went to was awful. The insinuation was that had I fulfilled my role in bed more enthusiastically, none of this would be happening. Would you believe it?'

Victoria shook her head, 'I've always thought that couples counselling can unearth things which are best forgotten or left unsaid. Unintentionally of course, but I have known it make fragile situations much worse.'

Rachel nodded. She picked up her glass, forgetting that it was empty, pulled a face and continued,

'Well tonight he came home with a fistful of estate agents leaflets and said he'd had enough and he was looking for another property for one of us – him or me, he didn't mind. I just lost it and made a complete exhibition of myself. I ended up running out of the room and getting in the car. I couldn't bear to be in the house with him any longer.'

She paused for breath. Victoria felt she should fill the silence.

'Oh dear. I'm so sorry. No, no more wine. It won't help.'

They talked until the clock struck midnight. By then Victoria knew more about Rachel's marriage than she would have wished. Privately she felt that had Rachel confronted Marcus right at the start of it all, rather than spending the last few months playing private detective and building up a mountain of suspicion and resentment, the marriage might have stood more of a chance. But there was little point saying that now.

'You'd better stay here tonight. The bed's made up in the spare bedroom and you're in no fit state to drive home. Do you want me to ring him to tell him where you are?'

Rachel shook her head violently. 'No. He wouldn't care anyway.'

Victoria prised the empty glass out of Rachel's hand, gave her the box of tissues and showed her up the narrow stairs to her room.

'Try to sleep. See how you feel in the morning.'

'Good morning. What sort of night did you have? ' Victoria was grilling bacon. A fortifying breakfast would do them both good.

'Awful.' Rachel was ashen. She came and sat at the table, her diminutive frame swamped by Victoria's second best dressing gown.

'Poor love. What do you want to do? You know you're welcome to stay here for a bit, if you think that would be the right thing.'

'Victoria, I don't know what I should do. I suppose I shall have to go back at some point. If I could just stay a few days…'

'You can stay as long as you like.'

Rachel smiled with relief.

'Thank you. I'll try not to get in your way. There's more to the story, obviously, but this feels like the end of the road. At the moment, if I go back, it will be to pack my bags and find a solicitor. It's good to be back in South Heath. I feel safe here. Has the village changed much?'

'Not hugely. The Hall has been turned into a school and that's where I work. I'm the Head's secretary now. There's a supermarket, that'll be new to you. The duck pond's still there - with the great-grandchildren of the ducks you used to feed. A couple of the pubs have become pretentious eateries where you can eat overpriced, miniscule mouthfuls off bits of slate, but the rest of them are just the same; the druggy one, the Sky Sports one and the Royal Oak, aka God's waiting room.'

'The one where they go to escape their wives and talk politics.'

'That's right. It's not the prettiest village in Somerset as you know. It has all the right features but assembled in the wrong order somehow. Having said that I'm still very happy here.'

'I bet the Mendip News hasn't changed.'

Victoria fetched her coat. 'Well, it's still complaining about the noise of the planes coming in over the village to Bristol airport and the amount of dog poo on the streets, but the current beef is all the new housing developments being proposed.'

She dropped her purse into her shopping bag and added, 'What always amuses me is that the most vociferous folk who don't want any more houses, themselves live in places built in the last forty or fifty years. Do you want to come with me? I need some milk and stamps.'

'Yes, it'll be good to have a wander. Just give me a couple of minutes to get dressed, I don't want to alarm the locals just yet. By the way, the cat seems to have taken up residence on my bed. Is that allowed?'

'It most certainly isn't. Throw it off and shut the door.'

'Poor cat. Why are you so horrid to it?'

'You just wait. As soon as the weather gets warmer the carnage will start and there'll be a steady supply of eviscerated, bleeding carcasses under the kitchen table - robins, blackbirds, frogs, toads and mice.'

'Ugh!'

'Exactly.

26

5

The weeks went by, Victoria began to worry that her lodger showed no signs of moving on. She suggested Rachel joined the choir. A new interest might help her friend to get back on her dragon.

'However hard it is to drag myself away from the fireside, I always come home feeling happier than when I left. Singing is the best therapy there is. It takes you to another place and you forget all the things on your mind. Give it a try.'

Rachel pulled a face. 'They told me at school I was tone deaf.'

'That's rubbish. I've heard you singing along to the radio. It's not pretty, but you aren't tone deaf.'

Rachel swiped at her with the tea towel in her hand.

'I'll try. Anything's better than squinting at your tiny television.'

'That's better. Show some spirit. You used to be such a fiery little woman. I was quite frightened of you way back.'

'I don't believe you. I looked up to you like an older sister.'

Victoria also found Rachel some part time work in a local bookshop. The news of her return to the village flew round and there was a lot of sympathy for her, especially from those who remembered Marcus.

At Rachel's first practice, Victoria took charge again. She spotted her friend making for the back row of the sopranos, where there was an empty seat right in the corner.

'Rachel no, not there.'

Rachel blushed and shuffled along the row to where Victoria was pointing.

After the practice, Victoria told her, 'It's no good you sitting back there. That lot sing like mice. You'll find sitting next to someone strong like Caroline will help you no end.'

Rachel nodded. 'I hate to admit it but you're right this time. Sitting next to someone who came in confidently and bang on the note made it much easier.'

Victoria dug deep in her wardrobe to check that the black dress she needed for the concert was clean. She called out to Rachel.

'What are you wearing on Saturday?'

'I've got my funeral dress. I'll put it on and you can see what you think.'

She accessorised it with a chunky ethnic necklace of red, blue and gold beads and went into Victoria's room.

'I like the necklace. Pity about the dress.'

'Oh for goodness sake. I'm fed up with you banging on about the black dresses. I think we'd look a right rag-bag of singers if we all wore what we liked. Black is smart and classy and suits most people.'

Victoria permitted herself a small smile. It was the first time Rachel had dared challenge her and she saw it as a sign her friend was getting her confidence back.

But Rachel hadn't finished.

'Sometimes, Victoria, you can be very judgemental.'

Victoria raised her eyebrows. Maybe it really was time Rachel found her own place to live.

On the night of the concert the two of them made their way up to the large Victorian hall, with its impressive hammer beam ceiling. The dust lay thickly on the huge oak beams and, when disturbed by a passing draught, would float down like snow on the unsuspecting heads beneath.

The audience shuffled into their seats, greeting friends and neighbours, some clutching glasses of wine from the bar to fortify themselves through what was to come. The hum of conversation subsided as the choir filed onto the stage.

Finally Alistair made his way onto his podium to polite

applause.

He closed his eyes momentarily. Victoria wondered if he could feel the heat and the tension from the choir as they waited for his signal. He raised his arms. Sixty deep breaths were taken.

The tenors came in, right on Alistair's cue, pure and sweet and absolutely in tune. Victoria relaxed a little. It was going to be fine.

The programme was built around songs from the musicals. Crowd pleasers, for those of a certain age - My Fair Lady, South Pacific and Oklahoma and, more up to date, Wicked and Les Miserables,

Alistair had arranged for a talented local child to play the flute and two elderly basses to reprise their party piece of Flanders and Swann favourites. He'd also persuaded Diana to sing 'Somewhere' from West Side story, but she was clearly consumed by nerves and struggled to stay in tune. Victoria felt embarrassed for her.

It was all over very quickly, and as the choir filed off the stage, Victoria enjoyed the usual surge of wellbeing that came at the end of a performance, regardless of how successfully - or not – it had been received.

As she put on her coat, she reflected that it was what brought them together to practise week after week; that special sensation, along with the feeling of union and complicity, when sixty voices harmonised and rose and fell in crescendo and diminuendo. Rapturous applause was welcome, but it wasn't essential. There was so much to get right – diction, timing, word endings, length of notes, accuracy of pitch – yet, when it worked, the resultant feeling was really good. It was lovely to go out on a Tuesday night and do something which required complete concentration and wasn't about work or family. They were a bunch of disparate souls, experiencing togetherness for a brief couple of hours before returning to everyday life.

'I wonder,' she said to Rachel, 'if it's the same thing as the high some people say they get from exercise?'

'Only sex ever did that for me,' smirked Rachel. 'I remember one boyfriend, long before I met Marcus, who ....'

'Shut up. I don't want to know. I do know what you mean, but I was trying to be a bit more cerebral here. It only ever happens in a piece one knows terribly well, that would tie in with the exercise, wouldn't it - when you are doing something on automatic pilot, leaving a part of your brain to run free. Volume helps too.'

Rachel nodded. 'We are told to be quiet practically from birth, so being encouraged to make a great noise is wonderfully liberating.'

In the pub after the concert, Keith, first to the bar, sat nursing his pint. Minutes later, more of the choir piled in and colonised the big table by the window. He smiled as Victoria came across to him and raised his glass in salute.

The girl behind the bar said, 'Hello Victoria, what's it to be; your usual?'

She handed over a large red wine.

'Are you going to spoil yourself with a bag of crisps tonight?'

'Do you know, I do believe I am. Salt and vinegar please.'

The girl returned with the crisps. 'I love your jacket. Is it new?'

Victoria smiled. 'Yes and no. I bought it yesterday from a vintage clothing stall in Bristol.'

She joined a coven of sopranos at a table who were dissecting Diana's poor performance at the concert. They asked her what she thought.

'It could have been better, but asking her to sing a solo when she's only been in the choir five minutes was possibly an error of judgement on Alistair's part.'

Someone said, 'Haven't you noticed how he's always standing talking her at every opportunity? People notice that sort of thing and tongues are beginning to wag.'

Victoria wondered if she should make an effort to get to know Diana better and try and integrate her into the group.

Fifteen minutes later she acted on her impulse and edged

her way back through the crowd to where Keith had Diana cornered by the bar and asked him to excuse them. She grasped Diana's arm and drew her away to a quieter area.

'I'm sorry to interrupt,' she said, 'but I thought you might need rescuing. Keith's harmless, but he can be a bit of a pain.'

'You thought right, thank you,' whispered Diana, 'I think I'll go home.' Victoria was disappointed. Her good intentions would have to wait for another day.

Diana found her coat and slipped out of the door. As she paused in the porch to put up her hood against the chill wind, she was startled by a voice from the shadows.

'Leaving already?'

It was Alistair. He added, 'No, I haven't come out for a crafty smoke. I just needed a few minutes peace to wind down. Did you enjoy the concert?'

'Yes, very much. It's amazing how much difference being in front of an audience makes. We really went up a notch, didn't we? I'm afraid I made a bit of a pig's ear of my solo though,'

She put her hand up to tousle her hair flattened by the hood.

Alistair reassured her.

'No, you were fine, just a bit nervous.' He hesitated.

'Would you like to come down to the Red Lion with me? There'll be hardly anyone in there and I'll buy you a whisky to warm you up.'

'That sounds lovely.'

He was right. Apart from two men at the bar staring silently into their pints, the pub was empty. The floral carpet was a touch sticky and years of nicotine had stained the walls and paintwork a sullen brown, but Diana didn't notice. She had him all to herself - she must make the most of it. She sipped delicately at the minute measure of golden liquid.

'I needed this,' and wondered what to say next. She knew men like to talk about themselves, so she asked him how he had become involved with the choir.

'I did a stint as their accompanist, then, when they needed

a musical director, they asked me if I was interested.'

He visibly relaxed, and settled back in his seat. 'Next question?'

'What do you get out of it? It can't be for the money.'

'No, it isn't. I actually enjoy doing it. It's a performance. I have to be all things to all people. The men should want to be me and the women,' he paused and looked into her eyes, 'the women should want to please me.'

Diana's eyes widened. Thoughts of how she might please him sprang unbidden into her mind.

'To be in control of sixty voices, making wonderful sounds, when it all goes right,' he grinned, 'is a very, very good feeling.'

'Don't they say that singing releases the same endorphins as sex and chocolate?'

'They do indeed.'

'Don't you get frustrated when we can't get it right, or don't follow your cues? Is it still worth it then?'

'Of course. Sometimes when the choir gets things wrong, it's my fault anyway, unlikely as that may sound. I tell you, if I won the lottery I'd probably still do it. I love the music, the drama, the power....' His voice trailed off.

She couldn't stop her eyes sliding to the ring on his wedding finger and she asked,

'Is your wife in the choir?'

'No, no. She isn't musical, I'm afraid – finds it all a bit of a bore now. She comes to the concerts occasionally. Now, let me get you one for the road.'

She watched him walk to the bar. What would it feel like to lie next to him, holding him close? He was clearly an accomplished flirt but did the banter go any deeper? Was he a challenge or a pushover? She couldn't help hoping it was the former. It would be more rewarding in the end.

They were still there at closing time. She looked at her watch then at the man opposite her. To break her train of thought, she excused herself and went to the Ladies where she leaned on the washbasin, and contemplated her face in the mirror. What was going on? She knew she was tired and maybe a little drunk, but this man was something special. He was getting under her skin. This was more than just flirting and it was scary. She shook his head and splashed cold water on her face. He was married. This really shouldn't be allowed to go any further.

'I'll walk you back to your flat.' He gave her his arm.

Should she ask him to come in for a nightcap? Would he accept?

It was after midnight when he left.

6

Even Victoria, who had sung in venues all over the area in her time, felt a shiver of apprehension as the village choir assembled in the cathedral under-croft on a bright May morning. This would be the first time they had performed away from South Heath. Would they rise to the occasion?

After a swift warm up, Alistair led them upstairs into the glory and the grandeur of the nave. Eschewing the choir stalls, he had them gather on the floor of the nave, very close to the audience. They expected just a few tourists and loyal friends but their audience had swollen to about fifty people sitting expectantly, if uncomfortably, in the pews.

By contrast with most cathedrals, this one was flooded with light. Victoria wondered if Cromwell was responsible for the original stained glass windows being replaced with plain glass. She was entranced by the sun's rays streaming into the white and gilded interior.

The choir struggled a little with their programme, perhaps overawed by their august surroundings. The tenors were a bar behind through a large part of 'Locus Iste', and the sopranos missed an entry in Rutter's arrangement of 'For the Beauty of the Earth.'

'He didn't bring us in,' hissed Victoria's neighbour. 'That wasn't our fault.'

Victoria knew their performance was not quite worthy of its splendid setting, but the highlight for her was the splendid acoustic, which allowed the final notes of each piece to hang thrillingly in the air for several heart stopping seconds.

Was the choir's original ethos of being a community venture, open to all with no auditions still appropriate? Should the pursuit of excellence have priority over the provision of a pleasant therapeutic singalong for those with boundless enthusiasm but little vocal training? This was something she had struggled with since the choir was set up. Her tendency to intellectual snobbery, she knew, was passed down to her from her mother and compensated her for her lowly position in the hierarchy of village society. Time and time again she had come down on the side of enjoyable, amateur warbling.

Last to leave the cathedral, Alistair spotted Diana, walking slowly, head down into the wind. Poor thing. She looks cold. He banished Helen's accusing face from his mind and drew into the kerb.

'Hello, would you like a lift home?'

She settled herself beside him, and exclaimed with delight as the heated passenger seat of his BMW began to warm up.

'My mother said never to accept lifts from strange men, but I'll make an exception for you.'

'Hardly a stranger, surely.'

She looked at him and ventured, 'We weren't very good were we?'

'Not at all. It wasn't perfect but the audience loved it. I had some very positive comments afterwards.' He paused. 'I can see this might be becoming a habit, but would you like to stop for a swift drink to warm us through?'

Diana nodded and gave him that sideways smiling glance that had attracted him before.

He turned off the main road and drove a few miles to a pub in an isolated village on the edge of the Somerset levels.

'I think you'll like it here. It's like being in someone's front room. They bring the beer up from the cellar in a jug.'

The little pub was busy but they managed to find a table in a corner. The barman said 'Hello, Alistair, nice to see you again. Keeping well?'

He took their order and said he'd bring their drinks over.

Responding to Diana's questioning eyebrows, Alistair said, 'This is my bolt hole when I need to get away from school or South Heath itself, and relax where nobody knows me.'

She made him laugh, talking about her job in the beauty salon, and describing some of the more outrageous 'holistic therapies' with which she indulged the ladies with money to spare. When she told him about Hopi ear candles, he accused her of making it up.

'When I was a penniless student I used to sing in some rather dodgy clubs. I had to learn how to cope with an audience who were just waiting for the stripper. I would have made more money doing her job, but I wasn't brave enough.'

Alistair fought against the image of Diana, in minimal clothing, breathing something sultry into a microphone. He should change the subject.

He glanced at his watch.

'Good Lord. Look at the time. We've been here hours.'

'Should you be driving?'

'Probably not, but we'll go the back way along the lanes. Don't worry, you're in safe hands.'

'If only.'

They left the pub, giggling at her innuendo, and scurried back towards his car. The rain had stopped and he grabbed her hand to jump over the puddles together.

By the time he dropped her off around the corner from her flat, he knew they had compounded their friendship, and with an awareness of the mutual frisson of attraction and desire, there was an unspoken understanding that they would meet again very soon.

His heart sank when he saw Helen standing by the kettle in her pyjamas.

'Where on earth have you been? I was about to start ringing the hospitals. Did the concert go well?' She reached into a cupboard for a mug. 'Horlicks?'

He shook his head.

'Yes, it went extremely well. You missed a treat. Pity you couldn't be bothered to come. Some of us went back to Keith's for a post mortem and then we all went for a curry. And it's pouring out there now, if you hadn't noticed. I'm tired and wet. I need a hot shower then a proper drink.'

Fifteen minutes later, whisky in hand, he looked at her.

'Those pyjamas don't do you any favours. It isn't even bedtime.'

Helen turned surprised.

'What? Don't take your bad temper out on me. I just fancied an early night,' and she took her mug up to bed with her, leaving him sitting, scowling into his glass.

As the warmth of the Glenmorangie seeped into Alistair's bones his thoughts turned back to Diana. Wasn't that just it in a nutshell? Helen was Horlicks, sweet but boring - and Diana had both the relaxing warmth and the dangerous promise of a good Scotch.

Back at home and fed and watered long ago, Victoria was thinking about Diana too. She went into the kitchen to put the kettle on, sufficiently deep in thought to remove the dead frog from under the table without communicating her feelings to the cat, who watched impassively from the windowsill.

She wasn't imagining that Diana always seemed to be standing with Alistair in the pub after practice. The others had noticed it too. There was definitely something in their ease together that suggested intimacy. She frowned. The feeling of foreboding was making her depressed and irritable. Pausing to raid the biscuit tin, she took her tea upstairs. She too would have an early night.

7

In the morning the rains had gone and stepping outside her back door into the spring sunshine, Victoria inspected all the herbaceous perennials she had planted the previous year, sturdily re-emerging for another summer. Her quiet moment of pleasure was interrupted by the ringing of her telephone.

She considered ignoring it, then went in and picked it up.

A man's voice said,

'Hello, Victoria. It's Marcus,'

She stiffened. What did Rachel's husband want with her? She did hope he wasn't going to come round and make a scene.

'I really could do with a chat Victoria, over lunch maybe? As Rachel clearly doesn't want to come back to me, there's a lot to sort out. I'm afraid we don't seem able to handle all this ourselves, without trying to score points. I promise I don't want you to act as a go-between or plead my case. I suppose I really need a sort of sounding board and you are one of the most clear headed and non-judgemental people I know.'

'I'm flattered Marcus, but I'm not sure I can be of any help to you.'

'Allow me to be the judge of that. The Crown in Langley Bottom is nice - good pub grub. Would Thursday suit you? I could pick you up at twelve.'

'Oh alright, but don't pick me up – I'd rather meet you there.'

She put the phone down, and felt a slight sense of disloyalty towards Rachel. She'd always got on well with Marcus when they were neighbours. He was the one to call when she was beset by small household emergencies, Robin being hopelessly inadequate on that front.

It was Marcus who had swept out the flooded kitchen and repaired the faulty washing machine hose that caused it; he'd traced the electric appliance that had caused all her fuses to blow, restoring heat and light to her home and he'd driven her to the vet with a dying cat on her knee, providing her with a clean white handkerchief to cry into. The two young couples, each newly married, had shared the fun and the problems alike.

Should she tell Rachel she was meeting Marcus for lunch? As she mentally leafed through her wardrobe wondering what she should wear, she decided it would be easier to keep quiet.

She disapproved of what she had heard about his behaviour as the marriage disintegrated. Should she tell him so? Was he using her to creep back into Rachel's good books? Bristling with sisterly solidarity, she decided she would hear what he had to say, suggest a marriage guidance counsellor or a solicitor, and send him on his way.

'Victoria. You haven't changed a bit. I've got us a table by the fire.'

Marcus kissed her enthusiastically on both cheeks. She sat down. She felt uneasy. Her instincts were telling her that Marcus was bad news.

Marcus pointed out the menu board and recommended steak and ale pie. Victoria, in common with many generously proportioned women, felt that when she was on public view, she should be toying with a few leaves.

She always imagined her fellow diners whispering, 'Look at what she's got on her plate. No wonder she's so plump,' and told Marcus that she would prefer a ham salad.

They made polite conversation.

'The last time I saw you must have been at Robin's funeral. What a tragedy that was.'

She nodded. What more was there to say?

He enquired if she was still working up at the school. Remembering he had been a lowly police sergeant back in the day, she congratulated him on his promotion to Chief Inspector. Contrary to the popular perception of policemen, Marcus was cultured and sensitive and, while she wasn't surprised at his steady rise through the ranks, she also knew he had a ruthless streak and was impatient with fools.

She watched him make his way to the bar for more drinks. His hair was iron grey now and it enhanced his surprisingly blue eyes. In that pale green cashmere sweater, he was really rather dishy. Victoria wished she hadn't been privy to Rachel's account of the disintegrating marriage. She found it hard to match her charming companion to the man described by his spurned wife.

She wouldn't let him sweet talk her or allow him to pull the wool over her eyes. She needed to keep out of this, it was too close to home.

It wasn't until they had finished eating that she addressed the reason for this meeting.

'So, Marcus, why are we here? I really don't want to be drawn into any wrangling between you'.

Marcus leaned back and picked up his glass. His face was reassuring.

'I'm not seeking to involve you in that way. I promise. I expect Rachel told you I'd had a bit of a fling? It was something and nothing. Val offered it to me on a plate and I was flattered. I wasn't looking for an affair, but it was such fun – all the intrigue and the excitement.' He took a long drink.

'Call it a mid-life crisis, if you like. It certainly did wonders for my ego. But it's over now. Why can't she accept that? All I got from her were long faces and endless sarcastic comments.'

Victoria frowned. 'Without wishing to be rude, Marcus, could you get to the point?'

'Yes, well the point is that I've had enough now. We need to sort things out. I see the break ups of colleagues at work and how infidelity leads to a desire for revenge. They hire solicitors who send accusatory letters and deliberately foster an adversarial climate, which is how they make their money, of course.'

His face was reddening and tiny beads of perspiration stood out on his forehead. His voice became lower and more urgent and he plucked at his napkin and screwed it into a ball.

'It really wouldn't be in either of our interests to go down that route. If we came to an agreement between ourselves, not only would we both save thousands of pounds in legal fees, but we'd also stand a chance of having an amicable relationship afterwards. The trouble with Rachel is that she does a nice line in playing the martyr and twisting the facts to support her grievances. I wondered if you could make her see sense and encourage her to talk to me rationally – let's get it sorted quickly and cheaply. Time to move on… as they say.'

Victoria held up her hands to stop the flow.

'No wait, I haven't quite finished.' Marcus felt in his pocket.

'Look, I've put our old house on the market – obviously Rachel will want her share and I've found a small bungalow which needs a bit of work. It would do me very nicely and keep me busy as well.' He passed a sheet from the local estate agent across the table.

'But this is in South Heath.' She scanned it and passed it back commenting, 'Is that a good idea? Rachel won't be very happy.'

He sighed. 'I know, but it's really difficult to find a property that's near enough for work and that I can easily afford once the financial settlement is agreed. This is the easily the best of the bunch. My plan is to do it up, then sell it for an enormous profit. After that I can move anywhere I like. Can you put a word in for me – sort of smooth the way.'

'Sorry Marcus. This is precisely what I didn't want to happen. You know Rachel is my friend and I really can't say how she'd react to the idea. You need to talk to her yourself. Thanks for a lovely lunch, I'm sorry I can't help you.'

She gathered up her things and almost ran to the car. Thank God she'd driven herself there.

On the way home awkward thoughts jangled in her mind. How come she could listen to Rachel complaining about Marcus but not the other way round? There were always two sides to every story. At least he was trying to plan a future and move on. She couldn't deny that Rachel's self-justifying, innocent victim act was beginning to grate. A position of complete neutrality, was called for. Her support for both would be limited to hospitality and social chit chat, and she should encourage Rachel to find somewhere permanent to live. Marcus could live where he liked as far as she was concerned. She'd had enough of her comfortable, well ordered life being turned upside down, and the time had come to admit to herself that enough was enough.

Lost in thought, Victoria rounded a bend a little too fast and almost knocked over a figure walking at the edge of the road. Cursing, she slowed down and saw in her mirror someone looking remarkably like Diana, on her own in the middle of nowhere.

She pulled in at the side of the road, and jumped out of the car.

'Diana, I thought it was you. I'm so sorry. I almost ran you over.'

Diana gave one of her funny little shrugs, as if to suggest that the possibility had occurred to her too.

'I missed the bus, and it's such a nice day so I thought I'd walk but it's taking longer than I expected.'

'Let me give you a lift home. I need to call in at the chemist first though if you don't mind.' She raised her eyebrows. 'You aren't in a hurry, are you?'

'No, it's my day off from the salon.'

Victoria wondered what someone like Diana did on her days off, whether she had friends and family tucked away somewhere. Diana didn't seem to be one of those people only too ready to spill out their life story to all and sundry.

Diana got into Victoria's car. She sneezed.

Victoria apologised. 'That'll be the air freshener. Sorry, it's new and a bit strong. You haven't been in South Heath long have you?'

'No.'

'Are you a local, or do you come from farther afield?'

'Bristol.' Diana folded her arms.

Victoria shot her a sideways glance and noted the defensive pose. She wondered, not for the first time, why this pretty girl was so uptight and unforthcoming.

Later, talking to Rachel, she said, 'She really clammed up when I asked her about herself. After all, I remembered her from the salon, when I had that massage, so I thought she'd be friendly. You'd think that joining the choir meant she wanted to get to know people.'

Rachel nodded sagely in that way that Victoria found so amusing.

'I've had a bad feeling about her since day one. She's trouble. I can feel in it in my water. I told you she'd come into the bookshop, didn't I? She was odd then.'

'You are so judgemental. She's obviously just painfully shy. I might just take her under my wing as a challenge.'

'For goodness sake, Victoria. Let it go. She's none of your business. I sometimes think you overdo the lady bountiful act. You collect lame ducks like I used to collect stamps.'

Victoria felt her jaw drop. How dare she say that? Wasn't Rachel one of her lame ducks once? She bit back an angry retort. She would ignore Rachel's ingratitude and concentrate on overcoming the barriers that Diana had so clearly erected.

8

The last thing Alistair wanted was for his choir to become stale and complacent. He told Victoria he'd seen it happen and that he'd been thinking about a trip abroad, possibly to Bruges, combining singing with more touristy pursuits.

He'd put it to the committee, sitting round the long pine table in the Chairman's kitchen. The wine was open and would, he hoped, have mellowed the naysayers.

'Why Bruges?' asked one, well known for her frugality. 'Why can't we go somewhere closer to home? I've heard Belgium is boring.'

He forced a smile to conceal his irritation.

'Obviously you've never been to Bruges, it's one of the most beautiful mediaeval cities in Europe. It's full of ornate houses, tree- lined canals, cobbled streets, stunning churches all floodlit at night and a magnificent market square.'

'I've been,' interrupted Maureen, the choir secretary. 'The chocolate shops are to die for and we did a tour of the old part in a horse drawn carriage. It was lovely.'

Alistair rubbed his eyes. This meeting was going on too long and he'd drunk one too many glasses of red wine. He always tried to keep out of the minutiae on the agenda and stick to musical matters. Very early on in his involvement with this choir, he'd decided that he wasn't going to get distracted by discussions about the dress code or how much, or how little, they were going to give to charity. In return he expected that decisions and choices of both music and venues were to be his.

'I've done a similar trip to Italy with my senior choir from the school, and I know what fun they can be. I suggest that we canvass choir members at the next practice to see how many would be interested.'

The following Tuesday night, his idea was met with enthusiasm from the ground troops and he got sufficient voices from each section to enable him to plan a suitable set.

Victoria offered to contact a firm who organised such things, would give them a costing and deal with all the travel details.

'We've got about thirty people signed up, Alistair, mainly those who aren't encumbered by small children.'

'Excellent, a long weekend of sightseeing and performing in a church in Bruges for tourists and locals will do wonders for morale. We've got six weeks to learn a couple of new things. Better check your passport Victoria.'

'Is Helen coming?'

'Yes. She adores Bruges. We went there when we were students. She loved the lace shops and the chocolate shops – the whole touristy thing. She never was a culture vulture.'

That was one of the reasons he'd chosen Bruges for their choral holiday. If he and Helen could recapture something of the intimacy that had made their marriage special, then maybe he would be able to resist the glorious Diana and walk away from the temptations she offered.

A late addition to the party was Marcus. He'd bought the bungalow and was busy involving himself in village activities. Somehow he'd heard that one person had dropped out and inveigled Victoria into adding him to the list. As it made financial sense she agreed on the condition that he didn't also join the choir. As it was, there had been sulky comments from Rachel. Victoria had to promise, 'He's just filling a seat as a tourist. We needn't have anything to do with him.'

Their coach left for Dover early on Friday evening. As it rumbled through the countryside, Victoria whispered to Rachel, 'Keith's driving me mad.'

'Is he? Why?'

'The running commentary on the route, the history of the

towns we're going through and the various points of interest we're missing with it being dark. Don't tell me you haven't noticed.'

Rachel hadn't.

Eventually to Victoria's relief, Keith fell asleep.

As the journey dragged on, Victoria reflected sourly on how it was that she, with her prudently packed travel pillow, couldn't sleep a wink, whereas Rachel, her head resting on a scrunched up carrier bag, was dead to the world.

Her restless legs were twitching and aching. She couldn't wait till the so-called 'comfort break' and she could walk about a bit and stretch them.

When they stopped, the rain was lashing down and there was a howling wind. Dismayed, the ladies swallowed their sea sick pills to prepare themselves for what was bound to be an uncomfortable voyage.

They arrived in Dover at midnight, only to learn that all sailings had been delayed due to the high seas. Victoria was longing to get out of the cramped seats, but reflected that she'd rather be on the coach than out on the English Channel on a night such as this.

'Whose daft idea was it to come this way? We'd have been there by now through the tunnel.' Rachel was red-eyed and grumpy. In a grey dawn they were finally allowed to board the ferry at six o'clock. The sea was still very rough and Victoria made her way up onto the deck where it was wild and windy, but so exhilarating. She clung onto the rail, enjoying the buffeting and the spray, pitying those who were huddled in the stuffy, hot saloon below decks battling nausea and the overwhelming smell of chips. She was joined there by Alistair.

'Have you got a minute – I could do with a chat - in confidence?'

'Of course.'

Oh dear, she hoped this wasn't about his marriage. Someone had reported seeing him with Diana in his car and jumped to a conclusion, and hadn't she herself entertained suspicions about their relationship?

The wind blew their words away and he gestured her to follow him, finding a sheltered corner underneath a suspended lifeboat. They sat on the deck and Victoria wrapped her arms around her knees.

'I'm struggling with something,' and he attempted a light laugh.

'I just wanted your thoughts. They say, don't they, that you can't love two women at the same time? That has to be nonsense. If you have two children they don't say you can't love both of them, do they? '

'What are you trying to say?'

'Come on Victoria, I'm not playing games.'

This was just what she'd feared. She rested her forehead on her knees wondering which tack she should take. They'd known each so long, ever since he was a fresh faced probationary teacher, and sought her opinion on things that troubled him. But this was major league stuff and she wasn't sure herself what he should do. She took refuge in semantics saying, 'It's a 'different kind of love' thing isn't it? Of course you will love lots of women. Your mother, your auntie, a sister......but, at the same time, in our society you are expected to love just one woman at a time sexually – as you well know. It's what keeps families together.'

He groaned. 'Oh, I know, I know. It's just so damnably difficult. I've got to play the dutiful husband this weekend in front of the choir and worry in case Helen picks up on anything.'

'Alistair, you're playing with fire. I can't believe what you're suggesting. For goodness sake, be careful.'

He shook his head.

'The sad thing is that I'd intended this trip to be a chance for Helen and me to relive some old memories. I'm finding it really difficult. I'm not a bad man – you know that.'

He got to his feet and extended a hand to pull her up.

'Let's pretend this conversation never happened. I'm sorry Victoria. You can't help me. Nobody can. I'll sort it out somehow.'

He walked off and she made her way back to the rail, looking at the boiling sea and wondering what it would feel like to jump overboard. Not that she wanted to end it all, but it chimed with the feeling she always had at the top of a tall tower. What if she flung herself off?

Should she have said more to Alistair? Robin used to laugh at her worries and tell her off for her tendency to catastrophise. But it was always sad when a marriage broke down. At least there were no children to be hurt.

The wind had dropped and sea mists closed in. She made her way back inside, none the wiser as to what, if anything, she could say or do to help him sort his life out.

They disembarked at Ostend and set off for Bruges, stopping en route for coffee and pain au chocolat. When they eventually arrived at the hotel tired, hot and sticky, Alistair stood up at the front of the bus.

Somehow, he was looking fresh and positive.

'Right everyone. You've got an hour for a quick shower and change of clothes, or whatever else you want to do, then we're back onto the coach. The driver is taking us to a bistro in the city centre where we're going to eat and have a few restorative glasses of wine. After that there's a boat trip along the canals.'

There was a vestige of a cheer, and a much happier group returned to the bus, which took them to sample the delights of Bruges before returning them to their beds.

Helen had checked the fire exits as soon as they arrived and inspected the room. It had seemed clean enough. Now she undressed and, while Alistair was in the shower she sat up in bed with her book propped up on her knees. When the sound of running water stopped, her heart sank. Alistair came out of the bathroom, a towel wrapped around his waist. He knelt on the bed beside her and spread his arms wide.

'Look – all nice and clean.'

Helen knew what that meant. She replaced her bookmark and turned to put the book on the bedside table. She wished him a good night and lay down, her back towards him. Sorry, was the unspoken message – not tonight.

At breakfast the next morning Victoria and Rachel surveyed the table piled high with assorted croissants and pastries. They each filled a plate and sat down to discuss how best to spend their few precious hours of free time in the afternoon. Victoria poured them both some coffee.

'Alistair said that this morning will be taken up by a tour of St Salvator's cathedral and then a practice run- through of the music for the lunchtime concert. We could find somewhere nice for lunch afterwards.'

Unlike her friend, Rachel wasn't a planner. 'Let's play it by ear. We'll have a wander and see what we fancy.'

Across the room, Alistair and Helen sat picking at their pastries. They had not slept well.

Helen looked around. 'They're a real mixed bunch your choir, aren't they.'

Alistair smelled danger. 'I don't know about that. They're a fairly representative group of the more mature I would have thought.'

'No, there are some who don't really fit in at all. That Diana doesn't seem to gel with anyone and Keith sticks out like a sore thumb.'

'We can't all be the same. Everyone just enjoys singing. They don't have to be best friends as well.' He didn't want this conversation.

'More coffee?' He took their cups over to the buffet.

When he returned, he changed the subject.

'What are you thinking of doing while we're at the cathedral? Or would you like to come and listen to us?"

But Helen wouldn't let it go.

'Someone told me she works in that massage parlour. What's it called – Bubbles?'

'Who?'

'That Diana.'

'I wouldn't know.' He crammed the remainder of the croissant into his mouth.

'Come on, we need to make a start.'

For God's sake, was she going to be like this all weekend? He was trying – wasn't he?

The coach dropped them off close to the cathedral and they approached it on foot, dodging horse drawn carriages of tourists and diverting from the direct route to walk up uncomfortably cobbled alleyways. Victoria grabbed Rachel's arm.

'Just look at that shop - wall to wall chocolate.'

Irresistibly drawn in, she sighed with pleasure at the aroma and the mouth- watering display featuring chocolates of every conceivable flavour and shape. Spoilt for choice she browsed happily for a while before returning to Rachel.

'I've bought a selection of chocolate caramels for Mr Next-door, he's feeding the cat while I'm away, and a small bag of truffles for myself. Here, will you tuck them away, out of temptations reach, at the very bottom of your rucksack.'

The old part of the city was enchanting and it was two happy ladies who eventually entered the cathedral with its soaring white columns. Victoria stopped to admire the Pieta and Rachel called her over to see a collection of stone coffins with painted interiors.

Alistair beamed at his little group of singers gathered on the sanctuary steps.

'This wonderful cathedral,' he told them, 'dates from the tenth century. So people have been singing here for over a thousand years. Just don't let their ghosts intimidate you.'

After the run through and when the time had come to perform, Victoria was delighted to see quite a respectable audience sitting waiting.

The choir began with Ave Verum Corpus, one of their favourites and warbled tunefully through Irish Blessings and Impossible Dream; but the climax for them all was singing Vaughan William's Antiphon, 'Let all the world in every corner sing' at full volume. Their voices resounded thrillingly in the sacred space and, for most of them; it was the lump-in the-throat highlight of the tour. Rachel nudged Victoria next to her and whispered, 'Wow, how amazing was that.'

Victoria nodded. She'd been watching Alistair intently as he conducted them, could see the fleeting frown when something wasn't quite right; and felt a glow of pleasure when, at the end of a piece that had gone well, he made a steeple of his hands and, smiling, bowed his head.

She reflected that for a choir to rise above the mediocre, they had not only to want to please their conductor but also to have that frisson of fear when they failed. If you didn't care then your performance would never reach out to the audience and move them in some way.

Alistair was waiting as they filed off. He was smiling.

'Go and enjoy the afternoon. There's plenty to see and do. You've earned it.'

Victoria and Rachel stood outside the cathedral, their ears still ringing with music. Marcus spotted them and approached.

'I'm off to climb the Belfry tower,' he announced. 'The view over the city will be stunning. Would anyone care to join me? Victoria, how about you? Are you fit enough to climb hundreds of steps?'

Rachel frowned and turned away, saying to Victoria, 'Go on - he's all yours. You two are bats anyway so a belfry should suit you down to the ground.'

She walked off and joined Helen and a small group of sopranos who were planning to go to the famous flea market, leaving Victoria alone with Marcus.

At the top of the tower, 366 steps later, she turned to him, her eyes shining and almost completely out of breath.

'How clever of you to suggest this. Just look at that view.'

'I didn't intend to split up your little group,' he apologised, 'so I'm glad you think it was worth it.'

They stayed a little longer, enjoying the waves of red tiled rooftops on the serried ranks of houses interspersed with church steeples which lined the canals. He kept putting his hand on her arm, whilst pointing with the other at landmarks and their shoulders touched as they stood together at the railings. Don't give yourself ideas, she thought, he's just one of those touchy-feely sort of people.

Back down at street level, Victoria looked from left to right.

'Which way now? I've completely lost my bearings.'

'If we go this way, we should come to the old market square. I shouldn't be a bit surprised if we find the others sitting in the sunshine stuffing their faces with waffles and ice cream.' He tucked her arm in his and set off.

He was right.

'My treat', he said and, warmed by their growing intimacy, they joined their friends and tucked in.

Across the cafe tables, Diana's eyes met Alistair's. He gave a barely perceptible nod. When Helen joined the shopping group, Diana seized her opportunity and, standing by Alistair as he paid for the coffees, she whispered her suggestion that he should forego the pleasures of the flea market and chocolate shops and do a little exploring with her, well away from curious eyes.

'Tell Helen you're going to visit some churches. Then she'll be only too happy to let you go off alone.'

He knew he shouldn't, but the promissory twinkle in her blue eyes and the curve of her smiling lips was enough to banish his good intentions.

'You're a wicked woman, you know that?'

'I do know. That's part of my allure.'

He stifled a laugh at her choice of words and nodded.

'Go on then. I'll follow you.'

Diana set off towards the canal and walked slowly along the towpath. Alistair stood and watched as the others headed off towards the shops then ambled in the direction she'd taken. Once they'd rounded a corner and were a safe distance from the centre, Diana took his hand and pulled it around her waist.

'Let's walk along the canal until we're far enough away from the tourist trail to be out of danger of being spotted.' She could feel the heat of his body.

They reached a little copse of trees, and sat on a bench facing the water. They lifted their faces to the sun. Turning her face to his she saw that his eyes were sparkling with the risk and danger of their situation.

Diana took his hand and kissed his long fingers one by one.

'Are you happy in South Heath?'

He stretched his legs before him and sighed.

'I was.'

'I sense a 'but'.'

'I need another challenge, Diana. The job's too easy. I could do it with my eyes closed.'

'What about the choir? Are you bored with them too?'

'Oh no, that's still fun. We're making such strides musically, I couldn't be happier with it. Especially now I've got you to look at on the front row.'

'Perhaps I should be your challenge?'

He got to his feet and walked to the water's edge. After inspecting the ducks for several minutes, he turned back to her.

He sat down and took her hand.

'This is so difficult, Diana… you and me. You're already a challenge. I can't compartmentalise you. I tell myself you are my middle aged folly but that doesn't help.'

'I just want you to be happy,' she nibbled the lobe of his ear to lighten the atmosphere, 'Don't struggle with it. Let's make the most of what we've got for now.'

Suddenly, from around the corner they could hear the diesel chug of an approaching canal boat and the unmistakeable sound of Marcus' roaring laugh. Diana froze. Alistair was quicker. He leapt off the bench and crouched down behind it in the bushes.

'Don't move,' he hissed, 'just sit there and wave.'

As the tourist boat passed, there were cries of, 'Look, there's Diana! Come aboard.' She waved and smiled as if it were the most normal thing in the world to be sitting alone at the side of a Belgian canal. No doubt she would face some questions from the more curious of the throng when they met up back at the coach.

The drama somehow put a dampener on their tryst. A chill in the air and the lengthening shadows caused them to stand

and stretch and set off to find their way back to the meeting place.

'I'll go ahead.' She picked her way down the cobbled alleyway. In her heart she believed that she had found her soul mate.

Alistair watched her walking away from him and wondered what it would be like to wake up beside her every morning.

He was the last person to arrive at the rendezvous, amid good natured jeering. He apologised and joked about getting lost in the red light district.

'Wrong city,' shouted Marcus.

'That's what you think.'

9

Marcus sat in Victoria's kitchen. She wasn't especially pleased to see him. She'd had a stern conversation with herself after Bruges and wasn't after upsetting any apple carts. His excuse was that he had come to bring her up to speed with his purchase of the new house. Didn't he know that women talk to each other, and that she might know more about him and his affairs than he would be comfortable with? He sat back in the chair and stretched out his legs.

'I can't tell you how much better I feel - now that I'm getting on with my life.'

The cat jumped up onto his lap purring obsequiously. He put it down on the floor and came over to where Victoria was standing rigid by the kettle, willing it to boil more quickly, and draped an arm casually around her shoulder.

'You know, Victoria, you were a real friend to me when I needed someone to talk to.'

Victoria turned to push him away, dismayed at the intimacy in his voice. Over his shoulder, she saw Rachel standing in the kitchen doorway, her jaw dropping like a descending lift.

Victoria took a side step. Marcus's arm fell to his side. Rachel's voice was high pitched and utterly unlike her normal tone.

'This looks very cosy.'

'Oh, for Heaven's sake Rachel. Marcus was just thanking me for lending an ear when he was down.'

She gave him a little push. 'Off you go now.' He retreated sheepishly, shutting the front door with exaggerated care.

Victoria sighed. 'Now, sit down and let me explain.'

Pink with annoyance, Rachel said, 'No need. I told you

what he was like, but I never expected you'd fall for his sob story. You know what your trouble is? You think you can be Mother Teresa to one and all. Well, count me out. You can find yourself another worthy cause, and, if it's a man you want, I'm sure you could do better than shagging my cast off.'

She gathered her chunky knit cardigan around her, and exited with as much wounded dignity as she could summon.

Victoria slumped down at the kitchen table and banged her head several times on the knotty pine. This was all completely ridiculous. How could Rachel think there was anything between her and Marcus? The tingle of pleasure she'd felt when he touched her was so momentary that she'd discounted it almost at once. She jumped up, and her chair crashed backwards onto the quarry tiles.

Fresh air was what was needed and she threw on her old green Barbour and marched out of the house and down the path, almost felling the postman who leapt aside just in time.

She took the bridleway which led up on to the folded hills and windswept plateaus of the Mendips, pausing several times to admire the view, refusing as usual to admit to herself that she needed to stop because she was quite out of breath. At the top of the ridge, she stopped and looked down over the valley. There was her cottage, her church and the grounds of South Heath School, lush and green in the morning air. She needed to get things into perspective. Generations had lived, loved and sinned in this landscape. Eventually they'd all be dead too; gone and forgotten.

There was no question that Rachel had completely over-reacted. She'd admitted her marriage was over, so she had no right to be acting as though Marcus was still her property.

Why shouldn't she remain friends with him? Maybe he's changed. Maybe he was the way he was because of Rachel. Who knows what goes on in other people's marriages? Admit it, the baser instincts of man, and woman too, change little over time, although people are less violent now. There was no gibbet at the end of Hangman's Lane. The stocks and ducking stool had long since been consumed by woodworm. But sex hadn't changed. She knew that. Sex was responsible for husbands leaving wives, men abandoning their children and even led to the abdication of kings. Now it was threatening to destroy what had become one of her dearest friendships. Was Marcus worth it? Probably not, was the answer; but she couldn't deny she was beginning to enjoy his company.

Drained of emotion and suddenly weary, she made her way back down to the village.

Once home, she consulted that day's list and began to attack the various tasks, seeking healing in the humdrum. Where was that damn cat? It must be three days since she last saw it. While she wouldn't wish it an uncomfortable death under the wheels of a car, she did rather hope it had found somewhere else to live – perhaps with a kind old lady, who didn't have a bird table and was happy to have it sit on her knee for hours getting in the way of her reading or crossword solving. She'd spotted two great tits in the ivy at the bottom of the garden this morning. If the cat was gone, perhaps they would come and nest there. She washed out the feeding bowls. With any luck she'd be able to put them in the next charity bag collection.

There was no official break in the summer months for the choir, though people disappeared for a week or two and returned tanned or otherwise, from Corfu or Cornwall. Their next concert would close the coming Arts Festival fortnight, which was something of a special event in the town.

Diana called in on Victoria that morning to pick up a copy of some new music that Victoria had spare. She asked Victoria, 'What is this Arts Festival then? There are posters up everywhere.'

Victoria brightened. 'Oh, it's amazing. There's a fortnight of events - music, drama and poetry, with a weekend in the middle when about fifty of us open our houses for artists, potters and jewellers to display and sell their stuff. This will be our seventh year.'

She rummaged in a drawer. 'I've got a programme from the

last one somewhere, it'll give you a flavour.' Failing to find it, she continued, 'we get about four thousand visitors, from miles around, over that weekend. Last year I had a potter in my house, the year before a silver-smith. Most people in the village get involved in some way or other with the Festival and the choir always does a concert.'

Diana pulled a face. 'I don't think I'd want every Tom, Dick and Harry coming into my flat snooping to see if there are any cobwebs.'

Victoria nodded, 'Yes, but it's as good a reason as any to have a clean - up.'

The two women went out into Victoria's garden. Diana admired the pelargoniums and said she had thought of getting some pot plants for her windowsill.

'Herbs perhaps, but I don't suppose I'd use them. Maybe something flowering and colourful like those you've got there.'

'You'll find they're quite expensive. Leave it to me,' said Victoria. 'Come round one Saturday morning and I'll do you some cuttings of these. They'll grow quickly this time of year and they'll flower for ages.'

'That would be lovely. One day I'll have a proper garden of my own.'

Diana spoke confidently, but as she walked home, the old feelings of despair and misery welled up again. Would she ever have a garden of her own? A man of her own? A home with a family? They all seemed as far away as ever. Maybe not quite so far away as ever. She quickened her step and determinedly hummed a little tune. Focus on the positives. It was all she could do.

Under the pretext of staying late at school for orchestra practices, junior choir and senior choir, a necessary part of his job, Alistair had, over the past couple of months, established a pattern of seeing Diana at least once a week.

The subterfuge, which the ascetic side of Alistair would once have found sordid and distasteful, was now an exciting means to an end. His desire to be with her, to touch her and be touched by her, began to occupy his mind night and day. He wanted to explore her body and, in turn, experience the exquisite sensations of her exploration of his. They had dangerous, uncomfortable sex in his car. They drove out into the countryside, walked in the woods and fields and made love al fresco.

'Naked as nature intended,' said Diana.

'Our summer of love,' said Alistair.

'Does Helen do this to you... or this?'

'I'm not sure. Do it again..... and I'll tell you.'

10

Alistair faced his choir. It was a sultry summer evening and already people were fanning themselves with their music.

He waved a score.

'Vivaldi's Gloria. Who knows it?'

A few hands went up - not as many as he had hoped.

'This is what we'll be singing in the first half of our next concert. I have booked a string quartet to accompany us and three soloists. It's a bit of a new departure for us – I promise you you're going to love it.'

They opened their copies. One of the altos expressed dismay at having to sing in Latin. Alistair pretended not to hear her.

'We'll begin at the beginning, starting with the basses. Listen while Jonathan plays your part.'

Vivaldi's harmonies were not too demanding and they rattled through the first section.

'Good. Do you like it?'

He nodded with satisfaction at the chorus of approval. He put his hands in his pockets and walked up and down in front of them.

'In the second half we're returning to more familiar ground. The theme of the concert is Hallelujah so we'll do the Leonard Cohen version and Handel's Hallelujah chorus from the Messiah, both familiar to us. The Handel will end the concert and I shall invite our audience to stand and join in with us.'

He returned to his music stand and leaned on it, enjoying the excited buzz running round the room.

'OK? Let's look at the Handel first. Remember, there are

a lot of words ending with 's'. No hissing. I'll bring you all off with my left hand.'

He stole a glance at Diana.

It was the beginning of October and all seemed to be under control. The last practice before the Festival concert. The string quartet was there for the first time which they all found both scary and thrilling. Alistair arranged everyone where he wanted them.

'We'll start with the Vivaldi. We still need to tidy up these ragged word endings Just watch me.'

Knowing that every good teacher is also an actor, he entertained them in his usual fashion with anecdotes from his past and snippets from his present, while also asking for their full attention and effort. Mostly, he felt, he got it. Respect was mutual. It was a lively practice and boded well for the performance.

On the night of the concert, looking dashing in his black suit and black bow tie, he followed the choir into the hall, jumped up onto his podium and waited for the applause to die down. He scanned the array of faces before him and flashed them all an encouraging smile.

Victoria, her senses heightened by the occasion, hoped they wouldn't disappoint him. Ever professional, he always maintained an outward calm but, watching closely, she had learned to read the quiet smile of satisfaction when something had gone well or the momentary grimace of dismay when a section missed an entrance or a tricky note was obviously wrong. The string quartet sawed away with brio and the soloists inspired the choir to new heights.

At the interval, she saw Diana draining her bottle of water and went over to her.

'Wasn't the Vivaldi super? Alistair doing what he does so well and us singing our hearts out. He really does have everything we need - brilliant musicianship, an engaging manner, the ability to inspire and loads of sex appeal. We're so lucky to have him.'

Diana sparkled with enjoyment. 'It was brilliant, I loved every minute. I hope the second half will be as good.'

They filed back out into the hall, and, as the lights went down, the audience settled themselves expectantly. Their confidence boosted by the success of the Vivaldi, the choir continued with songs of praise and celebration until all too soon, it was time for the finale.

'Gloria can be translated as Hallelujah,' Alistair told them, 'so, with the Hallelujah Chorus, we have come full circle. Please feel free to join in.'

A buzz of excitement ran through the audience as they rose to their feet.

He metaphorically crossed his fingers. For this, he'd got to keep together the choir, the string quartet, the three soloists, the pianist, the audience and the young man brought in to play the drums. Why did he take on these things? It could go so wrong.

But the resulting rapturous cacophony was thrilling.

He bowed and smiled and, turning back, saw that his breathless choir were cheering and applauding him too.

11

Alistair couldn't sleep. Helen always insisted on having the window open and he was aware of every car that passed and every plane that howled its descent to the airport. He got up, went downstairs and poured himself a small tot of whisky. He hungered for Diana.

Their relationship was escalating in intensity. It wasn't just the sex he told himself. Her unconventional attitudes and youthful enthusiasms stimulated him too. She made him feel as if he'd been living in a box for the past few years, plucked out every so often to do his musical thing, and put back when the performance was over, with the lid shut down tight and a fat lady sitting on it. It was unfortunate but, beside the dazzling Diana, Helen was frumpy, predictable and, if he were honest, mind-numbingly dull.

He knew his affair, should it be discovered, would be looked at very unfavourably by the school's governing body. This wasn't a state school where he imagined teachers with loose morals were ten-a-penny; he was taking a big risk – which was all part of the excitement.

The powers-that-be at South Heath were pillars of rectitude and righteousness. The Christian ethic was strong, and, mindful of the effect scandal might have on the paying parents, they were ruthless in cases of anything that deviated from an old-school, conservative norm. For a fee-paying establishment, gaining a bad reputation for any reason would be disastrous.

God knows he had committed no heinous crime, but he would not be able to stand up in front of a class as a known adulterer and a cheat. One of the drawbacks of a close knit community was that there were few secrets to be had.

Little by little, Diana was increasing the pressure on him. What had begun as, 'I wish we could be together forever. I want to wake up next to you every morning,' had inexorably progressed to 'When are you going to leave Helen? I can't bear this much longer.' He couldn't tell her what she longed to hear. Lying to Helen about where he was going or where he had been, was stressful enough, but his obsession with Diana was becoming harder to manage. He resisted the temptation of the whisky bottle and went back to bed.

The next morning Helen was up bright and early. She emptied the machine of its overnight wash and went outside to peg it out, taking care as she always did to see that each garment had a pair of clothes pegs of the same colour.

Once, years ago, while she was out shopping, Alistair had gone into the garden and swapped all the pegs round, mixing up the blues with the reds and yellows. Rather than laughing at his joke, she had patiently spent the next ten minutes re-pegging the whole line. She couldn't explain why this was, but why should she feel she had to? Didn't everyone have illogical habits? He wouldn't do that sort of thing now. He was changing. Perhaps she was too. Who could tell?

She made herself a cup of green tea and sat outside to admire the whiteness of her pillow cases. Somewhere near a dog barked incessantly, and a holiday jet descended with a roar of reverse thrust to Bristol Airport.

She went back inside. She would make the bed and tidy the bedroom, then reward herself with a little light lunch.

'Typical.' She clucked with annoyance. He'd left his suit jacket hanging over the chair again. She picked it up, found the coat hanger and went to get the clothes brush out of the drawer. There were several long blonde hairs on the sleeves. She despatched them expertly.

A disquieting thought quivered at the back of her mind. It grew until she couldn't ignore it. Surely there was a rational explanation. It was such a cliché. But, one by one, odd things he'd said and done, or not said and not done, attached themselves to her fear until a gelatinous mass sat heavily in her stomach and she felt sick.

Who could she talk to? Who would tell her she was being ridiculous? Victoria? No, too close to Alistair. Rachel? Too close to Victoria. She shivered, realising she was on her own with this one. She detested confrontations and would go to great lengths to avoid them, even if it meant storing up resentments for weeks and months. This was different though. Did she really think she could go on as though nothing was wrong?

When he came in from school, she was at the kitchen table with an opened bottle of wine in front of her.

'A bit early for you,' he teased. 'Having a bad day?'

'You could say that.' Her expression was as sour as the cheap wine she always bought. He made the effort.

'Pour one for me then while I go and get changed, and you can tell me all about it.'

When he came down, she was ready.

He listened to her and raised a sardonic eyebrow.

'Oh, come on Helen. It's not like you to have an over-active imagination.'

But by then she'd had time to reflect on various occasions when his behaviour had deviated from the norm. The blonde hairs on his jacket were by way of one warning too many.

She hid her clenched fists under the table.

'One night, I called you after choir practice. Your phone was switched off so I tried Victoria, presuming you were in the pub with the rest of them. I explained I wanted you to come home because I felt really poorly. I'd been throwing up since eight o'clock. She said she was sorry but you weren't there and suggested you might be already on your way home. But you weren't were you? You came in after midnight and said you'd gone back to Keith's for a nightcap. But that was a lie. I saw Isobel the next day and she said she hadn't seen you for weeks.'

She cited the times his phone would ring and he'd go out into the garden and walk up and down talking for ages.

'You said it was just school talk, and you didn't want to bore me. And, maybe, most telling of all, you haven't made love to me for months.'

She didn't add that she hadn't minded, and had reflected gratefully that it must be due to him getting older. Instead she went back on the offensive.

'I don't think my suspicions are unfounded. Are they? You're having an affair with somebody.'

She folded her arms, challenging him directly. 'For God's sake, Alistair, be honest with me.'

He got up and took his wine glass over to the sink. Here it was. The moment he'd dreaded. Could he lie his way out of it? He thought for a minute, then turned round and said, 'I've been seeing Diana.'

Helen's shoulders dropped. The forlorn hope that it had all been a figment of her imagination was shattered. She had to ask the questions. She needed to know the answers, but all she really wanted to do was run and hide.

How long had it been going on for? How often did they meet? Where did they meet? Did he love her?

The guilt was clear in his eyes. He made no excuses, and answered her questions simply. He was clearly sparing her the details. Devastated by the betrayal and the humiliation, her first reaction was,

'How could you do this to me?'

He had no answer to that.

'Who else knows?'

The lie came easily. 'No one.'

'So what are you going to do now? Have you a plan?'

She bit her lip and tasted blood. Never before had she felt so helpless.

He said, 'I'll end it. I love you. I've hated all the deceit.'

But she knew that it was her life, the life that had suited her so well that had ended. It would never be the same again.

Somehow, numb with pain, she carried on. She barely slept and had no desire to get out of bed in the morning. Even her routines and rituals of housewifery lost their attraction.

The front door would bang. That was him gone. Off to a rewarding day's teaching. Out every night. What had she got to do with her days? Wash his pants and iron his shirts. What had she done wrong that he would forfeit twenty years of comfortable marriage, his home and, quite possibly, his job, for a blonde bimbo? The daily rows, followed by sullen silences, were unbearable. She could hardly bear to look at him.

One night she told him. 'I can't go on like this any longer. You need to find yourself somewhere else to live for a bit and sort yourself out. Maybe a break will help us both.'

It was something of a test, born of desperation. If he had gone to live with Diana, that would have signalled the end of her marriage. To her relief, he appeared unwilling to draw the line and moved out to a poky flat above the butchers.

Diana, dismayed when Alistair refused to move in with her, spent as much time with him as she could, soothing him, cooking delicious meals, telling him how wonderful he was and making love to him creatively and inventively at every opportunity.

Mulling over his misery, Alistair recognised his feelings of besotted helplessness. When he was eight, his father brought home a boxer dog called Maisie and she became his best friend. She would climb up onto his lap, crushing him beneath her. She loved him so much and woke him every morning, covering his face with big slobbering kisses. She slept on his bed at night and waited by the front door every afternoon for him to come in from school.

Her desire to protect him from all comers led her to terrorise the milkman, the post lady and the window cleaner. She ripped to shreds anything that came through the letterbox and once chased an elderly lady down the road. Alistair, hearing the terrified shrieks, had rushed to the rescue.

His father said that the dog would have to go. So Alistair made himself some jam sandwiches and, together, he and Maisie set off up the lane. At the crossroads they met the vicar, a kindly man. Alistair sang in his church choir, and the old parson saw the child had been crying.

'What's the trouble Alistair?'

'I'm running away. Daddy says Maisie has got to go so we're going to find somewhere else to live.'

Luckily the vicar was a dog lover who already owned a Labrador. He took the boy's hand.

'Come on Alistair, let's go back and we'll see if Maisie would like to come and live with us for a bit. We'll persuade your father that I will be able to train your bumptious boxer into a sensible dog and you can come and visit whenever you want. If she settles then you can have her back.' Alistair didn't know what 'bumptious' meant, but he understood it as a word which fitted Maisie admirably. Alistair's father had his doubts about Maisie's trainability, but anxious to be rid of such a nuisance, agreed. The vicar's wife was even less enthusiastic but kept her thoughts to herself when she saw the boy's stricken face.

Alistair did visit, but it wasn't the same. Maisie never came back.

In the Headmaster's house Keith picked up Percy's lead and set off across the school playing fields. He needed to shake off this feeling of despondency.

It wasn't due to the days growing shorter and the chilly, misty mornings signalling the approach of winter. He quite enjoyed the drawing in of the nights, and pulling together the curtains to settle down by the fire for a cosy supper with Isobel. He even liked to kick at the piles of fallen leaves like a child, after a quick look round to make sure no one was watching.

Things were different this year. As Percy ran ahead of him towards the wood, he still felt the orange leaves crisp under his feet like bits of toast, but now even this annual pleasure had lost its charm. The everyday management of the school was continuing to be difficult for him. He was grateful that Victoria covered for his lapses of memory and tried to delegate as much as she could to his deputies, but he could sense that amongst the staff and pupils there was a feeling that things were not quite as they should be. In the past he'd been known for his coolness under pressure and ability to think on his feet, but these days he just felt weary and wanted it all to go away.

Alistair could make a good head. Pity that he didn't know where to draw the line. The memory came flooding back from across the years…Yvonne… but he'd known when to stop. He got home and went into his study. He had a decision to make. He would talk to Isobel first, but he already knew what her answer would be. She'd been hinting it was time to go for months. Percy, hearing footsteps on the gravel, barked.

Diana stood at his front door, plucking up the courage to knock. What she was about to do was probably a waste of time, but no straw was too fragile for her to her to clutch at. She was encouraged by his beaming smile when he opened the door and saw who it was.

'Hello Keith. Can you spare me a minute?'

'Come in my dear. Diana, isn't it? To what do I owe this not inconsiderable pleasure?'

'We've met before, over twenty years ago,' she began, following him into his sunny study and taking the seat offered. The room smelt of old leather and lavender furniture polish.

'Surely not, I'm sure I wouldn't have forgotten you.'

She ignored his clumsy gallantry and continued. 'My mother was a cleaner at Field View prep school. The Head let her bring me to work with her after school, because she saw Mum was struggling as a single parent. You were a new teacher, and you let me clean out the guinea pigs in your classroom, while you did your marking. I was about six.'

Keith's jaw dropped. 'Little Diana, of course, I remember. Fancy that. You have changed a bit since then. Well, well, well. You're right - it was a long time ago.' He got up from his chair, took her hand and pumped it up and down enthusiastically.

'How is your mother?'

Diana waved that away. That wasn't what she'd come to

talk about.

'My childhood was difficult, to say the least, but,' and she raised her big blue eyes to his, 'I felt safe with you and I thought of you as my grown- up friend.' She saw a flicker of apprehension on his face and rushed on.

'I take it you'll have heard talk about my relationship with Alistair?'

'I don't listen to gossip. One of my rules.'

'Well, he's worried about the damage that might be done to his career, although, personally, I can't see how his private life is any concern whatsoever of the Governors. I just wanted to ask you, as someone who was kind to me before, if you could use your influence to persuade them that once his divorce is through, we will,' she attempted a light laugh, 'become respectable.'

She was embroidering the truth a little. Divorce hadn't actually been mentioned, neither for that matter had marriage, but the risk that Keith wouldn't tell Alistair of her visit was one worth taking. Right on cue, her eyes filled with tears and she pulled out a tissue dabbing daintily as they rolled down her cheeks.

'You see, Keith, I love him so much and we just want to be together.'

She watched as Keith walked over to his French windows and surveyed his fine lawn. He turned and looked at her.

'I can't reveal school secrets, my dear, but there are changes afoot. Be assured that I will act in Alistair's best interests when the time comes. Now, if you'll excuse me, I am rather busy today. It's been lovely to see you.'

'Of course. I'm very grateful to you for listening to me. Thank you for your time.'

Diana left, not knowing whether she'd done any good, but pleased with herself for having tried. If she could stop Alistair from worrying about the gossips and rumour-mongers, he'd perhaps be more willing to move in with her and enjoy their burgeoning affair, while taking the necessary steps to end his miserable marriage.

12

Rachel glared resentfully at the green mountain of sprouts piled up in the supermarket. The loudspeakers shrieked for Wayne to go to the checkout and a pensioner pushed her aside to reach for a turnip. She should have gone to Waitrose.

She rounded the corner of the next aisle and there was a clash of trollies.

'Sorry.' It was Helen, who then tried to push past without acknowledging her.

'Hey, wait a minute', she grabbed Helen's coat sleeve. 'I've been thinking about you. How are things?' Helen looked at her dead eyed.

'Alistair's gone but I'm fine', she managed, 'absolutely fine. Now if you'll excuse me, I'm in a hurry.'

'Please Helen; I know what you're going through. I've been there, remember? Come and have a coffee with me. We can park our trollies by the café'. Helen shook her head.

'Sorry Rachel, I don't feel like talking.'

'We don't have to discuss Alistair. We'll talk about politics or knitting. Come on, I insist. My feet are killing me and coffee and a sticky bun will just hit the spot.'

Rachel was employing her inner bully, but it seemed to be working. Helen shrugged and together they made for the coffee shop at the far end of the store.

'Go on, you grab a table, I'll be right with you,' said Rachel. She gave Helen a little push and joined the queue. A few minutes later she carefully put the tray down. 'They're busy today.'

Helen was rubbing hand gel in. She whispered, 'Sorry, but I can't bear those trolley handles. God knows how many people have been pushing them around with their filthy fingers.' She put the little bottle back in her bag and leaned forward conspiratorially.

'I have a confession'.

'What's that?'

'I can't knit.'

The two women giggled. Encouraged, Helen ventured, 'Did you know I studied psychology at university? I wanted to be a therapist – before I married Alistair? Some therapist I'd have been. I can't even hold my own marriage together.'

Then she laughed as Rachel bit into her doughnut and jam spurted out, dribbling down her blouse. Rachel tutted with annoyance and scrubbed at the stain with a tissue.

Helen wondered how much she should reveal. She had nothing to lose.

'I went to see her, you know'.

Rachel's eyes opened wide.

'Diana? Oh my. What did she have to say for herself?'

'Nothing. As soon as she saw it was me, she tried to close the door. I stuck my foot in it to stop her and said we needed to talk. She wouldn't reply and just kept pushing on the door. In the end I had to walk away. I don't know what I was hoping to achieve. It just felt like the right thing to do. You know, woman to woman....' Her voice trailed off.

'She's nothing but a scheming, manipulative bitch', said Rachel, 'and she needn't think about showing her face at choir again.'

'Well yes, but it takes two you know. If our marriage had been solid he wouldn't have wanted another woman.' She sipped at the cup of rank coffee. She should have asked for tea.

'Ha! How many couples do you know with a perfect marriage? Do you want him back, or is that a silly question?'

'I don't know. He was the sweetest, kindest man I'd ever met. I would have put money on him never straying, but he has so......'

She stood up. 'Anyway I've got to think of myself now, not him. Thanks for the coffee. You can have my bun.'

Another marriage bites the dust. Rachel got up and found her half- filled trolley. She finished her shopping. Why, she thought, when we all have so much do we still want more? She wished she still had Victoria to share these moments with and wondered, not for the first time, whether she had been a little hasty in her summary rejection of the friendship.

Helen got home. She unpacked her bags. It was already dark so she turned the lights on. The evening was warm and all the windows were open allowing daddy-long-legs to come in to circle the lampshades. She hated them. What was almost as bad, was the autumnal visitation of enormous spiders had begun, in spite of the conkers she had scattered round the edges of her rooms. She closed the windows, retreated into the sitting room and turned on the television. The novelty of doing what she liked, when she liked, was beginning to wear off and the house felt empty. That night she had the recurring nightmare that had plagued her since childhood.

She was small and completely lost in a garden. The undergrowth was towering over her, with brambles reaching out to scratch her bare legs and huge trees blocking the sun. She was hot and sticky and sensed that, hidden among the jungle of leaves, were beady- eyed little men, watching her. There was even one beside the pond, fishing. Horrid little bearded gnomes - telling her to get out of their garden. There were flying things too. Moths beat their dusty wings in her ears, ants scurried up and down her legs and spiders sat fatly in their webs, waiting for her to blunder into them so they could rush out and suck her blood. She woke up screaming, and longed for Alistair to hold her and keep her safe, but there was only a one-eared teddy bear, lost in the tangled sheets.

13

Victoria was doing a little light dusting, but her mind was not on the job.

'What should I do?' Robin looked back at her silently from his frame on the piano.

'You always said I had lovely hair. You wouldn't think that now. I'm far too young to be going grey.'

She'd noted her propensity to talk more frequently to Robin these past few months and wondered why. A couple of months ago Rachel caught her out in the garden discussing the delphiniums with him. This time, in his soothing way, he put the thought in her mind that if she were unhappy with her hair, she should go and have something done about it. She rang the salon and booked herself a colour and a cut with Paul.

She and Paul went back twenty years. Once, depressed and low, she had called into the salon on spec and asked if someone could please just wash her hair for her. Not only did Paul find someone to do just that, but tuning into her mood, he told the girl to give her a long, soothing scalp massage as well. He had refused to let her pay and sent her away with a smile and said he hoped to see her again. Now, over two hundred appointments later, she had repaid his act of kindness with her loyalty. He knew more about her ups and downs than many of her friends, and, more importantly, he cut her hair more skilfully than any hairdresser she had ever had.

'Hello gorgeous! How are you? Come and sit in the chair of love. Is it to be the usual?'

Victoria submitted to having the voluminous black cape draped around her shoulders and felt, as always, like a giant toddler wearing a bib.

Paul rested his hands on her shoulders. 'You're looking wonderful. I see a twinkle in your eye. Come on, spill the beans, I know you too well .Something's happened to put that smile on your face.'

Victoria laughed. She adored Paul. He was better than a course of anti- depressants. But she prevaricated, 'There's nothing really – not that I'm going to talk about anyway.'

She looked at her face in his mirror. Usually, all she could see was her mother's critical face. Today though, she did look brighter. The morning session in her neglected garden; cutting back, clearing weeds and staking the Michaelmas daisies which were leaning over so disastrously, had done her good. Her cheeks were quite pink.

'Work your magic', she said to Paul, "I'm going out tonight'.

'Ooooh. I just knew it. Who's the lucky man?' He began to wield his scissors.

Victoria became conscious of ears around her beginning to flap. She sunk down further in her seat and wished she had kept her mouth shut. While she was beginning to enjoy her friendship with Marcus, she didn't want curious ears to pick up on it and make it common knowledge. Rumours flew swiftly in a small community becoming exaggerated and distorted. She knew that Rachel was bound to hear them and be unhappy about it.

Instead, as he began to snip, she ignored his question and encouraged him to tell her all about his recent walking holiday in Vietnam. She in turn told him, that, after an absence of four weeks, she'd been disappointed when the cat had walked back in, starving hungry and covered with ticks, but otherwise unharmed.

'Have a good night, my darling', he whispered in her ear as she got up to leave. 'I shall want all the details when you next come in.' He helped her on with her coat and said, 'You can tell how much I love you because I don't charge you for a blow dry after your cut.'

Amazed, she said 'Don't you? I didn't know.'

'Well, it's not really a blow dry proper - more of a waft,' and lowering his voice, he added,

'After all, I didn't have to get my tool out!'

He paused, 'I just used my fingers.'

Shaking her head in mock censure at his ribaldry, she fled, hoping he hadn't been overheard.

At home, she contemplated her daily 'To Do' list. On a notepad, next to her comfy chair, it told her to put a wash on, phone the vicar and cut back the ivy. Her other 'To Do' list, which existed only in her head, to be visited at 2am on sleepless nights, itemised more intractable problems. Chief of these was her friendship with Rachel.

Victoria was missing her and although it was Rachel who had stormed out, might she have calmed down by now and be missing her too? She should text her and suggest meeting up for peace keeping talks at the coffee shop. What's the worst that could happen? As she reached for her phone, there was a knock on the door. Rachel stood there looking contrite.

'I've come to make up. I know that I completely over-reacted.'

Victoria beamed with relief.

'Come in. You won't believe this but I'd just picked up my phone to text you to see if you fancied a coffee. You know Marcus being there really wasn't what it looked like. You jumped to completely the wrong conclusions.'

'I know. It's a dog-in-the-manger thing. I don't want him but I don't want anyone else to have him either. I remembered you both in Bruges, going off together…'

'As far as I'm concerned, Marcus is a friend and that's all. We spend time together occasionally, I enjoy his company, but we are not having an affair.'

Victoria picked up her cardigan and her purse.

'Come on, let me buy you a cappuccino and a sticky cake. The coffee shop shouldn't be too busy on a Monday. You and I have known each other for so long, we shouldn't be letting an ex-husband come between us.'

An hour later they were still there. Victoria could tell, that having caught up on the minutiae of their lives since they had last chatted, Rachel had more to say. She waited.

Eventually Rachel picked up her teaspoon and scraped the cold froth lingering around her cup.

'OK Victoria. I've been thinking about Marcus and how our marriage went wrong. I accept some responsibility, obviously, but I think that there are things about him you ought to know, which might have a bearing on you and him.'

Victoria interrupted. 'There is no me and him.'

Rachel waved her hand in dismissal. 'You say that now but you might yet be tempted because Marcus can be single minded when he wants something. When we met, he was wonderful. He couldn't do enough for me and made me feel very special. But there is a good Marcus and a bad Marcus.' She paused. Why did she want Victoria to hear this? She hoped it wasn't just so she could have the pleasure of saying 'I told you so.'

Victoria shook her head. 'Do we have to talk about Marcus?'

'Just let me just say this and then, I promise, I'll never mention him again.'

Victoria smiled wryly. 'I doubt that very much, but go on then.'

'I'm serious.' Rachel leaned forward. 'He has a low boredom threshold. When you are no longer enough for him, he will become very controlling. You'll hate that. I know you will.'

She looked at her watch. Was there time for another cup? She continued. 'I'll give you some examples. He wouldn't let me put my hands in my jacket pockets because it would stretch the material and spoil the hang. He didn't like me wearing trousers and, even in winter, he wouldn't let me wear anything in bed.'

Victoria laughed. 'That's enough.'

'No. Listen. You can mock, but these little things all add up. Suddenly you realise the element of choice has been taken away from everything you do. More importantly, when he's bored, he drinks too much and will upset your family and friends with vicious personal comments on their views and behaviours. You haven't seen it yet – but it will happen. We were all a lot younger when you knew him years ago. He's changed. He's the sort of man that if something is bad already, he will make it worse. If it's good, he'll spoil it.'

Victoria stood up. 'I'll bear all that in mind. But, as I said, there is no me and Marcus - at the moment anyway. I must be getting back. I need to hang out the washing so it'll be dry for tomorrow.' They hugged, but each was aware that, even after today, it would take time and effort if their relationship was to get back to how it had been.

Victoria pegged out the washing and reflected on Rachel's words. By now, she had indeed met Marcus a couple of times. Once for lunch, and the second time they'd had an evening walk along the Kennet and Avon canal, followed by a glass of wine in a canal side pub. Away from the village, she'd been able to relax, watch the ducks on the water and drink in the pleasure of undivided male attention. He had revealed that he played the saxophone with a small local group and had asked if she would like to go and hear them play in a couple of weeks' time.

'I've never been a groupie', she'd told him. He'd laughed and said something about widening her horizons, which she found a bit insulting. What did he know about her horizons?

He rang that night to repeat the suggestion.

'Saturday at the Green Dragon.'

'OK. I'll meet you there,' she told him, 'You'll be involved with stuff and I don't want to be in the way.' She'd also be able to leave when she wanted to, a necessity born of experience.

It wasn't easy deciding on the appropriate dress for the evening. She smiled, her mother would refer to her as an ageing hippy. Perhaps she would make a statement; give a hint that maybe there was something more to her than people thought.

Should she tell Rachel she was going? No. It wouldn't help.

One night out wasn't necessarily going to lead to another.

She hadn't consciously stopped eating but, despite all the cakes, the stress and tension of the last few months had crushed her appetite and she was delighted to find she had lost weight.

To celebrate, she bought a filmy tunic top in fine purple cotton with a silver thread running through it, and found some long silver earrings she had never dared wear before. She twirled in front of the long mirror in her bedroom and felt as if she was eighteen again.

Victoria decided she would also treat herself to a pedicure. Her relationship with Marcus had caused her to be more aware of the finer points of body maintenance. To her amusement she found herself depilating, moisturising and plucking areas which, previously, she had happily left to nature. The salon offered her an appointment at 1.15 with Diana. Victoria took it thinking it might be another opportunity to get to know this girl with the sad eyes.

She found Diana in professional mode. There was no hint of complicity as she greeted her client and invited her to soak her feet in a bowl of warm, gently fizzing, scented water. Victoria struggled to make conversation.

'Given that feet are often an unlovely part of the body, do you ever come across particularly horrid ones you'd rather not touch?'

Diana's reply was smooth. 'Certainly not. My job is to make people feel rejuvenated on the inside as well as on the outside. I can transform neglected feet and, with the massage and the relaxing experience, I can send my clients home feeling, and looking, better than when they came in.'

Turning the lights down low and the saccharine music a little higher, Diana suggested that Victoria should relax and think nice thoughts for a few minutes. She did try, but nice thoughts were hard to come by. Then Diana gently patted Victoria's feet dry and bent over her toenails, expertly clipping and filing them smooth. Then kneading her feet, she said, 'This cream is mint and ginger and will reduce any tiredness and swelling. Have you thought about what colour you would like your toenails painted?'

Victoria, too ashamed to reveal that she hadn't painted her toenails since Robin died, eyed up the array of little bottles glowing in jewel colours.

'This is really difficult. I'm not good at decisions at the best of times.'

The pinks were too pink and the reds too garish. She could see nothing that was subtle and muted as befitting a woman of advancing years. Finally she threw her inhibitions to the winds and chose a deep purple. For the first time Diana laughed and Victoria briefly saw another side to her.

'Good for you.' she said.

Victoria told her about a poem she had read that said when you grow old you should wear purple. She couldn't remember the exact sentiment but it didn't matter. Diana's eyes glowed with a sense of fun as she protested that Victoria wasn't that old.

Encouraged, Victoria decided to probe a little. 'Are you enjoying the choir?

Was it her imagination or did Diana draw back a little?

'Yes, very much.'

'How do you find Alistair…..some of the ladies are slightly intimidated by him – especially when he gets critical?'

Diana looked surprised. 'I can't say he frightens me. But sometimes I can see why it might be frustrating for him when we can't get things right. Now, are you happy with this colour?'

Victoria saw that the topic of Alistair had been closed down. Fair enough. She left hoping that maybe she had built a bridge between herself and Diana. A wobbly rope one - rather than solid stone, nevertheless a bridge. It was a start.

Saturday arrived. She downed a large glass of wine for courage and rang for a taxi. The taxi driver was in a talkative mood. When Victoria told him the name of the pub where the jazz club met, he knew it instantly. 'I used to go there', he roared from the front of the cab, 'I met my wife at that jazz club. Once a month, on a Thursday night, I'd finish early and end up there, watching her sitting with her mates and trying to pluck up the courage to ask her out.'

'Go on', said Victoria, settling back in her seat to enjoy the reminiscence, knowing it would take her attention away from feeling nervous.

'Eventually one of her mates came over and said Kylie wanted to know why I was staring at her. So I said it was because I thought she was bloody gorgeous. Pardon my French; I'd had a few by then. I watched her friend go back and tell Kylie what I had said. She just rolled her eyes and ignored me. I was gutted. She was there again, a month later, and this time I wasn't going to be put off. I cornered her at the bar, bought her a drink. Six months later our Dean were on the way and we got married.'

'A happy ending', smiled Victoria, her fears about the evening ahead quite forgotten, and tipped him a little more extravagantly than she might have done.

She found Marcus waiting for her just inside. He showed her to a table, saying,

'We aren't on until about nine thirty, so sit down and I'll get us a drink. What would you like?'

Victoria asked for a glass of white wine, she didn't want him to see her with red teeth, and while he was gone, she looked around hoping there wasn't anyone from the village there. To her surprise, she saw, in a corner of the room opposite her, Keith with two young women. After the initial shock she realised they were his daughters whom she hadn't seen for a couple of years, since they left home to go to university. The two gawky teenagers, with braces and bad skin, had matured into stunning young women with curtains of long hair and endless legs in very short skirts. She watched the three of them engrossed in conversation, the girls roaring with laughter at something Keith said. Catching his eye she waved across the room. He beamed and beckoned her over.

'Come and say hello,' he bellowed.

'Amelia, Cressida, do you remember Victoria, my right

hand woman? Of course you do. Sit down Victoria, we're celebrating me officially becoming an old codger.' He lowered his voice and moved in to whisper in her ear.

'Here's advance warning, just for you. I've given in my notice at school, but keep it to yourself for the time being. I shall recommend Alistair to the Governors as a worthy successor, once he's sorted himself out.' He sat back, beaming, and raised his glass to her. She gasped.

'Oh Heavens. This is a bit of a shock. Are you absolutely sure?'

'Yes, I am. I can't tell you how relieved I feel now I've made my mind up.'

'Well, I'm sorry to hear it. I won't say anything, I promise, until you tell me it's official.'

She tried to conceal her alarm. He was so obviously happy with his decision, and she stayed chatting with them for a few minutes more until she saw Marcus returning with their drinks. So she made her excuses and returned to their table, her mind whirring. This was going to affect all of them, not least Alistair. Marcus asked, 'Was that Keith you were talking to? He's looking a lot older these days.'

'I suppose he is getting on a bit. I must confess I'd hardly noticed.'

He laughed. 'We're all getting on a bit now. All the more reason to gather ye rosebuds…..'

'My sentiments exactly. Cheers.'

The band on the stage was telling her she was their sunshine and the singer seemed to be echoing that statement straight at her. She smiled and raised her glass to him. There was a small dance floor. A couple more glasses of wine and she'd be likely to be pulling Marcus up onto his feet. She did hope he was the sort of man who wasn't afraid to dance. So many were. When the set finished to loud applause, Marcus excused himself to her and went to join his friends onstage. Not much liking trad jazz, she was pleased that their style was more melodious and relaxed. The clarinet player was really rather good. She watched Keith's daughters being chatted up by young men at the bar, and then spotted Keith coming across to join her. He sat down.

'Well, Victoria. What do you think of my decision?'

She saw a small muscle twitching on his temple.

'I'll miss you, but we've had a good run. I think you're right to go now. Spend some time with Isobel, see the world while you can.' She could see he was relieved.

'Thanks, I intend to.' He took her hand. 'We were a good team, you and me, Victoria. I'll miss you.'

They both joined in the enthusiastic applause for Marcus and his group taking their bow. He then joined them, flushed and happy, and swept Victoria up onto the dance floor. She couldn't remember when she had enjoyed an evening so much. He had escorted her home and going to bed together had seemed like the most natural thing in the world. She definitely wouldn't be telling Rachel about that, especially after her denials when they'd last discussed him. Her attempts at self-justification rather failed to cover up her sense of guilt and discomfort. It was a problem she was happy to file away to be addressed another day - should it prove to be necessary.

14

It was Speech Day at South Heath School. Keith and his staff, resplendent in gowns and furry hoods, processed up the centre aisle.

Five hundred pupils in immaculate uniform whispered and fidgeted, until Keith stood at the lectern and fixed them with a basilisk eye.

He delivered the usual peroration on the school's successes in the year just gone; exaggerated the mediocre examination results; boasted about the student who had gone up to Oxford; lavished praise on the sports teams and thanked his staff for all their hard work.

Then, gripping the lectern, his knuckles showing white, he looked down across the rows of heads.

'I have an announcement to make.' He paused for effect.

'I have informed the Governors that it is my intention to retire at the end of this term.'

A murmur of surprise ran around the hall.

'I apologise to you all for the short notice. My decision is solely due to my poor health. Alistair McIntyre will be acting Head until such time as a new Head is appointed.'

Alistair sat, his expression of sympathy and regret concealing the excitement he felt at Keith's confirmation of his plan to retire.

Several days earlier, the Chair of Governors had approached him and told him of Keith's decision.

'In the strictest confidence for the moment, Alistair, would you consider taking on the role of acting Head? The headship will be advertised immediately. Should the successful candidate come from another school, he or she will have to give a two terms notice so the job will run from Easter. The Governors might want to appoint an internal candidate to ensure a swift succession, and maybe, Alistair, that person could be you. Being Assistant Head for pastoral care as well as the Director of Music amply qualifies you for promotion. So you've got the next couple of months to demonstrate your aptitude and enthusiasm for the job.'

Alistair nodded soberly to conceal that inside, his heart was dancing a jig of delight. But the Chairman's next words pulled him up.

'The governors very much hope you'll be able to sort out your, ahem, marital difficulties.'

He took the not very subtle hint was that if he wanted a chance at the top job, he would have to go back to Helen. The alternative, getting a divorce and turning his mistress into his wife, wasn't possible in the time scale.

Did he want to marry Diana? Although he would be proud to be seen about with such an attractive young woman, she was hardly Headmaster's wife material. He needed to be exuding gravitas, not flaunting a nubile second wife. On the other hand, maybe he'd be the envy of every red-blooded male in the school with her at his side.

As he sat through the guest speaker's attempt to inspire the pupils with the story of his own success in life, his mind was racing. To be head of this prestigious school, with the generous salary and the elegant Georgian house that went with it, would be to have reached the pinnacle of his career. He had spent the whole of his professional life after this prize.

He knew he was up to the job and he'd got lots of ideas for updating certain elements of the curriculum and attracting new students from the Far East and the Arab world. There'd been talk of building a sister school in Dubai. He could end up hobnobbing with sheiks and graciously accepting a Philippe Patek watch for getting that young Saudi princeling into Cambridge. What was the alternative? Turn away from the good life and live in relative penury with his bewitching lover? He'd be trading relative contentment and a life of luxury for firm young flesh and as much sex as any man could manage. How Victorian of the old biddies on the governing body to look down their noses at him if he left his boring old wife to live in sin with his lover.

None of their business of course, but the maintenance of tradition and the status quo is part and parcel of working in a school like this. He knew that. He could apply elsewhere for promotion - somewhere far away - where no one knew anything about his private life. He could even divorce Helen and marry Diana. It wouldn't be too late for them even to have a family. Dare he do that? No! The sensible thing was to try and convince Helen that it would be in both their interests to attempt a reconciliation. He couldn't pass up the chance of this Headship. He hardened his heart. Diana must be seen as a pleasing interlude. He hoped she would find someone else who would love her as much as he did. As soon as Speech Day was over, he would ring Helen and suggest lunch. He would take her somewhere they'd been to before in happier times, soften her up with a good wine and bring the full weight of his charm to bear. She must surely be missing him by now.

Helen had gone down the lane to pick the last of the blackberries. Probably a pointless exercise given her situation, but old habits were hard to break. She was remembering how she and Alistair had first met. Twenty five years ago this very month, she was studying Psychology at university in London and Alistair was doing his post-grad teacher training. They were introduced by a mutual friend, in a pub by the river.

Long after the others had gone home to their beds, they walked along the Embankment, leaned over Westminster Bridge and talked and talked. Helen couldn't remember what they discussed, but she did still remember the extraordinary feeling of homecoming and belonging with this man, who challenged her preconceptions and pronouncements. He was clever, she admired that, but he was also exciting and tactile and he had tucked her arm in his as they walked along as if they had been together for years. He was also by far the best looking of her boyfriends so far and she'd felt so lucky to be with him.

She'd better get back and make herself look presentable. Her hands were stained purple with blackberry juice. He was coming to take her out to lunch. She should make an effort. Should she let him see what he was missing? Did she care?

Wearing the cobalt blue shirt which Helen had bought him at Christmas, Alistair drove back to the marital home, his stomach churning. What a sorry mess he had made, and was he ever going to be able to sort it out without blood being spilt? Fancy thinking that the blue shirt would make any difference. It felt weird being there as a visitor, and an unwelcome one at that. Should he knock or just walk in? He decided to knock. There was no answer. He tried the door. It wasn't locked, so he opened it and cautiously went in.

He noticed the small changes she'd made since he'd left. Their wedding photo was no longer on top of the piano .He missed his piano. It was a good one and completely wasted on her. The framed pencil sketch done of him by a grateful pupil had disappeared from the wall. Where was she? The back door was open.

Down at the end of the garden, Helen sat fidgeting on a bench, her arms folded over her stomach to still the butterflies. Anger, resentment, jealousy and humiliation, were all jostling for position. Why does he want to come and talk to me? And why lunch? He must be coming to sweeten me up before suggesting we get divorced. It was unlikely to be to talk about reconciliation, or maybe he just wants to fill his car with the rest of his belongings. Hah, he won't get the piano in.

She saw him come around the side of the house and raise his hand when he saw her, sitting down by the compost heap.

'What are you doing out here? It's so cold.'

'Is it? I hadn't noticed.'

He walked across the lawn towards her. She saw her husband. But she also saw a man who had been sleeping with another woman behind her back. She couldn't forget that. A man with an ego big enough to believe that most women and even some men, fancied him rotten. He'd actually told her so in one of their rows. She faced him across the lawn. Alistair was smiling in supplication. She knew she was frowning. She saw his face fall as he registered her hostility.

'I've booked us a table at Le Pomme Vert, your favourite.'

'That's a bit OTT isn't it?'

Presumably she was being sweetened up for something. She fetched her coat and bag. They drove there in silence. He noticed her fists clenched in her lap. She noticed the sweet, familiar smell of his aftershave.

Once they were settled at a table in the window, overlooking the willow- edged river bank, with a glass of Chablis in front of each of them, he decided to plunge straight in with what he'd rehearsed the day before.

'Do you remember the night we met? We had such fun when we were students. Not a care in the world and completely wrapped up in each other.'

She looked steadily back at him. He related intimate moments which had stuck in his memory over the years, but there was little reaction. She sat still, stiff and cold. He struggled to hide his rising irritation. Finally, he leaned forward and put his hand over hers. It was now or never, the final plea. He held her eyes, and lowered his voice a semi-tone.

'I haven't been the husband you deserved, I know that. I've been weak and betrayed your trust. Diana was the folly of a mid-life crisis. You have no idea how much I regret not resisting her advances. She was very determined, you know. I didn't move in with her when I left home, did I? I rented that awful flat above the butchers. That was because I never stopped loving you... my wife... and my deepest wish now is that we should be reconciled.' He raised her hand to his lips.

'I want to woo you again – prove to you that I'm so sorry all this has happened.'

Helen didn't like this remorseful, puppy dog act at all. She was uncomfortable being in a position of power over him. She retrieved her hand and re-folded her arms, tacitly dismissing his sentimental view of their past and asked him, 'Why should I have you back? What sort of future have you in mind for us now? '

Alistair wasn't sure whether to reveal he'd been given the nod to apply for Keith's job. But such were the benefits, and so crucial to his case, that he had no option. He outlined his vision.

'They've asked me to be Acting Head for now, but also suggested I'd be a strong candidate for the Headship. Think of what that could mean to our lives. Firstly, the Head's salary would put an end to all the penny-pinching we've been accustomed to. We would move into the Head's house and maybe rent this one out as an investment and extra income. You could have a sports car and I could buy a Steinway. I would be in line for a fat pension which would enable us to travel the world when I retire and, finally, and perhaps most important of all, we'd have mutual companionship; loving and caring for each other in old age.'

Helen wasn't too keen on this practical, sensible Alistair either. Neither of the personas he was adopting came from the man she'd married. This was a stranger, attempting to manipulate her for his own purposes. The attempt at bribery was pathetic – a sports car indeed. They were interrupted by the waitress bearing huge plates of food.

'Why do they always give you so much?' Helen's face was disgruntled. 'I have no appetite whatsoever.' She picked at the salad on the side then pushed the plate away. She allowed him to talk on until, running out of his prepared arguments, he took her hand again and with his brown eyes holding hers, he pleaded.

'We're better together than apart, my love. The romantic side of me wants to sweep you off your feet again, but the sensible side wants to you to be realistic and appreciate all the benefits of us both, together, resurrecting our marriage and enjoying the next twenty five years. I have been so weak and foolish, but, honestly, I have learnt my lesson. Being faced with losing you has brought it home to me what is important and real. Please forgive me and allow us to come out of this mess stronger.'

Helen wasn't stupid. She intuited instantly that his chance of the Headship was dependent on their reconciliation. To have any advancement at all, he had to appear to be morally sound and above reproach.

For her, the months since he had moved out had been spent debating the pros and cons of trying to win him back. She had decided that the prospect of a reunion, until the next time his head was turned by a pretty face, was not one that appealed in the slightest. Some days she felt grateful for her single state. She didn't want to grow old in the company of someone who looked at her indifferently over the toast and Marmite while she wondered what he was really thinking. However, this promise of a new life altogether, and one that was privileged, financially rewarding and, possibly more interesting, certainly deserved her consideration.

She'd heard someone on the radio only that morning, whose husband had an affair with her best friend. When pressed by the interviewer to say why she hadn't thrown him out, the famous person had answered, 'Why should I? I've got what she wants. I'm not handing him to her on a plate.' Holding on to that thought and battening down her contradictory emotions – he loved her and wanted her back – that was the important thing, she said slowly,

'Well – this is the last thing I was expecting. I don't know. It might work. You would have to ditch the trollop. I mean really ditch, not just put her on hold. I'm sure you've been seeing her since you moved out, in spite of what you promised. I do miss you sometimes but I'd rather be on my own than go through the hell of the last few months again.'

She saw his face relax. 'Of course I'll do that. Oh Helen, you won't regret this, I promise. Leave it to me. I'll tell her it's over. We'll have a fresh start.'

They abandoned their half - eaten meals, both quite shaken by the momentous nature of their encounter and went back to the car. Alistair dropped Helen off at their house, and since he wasn't invited in for passionate lovemaking or even a cup of tea, he went back to his flat and began to plan the next part of his strategy. Where was the feeling of triumph? He'd got Helen to agree to a reconciliation. Why did he feel so flat and sad?

15

Helen did what she always did in times of trouble. She got down on her hands and knees in the kitchen with a bucket of hot water and a scrubbing brush, just like the one her mother had used. The physical exertion would disperse the adrenalin, and, as always, the sight of sparkling floor tiles lifted her spirits as nothing else could.

In addition to her renewed appetite for daily obsessive cleaning, she found herself confiding in Rachel, who seemed to be unwilling to leave her alone in her misery and, over the weeks that followed, often called by to see how she was.

'It's as though he's trying to woo me again with flowers and surprise outings. He's doing little jobs around the house. He got a plumber in to fix the dripping shower and the broken garden fence panels have been replaced. He's even painted the front door himself – not very well though. A waste of Farrow and Ball, but I didn't tell him that.'

Rachel was impressed. 'That's the silver lining I keep telling you about. And is it having any effect?'

'I suppose it is. Alistair, on form, is very hard to resist. You probably think I'm a fool but I've decided to give him one last chance. Not just because the tangible rewards are so attractive, but because, although I hate to admit it, I'm beginning to find that I don't much like living by myself. Now the novelty has worn off, I miss having someone to talk to. I babble away about inconsequentialities to disinterested shop assistants. I come home to an empty house, go to bed alone and wake up alone. Having sole charge of the remote control is great, but I think I'm willing to trade that for the presence of the man who has been in my life for so long. Being without him is like having lost a limb.' She paused for breath. Rachel opened her mouth, but Helen hadn't finished.

'I lie in bed and fantasise about putting dog shit through her letterbox. If I saw her in the street and I was in my car, I'd drive straight at her. That'd spoil her pretty face.'

Rachel felt she had to interrupt. 'You don't really mean to be so horrible.'

'Yes, I do. When I was at her house I wanted to find an excuse to go to the bathroom and wipe her toothbrush round the inside of the toilet.'

Rachel understood. Of course she did. She stifled a laugh. There was no value in remonstrating. Helen continued. 'The thing is, I feel so humiliated by what he's done. The concept of 'forgive and forget' is very hard for me. But, if I can convince myself that it's in both our interests to make a fresh start, I can surely get over my hurt pride. Embrace the practical me. What do you think?'

Rachel chose her words carefully. 'Well, of course, being offered the job of Acting Head will change his life certainly, but how much of your life will it change? And what if he doesn't get the actual Headship? He's already had one affair. What will prevent him having another when he needs his ego boosting again? As for being on your own, well, there's nothing like being in a loveless marriage to make you feel lonely, believe me.'

'I've thought about that. We got on pretty well together though, most of the time. It was probably our rotten sex life that caused all the trouble.'

She looked sideways at Rachel, 'If I were to swing from the chandelier a couple of times a month and wear suspenders, he'd probably be happy.'

Rachel thought it might take a little more than that, but kept her counsel. 'Well, good luck to you both. I agree that the single life has its drawbacks. But there's also a lot to like. I've got to go or the post office will be closed. I'll see you soon.'

There was a chill wind and Rachel pulled her coat close around her as she hurried into the village. Might Helen succeed in saving her marriage? Should she have tried harder with her own? Marcus and Alistair were very similar in some ways, though they'd not thank her for saying so. Both were attractive charismatic men, not above turning on their considerable charm for their own ends.

Only the other day Alistair had told her he desperately needed more men in the choir. 'Sadly Rachel, it's always the case. Men are more reluctant than women to come and sing. Would you mind very much if I asked Marcus to join us?'

She did mind but didn't want to appear spiteful and mean-spirited, so she'd assured him she was quite over Marcus and he should feel free to ask whoever he wanted to join the choir.

Her train of thought was halted when she saw Diana across the road. She looked pale and drawn and had her head down. Poor cow – another victim.

16

Diana got home and threw her bag on the floor. Friday night and no call from Alistair again. He seemed to be spending less and less time with her, no wonder they rowed when he did appear. When she rang him his mobile was switched off. Every so often she drove up to the school to see if his car was there. If it wasn't, she detoured round past his house. She knew that it made her a crazy stalker but it didn't stop her. She decided to make an extra effort and remind him that what she had to offer couldn't be matched by his milk-and- water wife. She spent the next day chopping, marinating and blending, and texted Alistair to come at seven that evening for, what she promised, would be a surprise.

Her little sitting room was furnished with what she laughingly referred to as 'shabby chic' and Rachel had commented to Victoria that it was probably just shabby. She festooned it with tea lights and pushed the furniture back, laying a tablecloth out on the floor. Around it she piled cushions for them to recline on, creating a Roman orgy scenario. On the cloth were bowls of olives, grapes and generous sun-dried tomato flatbreads. From the oven the aroma of simmering lamb tagine subtly hung in the air.

In the bedroom, lit by more candles, a white towel lay over the bed. The air was scented with patchouli and jasmine. At the bedside she had set up a little tray with massage oils. Celestial harp music was playing softly in the background.

She went through to the sitting room and looked around with quiet satisfaction, then naked underneath her filmy white dress, she crossed over to the window and stood watching and waiting. When she heard the familiar sound of Alistair's car pulling up outside, she turned up the Barry White and took another sip from the glass of wine she had been topping up for the last half hour.

She opened the door. He wouldn't come in. He stood there, shifting from foot to foot and avoiding her eyes. He looked past her and saw the feast laid out.

'Oh dear, you shouldn't have gone to all this trouble. If you'd said you were planning to cook. I would have told you not to bother. I'm here to tell you that Helen and I are going to try to rebuild our marriage and I hope to be moving back home very shortly.'

Her mouth dropped open and she shook her head. After a minute she said, her voice breaking, 'Is this some sort of joke? After all these months and everything you promised…'

'I'm sorry. I really am. But we can't go on like this. Believe me, I didn't want to hurt you, but there is no alternative.'

He still wouldn't look her in the face.

'Sorry? Is that it? Is that really all you've got to say? My God, Alistair. You're going to have to do better than that. You'd better come in. I don't want the neighbours to hear our business.'

If she could only get him in, she stood a chance of winning him round. He stiffened and thrust his hands deep into his pockets. 'No, I can't come in. I have to be somewhere.'

He turned and walked away. Diana took a few steps back into the room and sank to her knees. She curled up into a ball on the floor amongst the tea lights. Why did men always leave her? This place was all too familiar. She'd revisited it so many times throughout her life. She could barely remember her father. There had been a burly man who'd picked up and thrown her screaming with delight into the air. He'd had a prickly face and a smell of something sour. But he hadn't stayed around and the men who followed him into her mother's bed, banishing her to her bed in the little box room, had never stayed long enough for her to call any of them Daddy.

Her determination to do well at school and go to college

had been tested when her mother died of cancer. She became homeless and penniless, but by taking on various low paid jobs she'd made it through and passed her City and Guilds with ease. Lovers came and went. All she wanted, all she had ever wanted was a stable home and a man who loved her to the exclusion of all others. Was it so very much to ask? It would seem so. Damn him for being the same as all the others.

Alistair sat outside in his car. He'd told her. He hoped to God he'd made the right decision. Had it not been for the Headship, he would never had considered going back to Helen. So what sort of bastard had he become? An ambitious one, he told himself. He'd long known he had a hedonistic streak, and had deliberately pursued a career path towards an eventual high salary, in order to satisfy his longing for good wine, expensive clothes and exotic holidays. At the end of that awful episode of trying for children, one of the consolations was that, unlike his colleagues, he need never have to undergo bucket and spade holidays in cold, wet Cornwall. He started the engine and drove slowly away.

17

Victoria put down the phone and swallowed hard, a lump of pain constricting her throat.

Her brother had been brief and to the point.

'Hey Sis. This is a call I didn't want to have to make. You know I've not been feeling 100% for some time. The doctor sent me for tests and I'm afraid it's cancer. Stage 4 pancreatic cancer to be precise, and there is only a faint hope of remission. Would you be able to look after the boys while I go to London for a last chance attempt at extended treatment?'

Nathan and Luke were fourteen and twelve respectively and were well used to spending time with their Auntie Victoria in the school holidays. But this is different, thought Victoria. Could she cope with work as well as two boys who were now, no doubt, already traumatised from having a terminally ill father? She took care not to communicate her dismay to James, and immediately agreed. What else could she do? The boys had already lost their mother to breast cancer two years ago; to be fatherless too just didn't bear thinking about. This treatment might just work and they'd be able to go back home soon enough.

She recalled the conversation with James and Tina, when they asked her to be godmother to the boys. They told her that her chief duty, apart from renouncing the devil and all his works, would be to take on the care of the children should anything befall the two of them. At the time, they'd all laughed at the sheer unlikelihood of that happening. Now Tina was dead and who knows what might be the outcome with James?

He asked if she could come up to Salisbury in the next

couple of days, to discuss the wider picture and plan possible financial arrangements. Glad to have a little time to absorb just what she was taking on, she agreed.

Usually the drive up to Wiltshire to see James was a pleasure, but this time she gripped the steering wheel until her wrists ached and she felt the tension locking her shoulders. Her beloved brother was only fifty four, too young to die.

How would her ordered life be changed by becoming a family, should the worst happen? She got on well with the boys she encountered at school, but that was a very different thing from having two nephews living with her permanently. The days had long gone since she grieved at her inability to conceive a child with Robin. Wasn't she too set in her ways to cope with the disruption of her comfortable lifestyle?

Dismayed by the negativity of her thoughts, she turned on the radio. Jenni Murray was discussing a new book about the joys of retirement. Well, she could forget that now, couldn't she? She turned it off and considered the practicalities of the next few weeks, digging repeatedly into the bag of humbugs she had bought for the journey. Alas, there was no comfort in sugar.

James opened the door to greet her. She thought he looked pale. They clung together briefly and he led her through the house.

'I'll make us a cuppa. We'll have it in the conservatory, it's warm in there when the sun's out. You go and sit down.'

She remembered his complaining about feeling tired some months ago. At the time he had made light of it, saying that he'd been working too hard, and would be fine once he'd had a holiday. When he returned with the tea, she could see clearly now that her robust, stocky brother had lost a lot of weight and that his hands trembled as he passed her cup. His hair was sparse and wispy. He must be having chemo. Why on earth hadn't he told her?

He read her mind. 'I'm so sorry, Victoria, I should have let you know about this earlier. You know how I bottle things up. I really thought I could beat it.'

Victoria leaned forward in her chair, determined not to cry.

'You know that I'll do whatever I can, don't you?'

'Thank you. I was hoping you'd say that. My main concern at the moment is the boys. Up to now I've managed with friends and neighbours helping out. But if I am going to die…..'

He paused fighting for control of his voice, 'If I'm not going to be here for much longer, you are the only family I have.' Inwardly Victoria froze, her worst fears confirmed. She fought to keep her face passive. This was likely to be more than a temporary arrangement.

'What about Tina's parents, or her sister?'

'Her sister is still in Australia working somewhere in the outback, and her parents are practically gaga.' Victoria swallowed hard.

'Right. Okay. I didn't know that. Of course I'll have them. Give me time to work out the logistics. Teenage boys are a bit of an alien species I'm afraid. The ones at school are polite and respectful, but I know that's only a front.'

With an attempt at light heartedness she added,

'When you go in for this treatment, at the end of the month did you say, we'll have a practice run. After that I'll either be an old hand or I'll be ringing Barnardo's.'

James nodded. There was an unnatural stillness about him. Was that what acceptance looked like?

'If this final treatment doesn't buy me some more time, and you feel you can take the boys on permanently, I'll instruct my executors to sell my house. Some money can be put in trust for the boys, and the rest will go to you for their upkeep, school fees, holidays and all the expenses you'll be facing. You won't be out of pocket, Victoria, there are insurance policies as well which will cough up when necessary.'

He paused. 'If you really feel you can't do it, you must feel free to say so I can ring Tina's sister in Australia, but that would really be a last resort.'

'But James, surely they'd love Australia – all that surfing and sunshine?' Victoria knew she was clutching at straws.

'Don't you remember Tina's sister? She isn't remotely maternal. She's living in a commune in the outback doing something with kangaroos. It's nowhere near the coast. Remember, the boys will have lost both their parents within a relatively short space of time. I'm not sure that sending them halfway across the world into a totally new environment would be helpful.' He attempted an encouraging smile.

They talked for a long time, remembering their childhood; Tina with her wide smile and waist length brown hair, and the holidays the two families had spent together when Robin was alive. As darkness fell she left him with hugs and assurances that she would do whatever it took. He could rely on her.

When she got home she stood for a moment in the doorway, visualising rugby boots and sports bags in the hall and loud music pounding in the spare bedroom. She must try and be positive. Young people around would enliven the old cottage and prevent her from becoming set in her ways. They would ask her advice on their homework and, possibly, even be prevailed upon to take the rubbish out. It could be fun.

That night the fears returned. Why did everything seem worse at 3 am? The duvet had slipped down inside its cover, leaving an empty flaccid flap under her chin. She was too hot. She stuck her feet out. It was the time she felt most alone. She was not good at decisions at the best of times – now it was the worst of times.

Previously, she and Robin would have discussed problems together. They would have chewed over situations at the breakfast table and decided what to do. Now everything was down to her and, this time, the issue was huge and there were no choices. She couldn't get a man with a tool box in to fix it. Or could she? Marcus? No. She dismissed that notion immediately. She turned over, seeking a cold spot on her pillow. How could she, who had never had children, suddenly morph into a caring, knowledgeable parent? There'd be more washing, ironing, shopping, cleaning…. No more tucking into a bowl of cornflakes if she couldn't be bothered to cook. Two strapping lads would need a steady supply of nourishing food,

101

firm discipline and, presumably, emotional support. She couldn't do it. She would have to ring him in the morning.

Two weeks later, she collected two pale subdued children, clutching iPads and hauling enormous suitcases. She put on her best positive face.

'I've asked Mr Stevens if he will take you both into South Heath School as day boys, on a temporary basis. You already know a couple of local boys from when you've stayed before, don't you?'

'What? You're joking. We were looking forward to being off school.' Luke was indignant.

To begin with, they seemed unnaturally quiet. They spent, she thought, an inordinate amount of time hunched over You Tube and showing no enthusiasm to go out into the village to kick a ball about with the boys they knew.

One weekend, she drove them back to Salisbury to collect their bikes and some bits and pieces with which to make their new room more homely and child friendly. She had never envisaged the day when there would be a semi-naked pop princess adorning the wall of one of the spare rooms

'Victoria,' whispered Nathan, not long after they'd moved in. They had soon dropped the 'Auntie'.

'How long are we going to stay here with you?'

Victoria interpreted this as meaning what happens if Dad doesn't get better. They'd been told this was a final attempt at halting the progress of the disease. It was the unthinkable that demanded to be thought about. Cursing her cowardice, she ducked the question. There would have to be a conversation, but she would choose the time and the place.

'No idea, my love, she said briskly, 'but this will be your home for as long as you need it to be.'

When James' treatment was over, he was transferred back to his local hospital. They visited frequently and she could see he was becoming weaker. So, with a heavy heart, she made another decision. She went up to the school and asked to see the bursar.

'I'm sorry, but you know the position I'm in at the moment. Can I reduce my hours and go part time? Coping with work, the boys and hospital visiting is proving to be all too much for me. If it doesn't suit I can give in my notice altogether.'

The bursar agreed instantly to her request.

'How much could you manage? What about two days a week and see how it goes?'

'Thank you so much. James said money should not be a problem thanks to his insurances and sale of the house, but I don't want to rely on that completely. I see that as the boys' money and I don't want to have to buy my knickers with it.'

'You might want to come back to full time when the boys are a bit older. Yvonne can cover you for a bit. Just forget about us for now and concentrate on those poor wee boys.'

Night after night Victoria lay awake worrying. When Rachel called in, while delivering Christian Aid envelopes, she found herself invited in for a restorative drink. They sat glumly, hands wrapped round their glasses of brandy. Victoria broke the silence.

'I'm really not easy with all this. How will I deal with it when they are rude or bolshie? What's my position on drugs, alcohol, Twitter, internet porn......?'

'Hold on,' Rachel couldn't help laughing at Victoria's stricken face. 'They're a bit young for all that surely. You'll have a couple of years to practice on minor misdemeanours first.' Victoria shook her head.

'Don't you believe it. You see, I don't know how to discipline them. I've seen parents using the 'naughty step' on TV, but they're way too old for that.'

Rachel agreed. 'You'd probably be better off stopping their pocket money, but it's no good asking me. Haven't you got any friends with teenage boys you could ask?'

Victoria hadn't, but, ever resourceful, she bought a book on bringing up boys and consulted internet forums. She found much to alarm her and decided to rely on her common sense and feminine intuition. Marcus was also generous in giving his support. 'I'll come up on Saturday mornings and take the boys to the school's rugby matches and afterwards for pizzas. Luke might like to go for rugby training on Wednesdays. You never know – he might get into the Under XV team.'

Another friend, on hearing that Nathan was musical offered to give him guitar lessons. 'I'm not very good. But I'd be happy to start him off and we'll see how he gets on.'

18

Victoria wanted to know what the choir were to be singing at the Christmas concert. So after a break of a few weeks, she was back in her usual place on the front row of the sopranos, her pleasant face creased with anxiety, as Alistair, unsmiling and dressed completely in black, prowled up and down in front of them like a giant spider.

Uncharacteristically, he snapped at the sopranos for their inability to sing softly. One or two of the gentler souls looked mortified and Victoria wondered if she should have a word with him. But there was no need. At the end of the practice Alistair told them that he was resigning.

'This next concert will be my last. As I'm taking up the post of Acting Head at Christmas, I won't have the time or the energy to devote to the choir. I'm sorry to go, but I'm sure the committee will find a worthy replacement.'

Victoria heard gasps of horror from those who hadn't heard the rumours that had been going round and a cloud of unhappiness hung over most heads for the remainder of the rehearsal. The next thing they heard as they settled in their seats for a Tuesday rehearsal, was an announcement from the Chairman.

'We have a shortlist of four. By way of interview, they are going to come and give the choir half an hour's rehearsal of a carol, the title of which will only be revealed to them on the night. You will be canvassed for your opinions, but the committee will make the final decision.'

Victoria felt sorry for the four applicants. As she explained to Rachel, 'To lead sixty singers, some encouraging, some hostile, some experienced, and one or two barely able to hold a tune is demanding enough. But they'll also have to demonstrate musicianship, good teaching and conducting skills. Most importantly they'll have to win us all over with humour and personality. It's a massive ask.'

Came the night, one candidate failed to turn up; one was weak and beset by nerves, and so it fell to the remaining pair, one man and one woman to work their magic.

Jolly and well upholstered, Vernon had years of experience working with choirs and led them through the unfamiliar carol with practised ease.

Victoria smiled sympathetically as the female candidate took up her position before them. She clearly knew her stuff, but, in a choir where females outnumbered male by three to one, she didn't stand a chance. If women were to be dominated they clearly would rather it be by a man than a woman. So much for feminism, thought Victoria, there's still a way to go. Sure enough Vernon was offered the job.

'These things come in threes,' she told Rachel. 'First Keith, then Alistair. Who's next?'

She didn't have long to wait. Alistair told her that their gifted young accompanist was leaving the area to pursue his career in engineering. She knew that replacing him was going to be a lot more difficult to accomplish. For several weeks Alistair accompanied them himself. But while the choir loved it because he was such a brilliant pianist, he couldn't conduct at the same time and Victoria could see he was becoming very frustrated and annoyed.

In the break she overheard him telling the chairman that if an accompanist couldn't be found then the choir would have to fold altogether.

'Vernon won't take on the choir without one I can guarantee that.' The heroine of the hour proved to be Victoria. She rang Alistair the next day.

'I've found us an accompanist,' she announced triumphantly.

'David is an old friend of mine, he lives about ten miles away, but he's very competent and I've begged him to help us out as it's an emergency.'

'What experience does he have?' Alistair sounded wary. 'I'm not being rude, Victoria, but I've had my fingers burnt before with people's 'friends'.' Victoria tried to hide her annoyance.

'He's retired now but he used to play for the Huddersfield Choral Society. Is that good enough for you?'

Alistair laughed. 'It most certainly is. Give me his number and I can have a chat about what we're doing, and see how soon he can start.

'Don't worry. We've got four more rehearsals.' Alistair was exuding confidence. Wondering how genuine his belief in their abilities was, Victoria thought she recognised a strategy at work. Did he radiate positivity as a form of encouragement? Even his criticisms were wrapped in humour,

'I like your enthusiasm. Now let's do it again with the right notes.' They were working on the chorus, 'And the Glory of the Lord,' from the Messiah.

'Come on altos. This is your moment. Find the man inside of you.' His eyes flickered to Victoria – she was smiling.

He didn't tell them, but he was in two minds whether to drop this from the programme as it wasn't gelling together at all. It was true that on the night of a performance, the choir usually drew inspiration from somewhere and exceeded his expectations, but he daren't rely on it.

'No, no! Basses please! There was your speed, my speed and David's speed.'

David, accompanying them for the first time, laughed and nodded. They worked on the sections that concerned Alistair, and odd bits that various members found problematic. Eventually, looking at his watch, he said, 'We've got time for a last run through before we go to the pub. From the beginning. Stand up.' Everyone obediently leafed back to page 1. They had barely finished the first phrase when Alistair roared, 'Stop, stop.'

This time his exasperation was clear.

'You are watching me all through the intro, then as soon as it's time to sing, you drop your heads to look at the music. You don't need to do that. You know the first few lines. Look out at the audience; it'll sound so much better.'

'Is it my imagination, or did he get more and more edgy as the practice went on?' said Rachel as she walked home with Victoria.

'I think you're right. Maybe, because it's his last concert, he wants to go out on a high.'

Victoria fumbled in her bag for her torch. The alley which offered a short cut home was notorious for canine deposits lying in wait for the unwary.

She said, 'No, it's more than that. He's going around school looking really miserable.'

'Hasn't he moved back home?'

'Yes he has, but it doesn't seem to have done him much good.' She didn't ask Rachel in for a post mortem of the practice. She was feeling weary. Besides Alistair had told her he was going to persuade Marcus to sing in the basses as someone was leaving and they needed an extra voice. Soothing Rachel's savage breast when she heard about that was something she wanted to postpone for as long as possible.

19

Victoria stood outside her back door and smelled the last of autumn. She'd quite forgotten how pleasing a crisp chill could be after the humidity of the summer months. Her lawn was covered with crusty pillows of fallen leaves. She could smell the promise of Bonfire Night, smoky air and hot dogs.

Would the boys consider themselves too old for such things? Delighted with their response to her suggestion, she set them to building a bonfire at the bottom of the garden.

November 5th found her weeping copiously while chopping onions, when she heard the doorbell ring and went down the hall, wiping her eyes on a tea towel. A beaming Rachel thrust a tin of bonfire toffee into her hands.

'The boys told me about the bonfire so I thought I'd make them this. I've brought some black peas too. They are a Lancashire delicacy, a friend gets them for me. They need vinegar on them.'

'Oh Rachel, how lovely. Come in. Will you join us? It's only hot dogs and a few fireworks but we can open a bottle. I'm afraid Marcus will be joining us though – I want the boys to have a male figure around occasionally.' Rachel's smile faded a little.

'Of course. That's fine. I quite understand.'

She wiped the leaves off her feet, and accepting a glass of wine, took the toffee down to the boys who were calling to be allowed to light the fire. Victoria watched them through the kitchen window. They had both settled in well as far as she could tell and, all things considered, she was enjoying the challenge. They had enormous appetites, and fed her a constant stream of silly jokes and slanderous anecdotes about the goings on at school. Her gentle nagging was not having much effect on the presence of encrusted coffee mugs and general detritus in their bedroom, but that was a small problem, compared to what would, no doubt, come in time. Their father was still in hospital but showing some signs lately of regaining his strength. She took a box of matches out and let them start their fire, whilst reflecting on which of her male acquaintances in effigy she would like to see sitting on the top. Then while they sorted out their fireworks, she sat with Rachel, muffled up against the November gloom, clutching mugs of hot cocoa to warm their hands. The garden chairs were damp and soon their bottoms were too.

Nathan and Luke had built a good fire and it lit up the night with orange and scarlet flames. The boys ran round for a while with sparklers then asked, 'Can we have the proper fireworks now?'

'Yes, as long as you find a Catherine wheel for me. Rachel, what would you like?'

'I don't mind – something pretty. I don't like bangers.'

All was going well until Nathan put a rocket in a wine bottle.

'This one's called a Red Devil.'

As he lit it and stepped back, the bottle toppled over and the rocket flew horizontally up the garden towards the two women. It lodged itself between Victoria's thigh and the chair before exploding. It blew a hole in the wicker chair and burned through her trousers. As she jumped up, yelping with shock, Marcus came through the back gate. He took charge immediately.

'Come up to the bathroom. Take your trousers off and get in the bath. I'm going to turn the cold tap full on. Brace yourself.' Victoria, shaking with shock, shook her head.

'Is this really necessary? How embarrassing - sitting in my knickers in a bath of cold water.'

'It'll mitigate the damage from the burn. You might need to go to A &E.'

'Stuff and nonsense. They'll be busy enough tonight

without me taking up their time.'

But she did as she was told. After ten cold minutes he allowed her to get out of the bath and Rachel gently dressed the livid red wound, which was only bleeding slightly. Marcus made her a cup of strong tea. 'You were lucky. It's only a graze. It could have been a lot worse.'

It was a sad end to the little party although the boys stayed out till late, poking sticks in the fire, until there was nothing left but a pile of hot ash and some incinerated potatoes.

On Sunday morning Marcus was back.

'I've come to inspect the damage to your thigh and, if it shows any sign of inflammation, I'll insist you see a doctor tomorrow.'

She was both quietly amused and flattered, by all this attention. It had been a long time since she'd been cared for by a man, and to be honest, it was a relief for her not to be the person in charge and coping all the time.

'Sit down. I need to remove this dressing.' She shivered. His hands were cool and gentle. 'Am I hurting you?'

'No, no.'

'Right, that looks fine. You stay here on the sofa with your leg up and I'll take the boys to McDonalds to give you some peace and quiet. I'll just make you a nice filter coffee before we go.' She lay there, surrounded by the Sunday papers, thinking how extremely pleasant this all was. Dwelling on the concern on his face as he tenderly dressed her wound, and the feel of his hands on her skin, she chided herself. Good Heavens, Victoria, don't you go falling for him now. It had been over ten years since Robin died and she'd been inclined to treat the episode that had followed the jazz night as delightful, but strictly a one-off.

When Marcus returned with the boys, they asked if he would help them with some particularly vile maths homework. Victoria struggled to her feet from her place on the sofa and offered to make some scones for tea. While they were all sitting at the table, laughing at something Luke had said, the phone rang.

111

It was the hospital. James had had a relapse and was in the ICU.

'I'm on my way', promised Victoria. As she put down the phone she anguished whether to take the boys with her. She knew it should be their decision so she relayed the bad news and, as expected, they rose and got their coats. Marcus picked up his car keys.

'You shouldn't be driving with that leg and, besides, you don't know how long you will want to stay. I may need to leave you there and come back, but I'll do whatever it takes. You concentrate on James and those boys.'

Victoria looked sideways at his stern features as they sped through the countryside to the hospital on the outskirts of Salisbury, She prayed for James to recover and thanked the gods for providing Marcus in her hour of need.

When they got there, they left him to find a parking space, and raced down the long corridors to where James lay. The nursing sister met them at the doors to the ICU. Her face was grave. 'Follow me. James is not fully conscious but he may be able to hear your voices.' Victoria clutched at the nurses arm.

'He wasn't like this when we came yesterday morning. We even talked of him coming home for Christmas'.

The sister agreed. 'I know, but he took a turn for the worse early this morning. It happens. We aren't optimistic I'm afraid, but you can't put a timetable on these things.'

Luke pulled at Victoria's sleeve. 'Is Daddy going to get better?'

'We don't know darling. It might be time to say goodbye to him. Here, take my hand.'

The boys, looking awkward and scared, followed Victoria into the little side ward. James lay as though asleep, but terribly wasted, his skin tinged with yellow. A single sheet lay over him but there was heartbreakingly little for it to cover and Victoria feared that this really was the end. All the medical machinery had been taken away and the room was stark and plain. It was too hot and the smell of cleaning fluid hung in the air.

She looked across at the boys, unsure how they were

coping. They looked at each other, and then, together warily approached the bed. They leaned over their father and kissed his waxy forehead, then straightened up and looked at the nurse.

'Did you say he can hear us?'

'We think so,'

Victoria said gently. 'Why don't you sing to him? Don't you remember how he loved to listen to you when you were practising for the school choir? Try 'The Lord is my Shepherd,' that was one of his favourites.'

Tremulously, Luke sang. Nathan turned away to hide his distress, so Victoria joined in. James' breathing became intermittent. Victoria looked across at the nurse who shook her head slightly and murmured, 'Not long now.'

Victoria sat on the bed and took her brother's dry hands in hers. She whispered words of love and farewell. Was it her imagination or was there a faint answering pressure from his thin fingers?

'Don't worry about your boys, my darling. I'm making sure they are well and happy. You've been a lovely brother…the best ever.' When his breathing stopped, Victoria and her nephews sat quietly. She was aware of a sense of relief that his suffering was over. Eventually they were ushered into another room and someone brought them cups of tea. No one cried. Inordinate loss and grief had re-formed them now into a new, sad family.

20

Christmas that year was one of farewells. Alistair's final concert was a triumph. The choir looked up at him, as directed, and sang out with as much precision and attention to detail as they could manage. They wanted him to miss them.

He made a short speech at the end thanking everyone for their support and hard work. Victoria tucked a hanky into her sleeve in case she was moved to weep and was a little surprised when she remained dry eyed.

The Chairman said, 'You'll be able to come and sing with us now Alistair, we could do with another decent bass.'

'Maybe.'

Up at the school, Keith's final assembly also brought speeches, presentations and hyperbole. He was given a handsome antique clock. What a silly gift, thought Victoria, the last thing he will be doing now is clock watching. She suspected the traditional Isobel was behind that idea.

Victoria bought a small token Christmas tree which stood sadly in the corner of the sitting room. On the surface Nathan and Luke were quiet and polite, but Victoria still worried. She would almost rather have had slamming doors and rudeness than have the three of them tiptoeing round each other all the time. The only outward signs of grief were that the boys spent a lot of time in each other's company, closeted in Nathan's room, playing on their phones. Victoria's friends reassured her that that was absolutely normal behaviour for boys that age and she should be grateful they weren't yet into loud music.

Marcus came visiting more than was usual.

'Why don't we take them skiing in Austria in early January, before school starts again?'

Victoria, who had never set foot on a ski in her life, refused.

'It's very sweet of you but I'm struggling with all the paperwork and arrangements that still need to be processed on their behalf. God knows when it'll all be sorted.'

'All right, then let me take them on my own, a 'boys only' trip.' Feeling ungrateful and wondering what his motives might be, she shook her head.

'I'm sorry, Marcus. It's very kind of you but it's too soon and I need to get a handle on the finances before I can agree to funding expensive holidays.' The boys didn't seem to care much either way which, Victoria felt, endorsed her decision.

On New Year's Eve. Victoria sat with Rachel, waiting for midnight, in a reflective mood.

'Let's try to be optimistic,' she offered. 'We can look forward to the new Head up at the school, a changed choir and a brand new Health Centre, thanks to that housing estate. I wasn't convinced it would ever happen, what with all the petitions and objections from the Luddites about the size of the car park.'

Rachel said, 'There are still plenty of people who hate change. They were muttering darkly in the coffee shop this morning about extra traffic, the overcrowding in the Primary school and the influx of newcomers who, according to them, will be demanding a Tesco before the year is out.' Victoria refilled their glasses. Rachel drank deeply.

'Cheers. Happy New Year. I expect Marcus has told you how he hates New Year?'

Victoria shook her head. 'No.'

'He always said he hated the misguided optimism of a better year to come, free of bad habits and conspicuous consumption and that, in his experience, old enmities increased, new enmities developed and he was just another step nearer to dribbling dotage and impotence.'

'That sounds like Marcus. Miserable old fart. Has he told you about them wanting to demolish his bungalow?'

Rachel shook her head. 'No, what's that all about? Can they do that?'

'Apparently yes. It's in the way of the new development. He'll be offered a handsome compensation cheque to get out and then the builder will request a demolition order on it. As long as they don't find bats in the roof space or newts in the pond, they'll probably get permission, and then all he has to do is pocket the cash and find somewhere else to live.'

'Watch out Victoria. You'll be finding yourself with a new lodger.'

Victoria shook her head. 'I wouldn't mind a man in my life, but definitely not one in my house.'

The question of his relationship with Victoria was uppermost in Marcus' mind too. He was spending an increasing large part of his life with her and her nephews. Would it would be a good idea to press for a more permanent arrangement? They shared many interests, and the energy that had enabled him to have several affairs while he was married to Rachel, seemed to have left him. He prided himself on his expertise as a lover and rather thought that Victoria would be lucky to have him. Reading between the lines, it seemed to him that Robin had been a bit of a disappointment with that side of things. In fact, the more he thought about it, the more he imagined what a catch he would be. Good looking, solvent, practical, humorous and skilful in the bedroom department – she'd be crazy to turn him down. However, he would have to be subtle about his plan and contrive for the idea to come from her. He didn't want to wait too long. He'd accepted an offer from the developer and been given three months to relocate, but already the area around his house was being pegged out and diggers were removing hedges and flattening the surrounding site.

Forewarned that Marcus was looking for somewhere to live, Victoria was in two minds whether to offer him temporary lodgings until he found the right property. She had her misgivings about anything more permanent. Night after night she lay awake listing the pros and cons. She didn't want to de-stabilise the boys who were still mourning their father. She didn't want to upset Rachel any further, who would be bound to resent Victoria shacking up with her ex-husband in spite of her insouciance on the subject. And she didn't want to live with anyone or be forced into making all the compromises necessary to run a relationship before she was ready, if indeed that day were ever to come. In fact, apart from having a handyman around for household emergencies, she decided Marcus was likely to be more trouble than he was worth. The next day she bumped into Rachel outside the Post Office.

'There you are. We need a catch up. Have you time for a coffee at mine?'

Rachel, bundled up like an Egyptian mummy against the cold, nodded enthusiastically.

'I've always got time for a coffee with you. Are you offering biscuits as well?'

'Sadly, no. I baked some chocolate chip flapjacks yesterday and left them out to cool. When I got back from work, they'd all gone. I've told the boys they can bake their own from now on.'

They reached the cottage. Victoria said, 'Go and put a couple of logs on the fire. I'll make the coffee.' Rachel settled herself and stretched out her legs to the warmth.

'I have a story for you,' she said. 'Yesterday when I was driving home from Bristol, I got stuck behind a white van. On the back the logo said something like 'Home Solutions', and there was a list of jobs that this chap would do. Decorating, gardening, plumbing, cleaning things like ovens, carpets and windows. It struck me that those men posting profiles on dating websites have got it all wrong. Instead of listing off-putting things like cycling or going to the gym, they should post a list like that. I tell you, we'd be queuing up.'

Victoria laughed. 'Marry me now!'

'Exactly.' Rachel took a sip of her coffee. This was one of Victoria's best mugs. Was she being softened up for something? She didn't have to wait long.

'About Marcus and his notice to quit...' Victoria began. Rachel looked warily at her.

'He's been dropping hints about moving in here. You told me he would. He says the boys need a father figure.'

Rachel sniffed. 'Huh, more like he needs a mother figure.'

'That's what I thought. I've enough on my plate to be honest, with the boys and he isn't exactly suggesting a romantic partnership. In fact I think he'd like to be a lodger with extras on the side.'

Rachel looked around the room. It was warm and comfortable, the walls lined with book shelves and a sage green sofa big enough to get lost in. Privately she felt there were far too many pictures in the spaces on the walls. Could she see Marcus sprawled in an armchair, a glass of something alcoholic in his hand? She changed the subject, which was still raw and continued to have the power to upset her and said, 'You must do whatever you think is right for you. That's all I'm saying. Now, I was going to ask you about the boys; how are they settling in?'

'Well, so far, so good, really. They stick very closely together. But I've not seen open signs of them grieving. It's almost as if they live in the present. Their day to day life is what obsesses them – school, friends, computer games....'

'Perhaps they have short term memories like animals,' suggested Rachel.

'Is that true? No, I think they are just getting on with things. New chapters, new lives, moving on. The only things I'm putting my foot down about are sitting down to eat together and no phones at the table.'

Rachel gathered up her things.

'Good for you. I must get on. Do what you like with Marcus, but I warn you he's not the easiest of men to have around 24/7.'

'Mmm, that's what I suspected.'

Rachel headed out into the cold, hoping to get home before the forecast snow began. Victoria gathered up the mugs, thinking about friendship; and how much easier life was when blessed with the love and support of female friends. She would be crazy to risk losing her current comfortable life for the presence of a man – wouldn't she?

21

Vernon introduced himself to the choir. He was not a tall man and his shirt button strained uncomfortably across his stomach.

'Good evening everyone. I look forward to getting to know you all. My watchwords are commitment, application and excellence. You'll certainly get that from me and I hope I'll get it back from you. I've drawn up a programme for the Easter concert. We'll start with Moon River.'

He worked them very hard. For the entire two hours they struggled with the complex harmonies and changing time signatures in Henry Mancini's Moon River. Alistair had always presented several differing pieces to sing at practices, so by half past nine, everyone was sick to death of Moon River and, in the pub afterwards, faces were long and spirits low. Marcus came back with Victoria for coffee after the pub and as the boys were safely in their room, she seized the opportunity to tell him of her decision.

'About you moving in….I've thought about it but I'm sorry I don't think that it's the right time. I'm very fond of you, as you know, and I'm grateful for all your help with the boys. But I don't think you living here would work.'

She pushed the plunger down on the coffee pot and continued. 'My gut feeling is that Luke and Nathan need stability in the coming months. Having you living here would change our everyday lives and more change is the last thing I can cope with at the moment.'

She smiled anxiously at him, willing him to agree without rancour. By now, Marcus had experienced the delicious luxury of selfishness which came with living on his own, He'd been having doubts too. The thought of becoming just another cog in the family wheel had lost its appeal; although he kept that thought to himself, preferring the role of rejected lover.

'Victoria, you have broken my heart.'

He found a tiny one bedroom house to rent for the time being and consigned much of his furniture into storage. He still visited Victoria and the boys at weekends. The harsh winter meant there were logs to split, mountains of snow to clear from the paths and sledging to be had on the hills.

In the meantime Victoria found she was missing the social side of going out to work; the office banter and gossip. In the dark months of January and February, she couldn't get out in the garden much and the curtains were drawn and lights switched on by five o'clock. She found herself nodding off in her armchair in the afternoon, and scolded herself for becoming like an old person well before her time. Given that the boys had settled in so well, and there was no longer the need for hospital visiting, she resolved to ask up at school if maybe she could come back to work full time. She walked into the office and smelt the familiar work smells, the warm photocopier, instant coffee, Brenda's perfume. The bursar was delighted to see her.

'Victoria, we'd love to see you back. Are you sure you could manage five days a week? Alistair will need an experienced secretary and your stand- in is off on maternity leave soon.'

Alistair heard her voice and came out of his office.

'Hello Victoria, is this a social call?'

'Not really. I'm job hunting. Staying at home all day is driving me crazy. So I thought I'd see if you'd have me back.' Alistair looked across at the Bursar with his eyebrows raised. She smiled and said, 'I've told Victoria she'd be very welcome. Is that acceptable to you?'

'I should say so. You and I know each other so well Victoria, we'll make a great team. When can you start?'

In the marital home, Alistair sat at the breakfast table scanning The Guardian when he heard the ping of an email coming in. Was this the one he'd been waiting for? Yes! He licked marmalade off his fingers and did a little jig. Helen looked up, the tea pot in mid- air. 'What?'

'I've got an interview for the Headship up at school tomorrow week.'

'At last. Took them long enough,' but she smiled.

Maybe things were going to work out for them in the end, although she had yet to get the suspenders out. Alistair's eyes were shining and he said, 'The news on the grapevine is that the advert in the TES garnered twenty actual applications from which they're going for a short list of five. I remember the days when a job like this would attract at least fifty.'

Helen, standing at the sink, pulled the belt of her fleecy, full length dressing gown tighter around her and pursed her lips.

'I would imagine it could be seen as a pretty thankless task, what with fees not keeping up with costs, league tables and the dreaded Health and Safety. Still, now's your chance. I'll take your black suit to the dry cleaners. What time's your interview?'

'It's going to be a bit of an ordeal. The whole process takes three days. Day one is several short interviews each on different areas of Headship. Day two, we'll be observed teaching a lesson and then do a presentation on a given topic. That'll be the easiest day for me. Day Three, they'll shortlist from five to three, to face the final, formal interview with the Governors.'

'What a performance. Is all that really necessary?'

Alistair shrugged. He felt like one of those Alsatians which have to jump through burning hoops at dog shows. He'd done the obligatory leadership course. The key to success was to match his vision and aspirations for the school to that of the governors. He had pressed the right flesh at the right school events. He had even practically given up his sex life. What more could a man do? He went to the mirror and practised his serious, responsible face, telling Helen, 'I've been advised there'll be a role- play session, where a governor acts as an angry parent. I'll enjoy that if it happens. I'm good at performing. Victoria says there may also be an in-tray exercise, where we have to prioritise a range of issues that might land on a Head's desk and indicate our response.'

You shouldn't have any problems with that either.' Helen hid her alarm at the thought of the trial that lay ahead of him. On the morning of Day One he was up before dawn.

'I can't face any breakfast. Sorry, but I'm going in early.'

'It's only 7.30, it's going to be a very long day if you start now.'

She looked at the chocolate croissants she'd bought for him as a good luck treat and wondered how she was going to stop herself working her way through them while he was gone. She followed him to the door, wrapped the crimson scarf she'd bought him round his neck, stood on tiptoe to kiss him. He was wearing the black suit and his lucky tie that he'd worn first when they got married and then when he'd landed the South Heath job, and he'd polished his shoes to military perfection. He told her he'd walk up to school, so that he could rehearse in his head all the things he needed to say, but she insisted he took the car.

'All it would take is for someone's dog to jump up at you, or a passing car to go through a puddle and cover you in mud. You haven't got another decent suit.'

He'd struggled to hide his irritation. She was right. She was always right. That was half the problem. Diana was so deliciously, so wonderfully, wrong.

After he'd gone, the day dragged on for Helen. There wasn't a surface undusted or a cobweb to be seen. A perfect fish pie stood on the side in the pristine kitchen ready to go in the oven when he came home. Not for the first time, she wished she had a job. Something else to think about. She fired up the laptop and looked to see if there were any vacancies for counsellors. Relate were advertising. How could she talk to people with troubled marriages when her own was on a knife edge? Nevertheless, she dug out her CV and spent an hour updating it and fantasised about heading out into the world, suited and booted, to change other people's lives for the better.

By the time Alistair got home, he was completely drained and had no idea how well or how badly he might have done. It was so very different from his Director of Music interview, when he really did know his stuff. He snapped at Helen and left half of his fish pie on the plate. Later he went to the piano and played what Helen called his 'angry music'. She ran herself a bath to get away from it, but even there she could hear the powerful chords rattling the window frames.

At the end of day two the final five had been reduced to three. This time he came home jubilant.

'There's the token woman who knows as well as anyone that she has no chance of the Headship of a school like ours; the Head of a smaller public school just trying to advance his career and me. It's practically in the bag.'

On day three, the three candidates sat in the deputy head's office, which had been vacated for their benefit. Victoria came in with a coffee pot and a tray laid with the best china. She'd added a plate of fig rolls while doubting that any of them would want to face the panel with crumbs clinging to their teeth.

Alistair looked sideways at the other two. The female candidate was a tall, dark haired woman in a black suit and an aggressive metallic necklace. She made animated small talk and had a smile that didn't reach her eyes. He thought that, in the unlikely event of his being unsuccessful, he could work with her.

The other man was a Christopher Forbes-Martin, who had the saturnine good looks and patrician air of superiority so often seen in those holding positions of power. Alistair decided that if the chap hadn't been educated at Eton, he certainly had the confidence and aplomb of one who had. Definitely the one to beat. He looked quite a bit older than Alistair. Was that good or bad?

'The interviews were gruelling,' he told Helen, 'but I think my enthusiasm and knowledge of the running of the school impressed them. I'm feeling quietly confident.'

It was past seven o' clock when the phone rang. The Chair of Governors was apologetic.

'I'm sorry Alistair but you were not successful. The panel went for Mr Forbes-Martin who, as you know, is already a Head. You had an extremely good interview and I will be happy to give you feedback if you wish. We want you to know we are all very grateful for the hard work you are currently doing as Acting Head. You have my commiserations and I wish you the very best of luck with any future applications.'

Alistair put the phone down slowly. He couldn't believe it. That was his job. Hadn't the Chair said as much before Christmas? And Keith too, damn him. He turned to Helen. She, knowing instantly from his face what the verdict was, felt a cold shiver run over her. This disaster was not Alistair's alone.

22

Rachel was one of those at Vernon's first practice who felt that life was too short to spend two hours on one song. A friend rang her.

'I wondered if you'd like to come to the Black Cow instead of going to that choir. They are running a music night, with a live group, every Tuesday.'

'Why not.' She'd give it a try. Already dipping a toe into internet dating, maybe a night out once a week would increase her chances of finding a nice man. It was time to be a bit more pro-active. She went to see Victoria's hairdresser, Paul.

'I want you to do for me what you did for Victoria.'

He rose to the challenge, cut her untidy brown bob into shapely layers and highlighted them with subtle mahogany and copper streaks. She'd already discovered that having a broken relationship is the best way of losing weight there is. With some new clothes and an upbeat hairdo, she felt more than ready to face the world again.

The door of the Black Cow was open. Rachel hung back behind her friend, suddenly intimidated by the wall of noise. She saw him straightaway. Leaning against the bar with a pint in his hand - the most delicious man she had seen in years. Wavy brown hair, a skin tone which suggested the outdoor life, brown moleskin trousers and a woodland green open-necked shirt completed the look. His eyes twinkled as he saw her admiring gaze and he raised his glass in salutation. She grabbed her friend's arm.

'Who is that?' she whispered trying to look calmer than she felt. Her friend turned round.

'Where? Oh him, that's Richard. He farms just down the road. His wife is around somewhere. Is he giving you the eye? He's a bit of a lad.'

'No, no,' Rachel blushed, 'just someone I've not seen before.' She took the glass of wine her friend bought her and slipped back outside with it, hoping to cool her flaming cheeks. Someone came out of the pub behind her. Was it him? Of course it was. He introduced himself to her and chatted easily about this and that before, noticing her shiver, he suggested they went back in so that he could buy her another drink. Other people soon came up to talk to him and she moved away to find her friend.

'There you are. Where on earth have you been? I was just coming to look for you.'

'Just outside to cool down. I got chatting to the smokers.'

'The group's good isn't it? All the golden oldies.'

By the end of the evening, most of the crowd were on their feet dancing. Richard was watching her. When the singer announced the last dance he pulled her into his arms. Holding her close, he moved confidently and sensually. He smelt of sweet hay and fresh cut grass and cloudless skies. When the dance was over he pressed a bit of card torn from a beer mat into her hand, nuzzled her neck and disappeared into the crowd. On the card was a phone number.

She rang him a week later. She'd never come across anyone quite like him before. He told her that his farm was a small one that had been in the family for years, which appealed to the pastoral romantic side of her nature. He ran a dairy herd and had a few Jacob sheep. Alert and humorous, he was tall and strong and he made her feel twenty years younger. Seeing each other every week at the music night gave them the opportunity to get to know each better. She confessed her infatuation to Victoria and it brought an unwelcome reaction.

'I can't believe you're doing this. He's married. Whatever happened to female solidarity?'

Rachel sighed. 'I know. But he says the marriage isn't happy and they are only staying together until their girls grow up.'

'I bet that's what Marcus said to his lady friends too. That line is as old as the hills.'

'Anyway, I'm not looking to break up his marriage. I just want a bit of fun.'

'Wasn't that exactly what the woman Marcus had an affair with said?'

That shot hit home and Rachel took herself off before Victoria could make her feel any guiltier than she already did.

One warm April evening, leaving the little country pub they frequented, Richard turned the Land Rover onto a narrow track, heading higher and higher up into the Mendip hills. Rachel loved riding in the Land Rover, it took her back to her childhood when she cherished a dream of being a farmer's wife.

'Where are you taking us?' She settled back in her seat, her slightly tipsy grin stretching from ear to ear.

'It's a clear night. I thought we'd do a spot of stargazing.'

'Oh, not what I had in mind', she murmured, amused at her new found propensity for innuendo and flirtation. He smirked and swung the car into a gateway.

'Come on, give us your hand.'

He led her up through a clump of trees to the open hillside. He stopped and spread his coat on the close, sheep - cropped grass. 'Lie down.' He lay beside her. Above them a million stars twinkled and an almost full moon illuminated the woods and valleys below.

'There's Orion, look, and his belt. That big star is Mars, the planet.' He pulled her closer. Their love making, urgent and passionate, was heightened by the extraordinary setting and the chill of the night air. But he was married. Her feelings see-sawed from self- justification - it's a dog eat dog world - to the certain knowledge she was doing wrong. A few weeks later, at twilight, as they stood at the edge of a small copse listening to the owls, she took a deep breath.

'I'm sorry, but this has to stop.'

He smiled equably, 'OK. Bored with me then?'

'Far from it. But it's not right. You're married. I can't do it anymore.'

'That's a pity.'

Fortified by her foray back into the world of flirtation and dating, and buoyed by the newfound belief that maybe she was still attractive and desirable; Rachel returned to the internet. This time, she followed strict criteria when trawling her two chosen websites. He must have a degree, be able to spell, be taller than her, be solvent, cultured and look presentable. She was aware that the lovely Richard would have failed on several counts, but she wasn't looking for another roll in the hay with another woman's husband, but an unattached, long term lover. A husband of her own would be nice, but was not essential at the moment. Ned sounded interesting. He was a Scorpio which promised an interesting sex life, and wrote her long, engaging emails. The photo he sent showed him to be visually acceptable, if a little balding, and he owned his own company doing something with computers. He only lived twenty miles away so eventually they arranged to meet at Moreton Castle, a crumbling Norman ruin about half way between their respective homes.

'That was my idea,' she told Victoria.

'I thought if we can find nothing to talk about then at least we could enjoy the setting. I was so nervous. I saw him waiting on the bridge, so I walked up to him and held my hand out. He grabbed hold of me and thrust his tongue down my throat. It was horrible. I spent the next hour fending him off as he attempted to pull me into every niche, every dark corner of the castle for more of the same. All I could do was try and keep out in the open and make my excuses to leave as soon as I could. Even then, can you believe, he wanted to know when he could see me again.'

Victoria didn't know whether to admire her friend's sense of adventure or chide her for her folly.

Undeterred, but making a mental note to avoid Scorpios, Rachel continued her search and entertained Victoria with blow by blow accounts of her string of dates.

'There was an interesting sounding man in Midsummer Norton, but I learned the hard way that all men lie online about their height. He was at least four inches shorter than he claimed and the top of his head barely reached my chin. That, and his bushy beard, made him look like a garden gnome. He wanted to hold my hand as we walked along looking for a nice pub; so I had to hold onto my handbag on the side he was on. Why would I want to hold his hand? We'd only just met. When he cunningly switched sides so did the handbag. It would have been funny if it hadn't have been so embarrassing. It was another early night.'

She confessed, 'That one was the last straw. I must be cursed. I've closed down my memberships and decided that men using dating websites are all liars, short, rude or desperate.'

Victoria tried to be positive. 'You aren't cursed. Good men are hard to find. On the plus side, we've had such a laugh. I shall miss your stories.'

Privately she marvelled at Rachel's ability to detach herself from reality. She was never likely to meet a soulmate via a computer. On the other hand, if one is rooted in reality then nothing is ever possible. Negative 'what ifs' abound and there are always be reasons not to try. Maybe she was becoming overly pessimistic as she grew older. Or maybe she was just envious of Rachel's bravery. She sniffed, more like desperation than bravery, if truth be told.

23

The news that Alistair had not been appointed as Head of South Heath spread like wildfire. It reached Diana who, feeling friendless and alone, was struggling to adjust to life without him. He'd gone back to Helen because he wanted that job, and part of her was glad he'd failed – serves him right. But where did that leave her now? She felt like a minnow – too small to be of any use, so taken off the hook and thrown back into the river. There was literally no one who cared whether she lived or died. Every song on the radio was about lost love and heartbreak and if she went out to the shops, all she saw were couples holding hands or walking with arms wrapped around each other. She'd had enough. She was tired.

She made an appointment to see Dr Wright.

She sat in the consulting room, twisting a sodden paper tissue between her fingers, and wept - confessing she wanted to end it all. The doctor was sympathetic but brief, and prescribed anti- depressants and six sessions of counselling.

'We can't have you thinking these dark thoughts. The pills should take the edge off your distress but will take a while to begin to work. There is a waiting list for counselling, so no quick fix I'm afraid. Just remember there's always light at the end of the tunnel. Come and see me again in a week.'

Diana didn't think much of the cliché, and thought, Yeah, it's an approaching train, but couldn't summon up the energy for such an exchange. She walked through the afternoon bustle of the village to the chemists, clutching her prescription. She stopped at the kerb as a bus approached. If she stepped out in front of it all her troubles would be over.

Over the next few weeks, as the pills began to do their

work, the desperation receded. She just felt numb and tired and slept the days away.

The room into which she was ushered for her first meeting with the counsellor was sunless and bare. There was the obligatory box of tissues on a low table and a terminally ill pot plant on the windowsill. She disliked the bearded man in his baggy khaki shorts at first sight and felt disinclined to share anything at all with him. He did his best, but as she thanked him and left at the end of the session, she knew that she was unlikely to be returning.

On the way home, she called at the shop for some milk. Her eye was caught by the sight of the familiar packets of cigarettes she had smoked for years before managing to give up. It was so easy. Once home and fortified by nicotine and cheap cider, she wrote endless notes to Alistair, screwing them up and throwing them onto the floor – she knew there was no point in sending them. Her lovely blonde hair hung in rat's tails around her face and she wasn't surprised when her periods stopped and she lost weight. When she got a formal letter from the salon saying that as she'd been off for so long without sending them a doctor's note, they'd had no option but to replace her, she didn't care. She slumped in the armchair, listening to the rain beating against the window. How many tablets would it take to help her die?

Hardest to bear was the constant nausea. She vomited first thing in the morning for four days running. Was it possible she was pregnant? But he'd told her he was unable to father a child, and Helen's childless state had reassured her that it was true. There was one sure way to find out. She got up and dressed, scraped back her unwashed hair and secured it with a rubber band. There was no milk left for a cup of tea. With her sweatshirt hood pulled up in an attempt to be invisible she walked up to the chemist. She pushed open the door and flinched at the smell of scented candles. A line of old people, sitting waiting for their prescriptions turned and looked at her. On the shelf there appeared to be two sorts of pregnancy tests, some in pink packets and some in blue. Was that dependent on whether she wanted a boy or girl? What a thing to think at a time like this. She picked up the nearest one. Once home she went straight to the bathroom and did the test then sat on the side of the bath to wait for the result.

The two thin blue lines were unwavering. It could be wrong. Should she do another test to make sure? Wasn't the morning sickness enough to convince her? She put the kettle on and opened the window to let out the smell coming from the kitchen bin. She'd forgotten to buy milk. It'd have to be black coffee. There wasn't a clean mug so she rinsed one out under the tap and realised she was humming to herself. Was it ridiculous to hope Alistair might want to be a father? She pictured the three of them together. A girl perhaps with blonde curls like her mother or a boy with his father's dark hair and long pianist's fingers? But look at the state of her. He didn't fall in love with a gaunt, greasy haired girl who couldn't even wash up after herself. Stuff it. She went back to bed but in her dreams she abandoned new-born babies in unlikely places – under the massage table in the salon, where the crying upset the customers and behind the stage curtains in the church hall during choir practice. In the end she had to go back and see Dr Wright.

The doctor rubbed her hands together apologising for their coldness. Diana shivered as her unloved body was pressed and probed.

'By my reckoning, you are at least 20 weeks into your pregnancy. I'm surprised you haven't felt any movement though. I can hear a good heartbeat. We need to get a scan done as soon as possible. You're going to have to start taking care of yourself. Are you eating properly?'

Diana shook her head.

'I'll do a blood test now. I don't want to wait till the phlebotomist comes in. I wouldn't be surprised if you weren't a bit anaemic, as well as underweight. Get on the scales.'

Diana slipped off her shoes.

'Hmmm, thought so. Do you smoke?'

Diana raised her eyes and looked into the doctor's

impassive face. She nodded. 'Sometimes – not many though.'

She added, 'I did feel something odd in my tummy a few times, but I told myself it was just wind.' She recognised her denial. 'Is it really too late now to get rid of it?'

'Well, yes it is. Is that something you want to do?'

'I'm not sure, but I can't even look after myself, so......'

She could see that in her current state of self- neglect, carrying a child and subjecting it to copious quantities of alcohol and tobacco in the first vital weeks of gestation, was not giving it the best start in life. The doctor looked concerned. 'Have you anyone you can discuss this with? Someone to support you; parents, friends?'

'My parents are dead and I have no friends.' Was Victoria her friend?

'What about the child's father?'

'We don't see each other anymore.'

The doctor prepared a syringe. 'Sharp scratch.' Diana looked away.

'Right, that's done. I'll ask Susan Dean, the community midwife, to call round. She's very nice and easy to talk to. In the meantime, cut out the alcohol and the smoking altogether and get some nourishing food down you. I want to see you again in two weeks.'

Diana nodded. Bossy cow. How much worse were things going to get? On the way home she bought some carrots and two sausages. Money was running low. She would have to sign on for benefits. This was no longer just about her. She went into her sitting room and looked around. She'd done her best with the room. The furniture looked cheap but the sofa was covered with a bright paisley throw and she'd splashed out on some cushions to echo its burnt orange and green. There was a bookshelf with a few paperbacks on it and a small television. Could she see a baby there too – kicking on the hearthrug? Suddenly overcome with weariness, she lay down on the sofa and closed her eyes. She woke to a knocking on the door. Go away, whoever you are.

A voice called, 'Are you there, Diana? It's Susan Dean,

Community midwife.'

Would she hear the radio playing? Keep quiet. Diana got up and watched from behind the curtain as her visitor stumped down the path and drove away. She should have let her in. God knows it wasn't as if she had anyone else to talk to. But not sharing it with anyone else made it somehow less of a reality and just now she couldn't cope with reality.

A tiny part of her was excited at the thought of Alistair's child growing inside her. But she was in no fit state to bring up a child on her own, and she'd accepted that Alistair, now busy re-kindling his relationship with Helen, would not come back to her. Her neighbour, Tracey, was a single mother and never went out, never had any money and lived in a similarly squalid council flat. That sort of life was most emphatically not what she wanted for herself. She didn't even like children very much. When customers brought their new born offspring into the salon to be clucked and cooed over by the staff, she'd always retreated into the kitchen to make a coffee, and been glad when gathering up bottles and nappy bags and all the other paraphernalia babies seemed to require, they pushed their enormous buggies off down the street,

The pragmatic thing to do was to insist on a termination, go back to Bristol, get a new job and start again. But it was too late for that and, besides, she was carrying Alistair's baby. It was all she had left of him. How could she possibly kill his little son or daughter? If he knew, he might just leave that sanctimonious bore he'd married and come back to her. Was she just clutching at straws? And would he be interested in her growing bump? It was obvious that her attempt to break into his cosy middle- aged world had failed. But she loved him. He'd loved her too, hadn't he? She had to find out.

She washed her hair, put on her only decent clothes and walked up to South Heath School. Victoria was in reception making a phone call when she looked up at the window hatch and saw Diana standing there. She heard her ask if the Head was free. He was, and she watched curiously as Diana was ushered into Alistair's room. A few minutes later they both emerged. Alistair informed Victoria that he was going out but would be back in time for the staff meeting. Was it her imagination or had Diana been crying? The school secretary, sitting across the office from her, raised her eyebrows but Victoria confined herself to a shake of the head. There was no point in speculating. It could be something or nothing.

In Alistair's car Diana was trying very hard to be calm and strong. Men didn't like weeping women. But her trembling hands belied the illusion. His voice was cold, his tone peremptory.

'What's all this about? I haven't time to play guessing games.'

'We need to go somewhere we can talk. I'm pregnant and I don't know what to do.'

She heard a sharp intake of breath and he swung the car round to drive out of the village. He drove to an empty car park beside a nature reserve, glad to have something to do while he processed this bombshell. He backed the car into the far corner under the trees and turned to face her. He said quietly, 'I have to ask – how do you know it's mine? You know I've been told I could never father a child.'

'Because there has only ever been you, ever since we met. Do the maths.'

She sensed the rigidity of him beside her and willed him to soften and reach out. Surely he would see they were in this together? She put her hand on his arm. He flinched at her touch and turned to face her. His eyes were dead.

'Jesus, Diana, how could you have done this to me?'

She clenched her fists. Her nails dug into her palms.

'I can't believe you just said that. We made this baby together. How dare you suggest it's something I've done to you?'

Alistair banged the steering wheel with his fists. Staring straight ahead, his voice rising, he said, 'You clearly don't understand what a blow this is for me. I'm trying to concentrate on practicalities.' He took a deep breath.

'My first reaction is that you need to ask for a termination. You don't want to be bringing it up on your own.'

'It? For God's sake Alistair, this is your son or daughter we're talking about.'

How stupid she was. Why did she think he would be anything but horrified and angry? This complete and total disengagement confirmed her worst fears.

He went on. 'You told me you were taking the pill – presumably that was a lie. Didn't we agree we shouldn't rely on my fertility problems?'

She hadn't seen this side of him before. She had overestimated him. He was just the same as all the rest. Didn't they say you had to see someone in deep trouble before they revealed their true self? She decided to try another tack. Adopting a conciliatory tone she said, 'Of course, you're right. I can plead severe mental distress and insist they abort your child. The world doesn't need another little Alistair. Cute as he very probably would be. It'll be a late termination so I'll probably have to go into an induced labour, but he'll only be a tiny lump of flesh in a bowl and easily flushed down a sluice – never to grow up and call you Daddy. The days when a man needed a son and heir are long gone.'

He flinched. 'Christ Diana, you aren't going to make this easy are you?'

Struggling for control, she said, 'You need some time to think it all through. Take me home now and we'll talk another day.' The smell of the air freshener in his car was making her feel sick as well as reminding her of Helen. Oh God, Helen. How was she going to react? She fought the mad impulse to vomit in the foot well as an expression of her distress. As they drove back to the village, she glanced sideways. His profile was cruel; this ruthless Alistair new to her. She wanted to kill him.

After a week of sleepless nights, she went back to Dr Wright.

'I can't go through with this. I've tried but it's no good. I can't eat, I can't sleep and I do nothing but cry all the time. I want an abortion. I've talked to the father and he doesn't want this baby either. I can't do this on my own. I don't care how late it is.' The doctor shook her head.

'I'm sorry, Diana, that is out of the question now, but I am very concerned about your state of mind. I'll make an urgent referral to the hospital for an appointment to see another counsellor as soon as possible. In the meantime, talk to Susan Dean. She's very down to earth and practical. She'll support you all the way through.'

Diana walked back very slowly. Gin? Hot baths? Could she throw herself down the stairs? How difficult was it to dislodge a baby? Perhaps Alistair would feel differently once he'd got over the shock. Pigs might fly. There had been no hesitation in his reaction. She wasn't ready to go home so she went and sat in the children's playground and watched toddlers being pushed on swings and encouraged to climb the ladder to the slide. Young mums kept one eye on their phones and the other on their child. Was this to be her future?

24

Alistair sat in the conservatory waiting for Helen to come home. The stench of her tomato plants was already obvious. God knows why she insisted on growing those damn things year after year. He didn't even much like tomatoes and she always ended up giving them away. The plants were growing quickly, it was when they became six foot, stinking Triffids that he really loathed them.

How could he avoid having to tell Helen about the baby? If Diana had a late termination, as she'd suggested, then maybe he could get away with it. But all it would need was for somebody's sister, brother or cousin to work in the maternity unit. Not an option. It was bound to get out. The days were ticking by, but the problem wasn't going to go away.

He could pretend it had nothing to do with him and suggest she had a reputation for sleeping around. No, he was not a complete rat. He'd loved her once. Damn it – he loved her still. Had he made a terrible mistake?

Helen was walking home from the library. It was raining that fine wetting rain. She stopped to pull up her hood. She knew it made her look like a garden gnome but she looked worse with her hair flat and wet. Her route took her past Diana's flat. As usual, she tried not to look across the road, but there was a familiar figure there knocking at Diana's door. She turned as Helen approached and greeted her. 'Hi Helen. I almost didn't recognise you with your hood up.'

'Hello, Susan. Working late?'

'As usual. Will you be at Gardening Club tonight?'

'Yes. I expect so, unless something more exciting comes up.'

Twenty paces further down the street, Helen stopped. What was Susan Dean doing at Diana's front door? Stop it. There had to be a perfectly reasonable explanation. She continued on her way home, her mind consumed with alarm and suspicion.

'What are you doing, sitting in the dark?' She snapped the lights on as Alistair jumped to his feet.

'Sorry, I must have nodded off.'

'I saw Susan outside Diana's just now.'

'Who's Susan?'

'The midwife at the practice.'

She watched his face closely. He put his hands in his pockets and turned to look out of the window. The moment had come sooner than he'd feared. He turned back to face her. 'You'd better sit down. I've got something to tell you and it's bad…. Diana says she's pregnant.'

Her hands flew to her mouth. 'Oh my God.' Then, 'Are you sure it's yours? I wouldn't put it past her.'

His face twisted. 'It's not beyond the realms of possibility.'

'How long have you known?'

'A couple of weeks maybe.'

Helen turned and walked the length of the room and back again to face him, her face suffused with anger.

'You complete and utter bastard. I can't believe you didn't tell me before. What happened to 'no more secrets'?'

'How could I tell you? It was such a God-awful thing to happen – just when we're trying to make things work. I thought it would be too much for you to take.'

Helen folded her arms. This pathetic, red-eyed Alistair was infuriating.

'And do you know what she's going to do about it? I take it you and she are having cosy little chats.'

'Not really. I've seen her once. It didn't go well.'

'You need to make sure she gets rid of it, quickly before it's too late. Do you know how many weeks she is?'

Alistair shook his head.

'Oh, for God's sake, Alistair, this is dreadful. It could affect your job as well as everything else? What do you think the governors are going to say about one of their senior staff having a pregnant ex-mistress?'

'I'd tell them my private life is nothing to do with them, but you're right. I'll have to go and see her again, but you know Diana, she's not going to do me any favours, or you either for that matter - and she isn't thinking rationally at all.'

Someone was knocking. Diana opened the door frowning slightly, she wasn't expecting anyone, and welcome visitors were few and far between these days. It was Helen. She put her foot firmly in the door and said, 'I know you won't want to ask me in, but I'm equally sure you won't want your neighbours to hear what I have to say. I'm not here to cause trouble; in fact I'm going to help you with some good advice.' She pushed in past Diana and went through to the kitchen. She tried not to look at the sink piled high with dirty pots or the worktops littered with empty tins and curling crusts.

'I hear you're pregnant.' She didn't wait for an answer.

'Alistair won't leave me again, you know. I suggest you either get rid of it or have it adopted. Don't think of hoping to appeal to his better nature, because I can tell you now, as far as you're concerned he isn't interested. Don't you dare go anywhere near him from now on.'

She paused for breath, conscious that her voice was unsteady. The state of the kitchen was distressing her as much as her reason for her being there. Her hands itched for her yellow Marigolds and a sturdy scouring pad. She couldn't help herself. Automatically she turned on the tap and squirted washing up liquid into the bowl.

'What on earth do you think you're doing?' Diana strove to control her trembling voice.

Helen ignored her and carried on speaking. She felt calmer as she washed mugs and plates.

'I mean it Diana. You're on your own now and you've no one to blame but yourself. Sort yourself out. I suggest you leave this slum and go back wherever you came from. Alistair has told me he wants nothing to do with you.' She scrubbed at a saucepan.

Diana subsided into a chair. 'Leave my pots alone. How dare you…' but her voice lacked conviction. She started to cry.

'There's no point in crying. If you'd paid more attention to cleanliness and tidiness in your home and less to my husband, you wouldn't be in this state. Have you got a clean tea towel?'

Diana shook her head. 'Just go away and leave me alone.'

'Well, it's more hygienic to let them dry naturally.'

Helen turned away from the sink. Out of the corner of her eye she could see a sweeping brush by the back door. No, that might be a step too far. She folded her arms and regarded Diana levelly.

'There's no future for you here. I suggest you get rid of it and move away, out of this village altogether.'

Diana almost heard the sound as something snapped inside her. She stood up and planted her feet firmly apart, her hands on her hips. She'd had enough of this woman.

'How dare you tell me what to do, you barren bitch. You come here, all holier than thou, and tell me to have an abortion; then you say go and live somewhere else and all the while you stand there washing my pots! No wonder Alistair came to me. Go and interfere in someone else's life. You're mad. Get out.'

Helen turned and left with as much dignity as she could muster. She'd made a fool of herself, but she'd said what she wanted to say. There was no need for Alistair to know what she'd done. When she got home he was sitting listening to some unidentifiable gloomy music, so she cried briefly in the bath and went to bed.

142

25

'Hi Diana, I heard you weren't well and as I was just down the road at the doctors, I thought I'd give you a knock.'

It was Emma from the salon. She had been the only one amongst the girls there with whom Diana had felt she had anything in common, and they'd been out once or twice together before Diana had got involved with Alistair.

Conscious of the state of her flat, Diana said, 'Oh, I was just getting dressed to go out but I've got time for a coffee. Shall we go to the tea rooms?'

'OK, sounds good. Just wondered how you were. I've been missing our chats at work.'

Diana threw on some leggings and a loose jumper and the two women walked to the centre of the village. Once they were seated, Emma chatted on about the latest salon gossip, wondering if she should say anything to Diana about what she had heard on the grapevine. In the end she didn't need to. Diana said, 'I may as well tell you. I'm pregnant.'

Wise to the ways of the world, Emma bought some time by adding sugar to her coffee, then ventured cautiously,

'Is that a good thing?'

'I wasn't sure to begin with, but I'm feeling better about it now.'

Diana told Emma that she'd had an affair which was now over and that time had run out to have a termination. She began to shred the paper napkin that was in her hand.

'It's been hard – getting used to the fact of having a baby on my own. It's so not the way I expected things to go. You'll understand, being a single mother yourself. I can talk to you. You're not like the others.'

Emma was honest and realistic. She hid her shock at the state of Diana, previously so poised and glowing with health and said, 'It will be difficult. You'll have money problems. I did. Still do. But it helps if you can get a support network – being on your own is the hardest part, or at least it was for me.'

She fished in her bag and brought out a photo of a grubby little boy in red wellington boots standing in a puddle.

'This is Liam. I wouldn't be without him for the world.'

By the time Diana got home, she was reconciled to her lot. She would welcome her baby into the world without a father. She'd managed pretty well without having had one herself, hadn't she? She decided to buy something every week in preparation. She started off with a pack of three tiny vests. She hummed as she put them into her new baby drawer. She might enjoy being a mum – especially if it was a little girl. Alistair needn't be afraid of being left out. She would make him pay by seeking maintenance for the child; by disgracing him at school and by parading his love child in front of his frigid, barren wife.

It wasn't long before he, too, came knocking. Her stomach lurched when she spotted him walking down the road towards her flat. She hardened her heart as he rang the doorbell.

'What do you want?'

She saw him flinch in the face of her hostility.

'You'd better come in.'

Keeping her voice steady, she faced him across the kitchen.

'Right Alistair. I presume this is what you want to know. I'm told it's too late to have an abortion, so I shall have this baby with or without you. I never expected to be a single mother. But then I never expected to fall in love with a married man. Perhaps my getting pregnant is God's punishment to you - for your adultery.'

Alistair sat back in the chair and looked at her. How many hours had he lain awake since her announcement wondering what on earth he was going to do? In the end he had persuaded himself that with his having made the decision to stay with Helen, the best option would be for Diana to terminate the pregnancy. People did it all the time. But it seemed now the matter was out of her hands. Was it too late for him to try and change her mind? Perhaps a little negative reinforcement would push her to reconsider. It was worth a try. He raised a saturnine eyebrow.

'I've often wondered what it would be like to be a father. Perhaps it could come and stay with Helen and me at weekends - to give you a break.' He warmed to his theme and leaning forward to demonstrate his sincerity, he continued,

'We could take it on holiday with us as well. Helen's got some little godchildren who would love a real baby to play with. I can help you choose a name, and I wouldn't be surprised if Helen hasn't already started knitting little bonnets? Do babies still wear bonnets?'

Diana lifted her chin. She wasn't going to bear the burden of a child just so Alistair and Helen could play happy families when they felt like it.

'Fuck off Alistair. I'll do this without you.'

After he'd gone she picked up a bottle of wine. An inner voice told her to put the kettle on instead. She looked down at her hands. They were shaking.

Oh God, was she really going to go through with this on her own? Dare she carry on even if, as now seemed obvious, it wasn't going to bring him back? He'd made it clear what he wanted her to do. Surely they'd have to give her an abortion if she convinced them she was loony enough.

She changed her mind about that drink and went to run a bath instead. She lit some candles and poured in a generous slug of her favourite bath oil, admiring the irony; it was the one Alistair had bought her for Christmas. She lay there relaxing in the perfumed steam, stroking her swelling stomach and trying to picture the little creature curled within. How big is it? Does it looked like a proper baby yet? She'd have to buy one of those books that took you through all the stages of pregnancy. In fact she'd do it today. She got out of the bath, slipped on her white bath robe and, settling herself on her bed, switched on the laptop. As she waited for it to warm up she looked down at her stomach. Were those stretch marks? Never mind. Add some Bio Oil to the shopping list. No, too expensive. Maybe olive oil would do instead. Of course she could manage with a child. Would it be a girl or a boy? She'd better start thinking about names. A smile spread across her face as she pictured herself sitting in an old rocking chair with a contented babe at her breast.

She spent the rest of the day trawling the internet. She read the online posts from women who had decided to keep their babies, and women who had gone ahead and had an abortion. There were those who had given up their babies hoping that a better life awaited them. She read of the isolation, the banality and the repetition of bringing up a baby alone. She read of the sorrow and feelings of loss from those who had chosen not to bear a child this time and bitterly regretted their decision. But, conversely, there were those for whom it had been absolutely the right thing to do. Finally she ordered a book on pregnancy from Amazon. She closed the laptop with a snap. Enough. Her mind was made up. She was going to have a baby. This was no amorphous bundle of cells. This was a tiny child, a child who kicked and swam and hiccupped inside her. This child would love her even if its father did not.

Maybe this would be something good coming out of the mess of the past few months. Stopping the drinking and smoking was the first step. A few sessions a week at the salon would boost her income in the short term, if they'd have her back, and she could even consider something like bar work or waitressing before she got too fat for either. Then she could apply for benefits. That morning, as she lay in bed, she had that odd sensation of movement in her tummy she'd had before but now it was stronger. It came and went. It felt as though a butterfly was fluttering deep inside. Now, every time she became aware of it, it was an affirmation of her baby's presence. She spread her fingers across the tight mound of her belly, willing her baby to prove to her that it was really there.

She had her proof when she tried to zip up her jeans. She was going to have to find some money for maternity jeans or be creative with a bit of elastic and a long top to hide the gap. There was a new charity shop in the village. She could check that out. She wasn't above buying her clothes there. She'd heard the phrase 'pride is the luxury of the rich'. Now she understood.

Emma came round again and presented her with a bag of baby clothes.

'Liam has grown out of these; you may as well make use of them. There'll be other stuff that I'll have finished with by the time yours is born.'

Diana inspected all the impossibly tiny sleepsuits and little cardigans. She smiled as she folded them up and put them away in her special drawer.

That night she and Emma went out to a club in Bristol.

'Pregnancy isn't an illness', Emma had said,

'You're allowed to let your hair down once in a while. It's good for you.'

Diana was not so sure about that when, the next morning, she vomited from dawn onwards. Her clothes and hair stank of smoke and the £50 she'd withdrawn from the cashpoint had disappeared altogether. When the doorbell rang, she automatically went to open it, and cursed inwardly when it revealed the midwife.

'I don't want to see anybody just now. I'm not feeling very good.'

'I'm sorry to hear that. I just need to check that baby is growing well.' Susan gently pushed past her into the flat.

'We're both fine, honestly.'

'Can you just lie down on the bed for me?'

She straightened up.

'Well, baby's heartbeat is strong and your blood pressure is okay. I'm more concerned about your state of mind at the moment. I'll leave you these leaflets on extra benefits you're entitled to and I strongly suggest you come to the antenatal group I run for young mums.'

'I'm not stupid. I know what I should be doing....it's just not easy.'

'No, it isn't easy. I don't want to preach at you, it's just that a bit of support can go a long way. The other mums-to-be in the group are really friendly and it helps to share worries.'

Diana knew she was unable to share her worries with anyone, but she managed to smile and assure Susan she would think about it. She would start with a ban on boozy nights out.

26

The next day, Alistair rang Victoria. Her quiet wisdom and calm unflappability reminded him of an aunt he'd been fond of when as a very young man, life had seemed impossibly difficult. He had no recollection now quite what it was that had caused such anguish. In fact in retrospect, those years had been replete with sunshine and sex.

'Hello Victoria. Can I come round? Everything is a complete mess. I don't know who else to turn to.'

'Of course. Come whenever you like. I'm in all day. I'll put on my black steeple hat and light up the cauldron. You bring the spiders and eye of newt. We'll ask the spirits for advice.' Victoria put the phone down. Why on earth did he think she would be of any help? What did he expect given what he'd been up to with Diana?

He found her in the garden struggling to tie bamboo canes together to make a wigwam for her sweet peas. He held the edifice together while she tied the string saying, 'Can you smell this green string? I love it, it's the smell of garden sheds and grandfathers.'

It was easier to talk while his hands were busy. He avoided making eye contact.

'It's Diana. You know I'd ended it? Well, when she came up to school the other day she told me she was pregnant.'

Victoria didn't reply. He knew she would have heard the gossip, but she obviously felt there was nothing to be gained by telling him so. Fair enough. Someone's dog was barking and barking. He swore.

'Why doesn't someone shut that bloody thing up? What makes it worse is Helen and I not having had children of our own. We always assumed that, sooner or later, they'd come along, but we wanted to get a house and build up some savings before she gave up work. The plan was for her to stay at home and bring them up herself. She was adamant she wasn't going to farm her babies out to a nursery for someone else to enjoy. You know what she's like. Everything has to be done properly.'

He saw Victoria's lips tighten. She nodded and suddenly he wanted to shake her and shout, 'For God's sake come out of your cocoon of self-righteousness and help me here.'

He closed his eyes and took a few deep breaths. He needed to calm down. After a minute or two he continued.

'I've never told anyone this. When she stopped taking the pill nothing happened, so we went for help. I did my bit. The specialist was quite clear. I had a low sperm count, and it was unlikely, but not impossible, that we'd be able conceive a child naturally. My job gives me as much contact with children as any man could want, at least, that's what I thought, and Helen got on with things, as she does. She was revolted by the idea of a sperm donor. We just stopped talking about it.'

Victoria held up her hand to stop the flow.

'How is she taking all this?'

'Hard to tell. She's gone very quiet. She never was the type to throw plates. She went to see Diana but won't talk about what she said.'

'Poor Helen.'

They'd finished their wigwams by now and retired to the garden chairs under a wall of early roses. Alistair sat back and listened to the bees busy on the verbena and the salvias, while Victoria bustled inside coming out a minute or two later with two small glasses of her precious sloe gin.

'Circumstances like this demand more than tea. Cheers.'

'Thank you.' He took a sip and savoured the warmth as it slipped down his throat.

'That's so good.' He drained the little glass. 'Any chance of a drop more?' When Victoria returned with the bottle he went on.

'Believe me, I've run through every conceivable option in my mind. Could I leave Helen? Possibly. If I stayed with her, my child could be aborted. I may never have the chance to be a father again. Could Helen and I adopt the child instead? Would Helen be willing to bring it up as her own? Would Diana be amenable to that? Probably not. Her last words to me were unrepeatable.'

He paused, folded his arms across his stomach and rocked backwards and forwards in his chair. Torn between wanting to take his pain away and giving him a good slap, Victoria fell back on common sense.

'I wouldn't be surprised if Diana decides to keep the baby. And, if she does, now you've gone back to Helen, you will have to support Diana and the child, if only from a distance.'

She flicked a tiny spider off her arm.

'You know that it's Helen you should be talking to, not me. The poor thing has just had one of the worst bits of news a woman can have, and not that many months since the last disaster hit her. I can't possibly tell you what to do.'

Alistair nodded miserably. What she said was true.

'I know you're right. I don't know what I was hoping you'd say. Helen doesn't deserve this. She wasn't that bad a wife. But I only went back to her because I was promised the Headship. Perhaps it serves me right. You know I still think of Diana every single day.'

He drained the last few drops of sloe gin from his glass. 'Can I stay here for a bit, Victoria? I don't want to go home just yet.'

'You can have as long as you like. Contemplate your navel while I get out of these dirty clothes and try and dig the soil out from under my fingernails. Gardening, like life, is a messy business.'

Pleased with her tiny pearl of wisdom, she went into the house, leaving Alistair to his gloom. When he reluctantly left, she sat down heavily and poured another tiny glass of sloe gin. She had some decisions to make. Since when did she become the go-to source of advice for everyone? She was hardly a poster girl for successful relationships. She'd been sought out by both Diana and Rachel with their separate confusions, and now him. There were so many positions she could take. The romantic, the practical or the conventional – all had their attractions. The knowledge that she had the power to influence the course of lives was seductive and, as her innermost and dearest wish was to see Alistair happy, preferably with Diana, any intervention by her on his behalf would have to be concealed under a cloak of practicalities and subterfuge. He didn't need to know.

Helen also was struggling to know what to do. She dusted and hoovered on automatic pilot and reflected on her options. Firstly she had to talk again to Alistair. She'd tried to be a good wife. They'd had happy times. The house was clean and tidy, there was always healthy food on the table. True, she hadn't been keen on the sex – all that sweaty grunting, but she hadn't let herself get fat and lazy, like so many wives. The initial fury with Diana had abated and left her feeling humiliated and impotent. She could tell him to pack his bags again, but this time, he'd be sure to go straight to Diana. She needed to be like those politician's wives who bravely stood by their man when his sordid little affair with his secretary was exposed. How on earth did they do it? At least she didn't have the Daily Mail at the gate. How could she go on living here and run the risk of seeing Diana triumphantly pushing her husband's child around in a second hand buggy? Forgive and forget was all very well. She wasn't sure she could do either. He was looking for jobs elsewhere. Maybe that was the answer. Put it all behind them and move a long way away. She scrubbed so hard at fingerprints on the wall by the light switch that the wallpaper came off.

27

Victoria pegged out some sheets, then stood back to admire them flapping in the wind. As she grew older, she took great pleasure in the things which came for free – like this warm wind drying her washing. The garden was radiant with her climbing roses and intertwined clematis. Should she pick some flowers to take indoors to die, or leave them growing there where they would last much longer?

At four o'clock that morning, unable to sleep, she had got up and made a cup of tea and taken it outside. It was just getting light and the dawn chorus was in full swing. She could hear a blackbird and the great tits which were nesting next door, and wished she could identify more birds from their songs. She drained her mug. Singing reminded her of the choir which was fast going downhill, its membership diminishing. Why was she so worried about it? There was nothing she could do. She wished she didn't care so much. These things come and go. You could only stick so many fingers in other people's pies, as Rachel was always telling her.

In the distance she could hear a cockerel crowing. Maybe she should get some hens. She'd got plenty of room for a coop and a run. The boys might like that. She saw herself collecting eggs in a wicker basket and scattering handfuls of corn like that woman in the painting. It would be a welcome diversion.

She told no one of her idea, but set about researching breeds, unsure whether to go for pretty hens or the boring brown ones which were good layers. A visit to a farm sale provided her with a sturdy hen house and a roll of netting for the run. All she needed now was a handy man to provide the muscle. Marcus made it clear he thought she was quite mad but was happy to show how useful he could be.

'I've decided to have some Marans, those dark grey speckled ones that lay lovely brown eggs, a couple of white Light Sussex maybe two or three bantams.'

Marcus had looked at her fondly. 'You'll owe me free eggs for ever.'

Nathan and Luke gave all the hens names, but their enthusiasm for feeding, watering and collecting the eggs soon wore off. Victoria didn't mind. Most days she sat on the wall by the run watching them. The pretty ones spent all their time preening and arranging their feathers. The others were more industrious, scratching with their long claws in the earth, pecking at worms and beetles. There was Diana, pretty but watchful and solitary. Rachel cosied up to the others and followed them around just wanting to be liked. Which one was she then? Maybe the handsome Welsomer cockerel with his orange and bottle green finery. He cared for his flock, sorted out their disputes. Wrong sex though. She liked her metaphor in spite of that.

Vernon, the new conductor, was finding it difficult to fit a choir practice every Tuesday night into his busy schedule. Although one of the basses did his best to take the singers through the set list for the next concert, it was obvious to Victoria that people disillusioned with the lack of leadership, were voting with their feet. She cornered the Chairman after the latest miserable practice and asked him what the committee was going to do about it. He was a kindly man, with a fine tenor voice, and she was rather fond of him, despite her grumbles about some of the decisions made by him and his committee. Urbane as ever, he soothed her.

'Yes Victoria, I share some of your concerns and I wanted to have a word with you as well. You won't be surprised to hear that Vernon's three month probationary period will not be extended, with, I should say, his full agreement. We shall probably have to cancel the next concert and take a break until things can be sorted. I do have a few irons in the fire. One of them is the possibility of Alistair coming back to us when the new Head starts at South Heath. Do you think he might be interested?'

Victoria sighed and shook her head.

'Between you and me, I think he is looking for headships elsewhere. But I suppose there's no harm in asking. But it's not just Vernon though. Audiences are dwindling because we're charging too much for concert tickets – people just won't pay that much to hear an amateur choir. And, another thing, what happened to the fine words about raising money for charity? An annual raffle when we have thousands in the bank really isn't good enough. Other choirs make hundreds of pounds for good causes. Why don't we do that too?'

The Chairman tried to smile. He'd heard all this before.

'Well, if we have a break, those are considerations that can be discussed in the meantime. Now, if you'll excuse me...' and he glided away leaving Victoria in her customary state of frustration. Maybe she should have some time off. She'd miss the singing and the camaraderie with her friends though. Why did simple pursuits always become complicated bureaucracies?

Freed by the cancellation of the concerts, her thoughts turned towards doing something with the boys that would take them away from South Heath and give them the chance to experience something completely new. She had the germ of an idea, but would need to persuade Marcus to come with them. On a chilly evening she lit a log fire and invited him round for supper.

'Something smells good,' he said and went to stand in front of the fire, turning himself slowly as if on a spit.

'Oh, it's only a moussaka, nothing special', she said, not wanting him to suspect that he was being softened up for her holiday idea. When she deemed him to be sufficiently full of good food and red wine, she turned the conversation to Nathan and Luke.

'I've always thought' she began, tucking her feet underneath her on the sofa, 'that one of the things we should be doing in our lives is making memories.' Marcus was no fool. Tuned into Victoria as he was by now, he smiled at her to encourage her to unveil her latest idea.

'I'd like us to take the boys away. Away from their dratted phones and do something with them they've never done before.'

'I see. What exactly did you have in mind and what about your hens?'

'I want to hire a boat on the Norfolk Broads. Brian, next door, will look after the hens. I know it'll be wild and windy, but what an experience it would be for Nathan and Luke. Lots of fresh air, interesting places to explore when we moor up and they'll love to have a go at the wheel. I can't do it alone. Will you come with us?' Marcus laughed with relief.

'You had me worried. I was wondering what on earth you were going to come up with. I suppose you've looked into it? They might all be booked up by now.'

'Leave it to me. I've done some research and will get onto them first thing on Monday. I'm sure I can find something to suit.'

Marcus said 'I can arrange some leave and I'd be more than happy to get away if it means you stop obsessing about that choir and its problems.'

She gave him an old fashioned look, then smiled with relief. This was the part of their relationship that she enjoyed most. He gave her the security to plan adventures and the confidence to follow her plans through. By the weekend, the boat was booked. The question of sleeping arrangements which had briefly bothered her, was easily solved when she discovered the huge price difference between a boat that had just a double and two single beds and anything larger. Her suggestion to the boys that they should share the double bed was indignantly repudiated. Even the distaste that they might have felt about her and Marcus sleeping together wasn't enough put them off wanting a bed each to themselves. So that settled that.

She told Marcus, 'I've been on boating holidays on the

Broads before with Robin. Warm clothing and comfort food is essential. It might be summer here but they say the wind comes across to Norfolk straight from Siberia, so pack yourself wind proof and rainproof gear, plus a woolly hat and a hip flask. I'll bring the hot water bottles.'

Waiting for them in the boatyard at Stalham was a sight that impressed them all.

'Wow. Is that the boat we're having? It's enormous. Can we have a go at driving?'

Marcus's Yes and Victoria's No came simultaneously.

Displaying more animation that Victoria had seen for months, Nathan and Luke climbed aboard to explore.

'It's old school down here. Look at that TV and DVD player,' Nathan was not impressed.

'There's two showers though,' called Luke who was attempting to open the sliding sun roof.

'Come here, both of you and listen to Pete,' ordered Marcus. Pete, from the boatyard, instructed them all in the speed limit, mooring and general water etiquette and took them for a short practice run.

'That's it,' he said, deftly manoeuvring into the bank so that he could jump off.

'You're on your own now. Have a good holiday. You've got our number if you need it.'

The sun shone, the air was fresh and clean and Victoria's spirits rose in anticipation of the week ahead. Marcus took his role very seriously.

'I am the captain- as you can see.'

He doffed the gold braided cap he'd bought in the boatyard shop that morning.

'I shall be doing a Captain's round every day, after breakfast. If your beds are made and your cabin is spick and span, there will be a daily ration of sweeties.'

The delighted boys saluted him briskly and promised to comply.

'Now, Victoria, I suggest we splice the main brace right

away. Have you unpacked the gin?'

They motored south along the river and through several of the smaller broads. They passed derelict windmills, ruined abbeys and vast beds of waving reeds. As Marcus moored for the night, Victoria, with a flourish, produced the chicken curry she'd made at home the night before. Later, lying in bed, she nudged Marcus. 'Just listen to those boys chattering.' She raised her voice and shouted, 'Go to sleep!' In the sudden silence, she could hear the lapping of the water against the hull and the occasional cry of an owl as the boat swayed gently on its ropes.

Never one to lie in bed when there was something more interesting to do, Marcus got up every morning at seven o'clock, fired up the engine and chugged along through the early morning mist while Victoria and the boys slept. He loved it that there were no other boats about; his only company inquisitive grebes, coots, moorhens and the occasional heron eyeing him as he passed. This had to be the best time of the day. All he needed to feel utterly at peace was a mug of tea, fortified by a drop of whisky, and the passing landscape dotted with windmills, woods and reed beds. Could he get used to this family thing? Would the frustration of not getting his own way all the time be mitigated by the warmth and fun they had together? He could be looking at the next chapter of his life. What price freedom?

On the third day, once breakfast was over, he spoke seriously to the boys.

'This morning we'll be heading down Breydon Water. It's four miles long and notorious for strong currents. This wind will make it choppy and there's a strong tide running. You'll need to be very careful. If you go overboard, I won't be able to turn the boat and get to you before you drown.' He saw the look of alarm on Victoria's face.

'In that case,' she said, 'they'd better stay below.' He waved away her concerns.

'Nonsense. They'll have their life jackets on. As long as they hold on tight to the handrails, they'll be fine.'

As they drew closer to the huge expanse of grey water, Victoria could see white horses on top of the waves as the wind gusted and tugged at her jacket. A cold shower of fear washed over her.

'Marcus, please call them in. The deck's so slippery… '

Her words were blown away by the wind as the boat bucked and rolled in the swell. White faced, she stood by Marcus at the wheel, gripping the back of his seat and watching the boys at the front of the boat, yelling and waving as, exhilarated, they clung on for dear life. At last they reached the calm of the River Yare, and moored up for lunch. She took Marcus to one side and said, 'I never want to go through anything like that again. In future, I will make the decisions on safety grounds. Is that clear?' Marcus shrugged off her restraining arm, 'Have it your own way, but I guarantee you that's a thrill they'll remember for a long time.'

28

Victoria sat back in her chair and wiped away the tears of laughter with the corner of a grubby tea towel. Rachel pretended to be offended but without much success.

'You never told me about that one. How many more are there that I haven't heard about? Surely there must have been some normal, ordinary blokes as well?'

'None you'd look twice at. I tell you Victoria, it's like a parallel universe out there. They do say that you find someone once you've stopped looking, so maybe that's what I'll do. Or maybe I'll be perfectly happy not having to tiptoe round someone on eggshells all the time. Let's face it – men of our age, if they aren't married, are either somebody's rejects, gay or irredeemably damaged. Oh, sorry......'

She stopped, putting her hand to her mouth in mock horror at her faux pas.

Victoria chuckled, 'No offence,' and cut them both another slice of chocolate sponge.

Rachel waved the offered cake away and changed the subject.

'Tell me about the Broads. Did the boys have a good time?'

Victoria picked the chocolate buttons off the top of her cake.

'Oh yes, they did. One of the highlights for them was at bedtime when we'd moored up outside a pub and eaten our evening meal. Once the they were in their pyjamas, we put out the lights and with just a candle flickering in the dark Marcus told them a ghost story based on a dreadful deed done in that very pub, on that night exactly a hundred years ago. The story always ended with him giving a bloodcurdling scream and blowing out the candle. The boys would yell with fright and then laugh at themselves. That was great fun.'

Rachel's face betrayed a twinge of jealousy. 'I bet it was, but, be honest, there has to have been a downside.'

'Of course. I was furious with him when we went down Breydon Water. It was so rough and he seemed totally unaware of the danger of one of them falling overboard. It was obvious he thought I was fussing needlessly. I was so relieved when we arrived at the other end. Then there could have been another disaster when we moored up at the bottom end for the night. We'd been warned there was a very big rise and fall with the tide. Marcus said he had it all in hand but I spent the night worrying that, when we woke up, the boat would be dangling in mid- air, suspended by its mooring ropes.'

'He always was a bit gung ho about health and safety. Still, you all came back in one piece.' Rachel tried to keep the hint of envy she felt out of her voice. When she'd gone, Victoria loaded the washing machine with the third lot of muddy jeans, sweatshirts and socks that day. She cursed the fact that she'd offered to do Marcus' holiday washing as well as their own. She was right not to share her concerns about the amount he was drinking, wasn't she? She didn't want to admit to Rachel that every night, just as she had foretold, the amiable, laid back fellow she thought she knew, had become irritable and critical of everything she did or said.

It was the same now they were back at home. After a bottle of wine or several pints of real ale, there was only one way of looking at things, and it was his way. She thought it had taken took her so long to notice because he never appeared to be drunk. The only signs were when he began to argue with her about politics, criticise her friends, the way she was bringing up the boys – even the way she cooked spaghetti Bolognese. She'd snapped the long strands of pasta in half so they'd fit more easily into the pan and he had objected violently. He'd made her feel like a stupid child. Often she felt a huge sense of relief when he left to go home. There were times when they were at his house that she took herself off when he started to insult her or the things she held dear. Hardly a recipe for an ideal relationship. He told her that he had been brought up strictly by parents who never displayed any affection - either to him or to each other. He said that when he was sixteen and thinking about going to university, his father had sneered at him and told him that he would never amount to anything. He claimed that he was only too well aware of his faults now, and laid the blame squarely at the door of his upbringing. She was beginning to suspect that this excuse gave him the freedom to be obnoxious whenever he chose.

She thought back. There had been conversations years ago before Robin died, when Rachel had confided in her just how difficult Marcus could be. She remembered being surprised at the time, how this seemingly gentle, clever, funny man could be, according to his wife, miserly, foul mouthed and utterly unpleasant to her, her friends and her family.

'Rachel, why ever don't you leave him?' she remembered asking at the time. The answer that came back was simple: 'Because I love him.'

Victoria was glad she had held back from encouraging Marcus to move in. She began to doubt that they were destined to ride into the sunset together. But, for now, the good in their relationship outweighed the bad, so she tried to avoid the trigger points and make the most of what they had.

A few days later, Rachel called in on her way home from the bookshop. Victoria sat on the sofa, stretching her legs before her the better to admire her purple toenails.

'I'm disappointed no one has commented on these. Here am I, trying to shock.....'

'Mmm,' Rachel, taking off her jacket, wasn't listening.

'Rachel, talk to me. We both need cheering up. What can we do?' Rachel cocked her head on one side and regarded her friend.

'I know that look. You've already got a plan, haven't you? What's in your mind?'

'I thought we might have a day at that spa. You know, the

162

one that advertises in the Mendip News.'

'Oooh, yes, I'd be up for that.' Rachel had a vision of herself on a bed being massaged with essential oils by a burly Adonis with a six pack.

'We could have a treatment or two, swim and laze around in white towelling robes read expensive magazines...'

'Speaking of expensive...'

'Not terribly. There are lots of special offers and midweek deals. And, don't we deserve it?'

Victoria made a call. They were in luck. They drove up an avenue of trees and parked outside a stately pile.

'We were fortunate to get that cancellation. What a lovely place.'

Rachel was getting their bags out of Victoria's boot. Victoria looked across the car park.

'If your preferred style of architecture is Victorian Gothic, then yes. Get a move on. It says here the yoga class starts at 9am prompt,' She waved the glossy brochure at her friend in an attempt to hurry her up. Why was she feeling so grumpy? Perhaps a little eastern tranquillity would soothe her savage breast. She'd done yoga before. Who hadn't? But only in draughty church halls or cold community centres. If truth be told, she hadn't much enjoyed attempting to coax her unyielding body into the required postures then, so wasn't sure why had she signed up for it today.

The 'Relaxation Suite,' dripped with luxuriant greenery, low lighting and barely audible mood music. Their instructor, possessed of a perfect body and sinuous limbs, was gentle with them however. Watching Rachel out of the corner of her eye, Victoria noted with satisfaction that her downward dog was superior by far. Too soon, they came to the final exercise. Told to empty their minds of all their woes and unfinished business, and imagine themselves in a lovely, safe place, they lay on their mats and closed their eyes. She couldn't do this. She never could. While everyone else seemed to slip effortlessly onto a sunlit beach or into a wondrous garden, her mind would wander round frantically, looking for peace, and find only litter and jellyfish on the beach or weeds that needed to be pulled up in the flowerbeds.

Glad when the class came to an end, with Rachel in tow, she set off to look for the steam room. Normally, that would instantly relax her, as long as there was no one in there chattering. She was in luck. Nobody there. She told Rachel that complete silence was essential, and settled back, happy at last, in the warm tropical moistness.

It was six o'clock in the evening. The big pool was deserted except for Rachel doggedly swimming length after length. Their special offer ran out at eight, and Victoria was determined not to waste a minute. They'd both had a facial and a massage and spent time in the sauna and steam rooms, before taking a bike ride around the grounds. Now it was time for something completely different.

Victoria looked around carefully. Not a soul in sight. Rachel didn't count. She lowered herself into the plunge pool and swam through the passage that linked it with another pool outside in the gardens. Underwater lights glowed, and lush green vegetation flourished. It was like being in a jungle. Another swift look around. The coast was clear. She peeled off her swimming costume and indulged in one of her very favourite pastimes; a naked swim. She swam to the far end and stood under the waterfall, her body turning pale green in the lights. Rachel appeared and swam towards her. She stood up, shaking her curls and wiping her eyes.

'I wondered where you'd gone. Oh my God, Victoria, you can't do that. What if someone comes?'

'I don't give a toss. I can easily put my costume back on if necessary. Why don't you try it? It's a fantastic feeling.'

'I don't understand it. You're beginning to display some alarming tendencies. First the purple toenails, now naked swimming. I sometimes think you do these things just to shock,'

'Maybe I do, but perhaps I'm trying to shock myself rather than other people. Had you thought of that?'

'Wait till we get home. What's it worth to keep schtum?'

'No deal. The older I get, the less I care about what people think.'

Rachel gave up and with much splashing made her way back into the complex. Victoria, left to enjoy her solitude, thought that her little acts of rebellion were for her own satisfaction rather than a public declaration of non-conformity.

29

In addition to her three days a week at the bookshop, Rachel worked as a volunteer with a local community group. They ran a befriending service, and she visited two old ladies who needed nothing more than a familiar face to call in every so often and have a chat or run a few errands.

'Rather you than me. I don't much like old folk,' Victoria was dismissive.

'You're in denial. You're frightened of getting frail and forgetful yourself. You'll be glad of people like me one day.'

'No, I think it's like maternal instinct. It kicks in if and when you need it. Look at me and the boys. I didn't think I was in any way maternal but land two strapping teenagers on me and I've got a whole new lease of life.'

Rachel refrained from pointing out that Victoria had had very little choice in the matter, and her complaints about loud music and enormous appetites were frequent and heartfelt. She just said, 'Well, I enjoy the company of old people. Remember I looked after my own parents, and I'm very glad I did.' Not for the first time, she wondered how Victoria always managed to make her feel slightly inferior.

One morning her phone rang. It was the manager of the community group.

'Hello Rachel, I've got something which might interest you. Could you pop in to the office?'

Rachel put on her professional face and walked round. Rosemary made her a cup of coffee and chatted about the various projects the group were taking on. After a while Rachel said, 'You wanted to discuss something with me?'

'Yes. I've had an e- mail from Christopher Forbes-Martin,

the new Head up at the school. Apparently, he's a widower, and has an elderly mother who lives with him. You know that lovely half- timbered cottage down Church Lane? Well, he's bought that. He needs someone to go in several times a week and keep the old lady company and maybe take her out for jollies now and then. A sort of 'companion' as it used to be called. You've had experience in that area with your own parents, haven't you? And, of course, the experience you've had with us will stand you in good stead.'

Rachel nodded. 'Does his mother need nursing care?'

'Not as far as I know. He didn't go into much detail, just asked if I knew of anyone who might possibly be interested, and, if I did, to ask them to give him a ring and he would fill them in with what would be required.'

Rachel walked home with a phone number on a Post- It note in her hand, wondering whether she really wanted to take something more on. The old girl's probably gaga, and she didn't fancy emptying commodes and mashing up food. By the time she got home she'd talked herself out of the idea and wasn't even sure whether to phone the man at all. She called Victoria for advice.

'Oh for Heaven's sake', said Victoria, 'Just ring and find out what he wants you to do. I met him when he came for the interviews and he seemed extremely pleasant. Slightly arrogant perhaps, but that might have been nerves.'

Arrogant doesn't begin to describe him, thought Rachel as she put down the phone. There was nothing she could put her finger on, except he had been excessively formal and there was no warmth in his voice. But she agreed to his suggestion that she go and meet his mother. He asked for a DB check, which irritated her, even though it was a perfectly reasonable request, and grilled her on her previous experience. No more than I would do in his situation, she told herself, but the feeling of being patronised persisted and raised her hackles. His voice was smooth, with a cut glass accent, which, had she been talking to him in her days of internet dating, would have turned her legs to jelly. She loved a man with a posh voice.

However, to her, in this situation, it smacked of condescension. This isn't for me, she decided, but lacking the courage to ring back and tell him, she knew she'd have to go through with it and then, maybe, drop a note through his letterbox and politely decline the job.

Christopher Forbes-Martin finished unpacking the last box of books. He put them on the waiting shelves in any old order, anticipating the pleasure he would get eventually from arranging the fiction alphabetically by author and the non-fiction into categories. He knew that these days if he wanted to find something out, he just went to the internet; yet he couldn't bring himself to get rid of all his gardening and medical books, let alone the poetry books and his collection of biographies. He sat down at his desk and pulled his To Do list towards him. He crossed off 'unpack books' and ran his hands through his hair, realising he needed to add 'Get haircut.' That person who had phoned him about visiting his mother was due shortly and, if she proved suitable, would be another item to cross off the list.

He opened the front door to Rachel at the appointed hour. She remembered to smile and said, 'Good morning, I'm Rachel Williamson.' Dressed casually, he looked far less formal than he sounded on the phone and her nerves abated a little.

'Hello. Thank you for coming. We'll go through onto the terrace. Can I get you a drink? Coffee? I'm afraid everything is in a bit of a mess still, but as you can see, I'm working on it.'

'No, no coffee, thank you.' Rachel sat down on a bench against an old brick wall. The smell of the roses and the warmth of the late afternoon sun calmed her.

'What a beautiful garden.' She folded her hands in her lap and wished he would sit down too.

'I can't claim any credit for it, I'm sorry to say. We've only been in a few weeks. But I hope to be able to keep on top of it. Mother is having a nap at the moment, and I wanted to talk to you first anyway.' He perched on the edge of a garden chair.

'To begin with, you need to know that although she has rheumatoid arthritis, which makes it difficult for her to get about, there's absolutely nothing wrong with her mind. She is a highly intelligent woman and the mental stimulation you would provide is what I'm looking for more than the physical side of care. It's a long time for her to be alone when I am at school all day. I already employ someone to come in and bath her, help her dress and so on so that would not be required of you. You might find yourself having to make the odd cup of tea and perhaps take her out in her wheelchair if that's all right.'

He regarded Rachel with a quizzical air.

'How would you feel about that?'

'It sounds perfect. Actually I enjoy the company of older people far more than that of the young. I already do some work here with the elderly in the village.....'

'Yes, yes, that person in the community office spoke about that. Right, let's go inside and I can introduce you to each other.'

He stood up and gestured to her to follow him into the house. She saw how his hair curled at the back of his neck and how broad his shoulders were under the faded blue sweatshirt and made an attempt to return to practicalities.

'Are you offering me the job then?'

'No, sorry... not yet at least. Once you've had a chat with her, you can both make up your minds if you want to go ahead and, if you're both happy, then we can sort out the niceties. Come this way please.' He led the way back into the cottage and into a room where his mother was seated in an armchair. He was conscious of being pleased that this Rachel seemed to be intelligent and personable. Please God Eleanor would agree.

Rachel saw a tall woman who had clearly once been a great beauty. Her hair was carelessly gathered up into a chignon and she was dressed all in black save for a vivid, multi-coloured shawl draped round her shoulders. Rachel found it hard to conceal her surprise. She was expecting to meet a little old lady hunched in a hand knitted cardigan.

'Good afternoon. I am Eleanor; I see you've met Christopher. I hope he's painted me in a flattering light. He certainly speaks highly of you.'

Does he indeed, thought Rachel. Who's he been talking to?

'I'll leave you two to chat, I have some calls to make,' and with that Christopher disappeared into his study.

Rachel looked around her. There were shelves of books and richly patterned rugs on the polished oak floorboards. There were paintings on the walls. To her untutored eye they looked like originals. French windows opened into the garden and the sun streamed in.

'This is a glorious room!'

'Yes, as soon as I saw it I claimed it for my sitting room. I needed space for my books and Chris has been relegated with his to the little study, when he needs to get away from me. Would you like some tea? I can offer Earl Grey or builders.'

'Earl Grey would be lovely, thank you'.

Eleanor called out to Christopher, 'Earl Grey for two, my darling, when you've got a minute.'

'Right,' came the answer from afar. The tea, when it arrived, was in chunky stoneware mugs. Rachel smiled to herself. Where were the bone china teacups and matching teapot? Clearly this old lady was going to be full of surprises. They chatted easily for half an hour and, when Christopher came back into the room, both women were chuckling as Eleanor entertained Rachel with her trenchant views on political leaders. He sat down with them and told Rachel that, ideally, he would like her to spend some time with Eleanor three mornings or afternoons a week, except in the school holidays. Rachel, having instantly taken to this feisty old lady, agreed. After all, it was Eleanor she would be spending time with, not her son. Sipping her tea, she asked Christopher if he was looking forward to starting up at the school.

'It can't be easy taking over someone's job when every change you make will be taken as an implied criticism.'

He appeared stung by this and retorted swiftly, 'It's not my intention to begin by upsetting people.' Mortified, Rachel backtracked, 'No, of course not. It's just that Keith was such a traditionalist, I thought you might want to be a new broom, sweeping clean - and teachers are supposed to be notorious for resisting change.'

Conscious she was digging herself into a hole, she rose to her feet and bade goodbye to Eleanor who had been watching the exchange with an amused smile. As he walked her to the front door he raised the subject of remuneration, out of ear shot of his mother, and they shook hands in agreement for a trial period of three months.

'The important thing is that I really liked her,' she told Victoria, 'so the fact that I find him a bit intimidating is neither here nor there. I don't expect I shall see much of him once school starts anyway.'

When dressing for her first visit to Eleanor she took a little more care than usual. Looking in the mirror she saw a face that was worryingly grey and careworn. She smiled experimentally and saw a transformation. So she put on a suggestion of make-up and a squirt of her precious Chanel No 5 and resolved to smile more. She was uneasily aware that all this might not be for the sole benefit of the old lady.

30

Marcus stood, swaying slightly, in the kitchen and watched Victoria poking slivers of garlic and rosemary into the leg of lamb. She opened the oven door, pulled back from the blast of hot air and manoeuvred the tin onto the shelf.

'I can see you're busy. I'm just on my way home from the pub and I wondered if the boys would like a kick about before lunch.'

'No, sorry, not just now. They're upstairs tidying their rooms before we eat. I had to read the riot act, you've never seen such pigsties.'

He stepped past her into the hall and bellowed up the stairs.

'Nathan, Luke, down here now.'

Victoria started to speak but he brushed her protests aside. When both boys had clattered down the stairs and were standing in front of him, Marcus, his face reddening, said, 'I hear you two have been taking advantage of Victoria's good nature.'

'No, we…'

'I haven't finished. You need to go back upstairs right now. I'll give you twenty minutes to tidy and clean those bedrooms. I'll come up to inspect them and, if I'm not completely satisfied, there'll be no dinner.'

Nathan looked sideways at Luke and then turned to Marcus and lifted his chin in defiance.

'We don't have to do what you say. You're not our father.'

Marcus grabbed Nathan by the front of his shirt and put his face very close to the boys.' 'I'm glad that I'm not your father, but I am acting in loco parentis, if you know what that means … which I very much doubt.'

'That's enough.' Victoria pulled Marcus away. 'You two go back upstairs.'

She turned to Marcus and when she heard the bedroom doors slam, she hissed,

'How dare you? How much have you had to drink?'

'Seven or eight pints,' grinned Marcus, his anger disappearing as fast as it erupted.

He made a clumsy grab for her.

'Come here, give us a hug.'

Victoria twisted away from the beer fumes on his breath and opened the front door.

'That's it. I've had enough. Go home Marcus. You have absolutely no right to speak to the boys like that, drunk or not.'

He raised his hands in mock apology.

'Can't you see you're letting them walk all over you? I was only trying to give them a bit of discipline. You're making a rod for your own back.'

'What I can see is that I'm sick of your bad temper. You clearly have no idea of how obnoxious you are after a few pints. Get out.'

Marcus woke up the next morning with the unwelcome gift of perfect recall. He groaned aloud at the memory of Nathan's terrified face and the expression of shock and loathing on Victoria's. He had some serious apologising to do. Should he go round tonight after work?

No, he was due at a regional conference in Oxford and wouldn't be back until late. Anyway, he'd only been thinking of her when he disciplined that cheeky lad. Why couldn't she see how they were taking advantage of her good nature? It was like training a dog. A good kicking as soon as they strayed out of line, soon taught them how to behave. Her sweetness and generosity had attracted him to her in the first place, but the way she extended it to every waif, stray and hopeless case she came across was so bloody annoying. Things had never been the same since those boys came to live with her. The subtle change in the hierarchy was not to his liking.

He lifted his face to the stream of water coming from the shower. Rachel had told him that someone had described him as the most offensive man they'd ever met. He'd tried not to be that man in the years since, but clearly he was still in there. Perhaps he was just a bully, as his father had been to him.

He waited a few days before going back to Victoria. A mutual cooling off period would benefit both of them. By the end of the week, she might even be beginning to miss him. After work on Friday night, he came home and changed his clothes. Although she had joked about men in uniform, this wasn't the time to be light hearted. Was this shaping up to be the end of yet another relationship? Not for the first time his thoughts went back to his childhood.

He stood in the playground. It was cold and windy and an autumn chill was in the air. His mother held his hand although he tried desperately to pull it away.

'I'm five, Mummy, don't hold my hand.'

A teacher came over to them. She called to a group of watching children, 'Will someone look after this new boy? His name is Marcus.'

Then she moved away to see the lines of children into the school. No one stepped forward from his new class.

Another year, another school.

He stood in the playground, his hands firmly in his pockets. His mother explained, 'This is Marcus' third school, I'm afraid, we move around a bit for my husband's work.'

'He's a tall lad for seven. Come with me, Marcus. We'll soon have you settled in.'

Just words.

Once again, he stood in the playground alone. He hadn't got the right uniform on. The listening children overheard his mother say that due to their unsettled lifestyle, this would be his fourth school in five years, and they were merciless with their taunts.

'Gyppo! Do you live in a caravan?'

'Is it true you eat hedgehogs?'

'I bet your mother tells fortunes and sells pegs.'

He blacked that boy's eye. It put a stop to the bullying. But he never made a friend. Small wonder he didn't like people very much. He didn't possess the skills to maintain friendships as long as most people did.

It was one thing though to be intellectually aware of ones shortcomings. It was quite another to change the flawed adult that had grown out of that damaged little boy.

His relationship with alcohol was complicated. It dimmed the spectre of his cold, sneering father looking over his shoulder. It released his inhibitions enabling him to relax, make jokes and be tactile – essential with his women.

He reached Victoria's house and tapped on the door. It was a while before Victoria opened it. He hadn't expected a red carpet but he was still unprepared for the open dislike in her gaze and the height of her eyebrows.

'May I come in?' He didn't usually have to ask. She nodded and moved aside.

He sat at the kitchen table, in the chair he had come to regard as his and clasped his hands together in supplication, attempting to catch her eye. She busied herself emptying the dishwasher.

'Sorry Marcus, I need to do this now. I've had a busy day and I'm out tonight.'

He wondered where she was going and who she was going with but it was clear the information was not to be forthcoming.

'Victoria, look at me. Please. Don't make this more difficult than it already is. I'm sorry about the other day. I was only trying to get those lads to pull their weight.' He stood up, walked round the table and held out his arms to her. 'Don't be like this. I was only thinking of you.' She ignored his arms and went and stood with her back to the sink.

'I can't do this anymore Marcus. It's not just what happened on Sunday. I have enough drama in my life without you adding to it. I really think this relationship has run its course. I'd like us to stay friends. That goes without saying.' Her face was set.

He stared at her in silence for a moment.

Then he turned and walked away, his back rigid. He wasn't going to beg. It was her loss. She could be replaced.

That night Victoria lay in bed with memories swirling round. The fun they had in Bruges, love in the boat on the Broads, the feeling of his arms round her in bed. She had drawn in his sweetness as fast as her dry hands absorbed hand cream. How complex were human beings, that they could be so good then, in a breath, so bad? She considered the strategy of compromise. So many women did it, how else could marriages survive? She imagined how it would be if, when this latest spat had blown over, they continued as before. But she didn't want it any more, not like this, walking around him on eggshells, fearful of causing offence and flinching inwardly every time he reached to top up his glass.

She needed to get away.

Where could they go? It was nearly half term. They could all do with some fresh air, wonderful scenery and physical exertion. By the time the boys came home from school, she'd had an idea.

'How would you fancy driving down to Cornwall and staying near a surfing beach?'

His face alight, Luke said, 'Oh, wow, we've never done proper surfing. That would be amazing. Dad always said he'd teach us how to surf.'

Nathan looked thoughtful. 'Do you know how to surf Victoria?'

'I'm afraid not, but I know a man who does.'

'Oh no. Not Marcus.'

'Certainly not. There's lots of surf schools down there with young men who'll teach you how to do it, and they'll have all the kit you need as well, wet suits and so on.' She took out the ironing board.

'I could teach you how to iron your shirts though.'

Now she had made the decision, she needed a plan. She started looking for a holiday flat close to the sea. She'd left it so late that she began to despair. In the end a teacher at South Heath, hearing of her difficulties, offered her his family's holiday flat in Cornwall.

'Nobody's going down this half term. You did a wonderful thing, Victoria, taking in your nephews like that. I'm only too pleased to help. It's in Sennen – close to the sea front.'

'Where is Sennen, Victoria?' Luke was the inquisitive one.

To her delight, he returned her spontaneous hug.

'It's right on the tip of Cornwall, Luke, with a glorious beach, a surf school and near enough to St Ives for me to be able to visit Tate Modern and us all to walk the coastal path.'

'Cool.'

When the end of term came, she happily over- packed, safe in the knowledge there was no man, hovering over her shoulder, complaining about the number of bags and boxes.

As soon as they arrived in Sennen, the boys disappeared to the beach. She stood in the doorway and watched them running down the lane and envied them their youthful energy. After seven hours on the road, she was weary.

Tea first, she thought, then get started on the unpacking.

Before long Nathan and Luke returned, grinning from ear to ear with a gift of a dead crab for her, and she sent them back out to buy fish and chips for their supper.

That night she slept better than she had for months and woke in the morning to bright sunshine and the screams of the seagulls.

Happiness, she decided, was the sound of seagulls on the first day of a holiday.

A pattern was established where the boys spent the mornings at the surf school and, in the afternoons, they all set off to explore Cornwall. In the evenings, both boys were back out on the beach until dark, perfecting their new-found skills. Most nights, Victoria took a blanket and a flask of soup, and huddled on the beach, watching them and laughing as they fell off their boards over and over again. Sometimes they would stay out there until late and lie, snuggled together under the blanket, looking at the stars.

On their last day, she told them over breakfast,

'I don't believe my luck. I've managed to acquire three returns for the performance tonight at Minack in Porthcurno.'

'What's that?'

'It's an open air theatre, built into the cliffs overlooking the sea. It's one of my favourite places in the world. I promise you, you'll be gobsmacked. Don't let me forget to take cushions though.'

She was rewarded by their amazement at the stunning spectacle before them; the semi-amphitheatre on the cliff's edge curled round a small stage and the impossibly blue sea sparkling beyond.

'Wow, it looks like something the Romans built.'

That night, they sat on the vertiginous stone steps watching the Tempest.

'I can see why we needed cushions,' Nathan observed, 'my bum's gone all numb.'

Victoria, however, a boy on either side of her, her arms about their shoulders, under the full moon, sighed with deep contentment.

31

Rachel and Eleanor were getting to know each other. Eleanor saw something of herself in Rachel. She said to Christopher, 'So clever of you finding Rachel for me. I can tell her the story of my life and know that unlike you, she hasn't heard it all before and is stifling her yawns.'

Christopher, his back towards his mother as he expertly flipped an omelette onto a plate, smiled to himself.

One morning, Eleanor looked at Rachel over the top of her glasses.

'Did you read the piece in the paper about that dying baby?'

Rachel nodded while squinting at a needle with an impossibly small eye, which refused to be threaded.

Eleanor seemed to be in a mood to share confidences. 'It was very sad, but then we've all had our share of heartbreak, haven't we.'

Rachel put down the coat that had shed a button and waited.

'No, don't let me stop you sewing that button on. I can't see well enough to do it myself. You can listen and sew at the same time can't you? '

'You're bullying me again, Eleanor,' but she picked up her needle and thread.

Eleanor looked into the distance. The French windows were open and somewhere a robin was singing.

'It's a wonder to me that Christopher turned out as well as he has,' she said. 'I tried to shield him from the unpleasantness of the divorce, but he must have been aware of my distress. When we moved in with my parents it was very difficult. He was such a sensitive little boy.

She paused. 'Would you put the kettle on for me? I want to tell you my story and all this talk will make my voice croaky.' Rachel obediently did as she was asked. When she returned from the kitchen with two mugs of Earl Grey, Eleanor shifted in her seat to make herself comfortable against the cushions and continued.

'You young people seem to think you have a monopoly on misery. In my day we just didn't talk about it all the time. My misfortune was to have a husband with a wandering eye. I came across him literally *in flagrante* with my best friend. Christopher was only eighteen months old. I walked out with nothing but the clothes on my back and my baby under my arm. I had no choice but to move back in with my parents, in the face of their strong disapproval. To them, marriage was a sacred bond. They were extremely old school and actively discouraged any displays of physical affection, so I used to have a secret cuddle in bed with Christopher first thing every morning. A private treat for both of us.'

Rachel's eyes widened in horror.

'Poor little boy. How could they be so cruel?'

'They thought it was best for him if he toughened up. In their view I was spoiling him. He was always drawing and painting. They said that eventually he should go away to boarding school to learn how to play rugby and become a man, but I put my foot down at that.'

'Why didn't you leave?'

'Things were different then. Where would I go? I couldn't support myself, let alone a child. There weren't all the benefits and suchlike for single mothers that there are now. They insisted he went to the local prep school, at their expense, and I got a job as a receptionist in a very up-market car showroom selling Bentleys and Jaguars. It was there that I met Anthony who was the boss's son. We fell in love and got married, and he loved Christopher almost as much as he adored me.'

'It's like something out of a novel,' breathed Rachel entranced.

'But without the happy ending. Anthony died much too young, he had a heart condition and then it was just me and Christopher together against the world again. I'm not complaining though, dear, there's been plenty of happiness in my life as well.'

'Are all these pictures Christopher's work?' Rachel looked around at the landscapes and portraits around the room.

'Oh yes. He doesn't do much now, of course, he hasn't got the time. That one of me over there was my eightieth birthday present last year.'

'May I take a closer look?' Rachel got to her feet and stood in front of the portrait. 'He's really captured the twinkle in your eye. He's very talented. You must be so proud of him.'

'I am. All I would wish for now is for him to find someone to make him as happy as I was with Anthony.'

Sharing their life histories helped Rachel to keep her own troubles in perspective. Eleanor was the only person to whom she could admit her feeling of schadenfreude when Marcus' short lived relationship with Victoria came to an end.

'It was all too close to home, my best friend and my ex-husband. I needed to get away from him completely, not see him on her doorstep with bunches of flowers and a soppy look on his face.'

Eleanor cackled, 'I'd be willing to bet having you around dampened his ardour a bit too. He wouldn't have wanted you telling Victoria about his less salubrious habits.'

A few days later, Eleanor asked, 'Rachel, could you come on Saturday instead of Wednesday, as I've got a busy week ahead?'

'You've got more of a social life than I have, you lucky thing, but yes, of course. I've nothing planned for the weekend.' Rachel busied herself making some cakes to take with her while wondering if fruit would be a better gift. All this cake was showing on her hips.

'Good morning. It's a lovely day. I wondered if you would like a walk out to enjoy the sunshine.'

Rachel deposited the little plate of chocolate eclairs in

Eleanor's kitchen. She'd thought that, if Christopher was there, he could help her get his mother into her wheelchair. He might even like to come with them. In the event, however, there was no sign of him and Eleanor just wanted to sit and talk.

'My arthritis is giving me gyp today, my dear. Must be the weather. I'm not up to doing anything much at all. Come and sit down by the fire. I know it's an extravagance, when there are the radiators, but I feel the cold these days.'

'This is nice', Rachel stretched out her legs. Eleanor continued, 'I remember when we were children, sitting by the fire with our fronts all warm and toasty and our backs still cold.'

'Yes, thank goodness for central heating, although the frost patterns on the inside of the bedroom window were pretty.'

'We had hot water bottles which gave us horribly itchy chilblains on our toes, does anyone get them nowadays I wonder?'

'I bet they don't. But we still complain about things, don't we?'

Eleanor was on a roll. 'Our legs used to get all mottled from sitting too close to the fire. You don't see that now either.'

Rachel smiled and admitted, 'In winter I used to get dressed under the bedclothes. I don't think I'm agile enough to do it now. Then I ran as fast as I could downstairs to where the fire had been lit. If we were lucky, it had stayed in overnight.'

The women sat quietly for a minute.

Rachel heard the front door opening and turned towards the door, her lips curving into a smile.

Christopher came in ahead of a tall, willowy woman with dark brown curls and perfect teeth.

'Hello Rachel, I forgot you were coming today. Can I introduce my friend, Claudia?'

Rachel forced a smile and shook hands. Then she made her excuses and, told Eleanor she would see her next week. She walked home and chided herself for being desperate enough to look at any unmarried man as a potential partner.

Wednesday found her knocking at Eleanor's door with difficulty, balancing a tin of chocolate brownies on one arm and holding a small nosegay of russet chrysanthemums in the other. Eleanor looked delighted to see her.

'I've been on my own all week,' she told Rachel.

'Christopher is away in Italy for half term. I expect he told you. He sent me some photos the other day of Tuscan hillsides and plates heaped high with glorious food, so I'm feeling very sorry for myself stuck here. I don't suppose I shall ever go to Italy again.'

Rachel wondered if the fragrant Claudia was with him but didn't like to ask.

'Did you travel much when you were younger?'

'I had some wonderful holidays with my father in Germany just before war broke out. We stayed in the mountains in Bavaria. He was a great walker and the scenery was beautiful. I've got lots of photos from those times, I'll show you one day. All the town buildings were hung with swastikas and people greeted each other saying Heil Hitler.'

'Oh, my goodness. Weren't you scared?'

'Not scared exactly, but there was definitely an air of menace. I remember writing a poem when we got home. I've still got it somewhere, I could show it to you. My father said another war was coming. I was only young, in my teens, but I remember, the last time we went, he said we wouldn't be back the next year. And so it proved.'

She fell silent. Rachel thought this might be a good time for tea and chocolate brownies.

When they'd finished, she cleared the cups away and said, 'When I came, that first day, I looked at your bookshelves and noticed lots of poetry books. Would you like me to read some to you? Or, indeed, would you like to read some to me?'

'What a lovely idea. Let me think, what are my favourites? You could start with 'Sea Fever', I've always liked that, and I used to love the story poems – 'Flannan Isle' and 'The Highwayman.''

Rachel took The Golden Treasury down from the shelf, judging most of Eleanor's choices would be found in those pages.

She was right and the two spent a happy hour until Rachel looked at her watch.

'Is that the time already? I must be off. Next time it'll be my turn to do the choosing. I'll see you on Friday.'

'That'll be nice. Christopher should be back later in the day.'

Friday came. There was no sign of Christopher. Was she disappointed or relieved? She took Eleanor her morning coffee and sat down opposite her.

Propping up the books on one of the bookshelves was a curiously twisted piece of metal. 'Is this a sculpture?' she asked.

The old lady smiled.

'Yes and no, dear. I keep it to remind me of the horror of war.'

Now Rachel really was intrigued.

'You can't leave it there, Eleanor, what's the story?'

Eleanor was only too happy to reminisce. She pulled her crimson cashmere wrap snugly around herself.

'I was brought up in a big stone house on the outskirts of Sheffield. It was built as a hunting lodge for the Duke of Norfolk. There was a long drive and trees all around. It was a wonderful place for a child. Then the war came and, literally, brought our lives crashing down. My father was too old to join the services again, he'd done his bit in the First World War. He had a thriving business supplying shops but the government took his lorries and his men were called up.'

She paused and took a sip of tea.

'He struggled on with a horse and cart, working all the hours of the day. At night he went out with the fire fighters, stamping out fires caused by incendiary bombs. The phosphorus in the bombs stuck to his boots and burned through the leather to his feet. He had third degree burns from that. One Friday night when the air raid sirens began wailing, we all went down, as usual, into the cellars for safety. Sheffield was a prime target you know, because of all the munitions factories.' Rachel nodded her understanding.

'Suddenly there was an enormous explosion and all the walls shook .It was the loudest bang I've ever heard. We huddled together until the sound of falling masonry had stopped and eventually the All Clear sounded. The house had received a direct hit. We were lucky we were able to climb out of the cellar. There was rubble everywhere and the air was thick with smoke, dust and soot. We lost everything, but we felt lucky to be alive.'

Rachel held out the lump of metal in her hands.

'And this?'

'Is a piece of shrapnel from that bomb. I picked it up from a heap of roof tiles and rafters. My father told me off. He was never the same after that. His business never recovered. My mother always said his heart was broken.'

'You really have had quite a life, haven't you? Losing your home like that. Where did you go?'

'Mother's family had a property on the coast. They let us have that, albeit at an exorbitant rent. But beggars couldn't be choosers.' She dabbed at her eyes with a blue cotton hanky.

Rachel stood up.

'No more sad stories. Let's go out for a nice walk. We need a change of scenery and some fresh air.'

They sat by the village pond, feeding the already obese ducks on frozen peas as Eleanor had read somewhere that they shouldn't be given bread. They talked about music. Rachel made Eleanor laugh with some penetrating observations about the choir and its singers.

'I do hope the choir re-forms. I'll definitely come to the next concert. You make it sound such fun.'

32

Helen encouraged Alistair to redouble his efforts to get another job well away from South Heath. His applications for Headships were not resulting in his even being shortlisted, so, in addition, he started to apply for jobs as Director of Music. The world of private education was relatively small and he feared that word would get around of his indiscretion. Being a high profile character in the world of music education had its drawbacks.

One morning, after breakfast, he checked his emails. Helen had forbidden him to look at his phone while they were eating.

'I've got interviews for Headships at two schools. One's in Northumberland and the other in Hertfordshire.'

'That's good. Which one do you fancy the more?' Helen began to clear the table.

'Neither place fills me with much enthusiasm, the first one is too far north, the other too near London. But I'm in no position to be choosy. You take my best suit to the dry cleaners and I'll practice my lines.' He pulled a face.

Helen looked thoughtful. 'I don't really want you to get either of them. Desperate as I am to get away, I'm inclined to be choosy about where we live and, for me, a Waitrose and some leafy lanes are on the wish list.'

'We may not have a choice and anyway, how do you know there aren't leafy lanes and expensive supermarkets in Northumberland?'

He got up leaving half a piece of toast and a cup of coffee to go cold, picked up his briefcase and left without saying goodbye.

As soon as he'd gone, Helen got her coat and set off to

walk to the surgery.

She'd been wondering what on earth was wrong with her for some weeks. She was proud of the fact she seldom troubled the doctor, but this time, after she'd done some research online, she knew she had to make an appointment. The magazines in the waiting room didn't seem to have changed in the months since her last visit so she looked around at the posters on the wall.

One in particular caught her eye. It had a border of leaves, coloured in rather amateurishly with felt tip pens. It said:

Autumn Leaves are falling. Are you?

If so, come to our Strictly No Falling classes on Tuesdays and Thursdays.

She stifled a laugh.

'Helen McIntyre to Dr Wright, Room 2.'

Helen hesitated outside Room 2. The door was closed. Should she knock? She never knew whether to or not. She decided not and walked in.

Dr Wright looked up. 'Hello, take a seat.'

Helen wished she hadn't come. She looks weary. She'll think I'm a hypochondriac.

'I'm sorry to bother you, it's probably nothing, but I'm so tired all the time. I keep being sick, and this constant feeling of nausea means I'm barely eating. Could it be an early menopause?'

'What about your periods?'

'Um, I can't remember when my last one was. It's been a while, that's why I thought..."

'Have you done a pregnancy test?'

'What? No, of course not. Why would I? We were told we couldn't have children.'

'Do you think you could manage a sample for me?'

'Now?'

'Yes, if possible. Take this pot, aim for mid-flow, and come straight back in.'

Helen blushed and did as she was asked Twenty minutes later, choked with emotion, she came home wishing Alistair was there to hear her news. But he had driven north for an interview and wouldn't be home until late that night. She hugged her secret to herself, and resisted the temptation to call him. He had to be the first to know and she wanted to tell him face to face. This was too momentous for the phone.

He's here! She heard the car door slam and the sound of his key fumbling in the lock. She got up off the sofa, and stood waiting, trying to keep the delight from her face.

He went straight upstairs. She heard him banging about the bedroom, go into the bathroom and then back into the bedroom again. Unable to bear the tension any longer, she called up, 'Al, come down. I've had some amazing news.'

What if he's grumpy? Was he going to spoil everything?

He came into the room. His face was sour and resentful.

'What sort of news?'

'This should put a smile on your face. I kept it to myself until your interview was done, but if I don't tell you now I'll burst.' She paused for dramatic effect.

'We're going to have a baby.'

He stared at her, open mouthed. She sank down back onto the sofa. This wasn't the reaction she expected.

She watched as he turned away and went to the sideboard and picked up a glass. He poured himself a generous measure of whisky and came to sit beside her on the sofa. His expression was unreadable. 'This isn't some sort of joke?'

'Of course not. How can you even think that? '

His face softened. 'Come here,' and he held out his arms.

Relieved beyond belief, the words poured out,

'I went to see Dr Wright because I was so tired and nauseous. Remember how sick I was on Sunday? She agreed it could possibly be an early menopause, but she would do a pregnancy test just to rule it out. I told her she needn't bother as we'd been told we would never have children and, at forty four, it was hardly likely anyway. She did the test there and then. I just couldn't believe it.'

'Neither could she, I bet.'

Alistair disentangled himself and, walking to the end of the room, looked out of the window. Was that a line of tiny garments flapping on the washing line across the lawn and a swing hanging from the apple tree? Oh dear God, what now?

'She wants me to go for a scan because she can't work out a definite date. They need to measure the baby, which will tell them more.'

Still wordless, Alistair was struggling to say what she needed to hear.

Helen went on. 'I might be as much as twenty or more weeks. I'd noticed my tummy was growing but put it down to too many cakes.'

He took a deep breath. 'I just can't believe it. It's amazing - after all these years.'

But inside his head a voice was shrieking. What have you done? First Diana, now Helen. How on earth are you going to manage this?

Helen joined him at the window. 'She got me an appointment for the scan tomorrow. I did wonder whether not to tell you today and to present you with the picture afterwards. But I'd rather you came with me.'

'Of course, of course. I'm teaching tomorrow but I'll sort out some cover. No problem.'

She took his hand and pulled him back to the sofa beside her, snuggling up close.

'Are you really, really pleased?'

He put his arm round her and sought the words she needed to hear.

'I'm pleased and scared and excited and…I don't know what to say. I don't think I'll really believe it until I see it on the scan. Let's not tell anyone until after that.'

33

The call to say that someone else had been offered the job came the next morning. Alistair had no time to dwell on it as he had to take Helen to the hospital. Assailed by hospital smells and futuristic machinery, they sat in the radiography suite. On the screen, they were shown a tiny, amorphous shape with a lustily beating heart.

The radiographer took some measurements. 'I'd say you were about twenty two weeks – so due in early spring.'

It was suddenly all too much for Alistair and he broke down and wept.

He wept for the tiny foetus, he wept for Helen and Diana and to his shame, he wept for himself.

Another interview. Another failure. Aware he was driving like a madman, Alistair cursed the M5, full of caravans and family cars piled high with luggage. He put his foot down and kept to the outside lane, flashing his lights and hooting at anyone who got in his way. Who were these schools looking for? Superman? Or, in this case, Superwoman? Slim and toned, towering over him in five inch heels, this particular woman made him feel crass and provincial. Hailing from a successful London school, she made it clear she thought this was her job - and he was pretty damn sure she was right.

He couldn't face going home to face Helen's disappointment in him and, worse still, her clumsy attempts to pretend it didn't matter, that there would be plenty more chances. On a whim, he took the turning for Bristol and headed towards a pub he used to take Diana to, in happier days, a place where no one would have known them.

He parked himself at the bar. It was gloomy in there and the smell of beer, chips and something he couldn't identify, did nothing to lighten his mood.

He nursed his second pint and reflected on the mess that was his life. His reverie was interrupted by peals of female laughter from a dark corner. Irritated, he swivelled round on his stool to glare at the two women making all the noise. One of them caught his eye. Slowly she got up and came towards him.

'Hello Alistair.'

'Diana!'

Pregnancy suited her. Rounded and positively blooming, her eyes were bright, her pupils huge. For a split second he wondered if she was on something, but dismissed the thought as quickly as it came. She stood on tiptoe to kiss his cheek. He drank in the familiar smell of her perfume

'It's been a while,' she whispered, 'How are you? I've missed you.'

'All the better for seeing you', he said with a clumsy attempt at gallantry, 'May I buy you a drink?'

'No thanks, I'm heading home now. You can give me a lift if you like. I've probably missed the last bus by now. You'll save me calling for a taxi.'

Alistair shook his head to try to clear it. The image of Helen's accusing eyes flashed before him. What sort of a man was he becoming?

This evening was either going to get better and better, or go from bad to worse. The trouble was he didn't know which. The old animal magnetism was still there for both of them – he could feel it, and more dangerously, his battered self-esteem needed that special care that only Diana could give it.

Telling his conscience that he needed some time to sober up before attempting to drive home, he shepherded her out to the car which he'd left in a dark corner at the far end of the car park. The thin silky dress she was wearing hung loosely around her body. He peered at her as she slid into the car seat beside him.

'Where's my baby?' his voice was gruff. She pulled up the dress to reveal her tautly swollen stomach. Alistair leaned over and pressed his lips onto it.

'Get into the back, I want a proper look.'

He pulled into his drive two hours later, and tried desperately to concoct a plausible story for Helen, involving an accident and the closure of the motorway, the unavailability of a mobile phone signal and his wish not to disturb her, should she be sleeping.

Victoria reached for a bottle of Prosecco from the fridge as she saw Rachel and Helen coming up her garden path.

'Come in come in, time to celebrate,' she glowed.

'Sorry, not for me,' admonished Helen virtuously and carefully settled herself on to one of Victoria's kitchen chairs as if she were made of bone china.

'Of course not, stupid of me. I'll find you some juice. I think there's some orange left in the fridge.' Victoria marvelled at how Helen could be so annoying without even doing anything very much. How much damage could a mouthful or two of fizz do for Heaven's sake?

Helen had lost no time revealing her secret to her friends. She tucked her hair behind her ears and reached into her bag. With the air of a magician she brought out the little photo from the scan and passed it round.

'Do you know if it's a boy or a girl?' asked Victoria. Helen laughed.

'We told them at the hospital that we didn't want to know, and you certainly can't tell from that photo.'

'That's good. I think it's very sad that people want to know beforehand, even if it does make buying baby clothes easier.' Victoria was with Helen for once and nodded approvingly. They raised their glasses and toasted the health of mother and baby. Nathan and Luke came down to see what all the excitement was about. They were both embarrassed but fascinated by the scan. Victoria apologised for their awkwardness, but Helen laughed,

'It's alright. They don't like to think that people our age have sex!'

When the boys had disappeared upstairs again, Helen asked them both to carry on keeping it a secret between themselves, for the time being. She didn't stay long.

'It's time for my afternoon nap,'

Victoria went to the door with her and watched as Helen picked her way delicately through the burgeoning shrubbery. It's getting to be like Sleeping Beauty's castle out there she thought, and mentally added the job of cutting it all back onto her To Do list.

Rachel was waiting for her. 'Have I got this right? Both that Diana and Helen are pregnant and presumably Alistair is the man responsible for both?'

Victoria sighed. 'I'm afraid so.'

'How long have you known?'

'I've known about Diana for a while.'

'Why didn't you tell me?' Rachel complained. 'When Jean in the post office queue asked me if I'd heard, I didn't believe her.'

'Well I've been trying to support Diana, and I suppose I thought the fewer people who knew about it the better.'

Rachel raised her eyebrows. 'It's Helen I feel sorry for. If you're going to interfere then surely you should be helping Helen save her marriage.'

Victoria collected up the glasses and put them by the sink. 'Let's not fall out about this.'

But Rachel hadn't finished. 'Does she know Diana's pregnant too?'

'I would imagine so. Now, that's enough. It's all very sad and God only knows how it will all end. Off you go. I'm in dire need of an afternoon nap myself.

34

On Friday morning Christopher rang Rachel.

'Good morning. I hardly dare ask you this but I've got a problem. The carer I'd arranged to stay overnight at the weekend has let me down and the agency says they can't find a replacement at such short notice. I booked the hotel in London weeks ago, as a surprise for Claudia. I'm taking her to the Royal Opera House for her birthday. Could you possibly fill in?'

Mentally reviewing her distinctly empty diary, Rachel said, 'Of course. I can swap a few things round I think. Just as long as you don't make a habit of it!'

è

I have made a bed up for you in the spare room. Please find enclosed payment for these extra hours. There is a nice Pinot Grigio in the fridge. You'll probably need it by the time mother is safely tucked up in bed.

Chris

Victoria was outside the post office and Rachel, as usual, couldn't refuse the invitation for coffee and a chat. While Victoria fiddled with the cafetière Rachel told her about the note Christopher had left her.

'He's left me a cheque for £100.'

'It's probably less than he would have to have paid the agency for an overnight stay,' observed Victoria. 'Are the daytime people coming in as usual?'

'Yes, it's only overnight she needs me. It's just that being his friend, payment makes me feel a bit uncomfortable.'

'Don't be ridiculous. You're not his friend in this instance. You're merely working for him as his mother's carer. This is just a one- off for a few extra hours. I'd do it myself for £100.'

On Saturday night Eleanor said she was tired and went to bed early. Rachel went back down to the sitting room and leafed through the morning paper. What was she going to do now? She turned the television on and off again five minutes later. She must be getting old. All the channels seemed to be showing mindless rubbish. She got up and, as bidden, poured herself a glass of the Pinot. He was right - it was rather good. His bookshelves caught her eye. She'd always thought you could tell a lot about someone from the books they possessed. Christopher's books spoke of a man interested in the outdoors. There was a whole set of books on walks, on mountains and famous gardens. Another shelf had a collection of biographies – politicians, sportsmen, authors. Where was the fiction? She found those on the higher shelves, Ian McEwan, PD James, Lee Child.

She picked out a Pat Barker she hadn't read and thought she might take it to bed with her.

The phone rang, making her jump. It was Christopher.

'Hello, it's the interval, so I thought I'd give you a quick ring. Is everything alright?'

She felt guilty, as though he would know she was poking round his bookshelves. Conscious her voice had gone all squeaky, she said, 'Oh yes, Eleanor was all sweetness and light and I'm sipping a glass of your excellent wine. Are you enjoying the opera?'

'It's very good, not really my sort of thing - but Claudia likes it. I'd rather be at home in front of the fire with you.'

'You can't say that!'

'I don't see why not,' he sounded amused.

Was he flirting with her? What happened to all her good intentions? She gripped the phone hard and suggested Claudia would be wondering where he was.

'I'm in the drinks queue. She's in a queue for the loos. But I'll say goodnight then. Sleep well and I'll see you tomorrow.'

Rachel tiptoed up the narrow stairs, not wishing to disturb

Eleanor, and cursing her cowardice. Why couldn't she just flirt right back?

The little bedroom was a bit Spartan. When did she last sleep in a single bed? It took her back to her childhood. She managed to push open the window so that she could enjoy the dawn chorus. She sat up against the pillows and opened Christopher's book. Concentration proved impossible though so she put it aside and allowed her thoughts to run free.

Of course a good looking man like him would have lots of female admirers. Odd though, that he was still single. He was certainly out of her league. Had she been tall and willowy, like Claudia, with legs up to her armpits and a retroussé nose, then she might have been in with a chance. As it was, well, forget him. It was never going to happen. The best she could aspire to, it would seem, was the role of helpful neighbour.

Contrary to Christopher's instructions, she lay awake most of the night, alert to every strange noise, and conscious of Eleanor in the next bedroom.

In the morning, she made them both some breakfast then settled Eleanor in the chair overlooking the garden, surrounded by the Sunday papers and set off for home, telling her to call if there was anything she needed.

35

The beginning of the autumn term saw Christopher at last able to take his place as Head of South Heath School.

He rang Victoria.

'Good morning Victoria. Just a quick word. I've been having meetings with senior staff over this last couple of weeks of the holidays to give me a feel for which of them are positive and likely to be amenable to my ideas. The others I know from experience will be a longer term challenge. The important thing immediately, as I see it, is to establish a good working relationship with the key staff in the running of any school; my secretary and the caretaker. I've talked to Alistair and heard how competent and unflappable you were when you worked for Keith and then with him. Are you happy to stay on?'

'I'd love to but what about Yvonne?'

'Well, she's just let me know she doesn't want to come back when her maternity leave is over. So there's a job for you if you'd like it.'

'Thank you very much, I'd love to stay on.'

'Excellent. Would you call in to my office sometime, perhaps tomorrow if that's convenient, and I'll bring you up to speed with everything?'

Victoria walked up to school feeling a little apprehensive. Could she manage to continue full time with Nathan and Luke to look after? They'd just have to buckle down and help out more. It wasn't unreasonable to ask them to load or unload the dishwasher or clean their own bedrooms was it?

She found Christopher in his office. Dressed casually in jeans and a blue sweatshirt, he smiled widely when she walked in. He certainly was an attractive man. He'd do very nicely for Rachel. She'd play cupid if she had any idea how to go about it. The prospect of a new project, as always, set her thoughts humming.

'Victoria, come in. I want to put my stamp on this room.'

She understood, men needed to make their nests as well as women. He went on.

'Keith's musty velvet curtains will have to come down. I've seen a nice Bridget Riley print that'll brighten the place up. Those grim portraits of past Headmasters can go in a storeroom, I've got a couple of my own seascapes at home. I'll bring them in to start me off.'

He talked about some of his ideas to take the school forward and how he saw Victoria's role developing. After half an hour he glanced at the clock and said, 'Now, I need some greenery. I can't work without plants around me.'

So the two of them escaped for an hour to the local garden centre. Victoria talked him out of the glorious six foot tall weeping fig he hankered after, pointing out that no one would water it in the holidays, so he bought two smaller potted palms that he could take home when necessary.

Victoria was quietly confident the Governors had made a good appointment. She said as much to Alistair, who had rung to say how pleased he was to hear she was coming back full time.

'Rachel has told me how sweet and caring he is of his mother, and I can't help but be influenced by that. Too many people put their parents away in homes, for their own convenience, as soon as they become inconveniently needy. He lacks Keith's 'Hail fellow, well met' attitude, and he's got charm rather than charisma, and dedication rather than flamboyance, but you know as well as I do that Keith as Head was something of a roller coaster ride. Christopher seems altogether more grounded.'

'We'll see, shall we?' She detected a note of bitterness in his voice.

'Oh sorry. Well, of course, it would have been better if

you'd got the job, but given that unfortunately you didn't, I'm just saying I think Christopher will do us very nicely.'

She retrieved her work suits from her wardrobe and visited Paul for some rejuvenating highlights. Having to sit for forty minutes in the corner of the salon, waiting for the chemicals to do their thing, was her least favourite part of a visit to the hairdressers. Listening to his other clients bragging about their latest holiday in Sicily or which particularly expensive restaurants they had recently eaten at, made her wish she could afford the luxury of Paul coming to her home to do her hair in quiet intimacy.

She was in luck. This morning the salon was peaceful, and she took out the crossword from her morning paper. After ten minutes she was shifting in her chair. She was thinking too much again. Why did she do this to herself?

She worried about her boys growing up without the security of parents; and Rachel, too, with her lamentable love life, was proving to be immune to her creative machinations.

And Marcus. Did she miss Marcus? Yes, more than she would have believed possible, when she was away from him. But as soon as he reappeared, his domineering ways soon caused her hackles to rise. Better to be alone, she repeated to herself, than having to bear the brunt of another's moods and prejudices. Then she laughed to herself; she'd got quite enough prejudices of her own. When Paul came over to see if she was ready to be rinsed off, she told him about a sign she'd seen in a card shop which made her smile every time she thought about it.

It read *MISSING – Husband and dog. Reward for dog.*

Perhaps she should have bought it - to look at whenever she needed a smile.

Her sunny mood was dashed when Paul called over to a tall blonde woman who had paid her bill at the desk and was preparing to leave.

'So Annabelle, when do you go to Barbados? Is it this

weekend?'

She walked home and sat at the kitchen table, looking helplessly at her 'To Do' list. Barbados? Pah!

It was a relief when she heard a knock on the door. Even if it was only the window cleaner coming to be paid, she thought, it might break her train of thought, which was threatening to become dismal and self-pitying.

'Sorry to bother you.' Rachel stood on the doorstep, with what Victoria always thought of as her 'needy look' on her face. She said, 'Have you time for a natter? I've been with Eleanor all morning and need some normal conversation.'

'Come in. I thought you enjoyed seeing her.' Victoria led the way into the kitchen. 'I'm not busy. I was intending to make some bread but it doesn't matter.'

'Oh good. They sell bread in shops you know. No, I used to love going there but it's changing. Her mind isn't as sharp as it was and she gets upset easily. I have to be careful to avoid certain subjects. Have you got a bottle open?'

Victoria laughed. 'No, I'd decided to have an alcohol-free day, but if it's for medicinal purposes…'

She gave Rachel a push towards the sofa, fetched a bottle and two glasses and asked, 'Shall we go mad and have some crisps as well?'

'Ooh, yes please. I don't know what I'd do without you to keep me sane. Your hair looks nice.'

Rachel curled her legs up underneath her and let her head fall back on the cushions. She sighed and said, 'Do you mind if I ramble for a bit? I'm sick of being practical and serious.'

'If you can't ramble to your friends, then who…'

Rachel interrupted her.

'I've been making this list in my head', she began.

Victoria, well known for her lists, nodded with understanding.

'…of things that were once common, but now aren't. Am I making sense?'

Victoria nodded. 'I presume you mean 'common' as in lots of, rather than the opposite of posh?'

'Oh yes. For example, when I was a child I was terrified of moths. The way they flew around the light with their fat hairy bodies and rapidly beating wings and I was always scared they'd get in my hair. Now I don't remember when I last even saw a moth.'

'Yes, that's a good one. What else is on your list?'

Rachel needed no prompting. 'Mopeds, sparrows... They've disappeared too.'

Victoria took a contemplative sip of her wine.

'I've got one for you. Cars being towed on a towrope by another car. You used to see them all the time, but I was behind one the other day and it made me realise how rare a sight it is nowadays.'

Rachel nodded. 'I suppose everyone's in the AA now.'

They lapsed into silence.

'Have you heard anything on the grapevine about Diana lately?' Rachel finished the bag of crisps.

'Not a thing. I wonder how she is. I feel bad. I should have gone round to see her before now. In fact I might go this afternoon. Would you like to come with me?'

Rachel shook her head, 'No, I don't know her that well and I certainly wouldn't know what to say to her now. You go on your own.' Victoria picked up the empty crisp packets and put them in the bin. With her back to Rachel she asked, 'How are you getting on with Christopher now? I remember you were less than impressed to begin with.'

'We get on very well, thank you. Of course I am nothing more than his mother's carer, as you're always reminding me.'

Victoria, turning round, saw that Rachel's cheeks had gone quite pink. She couldn't resist saying, 'He's quite a hit with the female staff at school. I shouldn't be surprised if one of them doesn't snap him up.'

Rachel's flush had disappeared.

'Well they'll have to get past the lovely Claudia first. Goodness, is that the time? Thanks for the drink and the chat. I've promised to make Eleanor some raspberry muffins, so I'll be off.'

Victoria stood thoughtfully in the window and watched her friend bustle down the path. Did she envy Rachel's friendship with Christopher? She was happy enough in her man-free state – wasn't she? She wondered what Marcus was doing at the weekend and despised herself for her weakness.

36

Victoria acted on her decision to visit Diana who had been very much on her mind. Call her a busy body, but someone should be helping the girl, so it might as well be her. Rachel could wait.

She packed a capacious bag with all the things she might need and set out.

There was no response to her knock. Uncertainly, she turned on the door step, wondering whether to go round to the back.

'Victoria! What do you want?'

Diana came up the path behind her, a carton of milk and her purse in her hand.

'That's not very welcoming. I come bearing gifts.'

Diana had the grace to look ashamed.

'I'm sorry. I don't have many visitors – not the sort I welcome anyway.'

'Well, I'm definitely not one of those.'

She could see the indecision flit across Diana's face, but she unlocked the door and they went in.

Victoria looked around. She'd heard on the grapevine that the young woman was living in squalor, but what she saw was clean and tidy enough. There was even a solitary purple African violet in a pot on the window sill. Diana caught her gaze. 'I know what you're thinking. It's written all over your face. Well, I've turned a corner. I realised that I couldn't go on like I was. I'm even back doing two and a half days a week at the salon.'

Victoria looked at her. In spite of her defensiveness, Diana's eyes were brighter and she had a pretty floral dress on.

'I'm delighted to hear it. You're far too clever a woman to self- destruct in the face of adversity. I always felt that in my bones, you know.' In an attempt to lighten the atmosphere, she unpacked her bag.

'I've brought you some home cooking. I thought you may not feel up to doing much yourself at the moment. This one is beef stew, this is some chicken casserole for the freezer...' she paused, struck by a sudden thought.

'You aren't a vegetarian are you?'

'No, I'm not, but you really shouldn't have gone to all this trouble.'

Victoria ignored that and continued, 'I've put in some fruit, for your Vitamin C, some veg from the garden and a cake. We all need cake occasionally. In fact, put the kettle on. We'll have a cup of tea and sample it.' Over the next half hour she was pleased to see Diana visibly relax and display some of the charm and intuitive intelligence that so intoxicated Alistair. Eventually, she got up.

'I'll be off now. But I'll come again, I promise. I'm off to Wales with the school next week, but I'll come and see you when I get back. Look after yourself, my dear.'

She smiled to herself as she walked down the path, taking care not to tread on the daisies poking up through the cracks in the slabs. She'd done the right thing, for the right reason. Her next step would be to talk to Alistair.

As she passed the beauty salon, it occurred to her that a massage might calm her racing mind. She deserved it. Not with Diana this time, she'd ask for the other girl. There was a cancellation for the next day with Louise.

'Hello, come this way please.'

Louise was small and sturdy with sharp brown eyes like a monkey's. Victoria followed her into the treatment room, pleased to see there was no sign of Diana

'What sort of massage would you like?'

'I thought I'd try the hot lava shells, Louise, because it sounds faintly uncomfortable so it must be more virtuous.'

While Louise prepared the shells, Victoria asked if she saw much of Diana these days.

'Not really. She only does a couple of days a week, and she doesn't mix much with the rest of us. She's quite a private person.'

'Does she have any family?' Victoria pushed it.

'I don't know.' Louise turned away and left Victoria alone in the little room while she got undressed and lay on the bed.

It was clear Louise wasn't one to gossip. Did Diana have any friends at all?

She banished her concerns about Diana and focussed on the here and now.

Her poor body. How she'd neglected it. Blackened lungs from years of furtive teenage smoking and layer upon layer of fat laid down from delicious cakes and golden chips. She promised herself she'd look after it from now on, lots of vegetables and healthy walks.

She needed to quiet these additional thoughts in her head to make the most of the intense physicality of the massage. The smooth shells radiated their heat into her skin. When Louise tilted them to use their sharp edges, Victoria could feel little points of pain deep down in her muscles. It was over far too soon.

'Thank you Louise. My body feels so much better, but my head is still full of knots and nonsense. If only you could massage my brain as well.'

'Meditation will do that.'

'I know. Easier said than done though.'

She walked home slowly trying very hard not to dwell on the expense of such delights. A haircut, a colour and a massage came alarmingly close to costing a hundred pounds. But her car was a wreck and her last winter coat came from a charity shop, plus she didn't have exotic holidays, so what was the problem? It was okay to have different priorities from most people, wasn't it? She squared her shoulders and, thus consoled, enjoyed the extra spring in her step.

A week later Victoria sat on the top of a Welsh mountain and watched as Alistair and several children toiled up the slope towards her.

A couple of weeks ago he had approached her and asked, 'I wonder if you could help me out by taking Helen's place on a five day trip to Wales with six pupils from South Heath? She's not feeling very well, and she's no use to me if she can't help with all the activities. You know I've always been sorry for the children from places like China and Africa, who have to stay in school over half term. Like any school trip, it'll be hard work and Helen really isn't up to it this year. Would you like to come, with your boys too, of course?'

Her response was immediate.

'A break in Snowdonia, one of my favourite places, with one of my favourite men? You bet.'

They were staying at a tiny Youth Hostel, with very basic amenities, in the middle of nowhere.

Victoria looked around her. She could see the mountains; Snowdon and Tryfan and, in the distance, the thin blue line of the sea. A speck far above that was a skylark, with its song tumbling down to delight her. She lay back on the grass thinking that, right now, there was nowhere in the world where she would rather be. South Heath could be a million miles away.

Her peace was broken when the children joined her, panting and laughing with Alistair bringing up the rear.

'Miss, this is brilliant. Sir couldn't keep up with us. Can we have our picnic now?'

After they had eaten, Alistair and Victoria sent them off with a list of things to spot and identify: a bird of prey, a piece of slate, a butterfly, a wild flower and, hardest of all, the mountain rescue helicopter.

'It's good of you to do this,' said Victoria, 'These pampered kids, brought up by nannies and driven everywhere, they'll never have done anything like it.'

'I grew up in the city, and I never came anywhere as wild and unspoilt as it is here either. I just wanted them to get a taste of another world,' Alistair replied.

'Up here I can recharge my batteries and forget all my worries – if only for a while. I hope it does the same for them.'

Victoria seized her chance.

'I've wanted to ask you this for ages. There are an awful lot of us who are really missing our weekly choir practices. Now Christopher is Head, would you consider resurrecting the choir?'

Alistair frowned.

'I admit I've thought about it. I would want to make some changes though which might not be popular.'

'What sort of changes?' Victoria sat up, suddenly alert.

'I would want to change the ethos of 'every one and anyone just roll up and have a jolly good sing.' If we are to perform in public places and charge real money for tickets then, to be really successful, we need to be much better than we were. We need to cull, if that's the appropriate word, the weaker members. The choir may end up half the size, but the quality of the singing will be doubled.'

'Oh, my goodness.' Victoria said weakly.

Then, emboldened to reveal her own feelings,

'I can't pretend I haven't sometimes wondered if that would be a good idea myself. The way people can't be bothered to learn the words and instead sing with their faces buried in their music makes me so cross.'

Alistair nodded and went on,

'I agree. There are also too many people singing wrong notes and not following the timing. We'd have to do auditions to check that applicants can sing in tune and have some knowledge of basic musical notation.'

'But Alistair, this runs against all the principles under which the choir was set up,' Victoria objected, playing, as she so often did, Devil's Advocate.

'It will have to be made absolutely clear then this is not a resurrection of the old choir but a new, and different, choir – one which will follow the pursuit of excellence. Far better we help the community that way than churn out concerts of mind- numbing mediocrity which benefit no one.'

Victoria gasped.

'Come on Alistair, were we really that bad? That's so cruel. Don't you think some of the spirit of the choir would be lost?'

'I would rather have less spirit if it means fewer wrong notes and fumbled entrances. I want this new choir to be confident enough to sing without copies if needed. It'll make a world of difference to the performances. I'm sorry, Victoria, but I'm done with the old choir. My idea would be to have a meeting for those interested in joining a smaller singing group, with the express aim of delivering a diversity of music exceptionally well.'

'You'll leave a lot of people very disappointed.'

'I don't care. I wasn't put on this earth to make people happy, Victoria. Music is my passion. If there aren't enough folk interested, that's fine. I've plenty on my plate with the school choirs and orchestra.'

Alistair lay back on the springy grass with an air of finality.

Victoria examined her mixed feelings. This was a new ruthless Alistair, and she didn't like him very much. Neither did she altogether agree with him, she decided, and wondered what support there would be from the current singers for a new Super Choir. She rather wished she hadn't opened her mouth at all.

Then the children returned and clustered back around them asking for drinks and biscuits. The subject was shelved for the time being.

It was their last night. The children were in their rooms, if not actually sleeping. Victoria found Alistair in the tiny kitchen, attempting to remove burnt-on curry from the cooker top.

She supressed a smile. 'Where are the two on tonight's washing up duty?'

'I sent them packing. It's their last night and anyway they hadn't a clue how to clean up properly.'

'I rather thought that that was one of the reasons for the trip.'

'Have a heart Victoria. I've nearly finished.' He wiped his hands on a tea towel. 'We'll give them another half hour to chat tonight.'

'In that case, come and sit outside with me when you're done. I want to talk to you.'

Alistair rolled his eyes. 'Why does that sentence always fill me with dread - especially when it comes from a woman?'

She laughed. 'Sexist pig.'

When he joined her sitting at the picnic table she plunged straight in. 'Does Diana know Helen's expecting a baby as well?'

She wasn't sure what reaction she'd get. She'd never dared to broach the subject of his affair to him uninvited. To her relief he didn't snap at her, but shook his head.

'I don't know. I haven't seen her lately. No doubt the jungle drums will reach her eventually.'

Victoria decided to be gentle with him and resist the temptation to shake him until his teeth rattled.

'Perhaps you should be the one to inform her.'

'You're joking.'

'Far from it. Shall I tell you how I see it?'

He tried to smile. 'I have a feeling you're going to anyway.'

'Well, I've seen her a few times recently. She's having a very difficult time and, I have to say, I like her a lot. It seems to me that you only went back to Helen because of the Headship...'

He interrupted her, 'Look, Helen is my wife, and now she is carrying our child. There are no options for me here.'

'Yes there are. Of course there are. Whichever way you look at it, there is going to be a fatherless child.'

She leaned forward. 'You have to make sure that the woman you choose to stay with is the woman you want to spend the rest of your life with. Is Helen that woman?'

'Do you think I haven't thought of that?'

She persisted. 'Does Helen love you?'

He looked startled and getting to his feet, he walked away from her and stood looking out over the valley. She tried to soothe him. 'Yes, I expect she does. I just don't want you to make a decision that you'll regret for the rest of your life.'

'You're an interfering old woman, Victoria Dunn. Go and tell those kids it's time they settled down.'

She was glad to leave him and go inside. She enjoyed the fact she was encouraging him to do something that would be frowned on. If she'd planted a seed on Diana's behalf then all to the good. Time would tell.

Alistair left alone with the mountains looming over him, looked up into the sky and thought dear God, why me?

God said 'You know why.'

He was seized with fear for Helen and his unborn baby. However much he wanted to sweep all this under the carpet, he couldn't. It wasn't just about him anymore. Helen had been a good enough wife. She didn't excite him, but would any woman after living together for twenty years? He didn't know. A couple of centuries ago a man would be expected to have a wife and a mistress, and no one would have batted an eyelid. Just his luck to be born into a 'forsaking all others' era. Did he really want to be with Helen until death came knocking? He was trapped now. If only she wasn't … No, ashamed of his thought he went back inside. Sleep was a long time coming.

37

When they got back to school, Helen was there to meet him. She was brimming with suppressed excitement and told him their secret was now general knowledge.

'People kept asking me why I wasn't drinking. Then Marcus called in to borrow your foot pump yesterday and saw a Mother and Baby magazine on the kitchen table. The information was shared around and in the end I had to come clean. Mind you, my bump is growing so fast someone would have guessed before long anyway. Everyone is so thrilled for us, but I feel guilty you weren't there.'

Alistair looked at her. 'Go on with you. It must be a wishful bump. Your stomach is as flat as a board. Oh well, not to worry. We had to go public sometime.' He went up to Helen and put his arms round her waist.

'Pregnancy suits you. You've filled out and I love your hair like that, sort of long and thick. You're prettier now than I've ever seen you.'

She laughed and said, 'Wait until I'm the size of a house. You won't fancy me then.'

Helen made use of her surplus energy transforming the smallest bedroom into a nursery. Alistair wasn't known for his DIY skills, so if she wanted something doing, she had to do it herself. She wallpapered, painted and even bought a drill and put up some shelves. They looked slightly askew, so she took them down and re-measured and re-drilled until they were straight and true. It meant she had to fill in the holes that were wrong, but the feeling of pride in her workmanship more than compensated her for the extra time it took.

Relieved that her obsession with cleanliness was less in

evidence, she was finding other things she would rather be doing than battling unseen germs.

People were so kind. She'd had visits from several ex-choir members. They brought little knitted garments and well-meant advice. Without exception though, once the niceties had been dispensed with, they would bring up the subject they were really concerned about, which was all this talk of Alistair starting a new choir. They'd seen the notice up in the post office asking those interested to come to a meeting in the village hall. She tried to keep out of the panicky talk of auditions and such by telling them just to go along and hear what Alistair had to say. She supposed you had to be a pretty confident singer to submit to an audition and wondered how many would turn up for him.

On the night of the meeting, she could see that Alistair was anxious. He paced up and down rehearsing his justifications for changing the status quo.

When he returned, Helen was waiting.

'How did it go? Were there many there?'

'We got at least thirty, most from the old choir, but also a few new people. Don't look so worried.' He poured a small whisky.

'I explained my vision of excellence and the aim of improving musically as we go on. I talked about hard work and commitment, and I told them there were to be informal auditions to make sure they were singing in the right section.'

'How did that go down?' She stifled a yawn.

'OK, I think. Around thirty signed up for the auditions. One or two grumbled that what had started out as an informal community venture had become elitist and exclusive, but that was bound to happen.'

His next job was to conduct the auditions. Helen waited up for him. She needed to support him in this venture if their marriage was going to recover.

'You look exhausted. How did it go?'

He slumped down into a chair.

'I've heard everyone sing, and I think I've got a useful little group of twenty five who are keen and able.'

'Is Marcus in the chosen few?'

Alistair smiled. He knew she loathed Marcus.

'No, he isn't. Did I ever tell you that at one of the choir practices before I left, I had to make the tenors sing their part several times? In the end I told them that someone was singing the soprano line an octave lower and they must do it again. This time I noticed Marcus wasn't singing – and it was note perfect.'

Helen laughed.

'What about Victoria and Rachel?'

'Yes. They're both in. I've asked Christopher but he declined. He said he was sorry but he was snowed under with school stuff and his mother's poor health. I told him I needed him as I was struggling to find competent male singers. It's only two hours a week for heaven's sake. If he just comes when he can, he'll find singing is an excellent stress reliever.'

38

Marcus was on a mission. After being shown the door by Victoria he had foresworn the company of women. But this couldn't last. He enjoyed a drink in the pub with the other men a couple of times a week, but it wasn't enough. Besides, she might be missing him too. Although he teased her about her propensity to take in lame ducks, wasn't he a bit of a lame duck now? He couldn't bear the thought that he may never have sex with her again. Was she feeling the same? Besides, he missed her erudition and her baking.

The bottom line was that in the months since Victoria had shown him the door, he'd never met anyone else he remotely fancied. There were a few divorced women at work, but he wasn't about to waver from his rule never to mix work and relationships.

They had always had that certain chemistry between them. On the odd occasion they bumped into one another, she seemed to be pleased enough to see him and would kiss him on the cheek in greeting. The way back to her heart would be through those two boys. Sometimes she would go and have a drink in the local after choir practice on a Tuesday night. He would start there. He turned up at the pub freshly shaven, wearing the cologne she liked and the cashmere jumper she used to stroke – but no Victoria. The second week, the gods smiled down on him.

'Hello Victoria. May I buy you a drink?'

'Thank you, Marcus, that'd be very nice. A glass of Merlot please.'

Was it his imagination or was that a smile of genuine pleasure at seeing him?

'I've only just got here myself. I usually go to AA after work on Tuesdays.' He ordered her drink.

She seemed delighted. 'Oh that's brilliant. What do you do there, or is it secret like the Masons?'

'No, no. They've been very welcoming and told me that I can go every night if I need to. Shall we sit down?'

He picked up his glass of lime and soda, and steered her towards a table.

'We share experiences of alcoholism – all the lives we have ruined, all the cars we have smashed up, all the chaos we have caused. There's a sense of guilt in the room so palpable you feel you could touch it.'

'I've read about the 12 steps. Do you do those?'

'I don't. Well, I've done a few. They involve a lot of soul searching. The main thing for me is that it's somewhere I can be completely honest. We alcoholics are complete liars when we are drinking. We lie to our wives, our employers, to doctors, to everyone - to protect our alcohol.'

She looked around, not wishing their conversation to be overheard.

'Is it working for you?'

'So far, so good. If I get home from work and feel desperate for a drink, I just get myself down to a meeting and it reminds me what I'm trying to do and why.'

He drained his glass and hoped it would appear that he was enjoying it. Victoria was looking at him, her eyes were soft and warm. Was this working? He did hope so. She finished her wine and stood up to go. She kissed him on the cheek.

'I'm off now but I have to say that I really admire you, Marcus; you are such a nice man – when you are sober. Good luck to you.'

Getting the boys back onside proved not to be as difficult as he anticipated. Two old electric guitars and a battered, but still functioning, amplifier, dropped off at Victoria's with a casual query as to whether they might be interested in learning to play, saw him invited back into the family circle. He was careful to take it slowly. Victoria was a pushover. Nathan and Luke, though open to bribery, still had a wariness behind their eyes.

'The truth is,' he told Victoria, 'I see something of myself in Nathan. We both had difficulties with friendships in childhood and both experienced loss at an early age. I lost my parents at sixteen, not in a physical sense, but that was when I left home and never went back. I see a similar addictive personality in him. Haven't you noticed when Nathan takes up with a new interest, it consumes him to the exclusion of anything else. I used to be like that. I think he finds music to be as therapeutic as I do.'

He looked across at Nathan, bending over the guitar oblivious to their conversation. Lean with dark floppy hair and even darker eyes, he was fast growing into an attractive young man. With a twinge of envy Marcus imagined the life ahead of the boy; blessed with looks, talent and the ability to knuckle down to something until he got it right. He hoped that Nathan's persistence and perseverance would somehow rub off onto him, and help him regain his place in Victoria's heart.

It was the weekend. Victoria winced at the racket coming from Nathan's bedroom. There was no point in yelling up the stairs. She went in to Marcus who was mending a puncture in Luke's bike in the kitchen. Little by little he had managed to inveigle himself back into their lives, and, if she were honest, she appreciated his offers of practical help.

'Honestly, sometimes I rue the day you persuaded me to buy the boys those guitars.'

Marcus pretended to look hurt.

'Sorry, it's really good of you to give them lessons. I do appreciate the way you're still involved in their lives but....'

A fresh burst of an attempt at the riff from Layla drowned her words.

'Don't worry, Vic, the shed is almost ready to move into. We've cleared the accumulated junk and the lads swept it out this morning. They just need to stick all the egg boxes up. It's very primitive sound-proofing but it should make a difference.'

Victoria rolled her eyes. 'If it doesn't, the neighbours will soon let us know. And less of the 'Vic'. You know I hate it.'

As he'd anticipated the boys were thrilled with their new project.

'We'll buy you a bungalow in Bournemouth when we're rich and famous,' they promised Victoria.

'That'll be no good to me when I'm as deaf as a post. I shan't be able to hear the sea.'

Luke, rather to her dismay, had dropped the guitar and taken up drumming. Always the more physical of the two, he had an excellent sense of rhythm and spent hours in his bedroom practising. They had co-opted two other boys from school to play rhythm and bass guitars and Marcus had offered his expertise on the keyboards until they found someone of a more appropriate age.

39

'Good morning Eleanor,' Rachel sang out as she let herself in.

Eleanor was sitting in her usual chair, but there was no sign of welcome on her face. Clearly irritated at the intrusion she said, 'Who are you?'

Rachel's heart sank.

'It's Rachel, Eleanor. I always come on Mondays.'

'I've only got your word for that. Do you know I haven't seen anyone in days?'

'Now you know that isn't true. I've just seen Christopher in the garden so you must have spoken to him at least. I'll just go and put the kettle on.'

Rachel went out to find Christopher who was furiously sweeping up leaves. He turned towards her as she approached. He looked strained and tense.

Immediately he asked, 'Have you spoken to mother?'

Rachel nodded.

'How was she with you?'

'Not good, she asked me who I was and said she hadn't seen anyone all day. How long has she been like this?'

'Just this morning.' He scooped up the pile of leaves and dumped them in a wheelbarrow. The compost heap at the bottom of the garden was just too far away at the moment.

'Have you called the doctor? Sometimes confusion like that can be caused by an infection.'

'I phoned first thing. That's why I'm still here. She's coming after surgery. Do you know that damn receptionist asked if mother could make her own way to the Health Centre? She got the rough edge of my tongue I'm afraid. When the carer got her up this morning, mother asked her when she could go home and said she'd tell Antony never to bring her here again.'

'Antony?'

'Her second husband. He's been dead for forty years.'

'Of course. Oh Christopher, I am sorry.' She hesitated, adding,

'You know if she has got an infection, they will probably want her to go into hospital for a few days for intravenous antibiotics. When that happened to my mother, taking her away from home made her confusion even worse.'

'Is there an alternative?'

'Well, we can ask the GP when she comes. I'd better go back in now and chat to her.'

Rachel went back into the house to find Eleanor struggling to get to her feet.

'I'm going home. You can't keep me here.'

'Yes, alright Eleanor, but let's have a cup of coffee first and then I'll pack your bag.'

This had the effect of calming the old lady down.

'Look, I'm spoiling you today. Your favourite cup and your expensive biscuits.'

Eleanor managed a ghost of a smile.

'Have I ever told you about Antony and what a lovely time we had driving across Europe in a camper van, with little Christopher asleep in the back?'

She had, but Rachel, in the circumstances, was only too happy to hear it all again.

Then the old lady launched into an account of how she had had to send one of her carers away the day before.

'I'd never seen this woman in my life, and she pretended to know me and said she'd come to give me a bath. The cheek of her. I told her to leave my house and not to come back with her nonsense. She thinks I didn't know she had her fancy man in my kitchen. I could hear them talking.'

Rachel went into the kitchen to make the coffee. Sadly, there was no fancy man there. She put the breakfast pots in the dishwasher and looked round for more little jobs to make the time go more quickly. She could hear Christopher talking to his mother in a low soothing voice. Eventually Dr Wright turned up. She said it was most likely a bladder infection, as the symptoms had come on so suddenly. It took some time, but they managed between them to get a sample which the doctor tested.

'Yes, there's blood here,' she said. 'Given your mother's age it might be best if she was admitted for a couple of days to be treated. I'll give her an antibiotic to take now anyway.'

The following morning Rachel called round to see if there was any news. Christopher looked to be at the end of his tether. He told Rachel that he'd been awake most of the night, trying to keep his mother calm and stop her getting out of bed.

'I was terrified she would fall,' he confessed, 'if she broke her hip it would be the end of her.'

'Go and get some sleep,' ordered Rachel. 'I'll sit with her and I promise to call you if we hear anything from the doctor.'

His face softened as he looked at her.

'You are an angel sent from heaven', he said and went wearily up the stairs.

It was lunchtime before the phone rang to confirm that a bed would be ready for Eleanor if they could take her in right away.

Christopher emerged yawning from his room when he heard the telephone ringing. He went to tell his mother what was going to happen.

Rachel held her breath, expecting trouble, but Eleanor submitted graciously to the prospect of a few days in hospital. She insisted only that her best silk nightdress was packed and her very expensive night cream.

Rachel saw them out to the car, helping to stow the wheelchair in the boot. It wasn't easy. She admired Christopher for caring alone for his mother for so long. How much longer was he going to be able to do it, now that things had taken a turn for the worse?

She waved them off, promising Eleanor she would be in to visit her the next day.

When she got home she worked her way through a basket of ironing. Would it be presumptuous of her to call in on Christopher later tonight and ask how Eleanor had settled in and if there was anything she could do, for either of them.

She didn't want to intrude. She finished the ironing, made a batch of Eleanor's favourite butterfly cakes to take in when she visited, and put off making a decision.

At eight o'clock her phone rang.

'I've just got back in from the hospital and I wanted to thank you for all your help this morning, he said.

'She's settled in a side ward with two other ladies who seem harmless enough, and they've put her on a drip.'

'Oh, thank goodness, I've been so worried about her. Will it be all right for me to see her tomorrow?'

'Yes. She'd like that. It's Ward 7. Perhaps you should ring first and check on visiting times as you aren't family.'

She could tell he was aware that he sounded a little ungracious because he hastily added,

'And thank you again for everything you've done for her. Goodnight.'

Rachel went to visit Eleanor in hospital as often as she was able. One day, as soon as the nurse had finished taking her blood pressure and disappeared out of the door, she beckoned Rachel to come closer and whispered,

'She puts shit on my toast.'

Back home, warming up some soup for her lunch, Rachel couldn't get what Eleanor had said about the nurse out of her head. What was happening in the old lady's brain to cause her to use words that she would never have dreamt of saying normally?

Her fractured memory seemed to have held on to music more than anything else, and Rachel would sing softly to her the old songs from the Thirties and Forties. Sometimes her quavering voice would join in as Eleanor, eyes shining, revisited her youth.

One afternoon when Rachel arrived, Christopher was there at the bedside with Claudia. Eleanor was clearly distressed, telling Claudia,

'I don't know you. Go away. I don't like the look of you.'

Christopher hurriedly escorted Claudia away, apologising for his mother, and left Rachel to try and calm Eleanor down. It took her some time, and she was furious with Christopher for taking his lady friend to the hospital. Eleanor had made her dislike of Claudia quite plain months ago and she was staggered at his lack of sensitivity.

She tackled him on the subject at the first opportunity. She called round to collect a book Eleanor had asked her to get and to deliver some clean nightdresses she'd washed and ironed for him to take to the hospital. He glared at her, then dropped his eyes and shrugged.

'Claudia is very jealous of mother and her demands on my time. I thought maybe if they became friends then she'd be more understanding. She wants me to put mother in a home so we can go away more often, and possibly even live together.'

Rachel thrust the bundle of clothes into his arms.

'Well, I've never heard of anything more selfish. Your mother is a wonderful woman; she doesn't deserve to be treated like an obligation. You know what she thinks of Claudia. What on earth were you thinking to take her to the hospital with you?'

She clapped a hand to her mouth, conscious she had overstepped a boundary.

'I'm sorry. So rude. It's none of my business,' and she fled, embarrassed at revealing her private thoughts, leaving Christopher staring angrily after her.

She changed the times of her hospital visits after that, to be sure she wouldn't bump into him again. She couldn't imagine that, even if Eleanor were ever able to come home in the future, she would be able to resume her old job. She'd been proprietorial and bossy and he didn't seem the forgiving type.

Victoria was her usual pragmatic self.

'I don't understand why you are feeling so bad about it. The woman is clearly not welcomed by his mother and you told him so. Any friend would do the same thing. Perhaps he'll wise up to the fact that his canny old mother knows what's good for him and get rid of the girlfriend.'

Rachel saw Victoria's expression change. What was coming now?

'Rachel, have you fallen for him?'

'Of course not,' snapped Rachel. 'My only concern is that he does the right thing by his mother until she dies. Otherwise he'll bear the guilt for the rest of his life.'

She left. Victoria looked after her with both disbelief and sympathy on her face.

40

As the days passed, Christopher found himself missing Rachel more than he would have believed possible. He missed her calm efficiency in his home which without his mother there, was silent and unwelcoming, and he missed the laughter he used to hear when he came home from school to find the two women gossiping and reminiscing.

Most of all, he missed those evenings when Eleanor had gone to bed, and he and Rachel would sit companionably by the fire with a glass of something nice, talking about everything and nothing. He found her intelligence and quick wit stimulating, but also, in a perverse way, relaxing too. With her, he had no need to act a part, which was refreshing and in complete contrast to the way he had to be at school.

One night as he sat alone thinking about Rachel, the phone rang. It was Claudia at her most business-like. With resignation he tucked the phone between his chin and his shoulder and poured himself a whisky.

After the initial pleasantries, she launched into what he suspected when he thought about it afterwards, was a prepared speech. Her voice cold, she told him, 'Ever since we started seeing each other, you've made it clear you had no wish to marry. I accepted that, but I always hoped that I could make you change your mind. I've put up with your depressions and your negativity until now…' she paused and he jumped in.

'I've tried to be honest with you Claudia. I warned you from the very beginning you not to get emotionally involved with me.'

'That was easy to say. You've changed. What about this Rachel you keep talking about? Is she to be the next unfortunate victim?'

'Certainly not. I admit I've been trying to cool you off and in the process, I've cooled myself off too. Rachel has nothing whatsoever to do with it.'

'I don't believe you, but it doesn't matter. Goodbye Christopher. This relationship has run its course. There's clearly no future in it for me. I'll miss you but I've had enough of fighting your mother and that Rachel for your attention.'

She rang off. He slumped back down into his chair. In retrospect he should have called it a day with Claudia months ago. He'd been a loner all his life. Every relationship had ended prematurely for one reason or another. The fault lay with him and his need to be emotionally self- sufficient. Just living with Eleanor was drawing on all his reserves of empathy and forbearance.

But what about Rachel? He might have denied her to Claudia, but she was, unwittingly or not, insinuating her way into his head and his life. It had to stop before it got complicated.

She was too good for him, and the last thing he wanted to do was break her heart. She would be sure to want commitment and probably even marriage. That could never happen. Better not to become any closer. He would be friendly but nothing more. Time for bed, he'd drunk too much whisky, and he needed to sleep.

The next morning Rachel's phone rang. Her heart leapt when his name showed up. She summoned up her calm, business-like voice.

'Hello Christopher.'

He was brief and to the point.

'Good morning Rachel. I've just heard mother is being discharged on Friday. You'll be pleased to hear the confusion had completely disappeared and she's very much back to her old self again. She's very anxious that you continue to visit her at home. I hope I can rely on you not to disappoint her.'

'Oh. I rather thought we might have reached a parting of the ways. Are you sure you wouldn't rather get someone else, maybe a proper nurse?'

'I can certainly give it some thought but, in the meantime, Rachel, I'd be very grateful if you would resume your duties.'

Rachel got up the next morning her head full of Christopher's words. What a cold fish he is she thought. Nevertheless she went about the rest of the day humming happily to herself.

She picked a few chrysanthemums from her garden to take with her to the cottage. Walking through the village clutching her bouquet, she buried her nose in the crimson and yellow blooms and inhaled the distinctive scent. She felt almost bridal. What did she have in her bouquet when she'd married Marcus? She'd done her own flowers to save money. That, and the fact there was no wedding photographer, still rankled, even though it was their own fault for insisting on getting married as soon as they finished their degrees and hadn't a penny to their name. It might have been a spray of yellow and cream gladioli; how unimaginative was that? What would she choose if she were to marry again?

Eleanor's face lit up when she walked in. It was good to see her back in her usual chair.

'Oh Rachel, what beautiful flowers. These are my favourites. Are they from your garden? I love the colours – positively autumnal.'

'I'll put them in a vase for you.' Rachel went into the kitchen trying to hide her shock at Eleanor's appearance. Her face was gaunt and heavily lined, her hands clawed and trembling.

'I want them over there, Rachel, where I can see them. I can't tell you how good it is to be home. If I'd had to spend one more day looking at that poor old crone in the bed opposite, I'd have gone mad.'

'You are naughty, Eleanor, she was at least twenty years younger than you.'

At the end of the first week Rachel decided she needed to share her worries about Eleanor's deterioration with

Christopher. She waited until he would be back from school and, carrying a home- made chicken and leek pie covered with a tea towel, she walked down to the cottage. He opened the door frowning, but when he saw it was her, his smile was genuine and welcoming.

'Come in, Mother has been telling me of your adventures with her this week.'

'We haven't done anything much at all. Honestly, it's been really quiet.'

'Don't look so worried. I'd suspected there were flights of fancy involved. She isn't quite back to her old self yet. In fact she's upstairs in bed at the moment having a nap. Anyway, don't just stand there, come in and have a glass of wine with me. I've just opened a bottle.'

Rachel thrust her pie at him. 'I thought you might like this. I was making one for myself, and it was just as easy to make two. It'll save you cooking and I know it's a favourite of Eleanor's.'

'Thank you, that's very kind.' He took the pie from her and put it in the fridge. She peered over his shoulder. There wasn't much food in there. She wasn't sure whether to offer to go to the supermarket for him. She hardened her heart. There was nothing to stop him doing a bit of shopping for himself and his mother. Men were only as helpless as women allowed them to be.

'I couldn't help noticing she lost a lot of weight while she was in hospital.' She was determined to have her say.

'I'm not surprised, she complained often enough about the food.'

'Perhaps you should have a word with the health visitor. They could give her those protein shakes.'

He laughed. 'Can you see my mother drinking those? No, I'm trying to fatten her up with things she loves like smoked salmon and dark chocolate. Don't worry Rachel, I've got it all in hand.'

With relief she said, 'Glad to hear it. Of course you have. Can we go and sit out in the garden with our wine and enjoy the last of the sun?'

He nodded. 'I'll bring the bottle in case we need a top up.'

The wasps were busy in the rotting apples on the grass under the tree and Rachel had to swipe one away from investigating her glass.

She took a sip of her wine. He looked pale. Had he lost weight as well? He'd always been what her mother would have called a fine figure of a man. Now he almost seemed shrunken. Her heart went out to him. She wanted to put her arms round him.

'So, what are your plans for the garden?'

'I'm afraid it's a bit neglected of late. I'm trying to keep on top of it, but there's nothing new being done at the moment. I had all these ideas, but ...'

'The garden will still be here when you're feeling less stressed.'

'Of course.' He smiled at her. 'I can always rely on you for a dose of common sense.'

She smiled back to hide her irritation. She didn't want to be a 'common sense' person. Why didn't he think she was unpredictable, wanton, exciting?

Because you aren't, said the voice in her head. Look at you, with your sensible shoes and your comfortable cords. The last thing any man would want to do with you is take you to bed.

'I'll leave you to get on. You must have a hundred things to do.' She got to her feet.

'Must you go? Please sit down and have another glass. It's so nice to be able to relax and talk after the week I've had.' He topped up her glass.

'Are you sure? I'm always afraid I must be boring you.'

He reached out and put his hand on her arm. She flinched as a bolt of electricity ran all the way up to her shoulder.

'Don't ever think that, Rachel. I don't know how I'd manage without you. Don't go just yet.'

She changed the subject.

'Have you done any painting recently?'

'Not really. I did a small water colour of the garden. What

228

I would like to do...' and he hesitated, 'but I don't know how you'd feel about it – is a portrait of you. Mother's birthday is next month and I'd like to do her another painting. She's very fond of you.'

Rachel felt herself flush. He must be joking. Her, with her plain brown hair, her too-wide mouth and sturdy little body. Who in their right mind would want to paint her?

'Just think about it. I'm rather good at portraits. I'd take some photos and work from them. It'll save you sitting still for hours.'

Had he done one of Claudia?

They chatted on and Rachel managed to put the portrait question out of her head. She made him laugh with stories of Victoria and her cat.

'I'd thought of getting a cat as company for mother, I'm not so sure now.'

He looked at his watch. 'Would you excuse me while I take mother a sandwich and a cup of tea?'

He was soon back. 'I said you'd pop up and see her later.'

When it became chilly they moved inside and he made them both a hot toddy. Rachel crept upstairs to say hello to Eleanor but she'd gone back to sleep. It was almost midnight when Rachel stumbled home. She was grateful for the fact he had a relationship with Claudia. It meant she could just enjoy his company as a friend and employer. It made everything so much simpler. It was impossible he'd be interested in her and she was a fool to think he ever might be.

The next time she went to see Eleanor, she found her pie dish in the kitchen, sparkling clean with a little note inside,

Thank you. I was delicious. Please make me again soon!

41

Alistair sighed with pleasure. It was January and the first rehearsal with his new Super choir had just finished and most of them had headed off to the pub. He stayed behind to sort out some music, saying he would catch up with them later. It had been such a joy to work with people who knew the difference between a minim and a quaver; who watched him closely for guidance on dynamics and who could sight read sufficiently well to pick up the gist of a piece in minutes rather than weeks.

He heard the hall door open and turned thinking it would be the caretaker coming to lock up.

It was Diana.

'God, Diana, you made me jump creeping up on me like that.'

He could feel his heart drumming in his chest. How was it that she still had this effect on him?

'Alistair, I went past your house. Helen was in the garden,' her voice was shrill.

'Why didn't you tell me she was pregnant? Is that why you finished with me?'

'Damn it. You have no right to spy on me.' Alistair threw down the sheaf of music he was holding. He needed to stay calm.

'Look Diana, I'm sorry the way everything has turned out. I'm being torn in half here. I can't leave Helen now – she's so happy about the baby. Please try and understand?'

'You said you loved me.'

'I do. I did. Christ, I don't know. It's all such a mess.'

She came up very close to him. He could smell her

perfume, mixed with a little nervous perspiration. It was intensely erotic. She was wearing the tiny silver rosebud earrings he's given her in happier days.

She took his hands in hers and pulled him closer imploring, 'For God's sake, leave her, Alistair. She's got plenty of friends who'll support her. Think about it. We could go anywhere in the world; just you, me and our baby. We could be a proper family. I'm not like her. I can have more babies too, if you want.'

She was begging, but the time for pride had passed so she pressed his hands down onto her swollen belly.

'Can you feel him kicking? He's saying hey, daddy, I'm here.'

Alistair looked at her and saw the delicate beauty that had captivated him so many months ago. He felt their child restless under his fingers. Not for the first time, guilt rose like bile in his throat. He took his hands back and put them in his pockets. He so wanted to hold her in his arms. He tried very hard to say the right thing, but why did it feel so wrong?

'You must see ... I need to stay with Helen now ... the job, the baby and everything....'

Diana just looked at him, her eyes brimming with unshed tears.

He tried again. 'I don't want to lose touch with you. I will help financially with the baby, of course,' and, acknowledging the cliché with a wry smile, 'I will always be your friend.'

Diana snorted with derision. 'You're so pathetic. Damn right you'll support your child.'

She squared her shoulders and lifted her chin in defiance. She turned away from him and snapped, 'Go back to your stupid boring wife. I guarantee you'll regret it until the day you die.'

Then she was gone. Suddenly the room was cold and empty.

Alistair walked home as slowly as he could, his mind churning with regrets and justifications, putting off the moment when he had to fully embrace his old life.

Victoria was afraid that when Diana discovered that Helen was pregnant it might tip her back into depression. The sly glances and barely veiled whispers in the village would confirm her belief that everyone was talking about her and her reckless affair with Alistair.

She kept to her promise of regular visits and to her surprise she found Diana in a combative mood.

'It'll be impossible to avoid Helen if I stay here but I need to keep in touch with Alistair - if only for the cash when the baby comes. I want to be somewhere where his visits will go unnoticed but I've no intention of fading obediently into the background completely.'

'That's my girl,' said Victoria encouragingly. 'You've been really strong over this last few months. I can perhaps help you further later on, but it might actually be that fading into the background is just what you should be doing right now.'

Damn. Why had she said that? This was beginning to go beyond the Good Samaritan role she'd embraced initially. She said goodbye to Diana. Some objective thinking was called for.

She would go for a long walk and would not come back until she had made a decision. Was she going to continue to involve herself in Diana's affair with Alistair? And if she was, then how could she justify helping to break up a marriage. Especially one where a child was expected. She'd never liked Helen – with her stupid obsessions. Anyone who spent their life cleaning a house must be a nightmare to live with. She didn't deserve Alistair.

The path wound round to the hills, she could hear the larks and, higher up, the first lambs were bleating for their mothers. She shut them out. Concentrate.

She quite liked having a secret project. Nowadays everyone likes to think they know all about you, and want you to know all about them. The Facebook generation. No thanks. She'd built up an image; Victoria – solid, dependable, someone you knew where you were with. Hah!

Her head ached. The boys would be home soon. She needed to get back and start thinking about supper. A good walk wasted. She would play it by ear and rely on her usually trustworthy instincts.

It was almost dark as she walked up her path, and her back was hurting. She'd need a couple of her painkillers if she was to get any sleep tonight.

As she opened the kitchen door, she paused, switched on the light, and gave the floor its customary scan before stepping in.

'Oh God.'

There was the headless body of a blackbird, its entrails pooling in blood on the carpet and, circling the corpse, was the cat cowering with fear at Victoria's roar of anger. Grabbing the sweeping brush, she opened the back door and chased the cat out. Then struggling to overcome her nausea, she scooped up the body, found its head and deposited the bits in the wheelie bin. That's it. I'm ringing the Cat's Protection people first thing tomorrow.

'A waiting list? How long is it? You're joking – four hundred cats waiting to be re-homed? No, forget it. I'll try the RSPCA.'

The next day she drew a blank with RSPCA as well. So she turned her mind to the next item on her worry list. A trawl on the internet and a call to a letting agent found Diana a small flat above a shop on the outskirts of Bristol. Together they went to have a look.

'It's not perfect because it's on the second floor so you'll have stairs to deal with – not easy with a buggy and a baby. But you'll have some privacy – after all Alistair can't just drop by if you stay in South Heath.'

'Precisely. This will do me very well. I don't know how to thank you.'

Victoria waved her hand dismissively adding, 'Hopefully you won't be there for long and just look at that lovely view at the back, with the hills in the distance.'

'You always find something good to say about everything.

I do envy you your optimism. You're a real glass half full person.'

'I do try to be.'

Diana bit her lip.

'My glass is dirty, chipped and full of sour milk…. with a fly swimming in it.'

Victoria had to laugh.

'Now stop that nonsense. We'll go back to the agents and do the business. Good job it's empty so you can move in when you like. It'll be nice to come and see you without feeling the eyes of the neighbours on me. For the moment, as long as I can say I'm just popping in occasionally with the odd cake, we're keeping the worst of the gossips away, It wouldn't do for it to get back to Helen that I'm a regular visitor.'

'I did wonder if people asked you why you came.'

'Yes, one or two have but I just say you're a poor lonely soul and I'm doing my Christian duty. There's no answer to that.'

A couple of weeks later saw Victoria standing at Diana's door with celebratory alcohol and homemade Chelsea buns.

'I know it's an odd combination but I made the buns for Alistair's Governors meeting this afternoon and these were left over. They're always better fresh. I've brought some juice as well in case you aren't drinking.'

'Come in. No, I'm not supposed to be drinking but I'll have a small one with you Excuse the mess. I'm getting there…slowly.'

Diana found some glasses in a box and poured Victoria a large red wine and herself just an inch in the bottom of the glass.

'Cheers. Good health and a happy home.'

Victoria drank deeply. 'I needed that. How was the chap with the van?'

'He was brilliant. I don't know how I'd have done it without him.'

'I don't suppose you've seen Alistair?'

Diana frowned. 'No, we didn't exactly part on friendly terms. Has he said anything to you?'

'No, but he's stamping round school like a bear with a sore head. Listen, I've come to be useful. Let me help you tackle those last few boxes, then we can finish off the bottle – or rather I can.'

'Didn't you come in the car? You need to be able to drive home.'

'No, I caught the bus. I was thinking ahead.'

When everything had been unpacked and stowed away in cupboards and on shelves, Victoria went back to the bottle and found it empty.

'That's dreadful. You've been on the orange juice. I can't have drunk all that myself.'

Diana laughed. Victoria was definitely slightly squiffy.

'I've never seen you like this before. I had better make us some coffee.'

The doorbell rang.

'Hang on. I won't be a minute.' Diana put Victoria's mug on the table beside her and went to the door. It might be Alistair, except that he didn't know where she was. Shame – unless Victoria had told him. Dare she hope?

Her next door neighbour stood there piteously holding up a lacerated finger, dripping with blood.

'Sorry to bother you. Accident with the bread knife. Can you just wrap a bandage round this for me, I'm all fingers and thumbs.'

'Come in a minute.' Diana dismissed the pang of disappointment and dressed the wound, which wasn't too deep.

By the time she'd done, and the grateful neighbour had been despatched, Victoria was asleep and snoring softly, her coffee undrunk beside her. Diana covered her with a blanket and went to bed.

When she got up in the morning, Victoria had gone. There was a note on the kitchen table.

Sorry. Have rung for a taxi. Still drunk. Love V x

Now she wasn't answering her phone. Diana rang the school and was told that Victoria was not in the office. In the afternoon she got on the bus and, braving the curious stares of the village, knocked on Victoria's door. There was no reply.

Once back at home she texted Alistair saying she was worried about Victoria. After their conversation in the church hall, she wasn't sure whether he would respond, but his reply was instant. He demanded to know where she was and why she hadn't told him she was leaving South Heath.

He came round straight after school. It was as if their last conversation had never taken place. Clearly he'd left all his doubts and moral probity at home. Here, he was hers and hers alone. There was no doubting it.

When she started to explain the reason for her text, he waved it aside.

'First things first, I've missed you so much,' and he reached for her as if he were a drowning man coming across an unexpected life raft. Her burgeoning bump was no obstacle but instead a rather amusing diversion to be dealt with creatively.

'I always said sex should be fun,' he rolled away from her panting and smiling. Then he gathered her in his arms and settled back against the headboard.

'Now then, my lovely girl, what's your problem with Victoria?'

'At last! I'm not sure you've got your priorities right Mr MacIntyre. It's just that I can't contact her. She won't answer her phone and if I ring school they said she isn't available. It's been two days now.'

He put a finger under her chin and tilted her face up to his. He kissed the end of her nose.

'Come to think of it, I haven't seen her myself lately. I seem to remember someone saying she'd rung in and said she wasn't very well. What did you want her for?'

Diana hesitated. Her closeness with Victoria was not to be

236

shared. 'I just…'

He interrupted her. 'Will it keep? I need a shower first. Show me where to go.'

He got up from the bed. She was glad she'd cleaned the bathroom that morning.

It seemed an age before he emerged, his dark hair sticking wetly to his skull, a towel wrapped modestly round his waist. He lay back on the pillows, his arms behind his head.

He reached out for her.

'Cuddle up. I was thinking about Victoria myself. She's often intimated she doesn't like Helen very much. She once actually said she thought we were really ill-matched and I deserved a wife with more flair and personality.'

'I won't argue with that. Listen, this may sound fanciful, but do you think she's trying to rewrite the story?'

'In what way?'

'Use your imagination, dope.'

'The happy ending between the handsome musician hung like a donkey, the pretty young woman constantly rampant with desire and their expected love child?'

'More or less, though I'm not sure about the handsome.' She wriggled away from his teasing hands.

When he left he promised to find out where Victoria was and to let her know as soon as he had any information.

'Don't worry about her. It's not good for our baby. Victoria's old enough to look after herself. She's probably just have taken to her bed with a hangover after too much sloe gin and turned off her phone.'

42

Victoria, now recovered from the bout of alcoholic poisoning which had laid her low for two whole days, let it be generally known that she'd had a particularly severe migraine. She rang Rachel.

'Don't forget the Church Summer Fete will you. It's only a couple of weeks away. I've inspected my vegetable patch and decided to enter my runner beans and early carrots. I've got a few scores to settle from last year.'

'The Lord spare me from you competitive village women,' Rachel was dismissive.

'Oh go on. It's fun. You could try and win with some of your lovely jam.'

Rachel's strawberry jam was already potted up and labelled, so, in spite of Victoria's mockery, she found herself putting gingham caps over each lid in an attempt to improve its chances.

The day before the show, she tracked Victoria down at the bottom of her garden. 'I need three carrots – all matching, no rude ones.'

'Does Helen get involved in all this nonsense?'

'You bet she does. Her speciality is flower arranging. She takes it very seriously.'

Further down the lane, Helen came in from the garden and flung her secateurs on the table.

'Everything's ruined out there. I wish I'd never entered. Last night's rain has completely spoilt my roses. The petals are bruised and drooping, and the wind has blown down my delphiniums. They were a crucial part of my design.'

Alistair looked up from the paper and nodded

sympathetically.

'I don't know why I bother with it every year. It's Victoria's fault. She insisted I took part.'

He laughed. 'It's an opportunity for us middle class incomers to prove we're country folk at heart. The old parishioners, born and bred in South Heath, buy their jam and cakes in Tesco, but they still like to come along to see what people with time on their hands can produce.'

Helen set out her three favourite vases on the worktop.

'I know, but it's such a lot of work. When I came back from the shop they were trying to erect the Scout marquee in the rain. The wind didn't make it any easier. The vicar was there and some of the bell ringers. I told them I'd send you along to help.'

Alistair dropped his paper. 'You did what?'

'Only joking.'

The following day Rachel arrived at Victoria's slightly out of breath, having collected Eleanor in her wheelchair first.

'Sorry I'm late. Eleanor insisted on us coming the long way round.'

'Nonsense,' protested Eleanor, 'you kept stopping to talk to people. Don't blame me.'

Victoria laughed. 'Hello Eleanor. I see you've got Rachel summed up nicely. It's good to see you out and about again.'

By the time the three of them arrived at the school field, the rain had gone, the sun was out and there was a good crowd milling around. Children made for the bouncy castle, and the town band played songs from the musicals to an appreciative, uncritical audience.

They visited the tent where the local art group exhibited their inoffensive water colour landscapes and still life oil paintings. Rachel admired a view of the village duck pond until Victoria pointed out the price tag. Stalls were busy selling cakes, artisan bread, fruit curds and cheeses, chutneys and marmalades.

'Here's where all the working wives will cunningly stock

239

up with store cupboard items they'll pass off as of all their own making,' observed Victoria with her characteristic cynicism. Suddenly, she stopped dead in her tracks.

'Oh, good Heavens, Rachel, just look at that.'

They were by the stall manned by the local comprehensive school, which prided itself on its reputation for high academic standards.

'I can't see anything.'

'The sign, 'Sandwitches.' I shall have to say something. You know what I'm like about spelling.'

'I know what you're like about interfering,' Rachel was anxious to get on.

'Be as rude as you like. I can't let that go.' Victoria rummaged in her bag, pulled out a pen and corrected the offending word.

'Anybody would take you for a teacher,' scoffed Rachel, annoyed with herself for not having noticed the mistake first.

At last, the flap of the marquee was flung open and the judges emerged blinking into the sunshine. Everyone flocked in to see who had won and who had been spurned.

Victoria called across the tent. 'Rachel How did your jam do?'

'Nothing. Your carrots?' Rachel made her way over.

'No joy. I'm sure that Kevin got his from the farm shop. Did Helen win Best Flower arrangement?'

Victoria rather hoped she hadn't. Three flowers and two twigs didn't constitute an arrangement in her book.

'No, the vicar did.' Rachel had rather liked Helen's creation.

'Good. Come on, let's get out of here. These tents always smell of hot wet knickers. Let's overcome our disappointment with some calorific cakes from the WI cake stall, we can eat them over there on the grass.'

Rachel agreed. 'Excellent plan. My feet are killing me. I wonder if Eleanor would like a cake.'

'No, leave her for a bit. She looks happy enough over there talking to the vicar. Will Christopher be coming?'

'How would I know that?' Rachel tried not to sound

annoyed, knowing Victoria would read something into it if she did.

The tombola as usual proved disappointing and Rachel walked back to where she had left Eleanor. The vicar had gone and she was sitting entranced by the dog agility competition.

'Hello dear. Just look at that Border collie. He's amazing. What have you got there?

'My tombola prize. The lavender bath cubes. Victoria said they turn up every year, it's something of a standing joke in the village. It's my job to keep them for next year and pass them on.'

Eleanor chuckled. 'Did your jam win a prize?'

'Sadly no. The comment said it was too runny.'

'Never mind. You can give it me for Christopher – he loves home-made strawberry jam. Have you seen him? He promised he'd try and join us when he'd finished at school.'

'No, I haven't. What's he doing up there on a Saturday?'

'Paperwork, he said. He spends too much time up there if you ask me.'

'Come on, I'll push you up to the refreshment tent and treat you to tea and cake while you wait for him.'

Once settled with her tea, Eleanor fixed Rachel with a penetrative stare.

'Christopher is very fond of you, you know. I'm going to be cheeky, it's a mother's prerogative. Do you feel the same about him?'

Rachel felt herself stiffen and, uncharacteristically, she snapped back, 'Hardly relevant, Eleanor, surely, since he's seeing the fragrant Claudia. Anyway, I've told you, I'm done with men.'

She spotted Christopher in the distance advancing on them and jumped up, her cheeks flaming,

'Talk of the devil. Right, I'm off. No more matchmaking talk, if you want us to stay friends.'

'Alright dear – just one thing – did he tell you that his relationship, or whatever you would call it, with Claudia is over?'

As Rachel walked off as fast as she could without running, she was conscious of a feeling not unlike joy. She wanted to skip.

Alistair helped Marcus to take down the marquee the next morning.

'Is it worth all the trouble?' Marcus flinched as the heavy canvas billowed and flapped in his face.

'It certainly raises a lot of money for the church coffers,' Alistair was fond of their little church with its Saxon window head and fine Norman arch over the west door. His ambition had once been for his choir to sing there at Christmas, but the existing church choir jealously guarded its pitch.

'What's the new vicar like?'

Alistair laughed. 'Well, Victoria and Rachel were convinced he was going to bring happy-clappy hymns and lot of embracing to the services, but I think even they've been won over. He rolls his sleeves up and takes part in everything. When he encouraged people to bring their animals into church for Harvest Festival, he was the one who, with bucket and shovel, removed the evidence afterwards.'

'Shhh…here he comes.'

'Alistair, just the chap I wanted to see. I was wondering if you would like to join in the Harvest Festival service with your new choir. We only need two or three suitable songs and you can support the hymn singing too.'

'That would be fantastic,' said Alistair, his eyes gleaming. 'It'll be our first performance in public since the re-vamp. Thank you, Vicar, I'll tell the choir the good news on Tuesday.'

Nurturing this smaller group of singers had occupied his Tuesday evenings for the past few weeks. Grateful to have an excuse to get away from Helen's fretful anxieties over her pregnancy discomforts, he was drilling them in singing techniques and the correct ways of breathing, which involved muscles of the diaphragm that most of them hadn't even known existed.

In addition, drawn like a moth to a flame, he was visiting

Diana whenever he got the chance, assuring her that he would come up with a plan - if she would only wait.

43

Luke had the habit, when he got home from school, of going down to the end of the garden to check on the hens and collect any late eggs. But this day, the run was deserted, just a few feathers caught on the netting of the run, blew forlornly in the wind. Dotted about were small, still bodies. He dashed back up to the house to find Victoria.

'You've got to come quickly. Something horrible has happened.'

She walked slowly down the path. Did she want to see what was there? Usually by now she would be able to hear them chatting to each other. Instead there was silence. There was just carnage. She cleared up as best she could, and told the boys not to look in the wheelie bin. Bloody foxes. She'd loved her hens for the way they came clucking when she appeared with scraps; the way they scratched contentedly in the summer's dust and their excited calling to tell her they'd laid her an egg. Poor hens - what a horrible death.

She decided something positive was called for to cheer them all up. On Friday afternoon she ambushed the boys.

'How was school? Sit down both of you. I've had an idea. You boys spend too much time indoors. I'm taking you to Slimbridge.'

'Cool. Is it a theme park?'

'It most certainly isn't. It's a Nature Reserve. We'll sit in a hide and get close to all sorts of birds that you wouldn't see on our bird table in the garden. I'll pack us a picnic and buy you a spotter's guide when we get there. I'm offering a prize to whichever of you can tick off the most species.'

It turned out to be everything she'd hoped it would be.

They saw herons, swans, ducks and geese galore and Nathan swore he'd spotted an otter swimming, though Luke said it was a large rat. They walked from hide to hide to get close-up views of the various disputes over food and territories, and all enjoyed watching the ducks going bottoms up as they searched for food.

How long it would be before they balked at such family days out? She mused aloud. 'What a shame it is we can't have a pond in our garden, with our own ducks.'

'That'd be great. What's stopping us?'

'I'm most certainly not up to digging a big hole at my age, young man, and getting a digger in would cost a fortune.'

This had the expected response.

'We could dig it for you.'

'We could dig it deep enough for us to swim in!'

'Nice thought, Luke, but maybe just deep enough for fish to start with.'

She drove home. The occasional glance in her rear view mirror showed her two boys fast asleep on the back seat. Her heart ached for them. Was she doing alright?

The following weekend saw the boys excavating an enormous crater at the end of the garden and Victoria directing the spoil onto one side where she could perhaps build a rockery.

'Right, now we have a hole, we'll go to the garden centre and get a huge sheet of pond liner. After that your next job will be to spread some sand in the hole before we put the liner in.'

They made short work of barrowing the sand, from where the builder's merchants had deposited it at the front of the cottage, round to the back and into the hole.

'This is fun, Victoria. Feel my muscles.'

'Can we go and get some fish now?'

'Good Heavens no, not yet. Ben, our caretaker at school, made himself a pond earlier this year. He's coming to check on what we've done and tell me what I need to buy to complete the landscaping.'

She smiled at them. Youthful enthusiasm was contagious.

A few weeks later, it was finished. Small fish swam through the waterweed and a life size plastic heron stood guard over them.

'That's brilliant. Will you help me plant some spring bulbs round the edges?'

'Yes, and can we buy a bench or something so we can sit down here?'

'Good idea, Nathan.'

Later that night, all showered and scrubbed clean, they sat in their pyjamas and planned what they still had to do.

'We'll buy you a gnome for Christmas.' Luke snuggled up against her on the sofa. 'I've seen one with a fishing rod. We could sit him on the edge of the pond.'

'No thanks, my darling. No gnomes. Another couple of goldfish perhaps.'

The next day Rachel came round. 'I've just seen the boys in the paper shop and they insisted I came to inspect their new pond.' Victoria took her down to the bottom of the garden.

'Here it is. What do you think? And don't tell me it needs a gnome.'

'It's lovely, and it's so nice that the boys wanted to be involved.'

'I'm getting the hang of this, Rachel. We're beginning to have such fun - the three of us. I hope James is looking down and smiling.'

'I'm sure he is.'

Victoria had news but this wasn't the time to impart it to Rachel. She would hear soon enough on the village jungle drums. The message had been brief. The previous day Diana had given birth to a son.

She'd called him Theo. She'd had one visitor.

44

Helen confronted Alistair. He saw her cheeks were flushed with annoyance. Now what.

'I've just heard about this next concert. You know the baby's due around then. The last thing I want is for you to be out with your choir when I need your support. What if you miss the birth?'

'For God's sake. I shan't be far away. You can always phone me if you need me.' He was already half out of the door.

'Look at you. You can't wait to get away. You have no idea how difficult this all is for me. I'm supposed to be resting because of my blood pressure, I'm not sleeping and I've got this dreadful heartburn to put up with all hours of the day and night.'

'I'll be back as soon as I can.'

'Make sure you are.'

The door closed behind him. She rang Rachel.

'I've had enough now. I want to hold my baby in my arms, not carry it in a pouch like a massive kangaroo. I want my body back, and be able to run, or bend to pick something up from the floor. Most of all, I want to be able to go to sleep lying on my tummy.'

Rachel thought she too would be glad when it was all over.

'What if I go into labour and Alistair is nowhere to be found?'

'Then I'll come in with you and shriek 'push, push' and mop your brow.'

'It's not funny. You don't know what it's like to be like this. Sorry, I didn't mean to be rude. It's just that I have no control of when or how it will happen – and that's what's really scary.'

As her due date drew closer, so the pile of little knitted garments grew larger. This was the first baby to be born to their set of friends for a while, and she grew heartily sick of being asked, 'Are you still here?'

In her gloomier moments she thought that the interest was due more to the whispered rumours about her errant husband and her extreme old age as a new mother than from genuine neighbourliness.

She decided to go round to Rachel's. The coffee would be good and it would pass the time away.

Rachel opened the door. She had her coat on.

Helen was disappointed.

'Oh, you're on your way out.'

'I'm only going to Victoria's. Come with me.'

Helen hesitated. She wasn't entirely comfortable with Victoria, but Rachel took her arm and bustled her down the lane.

Victoria's smile seemed welcoming enough and she told them to sit down while she put her cakes into the oven.

'I'm experimenting. These are blueberry friands. If I've got it right they should be amazing.'

Helen was impressed. 'I'm no good at cakes. You'll have to tell me your secrets.'

'Isn't it odd how we respond to babies?' said Rachel as she poured the coffee.

'When I was at school, a man from the Times came to talk to us about newspapers. At the end, he held up a tiny facsimile of the Times. We all went Aaaaaah and he said that girls always respond like that, because it's a baby 'thing'. I remember being furious that we were so predictable. We must be hardwired to nurture the small.' She passed round the mugs.

'Did I tell you that I've asked Alistair to hang a towel in the bedroom window, pink or blue, if it's the middle of the night when he gets back from the hospital? It'll save us all bothering him when he might need some extra sleep the next day.'

Helen pulled a face. 'Good luck with that. He can barely tell the time of day at the moment. I don't know what's wrong with him. Anyone would think it was him having the baby.'

It was six o'clock in the morning and Helen, unable to sleep, was sitting in the little room she had decorated in preparation. There was a pretty wicker crib lent to her by the vicar's wife.

'I was keeping it for the grandchildren, but I'm happy to lend it out. You'll only use it for a few months till he or she's big enough to go in a cot. It's never worth buying one I always think.'

So kind, thought Helen. She shook some baby powder onto the back of her hand and sniffed it appreciatively. She opened the top drawer of the little chest which Rachel had bought, sanded down and painted for her. She looked at the tiny clothes, all washed and folded ready. Having chosen not to have one of the best surprises in life revealed to them beforehand, meant there were no pinks or blues in the pile of sleep suits and little cardigans. Instead there were garments in scarlet, green and yellow, far from traditional baby colours, but Helen loved them. Much of that was a rebellion against her mother, who would have been horrified at such a departure from convention. Even her marrying Alistair had been a disappointment to her mother.

'Don't ever marry a teacher,' she'd always said. 'You will never have any money.'

So when Helen brought home a gangling, six foot four, penniless, student music teacher for family approval, she saw her mother struggling not to show her consternation.

Sitting now, in the rocking chair Alistair had bought her for her birthday, Helen remembered her generous, prickly mother, who would have been so happy to have been called Grandma.

Her baby lurched and kicked inside her as she hauled herself up onto her feet and went back to bed. She disturbed Alistair. 'What's wrong? Have you had a twinge?'

''Fraid not. Go back to sleep.'

Her wish came true a week later. Alistair was out, of course, having a final rehearsal with his new choir. She was lying, feeling vast and porcine, on the sofa watching television, when she felt an unaccustomed slight pain which came every so often, hung around a bit then went. She didn't dare ring Alistair in case it was a false alarm, but checked her hospital bag was by the front door, and settled down to wait. He should be back in half an hour. When he rang to say he was just nipping to the pub, she told him he'd better come home instead. He was there within minutes.

'Have you rung the midwife or the hospital?'

'No, not yet, they say first babies always take ages.'

'Since when were you the expert? I'll ring them myself then.'

The hospital midwife was warm and reassuring.

'No, of course we don't mind you ringing. Tell her to have a relaxing bath and go to bed. She'll need all the rest she can get.'

Helen didn't expect to be able to sleep, so was surprised when Alistair woke her in the morning with a cup of tea and an expectant expression on his face.

'Well?'

'Ummm… the pains seem to have stopped.'

He took charge. 'Get up, we'll go for a walk and then I'll make you breakfast.'

'But it's still dark; don't be silly.'

'Just do as I say. I've read that exercise brings on labour and, if that doesn't work then one of my seriously hot curries just might do the trick.'

She heaved herself out of bed complaining. 'I don't know where you read that. Curry for breakfast is the last thing I could face, you idiot. I'm supposed to rest and sip raspberry leaf tea. What if I do start properly today? Have you got a stand in for the concert tonight?'

He turned and stood in the doorway. 'I've been worrying about that. There isn't any one I would choose to conduct my choir for an actual concert, and I'm refusing to believe that fate would be so cruel as to schedule a birth and my concert at the same time. But if the worst happens, they'll have to manage without me. I've rung into school to tell them I won't be in today.'

'Thank goodness. I think this is it, Al, and I'm so scared.'

He came and sat on the bed beside her and stroked the bump. It was tense and hard under his fingers.

He bent down and, putting his lips close to her taut skin, he whispered, 'Come on son, don't keep us waiting.'

This time, fate decided to smile on him. By nine o' clock, the contractions were every ten minutes and she was beginning to gasp and screw up her face.

'Do that breathing thing they taught you and I'll get the car out.'

He folded her carefully into the back seat.

'Hang on. Why can't I sit in the front with you?'

'Don't you remember, the mother- to- be should always sit in the rear of the vehicle in case things happen too quickly, and someone has to help deliver the baby there and then? I'm not taking any risks.'

Her laugh was extinguished by a groan of pain.

He drove to the hospital avoiding known potholes and sudden braking.

'It'll take me ages to find a space. I'll leave you at the door, park this and run back.'

'No need. Don't you remember they said there's a drop- off place? You can leave the car there and move it later.'

He helped her out, trying not to show the rising panic he was feeling. Dear God in Heaven, this is dreadful. It must be worse for her though. Helen stopped every so often to get her breath.

'Let me run on and get you a wheel chair,' he urged.

'No, don't leave me. I'll be fine, one foot in front of another, it was you, remember, who said exercise was good for me.'

He felt sick, he was as far out of his comfort zone as it was possible to be. When they finally reached reception and Helen had gratefully subsided into a wheelchair, they were directed to the delivery suite. More corridors to shuffle down and lifts to endure. He could feel his claustrophobia welling up.

'Hello, Mrs McIntyre? We're expecting you. Come this way, a midwife will be with you shortly.'

Alistair relinquished his burden to the professionals, happy to become just a bystander.

The midwife introduced herself and passed over a gown.

'My name's Adele. May I examine you? I need to see how far you've got.'

He saw Helen wince at the probing fingers.

'Think yourself lucky. Not that many years ago you'd have been given a bath, a shave and then an enema to round it off.' Helen shuddered.

'Well, you're about three centimetres so some way to go yet.'

He knew Helen had done her research, so he wasn't surprised when she'd pronounced she wanted to give birth as naturally as possible. A pool would be nice, she told the midwife, but definitely no epidurals. Was he imagining it or did the woman roll her eyes?

'I'm afraid the birthing pool has someone in it at the moment. Lie back. I'll just check baby's heartbeat.'

Alistair patted his pockets. 'Oh dear, that's my phone. I'll take it outside.'

Anything to get out of that room.

'Good morning, have you ever taken out PPI....?' He switched it off, but unwilling to go back in, he wandered up and down the corridor. It was filled with purposeful people striding to who knows where. He felt uncomfortable and out of place. Eventually his conscience forced him to go back to the delivery room.

He returned to her side, and struggled to subdue his revulsion at the hospital smells and fear of the array of high tech equipment on display. If only he lived in the days before fathers were expected to breathe through every contraction. Pacing the corridors and nipping outside for a soothing smoke sounded like an infinitely more attractive option. He could be here for hours.

'Let's have a go with the Tens machine. I put it in your bag.' He wired her up and played with the various settings. If nothing else, it was a distraction.

'Take it off, Alistair, it's useless.'

Time dragged on. 'Shall I massage your tummy?'

'No.'

'Your back?'

'No.'

'Would you like some water?'

'No.'

The hours went by. Helen's whimpering became screams.

'I can't bear this. I'm ringing for the midwife.' Alistair reached for the call button and pressed it firmly.

Why didn't she come? Was she drinking coffee somewhere? This was all so unbelievably primitive. Thank God I'm a man.

Adele bustled in. 'Is there a problem?'

'Look at the state of her. Surely you can give her something?'

'These things usually take a while, especially when it's a first. I could get you some paracetamol.'

Helen groaned. 'Paracetamol? You're joking.' Small beads of sweat glistened on her upper lip.

The midwife examined Helen again.

'You're still only five centimetres dilated. I'll give you some gas and air.'

'Honestly, I can't take much more of this.'

You and me both, thought Alistair.

In the lulls between contractions, he tried to soothe Helen as she raged at the conspiracy among women to conceal the hideous pain of childbirth.

'Why didn't anyone tell me that this would be agony for hours on end? And, more to the point, how dared they imply that I would be a failure if I took whatever pain relief I was offered? Bloody NCT.'

The midwife said she thought the baby would be a girl.

'What makes you think that?'

'You look like the kind of man that should have girls.' She suggested Alistair rubbed Helen's back some more and disappeared again.

Half an hour later, she was back with reinforcements.

'I've had a word and, given your age and the length of time you've been in labour, they've agreed an epidural might be helpful. Someone has called the anaesthetist.'

Alistair noticed all Helen's objections to medical intervention appeared to have vanished. Thank God for that.

When they arrived, to his delight he was asked to leave. He walked to the main entrance, went out and drank in the fresh air. Then he paced up and down the concourse. Guilt flooded in. He shouldn't be here. He should be up in that little room, suffering along with his wife.

It was just that he was used to being in control. This feeling of being completely superfluous was alien and demeaning. If men had babies, they'd have sorted out this process long ago. He had to go back in. Surely it couldn't go on for much longer. With a pang he thought of Diana. She went through this alone. Perhaps it was easier for her; she was younger. How would he have responded if she'd asked him to be there with her too? Dismayed at his turn of thought, he marched back in. He would do his best for Helen. Thoughts of Diana belonged to another day. Helen greeted him with a smile. 'The epidural has worked its magic. I thought you'd gone home, when the midwife said you were nowhere to be seen.'

'As if I'd leave you. Let me find something to pass the time. We could do the crossword. I've bought a paper.'

The midwife kept popping in to see how things were going.

'Have you chosen any names?'

He sighed. 'We've several girl's names, but we can't agree on one for a boy. I don't know why. How much longer is this going to last?'

Helen pulled at his sleeve. 'Calm down. I'm the one going through it, not you.'

'Shall I put some music on?'

He reached for the compilation he had prepared specially; some pastoral Elgar, soothing Sibelius and several Bach cello suites which he thought might enhance the occasion.

After only a few bars however, Helen fretfully demanded that he get rid of that bloody noise and give her some peace.

'This is all your sodding fault.' She slept.

Alistair sat in the uncomfortable chair wondering when all this was going to end. Perhaps he should go for another walk, but if she woke and he wasn't there, there'd probably be trouble.

At the other side of the room was what he presumed was an incubator. It had a radiant heater and temperature controls. He didn't like it. It looked like a baby oven.

Where's my phone? But the games with their tinny electronic music failed to engage him and he amused himself composing a text to Diana, which loyalty to Helen, snoring slightly on the other side of the room, prevented him from sending. Sometimes he really hated himself. When the midwife came in to see how labour was progressing, Helen opened her eyes. He seized his chance.

'Listen darling, I'm starving. I'm going to go and get something to eat.' He could see she wasn't impressed but he went anyway. There was a queue in the coffee shop and he'd only just sat down with his latte and chocolate muffin when a nurse appeared.

'Mr McIntyre?' Her eyes searched the room.

He stood up. 'Here.'

'I've been sent to fetch you. Things are beginning to happen.'

He attempted a joke, 'No peace for the wicked,' but she turned her back on him and disappeared away up the corridor. He got to the lift just as the doors closed. He jabbed furiously at the buttons of the one next to it. Why hadn't she held it for him? Forget it. He took the stairs two at a time. He'd be damned if he missed the birth after all these hours. He arrived panting at the delivery suite to find Helen even more out of breath then he was.

'I'm so sorry. I'm here now. What can I do?'

'Just sit there by her head and try and keep her comfortable. She's getting on nicely.'

Half an hour later after much brow mopping, hand squeezing and making encouraging noises, he watched transfixed as a tiny brown haired head emerged. Helen, sweating and red faced, squeezed Grace Elizabeth into the world. Minutes later the midwife handed him the tiny bundle all wrapped up. The mind numbing experience of the past twelve hours completely forgotten, he put his finger in her little starfish hand.

'Hello baby.' His tears baptised the tiny head. He handed her over to Helen, and hugging her, he murmured into her hair 'You are so wonderful, she's just beautiful. I can't tell you what this feels like.'

Then he straightened up and hugged the midwife.

'There were only three of us in this room and now there are four. How magical is that?'

45

Alistair lay on the reclining chair under the walnut tree with the Times Educational Supplement open at the jobs pages in front of him. He reflected disconsolately on his future. With his applications for headships being so spectacularly unsuccessful, he thought he would have to settle either for a deputy Headship, or run music departments which were larger and more prestigious than the one at South Heath.

A ladybird crawled up his bare arms. He flicked it off in irritation.

From the house came the sound of Grace crying. Why the hell didn't Helen go and see to her?

He had to do something. He was bored with South Heath, didn't care much for Christopher's style of leadership, and, while he adored his pretty little daughter, he was less enamoured with Helen .She had put on weight and appeared to have completely lost interest in him and his needs. The baby seemed to be permanently clamped to her breast and the house smelt of milk and urine soaked nappies. For reasons completely beyond him, Helen insisted on fabric nappies rather than the disposable ones, believing them to be more eco- friendly - her obsession with cleanliness replaced by her desire to save the planet.

He'd tried to make the best of a week in Cornwall at Easter, but St Ives was hideously overcrowded and the sea gulls pinched the ice creams from your hands. Getting to any other decent beach involved parking the car a mile away, and taking a steep path down, often with steps. No fun with a baby, a buggy, a beach umbrella, a windbreak, a picnic bag, towels, Factor 50 and the huge bags of nappies and wipes which accompanied them wherever they went these days.

Now he was back, he would have to carry on looking for jobs, maybe go on a course or two to widen his skill base, lose some weight and, in the absence of excitement and novelty, pursue contentment and serenity. It looked like it was time to grow up.

If only he could forget Diana. Thoughts of her disturbed his sleep and popped up inconveniently when he was trying to focus on something else. He'd gone back to Helen in order to get the Headship. That hadn't happened. Did he still have to stay? He could live without Helen. Could he live without Diana? But now, it seemed more relevant to ask could he live without Grace? He had a vision of her little smiling face and her tiny hand closing round his finger.

He remembered his mother forcing him to decide which of his toys he would give away, when she was engaged in one of her regular culls of the toy box. She used to say, 'If a giant came and said, in a big growly voice, Alistair, you must give me a toy. Which one would you choose? ' They'd laughed about his indecision at the time, it wasn't so funny now.

He narrowed it down to three simple statements.

Stay with Helen and Grace and never see Diana or Theo again.

Stay with Helen and continue his affair with Diana.

Leave Helen and start a new life with Diana.

Simple. Only it wasn't.

One job advertisement caught his eye. It was at a renowned public school in South Africa, in a different league from South Heath altogether. It had a big music department, with an orchestra, wind band, a chamber group and jazz band as well as three choirs. But the job was bigger than that. They wanted someone to run the whole Creative Arts Faculty.

He decided he would apply without mentioning it to Helen, who would be bound to complain about starting again in a strange country. Abroad was somewhere she regarded with suspicion and apprehension.

If the rumours circulating about South Heath School struggling to maintain its numbers were to be believed, the sooner he could jump ship the better. Perhaps it would be a lucky escape. He sat with his head in his hands. Grace was screaming now. He'd be leaving Diana. Not just Diana, but his son. His lovely sunny boy.

He stood up. Decision made – sort of. He would apply for jobs abroad. If he got one, then Helen would have to make the choice – not him. Let the fates decide.

Excited by the prospect of a possible way forward, he went back into the house and ignoring the crying baby, picked up his keys.

Helen came out of the utility room looking flustered.

He snapped at her.

'For God's sake go and see to Grace. Can't you hear her? I'm going out.'

He drove to Diana's flat.

She opened the door smiling, 'Good timing, darling, Theo's fast asleep', and she pulled the black T shirt off over his head.

Afterwards, she unwound her long legs from his and padded naked across the bedroom to pick up a furious Theo, now wide awake and hungry. She put him to her breast and Alistair watched, entranced by the primal beauty of the scene. For a split second he envied his son.

A picture flashed into his head of Helen with her pale, blue-veined breasts, her breast pads and nipple cream at the ready and one eye on the clock to time the feed. As ever with Diana and Helen, it was chalk from cheese. The one - earnest, uptight and anxious to do and be seen to be doing, the right thing. The other – natural, relaxed and elemental, a force of nature.

When Theo had finished, Alistair reached out his arms. 'Come here, son.'

Diana passed the baby over. She lay back down beside them.

Theo smiled milkily at his daddy and burped.

Alistair looked at his boy who had his mother's blue eyes but his father's aquiline nose and hair the colour of shiny conkers.

'You're a real looker, just like your Dad,' and he played peek-a-boo with Diana's discarded knickers until Theo smiled his gummy smile. He propped the baby up against his knees, put his arm around Diana and pulled her close.

'I've been thinking and I might have a plan.'

'Mmmm?'

Diana didn't want any serious talk. This was precious time for loving and sharing their baby.

'No, really, listen to me. If I got a job abroad – Canada say, or Australia, I just know Helen wouldn't want to come with me. The three of us could live together. It'd be a whole new life. Would you come?'

'It sounds too good to be true, but you know I'd follow you to the ends of the earth and back. Why don't you put Theo in his crib now and come back to bed.'

Lying on her side, with her head propped on her hand, she watched as he gently lay Theo down with a kiss. When he turned back to face her, she laughed softly when she saw the evidence of his readiness to return to her side.

46

'Alistair is busy applying for jobs, along with the rest of them,' said Helen, reaching for Rachel's teacake, 'but with no joy yet. I've been telling him he ought to look for a change of direction altogether, social work maybe or educational publishing.'

The three of them were in the coffee shop with tasteless cappuccinos in front of them. Rachel and Victoria were rather regretting the large toasted teacakes they'd ordered in a moment of weakness, so Helen was helping them out.

She looked at their faces, they weren't impressed by her ideas.

'Listen,' she said, 'anything's better than his other idea, which is to go abroad – Australia maybe he says or Canada.' She glanced across the kitchen to where Grace lay asleep in her buggy.

'Why would that be such a bad thing?' asked Victoria.

'It wouldn't be – for him. But I don't want to live abroad. I love England. I love the weather, the history, the country side, our culture and every single time I've been abroad on holiday, I can't wait to come home.' She tore another chunk off Victoria's teacake.

'To be honest, I've never really forgiven him for the Diana thing. For all I know he's still carrying on with her. If he isn't, then I'll live on tenterhooks waiting for the next woman to come along, flutter her eyelashes at him and tell him he's the most wonderful man she's ever met. I'm tired, you know? Tired of worrying about my weight; tired of always having to be willing to make love even when it's the last thing I feel like doing, and tired of having to second guess his moods and wishes.'

She examined her friend's faces to gauge their reaction. Rachel exclaimed, 'I had no idea things were that bad. Is anybody round here happily married?'

'Helen, do you love him?' The question came from Victoria. Helen ignored her. She had a nerve asking that.

She pressed on. 'We had a blazing row last night. I tried to persuade him that running away wasn't the answer. It ended with me telling him that if he wanted to go, he'd go alone.'

'You didn't mean that – did you?' Rachel's eyes were as big as her teacake.

'Well, he spent the night in the spare bedroom and had gone out when I woke up next morning.'

Helen blinked hard. What was the answer to Victoria's question?

Rachel asked, 'What's wrong with abroad?'

'Everything. I don't feel clean in foreign countries, there are flies everywhere and beggars on street corners. I don't understand the money or the language. I just feel terribly insecure.'

'Would you really not go with him?' Victoria was insistent. 'They speak English in Australia and Canada anyway.'

'I said it in the heat of the moment, but I've thought of nothing else all day, and I've decided it's up to him. If he can't get a job in this country, I'm not going anywhere else. This is my home, my way of life, my friends on the line - I'd manage somehow. I've still got some of the money my parents left me put away. Maybe that rainy day has come.'

She wiped her eyes and tightened her lips. 'He's messed me about too much. I can do without him if I have to.'

'What about Grace?'

'She'll stay with me obviously. He can come back and see her whenever he wants. When she's older, she can travel out to see him – wherever he ends up.' She scooped up the froth from the bottom of her cup with her teaspoon. It was cold and slimy.

Grace began to cry. Helen got to her feet. 'I'd better go. I'm not feeding her here whatever that notice says.'

They all walked through the village towards their respective homes. On the corner, where their ways parted, Rachel hugged Helen saying, 'Maybe things won't seem so hopeless in the morning. Give me a ring if you need tea and/or sympathy.'

Victoria said nothing.

Rachel waited for Helen to turn the corner and said, 'I can understand her wanting to live her life as she wishes, rather than as Alistair wishes, but I didn't realise she was quite so anti foreigners.'

'She's scared and insecure. There are drawbacks to staying though. She'll be lonely. She'll have to work on keeping up her friendships.'

Victoria reached her own garden gate and said goodbye. Rachel wondered if she was speaking from experience. She'd inwardly rejoiced when her friend's relationship with Marcus hit the rocks. Maybe that was unworthy of her. How old did one have to be before never wanting to have sex again?

She saw movement through Christopher's cottage window as she passed and for a moment, she toyed with the idea of knocking on his door. Then she hardened her heart and quickened her pace until she was home. Her latest folly as Victoria unkindly put it, a rescue dog called Bertie, was there to welcome her and giving him his expected fuss drew her mind away from worrying about the future.

Meanwhile Helen was occupying herself with diversionary tactics. She fed Grace and put her down, emptied the dishwasher and filled the washing machine. She changed the beds, cleaned the bathroom and hoovered. It wasn't working. Victoria's question had to be answered. Did she love him?

She tried a mental questionnaire.

Could she live without him? Yes.

Would she give him one of her kidneys? Maybe.

If she had the opportunity, would she sleep with anyone else? Certainly not.

Did she hate him then? Sometimes.

He was calling her bluff. She'd got used to the way their lives had settled. He did his creative, show- off thing, she was happy to be in charge of the mundane, workaday side that kept the partnership going. She had faults, areas where maybe she wasn't quite up to scratch, but she persuaded herself that her competency in other areas made her an acceptable wife. Nobody was perfect.

Grace's toys were tidily in their basket. His shirts were ironed, pristine and crisp, hanging in his wardrobe. She cooked healthy, nourishing meals. For God's sake, why wasn't that enough?

47

It was late September and Alistair, back at school, set 3B some theory exercises. That should keep them busy. He walked over to the window of the music room and stared out unseeing.

Last night Helen had allowed him to make love to her. He'd had to imagine it was Diana to avoid embarrassment. That had never happened before. When she'd got up to go to the bathroom he'd spread out like a starfish, enjoying the space she left him. He'd fantasised that it was Diana who had lain beside him and would be back in a minute. He would stretch out his arm across the bed so that when she lay down he could pull her close. He'd dozed.

When Helen returned, smelling of soap and, no doubt, well- scrubbed, he buried his head in the pillow consumed with guilt and self- pity. How much longer could he go on like this?

Decision time came for Helen sooner than she expected. She'd noticed that Alistair had taken to hanging around when the post was due, and one morning she saw him pounce on a letter. He opened it and waved it excitedly at her.

'How do you fancy South Africa? They want me to go up to London for an interview. There's a job in Capetown. I had an e-mail yesterday, this is the confirmation.'

She stared at him. 'You know what I think.'

He added hastily, 'It's not like those hot Latin countries you know.'

She took a deep breath. How should she put this?

'I have to say that, of all the countries you might choose,

South Africa is the last one I'd want to go to.'

She picked up her car keys twisting them around her fingers.

'It's probably not politically correct to say so, but I hate the accent, the crime rate there is horrendous and I've never met a South African who wasn't a racist bigot. Is that enough for you? You can report me to the Guardian if you like. I'm going out. You can mind Grace while you still have the chance.'

She could feel her lips set in a thin line as she left the house. The banging of the door provoked an angry yell from upstairs. Good, let him deal with her while he's still here. She revved up her little Citroen and drove off.

'Come on, my lovely. Let's get you changed, then Daddy will take you for a walk.'

Grace refused to make it easy for him, wriggling and kicking as he fumbled with the nappy. Would she miss him, or was she too young? If he had to go, perhaps it would be best to go now. A couple of years as the Head of the Faculty of Creative Studies in the sun would set him up nicely for a Headship when, or if, he returned. Angrily strapping Grace into her buggy; he thought how he'd spent his entire life doing what other people wanted; his parents, employers, now Helen. He strode down the village, his long black coat flapping, Grace clinging on for dear life.

This worm was going to turn. It could be his last chance for an adventure. He'd got the chance to get away from this incestuous place and all the gossips, and please himself for once. He'd done the decent thing and asked her. That was risky in itself. She might have said yes.

He gave a bark of laughter and deftly steered the child across the village green scattering fat ducks in his wake.

Ignoring Helen's adamant refusal to countenance a new life in South Africa, he went ahead and did some research. Seduced by the promise of a wonderful climate, stunning scenery and a vibrant ex-pat community, he attended three days of gruelling cross questioning in London. He was thrilled to be offered a job at what was one of South Africa's most prestigious boarding schools. When he got the call, he shouted for her. 'Helen, where are you?'

He found her at the bottom of the garden, with Grace on her hip, inspecting her lettuces. She must have heard him coming but she didn't respond.

'They've offered me that job! They want me to be Head of Creative Studies; that's English, Art, Music and all the technologies. The salary is enormous and the lifestyle is amazing.'

He was shocked to see her turn away from him. He reached out and grabbed her by the arm.

'Listen to me Helen. This isn't the time to play games. I can't turn down an opportunity like this. It's not wrong to be ambitious. Look what I did with the choir. I weeded out the weakest because I wanted the best. And it worked. I've got to move on.'

What was the matter with the woman? Anyone would think he was suggesting they relocate to some backward third world country.

Helen looked at him standing there. Am I punishing him for Diana? If she let him go alone, the ordeal of a long flight with a small child, never mind the expense, would mean she wouldn't see him for months. Was she about to sabotage her marriage because she didn't like Abroad? Was she really so narrow minded? There would be nothing to stop her coming home if she hated it. They could let the house on a six month lease. She'd know by then if she were a stayer or a quitter. She saw the furrows between his eyes. He looked anxious. He'd always had the power in their marriage. For the first time ever, she felt the power was hers. It was a good feeling. Perhaps she should be magnanimous. She sat Grace down on the grass and faced him, her hands lightly on his shoulders.

'Look, getting cross with me isn't helpful. Tell me about the school and the area where we'd live. Let's go on the internet and look at some pictures. Convince me that I might be happy thousands of miles from home.'

That night, after choir practice and the pub, Alistair was

very late home. He was drunk and had forgotten his keys. As he stood cursing on the step, Helen opened the door.

'Sorry, darlin', didn't want to wake you…'

'That's alright. I was waiting for you. I've got something to tell you. Sit down.'

'What is it? To be honest, I just want to go to bed.' He lurched towards the sofa and lay down.

'I've made a decision.'

She stood over him. Her eyes were bright but anxious.

'I'll come to South Africa with you. Grace needs her father and I need to be brave and see for myself what it's like.'

He sat upright, instantly sober, 'After all you said? I don't believe it.'

Where was the pleasure on his face?

Although initially nonplussed by his reaction, she was nevertheless touched by what she decided must be his relief and delight at her decision. He was perhaps just in shock. Perhaps she should have waited till the morning.

'We've come too far to break up over this, besides Grace would miss her daddy.'

She sat down beside him. Her eyes searched his face.

'I've spent hours thinking about this. I need to be brave. I don't want to be responsible for the end of our marriage. We need to do a deal. I'll be more the wife you want – and you must be tolerant and supportive 'cos it won't be easy for me.'

He ran his hand through his hair.

'It's wonderful. I can't believe it.'

He gathered her into his arms and rested his chin on top of her head, gazing into the distance.

Her voice was muffled.

'You've got Victoria and Rachel to thank for this. They helped me to see sense.'

In bed that night, as Helen turned her back on him, he'd lain staring at the cracks on the ceiling. What was Diana doing, was she lying awake too?

When Helen called round the next morning and divulged her change of heart, Victoria's first thought had been of

Diana. She knew she had to get to her before Alistair did. If she had due warning, Diana would be better prepared when he delivered the devastating news.

It was raining, a fine wetting drizzle as she bustled out to the car. At the flat she found Diana sitting amidst cases and boxes, looking happier than she'd seen her in months.

'I don't know where you'll sit but come in. I thought I'd make a start. I bet you think I'm mad, but there's a lot to do.'

The situation was worse than she expected. She'd encouraged Diana to think of joining Alistair sometime in the future, but yet again, it seemed she'd underestimated her. It was one of the few times in Victoria's life when she struggled for words. She walked across the room to Diana and took a deep breath.

'I'm afraid I have some bad news for you. I wanted to warn you, but I had no idea things had gone this far, I thought you might join him later.'

'No, I'm planning to fly out the day after him. Why, what's happened?'

There was no easy way to tell her.

'Helen's changed her mind. She's agreed to go with him. She wants to save her marriage.'

Diana turned away from her and looked out of the window. When she turned back, her mouth was set in a tight line and the sparkle had gone from her eyes.

'Okay, you've told me. Now go and leave me alone. I'll be fine.'

Later Victoria was to feel ashamed at her willingness to interfere in the lives of others. Assuring Diana she was at the end of a phone or happy to come again at any time, she'd fled, unable to mitigate the young woman's pain. She'd done what felt right at the time. What more could she have done? Perhaps she should have done nothing. She rang Alistair. No answer. She wouldn't tell Rachel about this. There had already been several pointed comments from that quarter on her inclination to attempt to help other people with their problems.

It took Alistair a while to summon up the courage to knock on Diana's door. When he did so, the next morning, there was no reply.

A neighbour poked her head out and said, 'She's gone away.'

'Gone away? Where? Did she say when she'll be back?'

'She isn't coming back. She left last night in a taxi, late, with the baby, a couple of cases and several bin bags.'

Clearly relishing the drama, she leaned against her door post and looked Alistair up and down speculatively.

'Did she say where they were going?'

'No, she just said if anyone asked, to tell them she was leaving for good.'

'Oh my God. How did she seem?'

'She seemed in a bit of a state to be honest. In a hurry, but with the baby screaming and the taxi waiting, I didn't like to ask too many questions. Not that she'd have told me - kept herself to herself that one.'

Alistair made his way back to his car as though he was walking through jelly. His beautiful girl. His little son. Not wanting to drive home and face Helen, busy fussing and making lists, and doubtless triumphant should she hear of Diana's departure, he drove out of the city towards Portishead.

The beach was deserted, the cold wind and sea mist over the estuary deterring even the dog walkers. He sat on a bench and watched the waves push forward, slap down and back away. Restless, he got to his feet and strode along the hard wet sand marked with ripples from the receding tide, his anger growing.

This was all Helen's fault. Agreeing to go after making all that fuss. He'd come to relish the idea of a fresh start, teaching his boy to swim and fish, and escorting his attractive partner to all the ex-pat parties. His new life was over before it had even started. He'd banked on Helen not coming with him. He should have held back on selling her the move. He'd been convinced she wouldn't change her decision to stay, and was just going through the motions.

He returned to the car, chilled through and damp. He needed to find somewhere warm where he could drown his sorrows.

There was a small hotel overlooking the sea and he settled himself in the corner of the bar, ignoring curious looks from the two old couples drinking tea. He ordered a double whisky, followed by another and another. His phone rang twice, both times the display said 'Helen', so he switched it off.

When he got back to the car he ripped the parking ticket off the windscreen and screwed it up. Let them find him in South Africa. He was not so drunk he didn't know he was unfit to drive, so he tipped his seat back, closed his eyes and fell asleep. He was woken by a knocking on the window. It was dark, but shiny buttons reflected by the street lights suggested the man was in uniform, so he lowered the window.

'Are you alright mate? I'm locking this car park now and you aren't allowed to stay all night.'

'Sorry, yes, I must have nodded off. I'll go.'

'Hang on a minute, Let me give you this,' and a fresh parking ticket was posted to him through the window.

Alistair stopped at the first garage he came to and bought a bottle of water. Draining it in one, he took the road back to South Heath and put Mozart's Requiem on to calm the tumult in his head. It started to rain and the rhythmic beating of the windscreen wipers were oddly calming. Pragmatism was called for. He could do it.

Gradually, the pain and loss subsided and he looked at what he still had. A wife and daughter that any normal man would be proud of; an exciting new job, away from the small-minded, middle class society in which he'd struggled to settle, and a salary almost double his current one. That should pay for some of life's little luxuries.

Think positive. In many ways, Diana had been a disaster right from the beginning. Hadn't he always known that? The affair had been thrillingly subversive and chaotic, but he should have met her twenty years ago. By the time he pulled up outside his house, he had almost persuaded himself it would all be for the best.

Helen was incandescent.

'I've been calling you all day. Where the hell have you been?'

'Where's the fire? I needed some time on my own, that's all.' He hung up his jacket.

'I need a whisky. Did you remember to get another bottle?'

48

'Good morning Rachel, come in. Am I glad to see you? I'm at my wits end with mother.' Christopher looked as if he hadn't slept for a week.

'She's been trying to get up in the night. I've had to put chairs against the bed. You know how unstable she is, even with her sticks. The carers have got her up now, and I really have to go into school. I'll come back at lunchtime to make arrangements for more care. Do you think you'll be all right until then?'

'Of course I will. Leave her to me,' said Rachel bravely, though her heart was sinking.

Eleanor was sitting in her chair. Her face broke into a smile when she saw Rachel.

'Hello, Rachel. I'm worried about Christopher. He seems awfully het up about something. I've told him I'm perfectly capable of running the house while he's at school. I'm going to make him a nice stew for tonight when he comes in.'

Rachel thought it was probably five years since Eleanor had been able to make a 'nice stew' but she just smiled and said that sounded lovely. She went into the kitchen to put the kettle on and heard the doorbell ring. At the same moment there came a thud from the sitting room. Eleanor was on the floor whimpering with pain. Rachel stood frozen to the spot. The door opened. It was Dr Wright. 'Just passing,' she said with a smile, 'and thought I'd check on Eleanor.'

'Oh thank God it's you. She's just fallen. I don't know what happened. I was in the kitchen making her a cup of coffee.'

Dr Wright was already on her knees beside Eleanor, murmuring words of comfort. She looked up at Rachel.

273

'She needs to go to A&E. I'll ring for an ambulance; can you let her son know?'

'Yes, of course. I only left her for a minute. She was sitting quietly…'

'She may have been trying to answer the door, she saw me through the window coming up the path. Don't worry. We'll get her checked over. With any luck she'll be sent back home tonight.'

A few minutes later Christopher burst in through the door. Eleanor lay by her chair in a crumpled heap.

'What happened? I only left her half an hour ago. Why is she on the floor? Can't you get her up?'

The doctor stood up. 'We mustn't move her before the ambulance arrives. You can follow it to the hospital and stay with her until they've done an assessment and checked that no bones are broken.'

He turned on Rachel, his eyes blazing.

'I left her in your care. I told you she was likely to try and wander about. Why weren't you watching her?'

Dumbfounded by this attack, Rachel didn't know how to respond. Luckily at that moment the ambulance arrived and the old lady was loaded gently onto a stretcher and into the ambulance.

Christopher said, 'You haven't heard the last of this,' and swept out of the house.

'Don't take it to heart, he's just shocked,' Dr Wright soothed. 'I'm sure you'll get an apology when he's calmed down.'

On automatic pilot, Rachel tipped the just-made coffee down the sink, washed the cups and wrote a short note to Christopher for him to find when he came home.

I'm sorry for what happened. I really wasn't at fault. Please let me know how she gets on, and if there's anything I can do to help. R.

At ten o'clock that night, she was sitting by her fire, examining her feelings for Christopher. Was she being a fool?

No question. Was he worth it? No…. maybe.

There was a tap on her door. She jumped up to answer it - hoping. He stood there shamefaced.

'I owe you an apology. I was completely out of order speaking to you like that.'

'Come in. Apology accepted. Sit down, let me get you a drink and then tell me how she is,'

His eyes downcast, he took a sip of brandy and sat back in the chair, momentarily closing his eyes.

'She has fractured her pelvis. They've kept her in, obviously, and…'

He swallowed hard, determined not to break down in front of Rachel. Wanting to give him permission to cry, Rachel went over and knelt down in front of him. Taking his hands in hers, she said,

'You know she's in the best possible place. They'll sort out some painkillers and have her fixed up in no time.'

'They did seem very kind. She went down to X-ray and they took great care not to hurt her when they had to move her. But she didn't know where she was and kept asking for Anthony. The thing is, will she ever come home again? They say it's a stable fracture and, with bed rest it should heal. But it will be a long job. I really don't want her to go into a nursing home. You hear such dreadful stories and she'd made me promise never to send her away.'

'There's no point worrying about that now. Whatever her needs will be when she comes out of hospital, you'll do your best to meet them. I'll do as much as I can to help. You need to stay strong for her, so go home and get some sleep.'

He stood up and faced her, his face stricken and pale.

'Thank you, Rachel,' he said simply and bent down and kissed her cheek.

Rachel approached ward 7 hoping that Eleanor would be having a good day. A nurse was bending over her and, when she straightened up, she was smiling.

'Hello, this one's quite a character isn't she?'

Rachel smiled with relief. 'She certainly is.'

'She's been entertaining us all, haven't you Eleanor?'

Eleanor nodded. She seemed to have shrunken into the bed but her eyes were shining.

'I've been singing,' she announced proudly.

'She even got Mr Blake, the consultant joining in. Well, your blood pressure is fine. I'll leave you in peace.' The nurse bustled off. Within minutes Eleanor fell asleep and Rachel crept away.

Two nights later, Rachel was boiling an egg for her tea. She knew it was an uninspiring choice but she felt so low and tired it was all she could manage.

Her phone rang. It was Christopher.

'I'm sorry to bother you, but I don't know who else to ring,' his voice was thin and strained.

'I'm in London at a Heads' conference and the hospital has just rung me to tell me that mother has developed an infection and is gravely ill. Could I possibly ask you to go and sit with her until I can get back? There's a train shortly, but I'll still be a couple of hours at least. I'd get a taxi but I think the train will be quicker in the end.'

Her reply was instant.

'Yes, of course. I'll go right away.'

'Thank you. The consultant said the other day that he was concerned about her breathing, but when I asked him if I should cancel going to this conference he said there was no immediate danger. It would seem he was wrong.'

Every traffic light on her route to the hospital turned to red as she approached. It began to rain hard. Was everything going to be against her? She banged on the steering wheel in frustration.

It was still visiting time when she got there and all the car parks were full. Rachel drove round and round. Surely people would be leaving soon. She decided to try the back streets. She left the hospital and turned left onto the main road and then left again. She wasn't the only person to have had that idea. Street after street was lined with cars parked nose to tail. Eventually she found a space. It was tight. She got in. God knows how she'd get out again. No time to worry about that. She locked the car and ran along the wet pavement.

Visiting time was ending and she had to push her way through people streaming out of the doors. When she got to the ward someone stood up at the nurse's station and said, 'I'm sorry but visiting time is over.'

She swallowed the words that sprang to her lips and said, 'I've had a call to sit with Eleanor Forbes-Martin. Her son is on his way.'

Luckily one of the nurses recognised her from previous visits and told her to go on in.

Eleanor was lying propped up on pillows, her cheeks sunken and her breathing laboured. Rachel was shocked at the change in a matter of days. She pulled up a chair and, taking Eleanor's hands in hers, she stroked them gently.

'Christopher is on his way, my darling, and I'm going to keep you company until he gets here.'

She couldn't tell if Eleanor was asleep or unconscious but a nurse, who came to check on her, thought she was just sleeping. Keeping her voice low, Rachel talked to her of happier times, though the lump in her throat felt enormous and her voice quavered and faltered.

The hours passed. Where on earth was he? Periodically she went and got coffee or tea from the machine – more for something to do than for any pleasure she would get from drinking it.

Eleanor stirred.

'Hello, how are you feeling?' Rachel stroked her thin hair aware of how upset she would be with its tousled state if only she knew.

As if reading her mind, Eleanor said querulously,

'Where's my hair brush? I don't want to go home looking like I've been dragged through a hedge backwards.'

'I'll find it.' Rachel, glad of something to do, rummaged in the locker by the bed. She found it and gently brushed the old lady's hair.

'There you are. You look a real bobby dazzler now.'

Very soon Eleanor was asleep again. The door opened and a doctor came in accompanied by the ward sister.

'Are you her daughter?'

'No. Just a friend. Her son is on his way. I can't imagine why he isn't here yet. He got a train from London ages ago.'

'There's been a crash on the line from Paddington apparently. Perhaps he's caught up in that.'

He bent over the bed. 'Now then, Eleanor, I need you to wake up for me.'

His face grew concerned as Eleanor failed to respond.

'Her pulse is very weak,' he said.

'I don't think she's just asleep. I can try giving her something,' and he turned to instruct the sister who left the room, returning with a syringe in a dish. He put his stethoscope in his ears and listened carefully to Eleanor's chest.

Rachel sat, she could hear her heartbeat thudding in her ears.

'What is it? Why won't she wake up? Isn't there any more you can do?'

'I'm sorry. I don't think there is. It sounds like she's developed a chest infection. It's a bit wheezy in there. I'll give her a shot of antibiotics and we'll set up a drip. I can't do any more. I need to finish my round. I'll be back as soon as I can.'

Rachel noticed that every so often Eleanor missed a breath. Soon the gaps between the breaths grew longer and, when the breaths stopped altogether she went to find a nurse.

'I think Eleanor has died,' she said.

The nurse rushed over and, absurdly, Rachel thought, apologised for not having been there.

Rachel sat for a long time holding Eleanor's hand. Poor Christopher. He's going to feel so bad that he wasn't with her.

She heard voices coming closer down the corridor and Christopher burst through the door, his hair wet and his cheeks glistening with raindrops, or tears. He went straight to the bed where Eleanor lay.

Rachel got up to leave thinking he would want to be alone with his mother. But he grabbed her hand.

'Don't go. I should have been here. I really tried to make it in time. They stopped the train at Reading and I got off and went to find a taxi. But too many people had the same idea and it was impossible. They laid on buses for us but the roads were clogged with emergency vehicles, police, ambulances and fire engines. It was chaos. I tried to ring you over and over again but you didn't answer.'

Rachel confessed she had left her mobile at home in her rush to get to the hospital.

'I'm so sorry.' What else could she say? 'Shall I go and leave you alone?'

'No!' His vehemence surprised her. 'Stay here with me.'

He sat silently beside her for a few minutes then burst out angrily. 'I can't believe I wasn't here for her. Just when she needed me.'

'She wasn't alone. I was here.'

He recovered himself and dropped his head into his hands. His voice was muffled and Rachel leaned forward to hear him. She wanted to put her arms around him.

'Yes. I know. I'm sorry. But Rachel, what's the bloody point of it all? She lived, then she died. Is that it?'

She tried to soothe him.

'I thought exactly the same thing when my father and mother died. I decided the point was the love they left behind and the people whose lives they touched and, hopefully, made better in some way. There'll always be a bit of Eleanor in me, and lots more in you.'

He reached over, took her hand and put it to his lips. 'Thank you. You always know what to say.'

They left the hospital and Rachel tried to remember where she had left her car.

When she pulled up outside the cottage, he said,

'Don't leave me just yet.'

They went in and tried not to look at the empty chair by the fire. He offered brandy, she shook her head and made some tea instead. They sat for a while and then, as they were both exhausted, he allowed her to go home and get some rest.

She obeyed but sleep was slow to come and she lay awake remembering Eleanor as she used to be – vibrant and interested in everything and everyone around her.

She called round the next morning. Both were very aware of Eleanor's presence in the cottage. Rachel opened all the windows. It was silly, but her granny had always said it should be done when there was a death, to allow the soul to fly away.

Again, Christopher didn't seem to want her to go. He made a pot of coffee and suggested they sat outside in the sunshine. He talked about his mother and thanked Rachel for the past few months of friendship she had had with her.

'My mother really took to you. I confess I was surprised how you were both instantly so comfortable with each other.' He took a deep breath,

'She loathed Claudia from the outset. I should have known she was a better judge of character than I was.'

He hesitated. 'I should perhaps tell you that I am not seeing Claudia any more. I shall not get emotionally involved with any one again.'

Another of those unsubtle warnings. Rachel took a deep breath. She needed to grieve for Eleanor on her own. Aware that he had had a double loss, she hadn't wanted it to appear that she was waiting in the wings to step into the vacancy in his life. Now he was saying that there was now no place for her anyway.

She made her excuses, 'I need to go home, Christopher, I've things to do. Let me know if you need any help with the funeral. The undertaker in the village is supposed to be very good and the Black Cow does an excellent buffet if you don't want to have people back here.'

Christopher looked up at her with such anguish on his face that she forgot all her good intentions and said gently, 'I'll drop by again tomorrow if you like and we can talk then. Just rest today – there's no need to do anything unless there are relatives or friends you need to inform; though maybe even they can wait. I think we both need to cry and I'd rather do it on my own. I'm sure you would too.'

He spread his hands helplessly,

'I'm sure you're right. I've taken up enough of your time – and thank you.'

She walked slowly home conscious that Eleanor had been her link with Christopher. He wouldn't need her anymore. Was this going to be the end?

49

At ten o'clock the next morning her phone rang.

Christopher was back in business mode. He had found solace in making arrangements.

'I've sorted the funeral place and spoken to the vicar. The funeral will be on Friday and I've put a notice in the local paper and the Times. Some delightful girls are going to do us drinks and bits to eat here afterwards.'

'Well done you', said Rachel warmly.

He went on, 'I don't expect there'll be many turn up. After all, we haven't been here long, and so many of her friends from way back are gone already.'

'Are you having flowers?'

'Indeed I am. I know people think they're a waste of money and it's better to give a donation to charity, but mother loved flowers and I think she'd approve.'

Rachel smiled at the determined tone of his voice.

'I couldn't agree more. When my father died I took great comfort from the beauty and colours of the wreaths and bouquets. Well, I'll let you get on. You know where to find me if there's anything I can do to help.'

She put the phone down firmly, before she forgot herself and revealed the depth of her feelings for him. She wanted so much to go round and take him in her arms and weep with him, but told herself that she should be sensible and keep her distance. If he needed her he had only to phone.

She picked up the tin of freshly baked shortbread and went round to see Victoria. Her response to Rachel's emotional confusion was typically blunt. 'I think staying away is exceedingly foolish, there'll be plenty of women out there looking for a vulnerable male to take to their bosoms. They'll be queuing up with their casseroles and flapjacks, mark my words. Then you'll be sorry you didn't go for it.'

'They'll be wasting their time then. He's made it quite clear he doesn't want a relationship with me, or anyone else. So that's that.'

'Oh, that's just the grief talking. Hang on in there and win him round with your charms. You know you want to. Golly, this shortbread is good.'

Her eyes twinkled. 'Perhaps you should take some round to Christopher.'

Rachel shook her head. 'I don't know. I was brought up to believe you waited for men to run after you, not the other way round.'

'For goodness sake – his mother has just died. You have the perfect excuse to minister to him without it being obvious.'

Rachel picked up her tin. 'I don't know. I'll think about it.' She went home and, ever the procrastinator, she cleaned her downstairs windows instead.

Friday came soon enough and as she walked up to the church with Victoria, to the sound of the tolling bell, Christopher was waiting under the lych gate for the hearse to arrive.

'Rachel, I've been looking for you. I want you to sit with me.'

Nodding to Victoria to go on in, he drew Rachel aside and asked if she would also walk in with him behind the coffin.

'My mother was very fond of you and I know this is how she would want it. The service will be nice and simple. An old friend will speak about Eleanor as a young woman and I will pay tribute to her as a much loved mother. The vicar will say a few words as well. He used to call in and see her for a chat when she wasn't able to get to church. I have to say he's been very supportive helping me with the funeral as well.'

Rachel wondered, as she always did at funerals, how many

people would come to mourn her when her time came. Funny, old fashioned word 'mourn'. They tended nowadays to want to call it a celebration of a life. Though she always found it hard to celebrate when someone close to her died. Perhaps she'd celebrate at Marcus' funeral. Ashamed of her train of thought, she tried to remember Eleanor instead. There had been a lot of laughter. The old lady had poked fun at Christopher's tendency to pomposity - 'just like his father,' and loved to hear the latest story from the running saga of Victoria and her murderous cat. She'd come to all the choir concerts and given Rachel feedback on the performances in her typically forthright manner.

The service was soon over and the burial, in the corner of the churchyard in dappled shade, was melancholy but dignified. Rachel and Victoria lingered to look at the glorious flowers lying on the grass by the old stone wall; lilies from Christopher and white roses from Rachel among them.

Christopher came up and took a firm hold of Rachel's arm, and together with Victoria they walked back from the church to the cottage. He insisted she came in, brushing aside her reluctance.

'I want you to meet two old friends of my mothers who have played a large part in my life as well.'

Victoria thrust a large glass of white wine into her hand and Rachel looked around to see who was there. Only a dozen souls had come back to the house. A couple from the village but most were strangers to Rachel and most were old. Presumably Eleanor's friends she thought. Odd that there didn't seem to be a wider family, but maybe that came with being an only child.

Suddenly her eyes widened and she nudged Victoria.

'Look who's just walked in.' and she desperately scanned the room to see where Christopher was. He was standing over by the French windows with his back to them.

The woman walked up behind him and put her hands over his eyes. 'Guess who?' she said.

Christopher turned awkwardly.

'Claudia!' There was the slightest pause before remembering his manners, he said, 'Good to see you. How kind of you to come.'

'Well', drawled Claudia, 'Your mother never had any time for me but I thought I should pay my respects anyway.'

'Is that who I think it is?' Victoria hissed in Rachel's ear.

'It's Claudia. I told you about her....'

'I thought it must be,' said Victoria. 'What's she doing here?'

They watched as Claudia talked animatedly to Christopher. Her tinkling laugh carried across the room.

'You go and top up people's drinks or something,' said Victoria, 'I need to pop in the kitchen, someone's calling me.' She came back out into the room and saw Christopher looking around. Was he looking for Rachel, or a means of escape? Either way, this was her moment. She walked up to them.

'Excuse me Christopher, I wonder if you could help me in the kitchen. One of the catering girls has burnt her hand. Have you got a first aid box?'

'Oh yes, Victoria. By all means. Excuse me Claudia.' He seemed grateful for the intrusion.

But Claudia wasn't so easily beaten. She followed Christopher into the kitchen. 'Maybe I can help. I did a first aid course once.'

Victoria elbowed Claudia aside and took control. She led the girl to the sink and ran the tap over her hand. 'Have you got some lint?' she asked Christopher. She covered the burn and held it while he found a bandage.

'There you are, keep it dry. Christopher, would you tell Rachel where I am and say I'll be with her in a couple of minutes.'

Christopher held Victoria's gaze for a moment, then nodded and walked away.

Claudia gave Victoria a hard look, turned on her heel and left the kitchen. Through the doorway Victoria could see Christopher talking to Rachel, his hand on her arm. By the time she re-entered the living room Claudia was nowhere to be seen.

Rachel came over. 'What did you say to her?'

Victoria spread out her hands. 'Nothing, honestly, why? Where is she now?'

'Well I was talking to Christopher and I saw her over his shoulder. She just stopped and looked at him, then at me. Her eyebrows went so high they practically disappeared into her immaculately coiffed hair and she was off out of the front door.'

'Result', chortled Victoria. 'It would seem she got the message.'

'God, you are so embarrassing. Christopher will be furious.'

'I think you'll find he's extremely relieved.'

Rachel didn't want to stay to find out. If Christopher thought she had anything to do with Claudia's abrupt departure he'd probably never speak to her again. The gathering was beginning to break up so she waved at Christopher from across the room and fled.

Once home she changed out of her funeral clothes. Defiantly, she put on her bright red trousers and purple fleece. If these don't dispel the gloom, nothing will, and she went out into her tiny garden, secateurs in hand and busied herself cutting back the fading herbaceous perennials and tossing any snails she came across out into the road. Hopefully, they would get run over before they managed to find their way back into her garden.

The previous occupant, an elderly gentleman, had most of the garden paved over. Rachel hated it and, one day, when she had sufficient funds, she was going to have it restored to grass and flower beds. In the meantime she had a multitude of pots of varying sizes and provenance filled with lavenders, geraniums and huge waving ferns in summer and bulbs in the spring.

Who knows, she might even be able to fit in a tiny pond. In a barrel perhaps? She re-filled the bird feeders then, suddenly overcome by a wave of sorrow and fatigue, she slowly and reluctantly went back indoors, and poured herself a large brandy before subsiding into her armchair. When she woke up, it was past midnight and the brandy remained untouched.

50

Victoria stood at the kitchen sink looking out of the window. Her mind was not fully on the encrusted roasting tin she had been hoping to restore to its former glory. She was also watching the pair of blackbirds who had nested that spring in Mr Next Door's ivy. Their chicks had long since flown the nest but the parents had stayed and were worm hunting on the vegetable patch. The two birds reminded her of Rachel and Christopher. Him - dark, handsome and slightly self-important, her - small, brown, busy and self- deprecating.

A little subtle matchmaking could do no harm surely. Those two were made for each other. It wouldn't be the first time she'd facilitated a relationship. She should do better with those two than she had done with Alistair and Diana.

Soon it would be Luke's birthday. If she had a party for him, he could get his group together and play for them, for a short while anyway, and if the evenings stayed warm they might have a barbecue in the garden. She could ask Marcus to be head chef as long as he was still on the wagon, and invite Helen and Alistair, Christopher and Rachel and a few other friends from the choir. If all else failed, they at least would have the personnel for a jolly good singsong.

She rang Rachel. 'Everyone seems to think it's a good idea. Do you fancy coming food shopping with me? We'll need steaks and salad stuffs and some extra bits and pieces.'

She sneaked a few luxuries of choice into the trolley when Rachel wasn't looking, and smiled to herself when she saw Rachel concealing some giant tiger prawns under the new potatoes.

'What about drinks? Should the whole evening be an

alcohol free zone?'

She was relieved when Rachel disagreed.

'OK. Silly idea. We'll get several bottles of delicious non-alcoholic beverages for Marcus, Helen and the boys, and compromise with some bottles of wine to be kept hidden in the larder, for the chosen few.'

'One should only be asked to sacrifice so much for one's friends,' giggled Rachel, knowing full well that she would need some Dutch courage to be able to maintain equanimity in front of Christopher. She had seen very little of him since the funeral and she'd decided to leave it to him to get in touch.

'He knows where I am,' she told Victoria. 'It strikes me he's got enough women in his life. For all I know he's back with Claudia. Why else did she turn up at the funeral?'

But he was beginning to haunt her dreams. Thoughts and feelings she'd thought were way behind her, surfaced again with the same intensity. She chastised herself for wallowing in adolescent nonsense, but the pain had an addictive pleasure to it and she couldn't help herself.

Wishing she was one of those petite women who could wear a bin bag and still look desirable, she lay awake at night worrying. Skirt or trousers? Pretty floaty top or sensible T shirt with her new kimono jacket. It was bound to get chilly later.

'It's alright for you,' she complained to Victoria. 'You're tall enough to carry anything off. It's impossible for a dumpy person to look elegant yet casual.'

'Nonsense. I'd give my eye teeth to be small and cuddly. Men love a little woman, it makes them feel all protective. You need to look amazing. What have you got that's feminine without being frilly?'

'I've got that pale pink skirt. I could buy a white top to go with it.'

'Just the job, pretty without being fussy. Out to impress anyone in particular?'

Victoria stood on the patio welcoming her guests. She clutched a glass of white wine which was masquerading as the non-alcoholic punch Marcus had made. Thank goodness it was warm enough for them to be outside.

Helen sat in a chair under the apple tree, and irritably swatted a fussing Alistair away as she would a midge.

'Go and talk to Christopher about education.'

Christopher was only too happy to oblige. Probably a distraction for him. Victoria, watching, could see his eyes following Rachel, who was flitting from person to person with dishes of nibbles and managing to avoid him altogether.

She marvelled at the lack of animosity between the two men. Good for Alistair, he could so easily have resented Christopher getting the job that had been promised to him. Could the opportunity to continue his affair with Diana have acted as balm on the wound to his ego?

When the music started, her heart swelled with pride as, looking very serious, her boys bent over their instruments. Yes, it was too loud and mostly unfamiliar but there was no denying their enthusiasm.

By the time they had eaten and sung Happy Birthday to an embarrassed Luke, dusk had fallen and she suggested that Marcus got his acoustic guitar and played some more melodious music, in keeping with the somnolent mood of those who had eaten and drunk too well.

Rachel though had had enough. The sight of Christopher laughing and chatting almost within arm's reach, sent her down to the bottom of the garden, nursing her glass of red wine and wondering whether to try and cadge a cigarette from someone to calm her down.

'Penny for them?'

She jumped and turned, spilling wine down her pink skirt. 'Oh Hell!'

'I'm so sorry. I didn't intend to startle you. Here, let me....' And Christopher dabbed ineffectually at the stain on her thigh with a large white hanky.

'Never mind. Leave it. It'll come out in the wash.'

'I looked round and you weren't there.'

'No, I'm here.'

He looked down at her, an unreadable expression on his face.

'Rachel, I've missed you. I hope mother's death doesn't mean we don't see each other anymore.'

Her mind raced. Should she play it cool or confess that she was missing him? She only gave it a second thought. Emboldened by an excess of alcohol, she followed her instincts. To hell with her doubts and fears. She lifted her eyes to his, challenging.

'Kiss me then.'

He looked speculatively at her, a slight smile on his lips, and, putting a finger under her chin and gently tilting her face up towards his, he bent down whispering, 'Lovely Rachel. I think about you every single day.'

Back up by the house, Victoria was peering anxiously into the dusk. She watched the two figures become one in the darkness, and, rubbed her hands together, smiling with satisfaction. When the party broke up, she saw that they left together to walk down the lane. Was that his arm round her waist? This was looking better and better.

51

Christopher put his head around his office door.

'Victoria, have you got a moment?'

She abandoned her attempt to find a date for Speech Day that suited everyone and went through. Her smile faded when she saw him sitting at his desk with his head in his hands.

He looked up and motioned her to sit down.

'Troubling news I'm afraid. It affects you directly, which is why I'm speaking to you first, before I make an announcement to the staff. You'll have seen the police here this morning.'

Victoria nodded. She'd seen the two constables going into school ahead of her as she walked up the drive and thought nothing of it. They occasionally came to give talks to the pupils.

'Well, it appears they were called out to a rowdy party at the weekend because lads were fighting on the front lawn. Inside, they found drugs being sold as well as taken. Five of the young people are boarders at this school. As soon as I heard I arranged for the boys' rooms to be searched. Drugs have been found. I shall have to contact the parents. I'm sorry to say, Victoria that that Luke and Nathan are implicated.'

Horror spread across Victoria's face, her midnight fears realised.

'Nathan and Luke? Drugs. Surely not.'

But they had both gone out on Saturday – to chill out with friends they'd said.

'What sort of drugs?'

'Marijuana mostly. They found some cocaine and various so-called legal highs as well. The thing is, Victoria, I am forced to take a stand on this. Publicly we have a no tolerance policy towards possession of drugs in school. The parents expect us to take a tough line and at all the top fee paying schools, the penalty for having cannabis on the premises is expulsion. The trouble is, that once it is their own kids involved the parents then expect leniency.'

Victoria struggled to marshal her thoughts.

'They say that half of all secondary pupils have tried drugs, don't they? What are the police going to do?'

'Probably nothing more than giving them a stern talking to, a cannabis warning, but, in theory, they could give a caution for a first offence. If cocaine is involved, they'd be lucky to get a caution. They would most likely be charged. I'm going to have the five of them in today and I shall send them home pending discussion with the Governors.'

At the end of the day Victoria walked slowly home.

How was she going to deal with this? She could do angry or disappointed. She felt both. Which would be more helpful?

Christopher had already spent the afternoon closeted with the little group, but she'd kept well out of the way in her office. She would talk to her two at home.

She could ask Marcus for back up, but the last time he got involved with a disciplinary matter, it was a disaster. He was sure to hear about it on the police grapevine, but she hoped he would leave her to handle it her own way. This was something she should do on her own.

It was only last night that she'd put down her book and looked affectionately over the top of her glasses at the boys, lying on the rug in front of the fire. Luke, sensing her gaze, gave her a small smile before looking back down at the chess set between them. Nathan, with his back to her, had his head lowered, deep in thought. His narrow neck, covered in a fine down, looked impossibly vulnerable, and she'd wanted to reach out and stroke it. As always, he tired of the game first and hoisting himself up on to his long legs, he offered to make them all a drink.

'Thanks Nathan, you're a star. Cocoa for me please.'

Most days when the boys came in from school, doors would be slammed and bags dropped on the hall floor as they made for the kitchen. Victoria would attempt to discuss their day and, answering in monosyllables, they would raid the fridge and the cake tin. This time however, doors had been closed quietly and she heard stealthy footsteps going straight upstairs. She took a deep breath then went and called up.

'Nathan, Luke, down here, please, both of you, now.'

She had mentally prepared herself for either exaggerated protestations of innocence, or a sulky withdrawal and a refusal to discuss the matter. What she wasn't expecting was Nathan's fury at what he saw as the disproportionate reaction from the police, the school and, inevitably, Victoria.

'For fuck's sake. The whole thing is just ridiculous. A few puffs on a joint. Everybody does it. Would you rather I got smashed on cheap lager every weekend? Or do you think the next step is heroin? We weren't even on school premises.'

'Nathan, calm down. Like it or not, at the moment, possession of cannabis is a criminal offence. Where did you get it from?'

'It's none of your business. Just back off and leave me alone.'

He turned and walked out of the kitchen. She heard the front door slam.

She swivelled round and looked at Luke.

'I don't know anything about it, honest. I've seen him smoking with his friends, but he said it was his own tobacco and I wasn't to tell anyone.'

'What do you mean, 'his own tobacco'?'

'He and Guy have got some tobacco plants on his grandfather's allotment. Oh, please don't tell him I told you. He said it was all right if you grew your own.'

'For goodness sake, stop snivelling. Don't they teach you about drugs at school? No, forget that, I know very well they do. Which allotment belongs to Guy's grandad?'

Five minutes later Victoria was striding down the village. She knew Guy's grandfather slightly. He was a keen gardener and specialised in enormous vegetables, with which he won prizes all over the county. The old man was leaning on his spade. As Victoria approached, a broad smile creased his weather beaten face.

'Guess I know what you've come about,' he said amiably.

'You knew?'

'Oh come on. I heard they'd been busted. The lads asked if they could grow a plant or two in my greenhouse. I figured it was better to do that than get involved with those dealers. Be honest now – a bit of wacky baccy never did anyone any harm.'

Victoria drew herself up and folded her arms.

'I call it harm if they end up with a police caution on their record. How will that look when they apply for jobs, or even just want to visit America? The law is the law and you are stupidly helping them to break it.'

'Get down off your high horse, lady. The plants have long gone now. If we keep our mouths shut then it'll all be forgotten.' He turned away from her and ambled off.

Victoria felt sick as she walked home. Not only had her boy been caught smoking an illegal substance, but he'd actually been growing and, presumably, supplying it to others as well. Did Christopher know about the horticultural enterprise? Taking a detour she knocked on his door, unsure whether he might be still be at school.

'Hello Victoria, I've just got in. Drink?' Victoria accepted a glass of wine, aware that she too, tended to rely on a drug of another sort in times of stress.

'I'm sorry to bother you. I'm so worried about Nathan. I wish his father was here to deal with it.'

'That's understandable. Sit down and I'll tell you what I'm going to do. I've spoken to a couple of my colleagues and it's very much a common occurrence in both state and fee paying schools. I've decided that as the smoking wasn't done on school grounds, there'll be no expulsions. They'll get a final warning, I shall inform their parents and I've asked the police to give them a good talking to as well. We'll set up an improved drugs education programme, which will be wider-ranging than the one we have at present.'

When she arrived home she could hear loud music coming from Nathan's room and read it as a clear 'keep away' signal.

She decided to obey. Christopher would be talking to them in the morning and she had had enough for one day.

Predictably, her night's sleep was punctured by unanswered questions. She had seen cannabis farms being raided on the news and a lot of heat and light was involved. Could they now be growing it somewhere else, or was she being ridiculous? There was only one place where they could have any control over the environment. She could easily check that out right now and, hopefully, put her mad theory to rest.

The big shed at the bottom of the garden which they had converted to a band practice room, was kept locked because some of the instruments were stored in there. Victoria struggled to find the key which was not in its usual place on the hook by the back door. She remembered that Marcus had given her a spare at the time they bought the padlock, found it in her key tin on the dresser and, pausing only to pull on a fleece, set off down the path. Her breath clouded in the cold night air. She must look like a fire breathing dragon. This wasn't what she'd signed up for. The lock was cold and stiff, and she struggled to turn the key.

As soon as she entered the shed she became aware of faint warmth compared to the chill of outside, but knew there was a basic heater on a very low setting. A swift look round revealed nothing amiss. Thank goodness.

Relieved, she turned, to go, then suddenly froze. There was a smell, a strong herbal smell, in the air. In the far corner her large, old kitchen cupboard loomed wide and tall.

Victoria strode over and pulled open the doors. Light from an enormous lamp flooded out and the overwhelming odour of ripening marihuana from the dozen or so large plants caused her to gag.

Sick with rage, she reeled and clung to a door for support. This was worse than she imagined. She burst into action and ran back up to the house to fetch a roll of black plastic sacks. Returning to the shed, she pulled the grow bags out of the cupboard, stuffed the burgeoning plants into the bin bags and ripped out the wires leading to the big arc lamp. Panting with the unaccustomed exertion, she put the bags in the wheelie bin and sat down heavily at the kitchen table to consider her next move.

Nathan and Luke would soon be getting up for school. Not ready to face them yet, she pulled on her Wellingtons and left the cottage to walk up on the hill. There was only the milkman to see her with her nightie hanging down below her coat.

From the summit, she could see the tops of the trees sticking up out of the layers of mist like icy lollies.

It was simple. She could go to the police, thereby upholding the law of the land – as she had tried to do all her life - or she could do her utmost to protect her boys from the consequences of their folly, by concealing what they had done, and hope they would learn a lesson from their close shave.

It was a no-brainer.

If she told the police that Nathan was growing and supplying an illegal substance, the consequences could be catastrophic. He'd be expelled, hauled up in court and have a criminal record for the next few years at least. That would impact on his chances of going to university, be a factor in making him ineligible for all sorts of jobs and crucially, make him hate her for the betrayal.

She'd have to go home to talk to him, make him aware of the seriousness of the situation and admit she was probably committing a crime by concealing evidence on his behalf.

By the time she got back, the boys were up and she found that all Nathan's bluster of the day before had subsided. White faced, he listened to what Victoria had to say.

'They will probably also find out about the plants at Guy's grandfather's allotment, it depends if any of your friends spill the beans. You'll have to pray that your little enterprise in my shed stays undiscovered. You can both come with me to apologise to Christopher for bringing the school into disrepute and promise him you'll knuckle down and concentrate on your studies.'

Nathan nodded.

'And if you've made any money, I suggest you pass it on to a charity. Narcotics Anonymous perhaps?'

'Okay, Victoria. It's a deal. Thanks, and...I'm sorry. It won't happen again.'

She looked at him. With relief, she saw contrition and shame on his face.

'Come here.' She put her arms round him and he twisted uneasily in her grasp. Had she not hugged them enough? At least she'd resisted the temptation to ask him what his father would have thought. That would have been a low blow. She released him and he escaped up to his room. She felt very alone. Oh James, what would you have said to him? Have I said enough? Will this really be the end of it?'

52

Christmas that year, for the choir, was a low key affair. The concert hall, usually decorated for the occasion with a Christmas tree and festive troughs of poinsettias, was completely unadorned. The capacity audience may not have noticed that anything was different. The choir had learnt new carols and the old ones were given their due prominence. But Victoria could see that Alistair was distant and his usual zest for performing had lost its edge.

She had watched, with more than a twinge of guilt, the lingering aftermath of the drugs scandal with Christopher battling his governors, the press, complaining parents and the police. At the end of January she went into his office. He was at his desk, his head bowed and his hands clasped in his lap. Had his hair always been greying at the temples? She wanted to comfort him. Inappropriate. But she knew someone who could, and would, with just a little encouragement.

'You need a break. Why don't you get right away for a few days? At half term perhaps? You could take Rachel somewhere.'

He looked up at her, eyebrows raised, then shook his head.

'It's a nice idea, Victoria, I could do with a change of scenery, but I don't expect Rachel would be interested. We don't have that sort of a relationship really. She's very independent.'

Victoria was exasperated. Why were men so obtuse? She turned on her heel and went to the door. With her hand on the knob, she said over her shoulder, 'If you don't try, you'll never know, will you?'

Her comment unsettled him. He stood up and stood in the

window looking down the garden. The rose bushes were almost leafless, bleak and spiky, giving no hint of the splendour in waiting. Could that be a metaphor for his life?

Although, on the face of it, he and Rachel had become close again, if they were to spend increasing amounts of time together, he would have to warn her not to hope for exclusive rights. Perhaps he should reveal the reasons why his feelings about their lack of a future together hadn't changed? It was all so difficult. He was fond enough of her to want to spend time with her, but he did not want a wife. He needed to feel free. Had he not promised himself that no woman would ever be in a position of power over him again?

That night they'd walked home together from Victoria's party, taking her to his bed had seemed to be the most comfortable and obvious thing to do. To be honest, he'd expected gentle, demure lovemaking - the culmination of a pleasant evening, rather than grand passion. She had surprised him with her enthusiasm and willingness to have fun. Twice they had even fallen off the bed together in a tangle of limbs and shrieks of laughter.

He hadn't pursued it in the weeks that followed – but to be fair, neither had she. With the memory of that night at the forefront of his mind, and for once obeying his heart and not his head, he picked up the phone.

'Rachel, I'm planning a cull of some of Eleanor's books. I hate to do it but I need the room and some of them might be suited to other readers. I wondered if you might like one or two perhaps. Would you be free, say Saturday morning?'

Since Victoria's party Rachel only seen Christopher once or twice in the distance, and had decided he must be regretting taking her home to his bed that night. Why wouldn't he? She was hardly a lissom lovely and, even in the dark, he must have been repulsed by her. Still, now he wanted to see her again, so maybe she hadn't disappointed him after all. She permitted herself a glimmer of hope. Thinking she might replace her usual Saturday jeans and jumper, for a pretty flowery blouse and denim skirt, she consulted Victoria.

'I don't want to look like mutton dressed as lamb.'

Victoria had laughed. 'I haven't heard that phrase since my mother was alive.'

Rachel pretended to be offended. 'Are you saying I'm old fashioned?'

Saturday came and she stood shivering in his garden. She'd have been better off with her jeans and woolly jumper after all. She cradled a mug of coffee to warm her hands. He seemed to be in a reflective mood and she was able to mirror it.

He broke the silence.

'I feel closest to her out here. The daffodils in spring were always her favourites. I used to buy her a bunch every Christmas. I can't remember where they came from, at that time of year, the Isles of Scilly probably, but she always said it was the best present of all. I never imagined I would miss her so much. She could be such a pain – but she was my pain. I suppose that sounds stupid?'

'Of course not. I miss her - it must be a hundred times worse for you.'

Needing something to do, she broke off some twigs of forsythia.

'Take these in and put them in water. They'll flower in a few days in the warmth of your kitchen.'

What else could they talk about? Was Eleanor the only thing they had in common now?

He walked away from her and collected the bird feeders which needed to be refilled. When he returned to her side, he hesitated then asked, 'Listen, before we look at the books I've had an idea I'd like to run past you. Would you fancy a bit of an escape at half term? Friends of mine have a small flat in Majorca, near Palma. There are lots of lovely places I'd like to show you.'

Rachel's jaw dropped. This sounded like an escalation of the relationship. What an unreadable, contradictory man he was. As if he was anticipating her rejection, he added, 'Of course if you'd rather not, please just say.'

She looked at his kind face and his anxious brown eyes. She wanted more of this clever, fascinating man, despite his obvious commitment issues.

'That sounds wonderful. I've never been to Majorca.'

His face cleared. 'I can promise you, you'll love it. There'll be very few tourists in February, hopefully some sunshine and stunning scenery.'

That didn't fit the image Rachel had in her head at all. She'd always thought of Majorca as a Spanish Blackpool, over run with drunken stag parties and enormous hotel blocks.

She confided her preconceptions to Victoria, and found herself being gently chided.

'Sometimes Rachel you're an even bigger snob than I am. Yes, there are touristy bits, but it's a huge island and it's easy to avoid them. Why do you think it's such a popular place if it's so ghastly? I'd love to go again. Tell Christopher I'll happily take your place if it's a bit downmarket for you.'

'Sorry. Point taken. I suppose I'm being judgemental without the facts.'

She was grateful that Christopher dealt with all the booking and that all she had to do was find her passport and pack a case. Meanwhile she took the opportunity to splash out on pretty new underwear.

As the plane thundered down the runway, she whispered to him,

'Hold my hand.'

'Why?'

'Because I'm scared.'

'But so am I.'

Rachel wasn't sure whether she admired his honesty or was unimpressed by his unmanly fears. Nevertheless she clung on to him until the Somerset levels below had disappeared and they rose above the clouds. They chatted for a while then, as Christopher dozed, she took out the novel she'd bought at the airport. There was a time when she'd have bought something worthy to impress her companion, but not anymore. The latest best- selling chick-lit would occupy her mind during the tedium of the flight and maybe send her to sleep as well.

They stepped off the plane into a wall of warmth. Blue skies and sunshine banished the memory of a cold, damp English spring.

He professed himself disappointed with the hire car he had booked.

'This has seen better days. I might see if I can get us something better.'

'No, leave it. This'll be fine. Let's get out of this airport and on our way.'

They left Palma and headed down the coast, along avenues lined with palm trees and caught tantalising glimpses of a blue sea between them. They looked at each other and grinned with anticipation and delight. He fumbled for his sunglasses and said, 'We're heading for Santa Ponza. It was just a small fishing village before the tourism boom. When we've found the flat, we'll drop off our bags and go and explore. We'll find a pavement café down by the harbour and watch the boats coming and going.'

In the still of the early evening they walked down the narrow streets. Delicious smells came their way from restaurants and tapas bars. Rachel stopped and inhaled deeply.

'I don't know about you but I'm starving. Can we find somewhere to eat?' She tentatively tucked her arm in his, he didn't seem to mind, and they wandered along looking at menus pinned up outside the cafes. They found one where they could sit outside under a red umbrella. Christopher laughed at her inadequacies with the Spanish language of the menu and ordered for them both.

'It has to be something from the sea,' he said, 'and it'll be freshly caught. I promise you'll love it.'

Rachel was alarmed by the large orange fish, complete with head and tail, which the waiter carefully placed in front of her. She tried to sip casually from her glass of wine while watching how Christopher dealt with his.

'This is a messy business but I'm doing my best. I love all

these different textures and flavours.' She mopped up the garlicky juices with her bread, and sighed with pleasure.

Christopher watched her as she tucked in. He was interested in this different Rachel. Gone was the brisk, confident woman he thought he knew. Here, he sensed her vulnerability, her concern at the unfamiliarity of her surroundings and her touching reliance on him to keep her safe. He had promised himself that he would be honest about his position. Should he be straight with her quickly and be done with it, or wait until the end of the holiday?

They walked back up the cobbled streets to the flat. He would talk to her tomorrow. Tonight he would hold her in his arms and relish their love making. Tomorrow's conversation might just change everything. She wouldn't like what he had to say.

Rachel, could see that he had something on his mind and was afraid he was disappointed in her. She was so different from the two women she had met from his past. They'd both been glittering, clever and exotic; so what on earth was he doing with her – a homely soul with no dress sense and even less sophistication? Her worries were swept aside as, laughing at her screams on discovering a large Spanish spider in the shower, he pulled her down onto the bed.

In the morning, sated and glowing, she slipped out of his arms and pulled on some leggings and a yellow sweatshirt. She went down into the village and, with much gesticulation, pointing and smiling she managed to buy bread, cheese and grapes for a picnic lunch. Feeling quite the local, she strolled back to the flat enjoying the sun and the bustle around her. She heard her name being called and looked up to see Christopher standing on the balcony waving.

Back in the flat she scolded him. 'You shouldn't stand out there in your underpants. There could be pupils from your school walking past.'

'You're right. It wouldn't be the first time I've bumped into kids or parents in unlikely places.'

He put his arms round her.

'But I woke up and you were gone. Now come back to bed, you wanton woman.'

'Certainly not. The sun is shining and there's a beautiful island out there waiting to be explored. Get some clothes on and let's go out.'

They headed towards the mountains.

Would you like to take a turn with the driving?

'Don't be ridiculous. They drive on the wrong side of the road to begin with. I've never driven abroad and I'm not about to start now.'

The road wound up and up, round hairpin bends and with vertiginous drops to either side. She wanted to shut her eyes but if she was going to die in a fireball plunging down into the abyss, she'd better keep them open.

'Please slow down a bit'.

'I asked you if you wanted to drive.'

'And I said I didn't. Neither, though, do I want to die.'

The monastery at Lluc, although it was early in the year, was busy with pilgrims and tourists. Christopher parked the car and chose to follow a steep path leading away into the wooded mountainside. They walked until they found a glade, green with moss and with a trickling stream making its way downhill. He laid out Rachel's picnic, making appreciative noises.

'Have you noticed how much better food tastes outside? This bread is so good.'

When they had eaten and drunk, he tidily packed everything away, and turned to her, saying, 'Right, I want you to know more about me. There are things that have happened in my past which have made me feel the way I do today. I think I owe you an explanation.'

He paused, twisting his hands together. She reached over and covered them with her much smaller ones.

'There's no need to tell me anything,' she offered, adding with an insouciance she didn't feel. 'You'd be surprised what skeletons there are in my cupboard.'

'Sorry, but I do need to tell you. I'm very attracted to you, Rachel. I don't find relationships easy, as you well know. If you understand why I am like I am, then it'll help you not to expect anything more than I'm able to give.' He sat down beside her.

'I married far too young. It was what you did then. I worked long hours and taught evening classes at night as well. Despite what people say about teaching, it's not an easy job. Difficult kids and stroppy staff can really grind you down. And I haven't even started on pushy parents.' He tried to smile.

'In time I bought the beautiful house she wanted. Everyone thought she was marvellous, but she wasn't happy with the wifely role. She didn't cook. Rarely was there a meal when I got home from work. She insisted on having a cleaner, thought she was above cleaning, and wasn't terribly interested in the bed side of things either. She spent most of her time playing bridge with her friends. Worst of all, as far as I was concerned, she didn't want children.'

He sighed. 'Perhaps I shouldn't be telling you all this, I've never told anyone else, but I want you to understand me.'

He dug the wine out of the basket and drained the remains of the bottle. 'God, that's sour.' He wiped his mouth with the back of his hand and continued.

'I wasn't particularly happy and neither, it seems, was she. She got more and more involved with gambling and started playing bridge at private clubs in town. Sometimes she wouldn't get in 'till three in the morning. Then, after twenty years of marriage, she told me she was leaving me for someone she'd met there.'

Rachel, listening with an awful fascination, felt she ought to interrupt him. 'Look, you really don't need to…...'

He silenced her with a gesture.

'Let me finish. As far as I am concerned, marriage is a contract and, as I try to be honourable, I would never have broken that contract. Besides, I still loved her or thought I did. I'd envisaged us caring for each other in old age, mellowing over time, ironing out the differences. But she had other ideas.

She found a top divorce lawyer and took me for almost every penny I had. She got the house as well. Refusing to go out to work paid off for her in the end. I ended up losing most of what I'd spent all those years earning. My Head's salary helped me start saving again.'

'It's not unusual. Lots of marriages break up.'

He picked at a fingernail, his mind far away.

'You must understand. I went into teaching late. When I left university I had various jobs, none of which paid very much. My father wouldn't help, not that I'd even ask – too much pride. For me, money meant security. Even now, I'm a saver not a spender. She took away the security blanket I'd built up over the years. It was a devastating blow. It was the worst thing she could have done – and she knew it.'

He stopped and got to his feet. He walked away from Rachel to the edge of the glade, where the land dropped away and stood for several minutes looking down into the wooded valley, wondering what effect his story was having on this honest, straightforward woman who was becoming so special to him in spite of his best efforts to resist.

Rachel stayed where she was, sitting on his coat on the ground. She leaned back on her hands and lifted her head up towards him.

'Let me get this right. Your marriage broke up; you feel cheated and bitter, quite understandably, and this is why you never want to try again?' He turned on her. 'Don't trivialise it. I don't want your observations. I merely need you to understand why no woman will have the opportunity to take me for a fool ever again.'

'Right. So, is that it then?' Now she was annoyed too. He had stopped talking but she could feel his eyes on her. He continued. 'Not quite. Once she got her hands on my money, she married that chap. My father had died and Mother was on her own so she offered me a home temporarily, and it suited us both so well, I've never moved on.'

In more ways than one, thought Rachel.

'Where is she now?'

'Oh I don't know. I think they went to live abroad to start with. I don't want, or indeed expect, to ever see her again. '

Rachel got up and began picking up their picnic bags. Her mind was racing but she wasn't sure whether now was the time and place for getting answers to the questions that were bubbling up in her mind. Why couldn't he just have been a nice, simple man who loved his mother? What made him think she wanted to marry him anyway? She entertained a brief fantasy where he proposed and she turned him down.

Christopher sensed that she was irritated with him.

'Tell me what you're thinking.'

She put down the bags, turned and stared at him, hands on hips. 'Where do I start? Firstly, why did you say you were a widower?'

'I never actually said that. At the Headship interview I merely said that there was no longer a Mrs Forbes Martin. Someone must have presumed I was widowed rather than divorced, and spread it around. Who told you?' Rachel racked her brains.

'I think it was Rosemary in the Community office, when she asked me if I wanted to visit Eleanor. But I don't know where she would have got it from.'

'Well, once I heard that was what people thought, I decided to leave it at that. It seemed preferable to be seen as a widower, and as I had no intention of marrying again, it didn't matter anyway.'

'Oh, so what about Claudia?'

She could hear a tinge of jealousy in her voice and tried to cover it up with a non-judgemental smile.

'She was just an expensive distraction. It was nice to have someone to go to the theatre and on holiday with, to get away from school. But we were hardly soul mates.'

He put his hands on her shoulders and forced her to meet his gaze.

'Right, now you know all there is to know. No more secrets.'

Rachel felt that this was probably the most important

conversation of her life – and yet she didn't know how to respond to him.

He continued. 'You see now that both the women I loved left me? Perhaps now you understand why I've vowed to spend the rest of my life on my own? I am being completely honest with you, Rachel. This is my position, and, believe me, I've not arrived at it without a lot of thought.'

'Your mother died because she was old and ill. You can hardly claim abandonment there.'

'I didn't say my feelings were logical. Feelings often aren't.' He searched her face.

'You should look on me as a temporary necessity. I am unworthy, depressive – and no use to you or anyone. Believe me, there is no future for us.'

At these harsh words, Rachel's stomach twisted.

'How can you say that and then make love to me the way you do?'

'You tend to get fond of someone you sleep with.' He threw the line away and shrugged his shoulders.

Rachel was determined to maintain her composure with him. Her annoyance had drained away and she saw a complex, damaged, but fundamentally honest man, who was scared of heartbreak and protective of his independence, who had loved and lost his wife, and his mother. She saw a man who had held her gently, and who looked at her with love in his eyes, despite the words of denial on his lips. She was emotionally bound to this man for better or worse. She reached forward and took his hand. They walked back to where they had left the car and drove home.

53

When they got back to South Heath Rachel had plenty to think about. She hadn't seen Christopher and wondered if he was avoiding her. The train of thought trundled miserably through her mind at all hours of the day and night.

Why should she expect him to maintain an interest in her and indeed even ever want to marry her? She wasn't clever. At school they'd said she'd be lucky to get any 'A' levels, and the alternative for girls such as her was to take a secretarial course. Someone with a different character might have taken that as a challenge. But Rachel was inclined to take herself at other's estimation. She spent several mind-numbing years in an office until she met and married Marcus. She left her hated job and waited for the babies which never came. She wondered if things would have turned out differently if they'd had a family.

Christopher would want a woman who stimulated him intellectually, someone who had lived a bit and was wise to the ways of the world. She put on her coat and went to the newsagent and bought a Times. Next time she saw him she intended to impress him with her grasp of current affairs. On the way home she saw Victoria's front door was ajar. She walked up the path between the mounds of lavender. Her breath caught in her throat and she hesitated on the doorstep. Perhaps she should try for once to bottle things up.

'Hello.' Victoria appeared in the doorway. She saw Rachel's drooping shoulders and hangdog expression and said sympathetically, 'Do you need to talk?'

'No. I need to scream.'

'You'd better come inside then. We mustn't frighten the neighbours.' She turned and led the way into the kitchen.

'Sit down. Has something happened? I take it this is about Christopher?'

Rachel didn't want to sit down. She prowled round the kitchen.

'Am I so obvious? Yes, of course I am. It's just that he never seems to be around these days. I went to the cottage a couple of times but he wasn't in – either that or he wasn't answering his door. Should I be taking this personally or is there some other reason?'

She watched Victoria's face as her friend hesitated before replying. Sometimes Victoria revealed what she was thinking through her expressions before the words came.

So for good measure she added, 'I expect he's bored with me and can't bring himself to tell me.'

Victoria shook her head and said, 'He's staying very late at school most nights and has a lot of meetings in London and Bristol.'

'You're saying that to put me out of my misery.'

'No I'm not. Look, it's nothing to do with you. I'll tell you, but please keep this completely to yourself for the time being.'

She switched the kettle on and got out the biscuit tin to give herself time to choose her words.

'Sit down for Heaven's sake. You'll hear soon enough. The school is struggling to balance the books. Numbers are dropping and there has been a big fall in pupils from overseas. The school hasn't kept up with the times, if truth be told, and parents want all the latest bells and whistles in exchange for the school fees which keep going up. Excellent teaching isn't enough nowadays, it would seem. Christopher has been trying to get some investment to upgrade facilities but, I gather, without much success.'

'Why hasn't he told me about this?' Rachel's indignation was almost comical.

'Oh come on. You know Christopher by now. He keeps things to himself, and he probably didn't want to worry you. Besides, it's not a new problem. He was warned when he was offered the job that the school was facing an uncertain future with wages spiralling, fees going up and stiff competition from the state schools in the area. He was hired in the expectation he would turn things around.'

'You could have told me all this ages ago and I would have been more supportive.'

Victoria sighed. 'We were told not to discuss the situation with anyone. I shouldn't even be telling you now.'

Rachel left Victoria's realising that not everything was about her, and understanding that Christopher had concerns of his own that demanded his time and attention. It would have been nice though, she thought, if he had felt able to confide in her. Victoria certainly seemed to know all about it.

She battled with herself over whether to stay quiet or go to him and reveal that she had heard rumours. She decided to take the easy option and do nothing. Let him come to her.

A few days later she was down on her knees in her vegetable patch, putting in some radishes and lettuce, when she heard him calling her name.

'I'm in the garden,' she yelled, 'Come round.' She scrambled to her feet to greet him. Her face was shiny, her hair needed washing and her body odour was less Chanel No 5 and more human perspiration. Why couldn't he have rung first?

'I'm sorry. I can see this is not a good time. I just thought I hadn't seen you for a while.'

'That's alright. I need a break. I've been at it since lunchtime. I don't know why I plant these every year – the slugs will eat the radishes and the lettuces too. Come on, I'll get us a drink.'

She made two mugs of tea and carried them out with a packet of biscuits, to the table in the shade of her little pergola. Her favourite rose, Munstead Wood, scented the air with a velvety deep perfume. She sat opposite him. His eyes were closed and there was a small smile on his lips.

'Oh Rachel, you are so good for my soul.'

'Well, sit there and commune with your soul, I need to clean myself up a bit.'

Five minutes later, hair brushed, armpits deodorised and

wearing a clean, cotton shirt, she sat down next to him. She fished a fly, swimming for its life in her now cold tea and waited to hear the reason for his visit.

'I must confess this isn't only a social call. I need to ask a favour. I'm going away for two weeks. Would you be able to water my pots and hanging baskets?'

His eyes were rimmed with red as though he hadn't slept for a week.

'Of course I would. Is it a holiday?'

Should she tell him how awful he looked? She decided against it.

'Sadly, no. I'm going to the Far East, to do some publicity stuff for the school. The governors have decided there is to be a recruitment drive so I'm off to Hong Kong, Singapore, the Philippines and Japan. I'll be doing local TV, lots of press interviews and speaking to various businesses in the hope they'll sponsor some pupils to come to South Heath.'

'Good heavens. I don't know whether to envy you or commiserate with you. Presumably there'll be rest days every so often? Isn't it awfully short notice for the new term?'

He gave a tired smile.

'You're right, it is, but it's worth a try to catch those who haven't got places yet. It has to be done if the school is to survive. The books aren't balancing. If things don't improve we could be closing altogether.'

Rachel feigned astonishment, and dunked her chocolate digestive while she decided whether to admit she'd heard rumours.

She came clean, but didn't mention Victoria's name.

'What? If gossip like this gets back to the parents, they'll start pulling their kids out, new kids won't start and in no time at all it'll all be over. Who told you all this?'

She was forced to reassure him that it had only been Victoria, in response to her own worries about his preoccupied mood.

'I thought you were getting bored with me. She wouldn't dream of telling anyone else and swore me to secrecy.'

He shook his head in exasperation.

'I'm disappointed in her. She should have known better. Why do you think I didn't say anything to you about it? If the Press will get hold of it then we may as well start packing. Are you aware how many people round here depend on the school? Not just the teaching staff, there are cooks, gardeners, cleaners, housekeepers, the maintenance man... it'll affect the whole area.'

Rachel apologised, but couldn't let it rest. 'What about you? What would you do - start looking out for another Headship somewhere?'

She tried to sound matter-of-fact, but inside there was a voice screaming - Nooooo, I've only just found you. You can't go to the other end of England and leave me here.

His gaze softened as he looked at her. Had he intuited what she was thinking?

'When I was appointed I promised the governors that I'd fight tooth and nail to get South Heath back on to a sound economic footing. And I have been doing just that. There are lots of things we can do; selling off some land is one. We're reviewing the financial situation monthly. Let's just hope my recruiting trip is successful. The overseas students are where the money lies nowadays.'

He got up to leave.

'When are you going?'

'At the end of the month. It's been planned for some time, but it's all been kept very hush hush. It was actually on the cards before Keith left. I wouldn't be surprised if that hastened his decision.'

'Was he pushed?'

'Let's just say it was hoped a new Head would be able to turn things around.'

He raised his hand in farewell and was gone. He called her again before he left. 'Can you come round and I'll show you what might need watering.'

She walked down to the cottage. Should she show how

314

much she would miss him?

'Would you like me to take you to Heathrow?'

'No, school is paying for a taxi.'

'No wonder they're hard up.'

'Don't be flippant Rachel. It doesn't suit you.'

But he was smiling. He bent down and gave her a peck on the cheek. 'I'll keep in touch.'

From: christopherforbesmartin@all.com
To: rachelwilliamson@bt.co.uk

Arrived Hong Kong safely – not too jet lagged. This place is overwhelming. Noisy, colourful, crowded. A real attack on the senses. It's the monsoon season and the humidity is unbearable. When it rains it's as though the heavens have opened, then ten minutes later the streets are quite dry again. Luckily my hotel is air conditioned. Have done a bit of sight- seeing, the giant Buddah and was taken on the Star ferry last night on a cruise round the harbour. Tomorrow I have my meetings with the students' representatives. They have never heard of South Heath obviously but they have all heard of Oxford and Cambridge and they see coming to an English public school as a stepping stone to higher things. Let's hope I can convince them to choose us.

I hope all is well with you.
Christopher

From:christopherforbesmartin@all.com
To:rachelwilliamson@bt.co.uk

If it's Tuesday, it must be Japan! I can scarcely believe I'm here doing this. Way out of my comfort zone, immensely challenging though. Have been in meetings and giving presentations all day and am being taken out on a trip on the bullet train to see Mount Fuji and Lake Ashi tonight.

Had seven students in Hong Kong expressing a firm interest, but expect some to fall by the wayside. The Japanese seem more wary, but who knows?

They talk about the inscrutable Orient don't they? I have another full day tomorrow then a 6pm flight to Singapore. Am absolutely exhausted, the heat doesn't help, and want nothing more than to be sitting in my garden with you in the peace of an English summer's evening.

Yours Chris.

From:christopherforbesmartin@all.com
To:rachelwilliamson@bt.co.uk

Am surrounded again by towering skyscrapers, teeming multitudes, traffic and noise. I can't imagine what the students who choose to come to England to study will make of our rural backwater. I am suffering from severe culture shock. Some of our party are going on to Korea and Taiwan after this, but I've done all I can. I need to put in my earplugs now and try to get some sleep. Tomorrow is another packed day, and only the thought that I shall then be on a plane home will get me through.

Your very weary friend,
Chris. x

Rachel read and reread the emails. She had kept her replies brief – a sentence about the weather, his garden and a light anecdote about village life since he'd left. The small kiss at the end of his email gladdened her heart. She'd always signed off with a kiss. Maybe it was contagious.

54

Victoria spent a couple of hours up at the school sorting Christopher's post and checking there had been no disasters while he'd been away. When she got home Rachel was there at her front door.

She followed Victoria in, sat down heavily and kicked off her shoes.

'That's better. I need a sit. I've been awake half the night worrying about Christopher. He rang me from the airport on his way home, sounding absolutely exhausted. I'd have liked to have picked him up when he lands but they're sending a car.'

Victoria risked asking, 'So you've missed him quite a lot then?'

Rachel picked at a scab on her knee from when she tripped over a rake in the garden.

'Yes, of course. But you know what it's like when you've lived on your own for any length of time; it's also nice to be able to be selfish again and be without the irritants of other people's ways and opinions. I sometimes wonder if I could ever actually live as part of a couple again. I'd have to work very hard on my tolerance and compromise levels. Besides, Christopher isn't looking for a wife. He's made that quite clear.'

'Have you any idea how successful he was in the Far East?'

'I think he's quite optimistic, but it's early days. I'm just on my way round to his place to open a few windows and take some bread and milk. There's nothing like your first cuppa at home after you've been away for a while.'

Christopher let himself into his office. Back to the grindstone. He wondered if it would prove to have all been worth it. Only time would tell. He looked at his post and the messages Victoria had deemed important, then he had to go and talk to the staff, who were gathering for a pre-term staff meeting.

The view from his window into the Headmaster's garden, past the rose beds and down to the lake, and the beginning of autumn colours spreading across the English landscape, lifted his spirits as always. But parents wanted state of the art science blocks and top class sports facilities, not ornamental lakes and dormitories which, although refurbished and updated, still bore traces of their Victorian origins.

Although he'd known that the school was in dire straits for months, he'd been too wrapped up in his mother's declining health and his involvement with Rachel to focus on the problem as he perhaps should have done.

Now his mother had gone. Only Rachel remained. He didn't know what he should do about her either. He went to the bottom drawer of his desk and took out the bottle of single malt. It was there for moments such as this – to calm his racing mind and dull the strain. For a moment he thought he could do an Alistair, not South Africa, but New Zealand maybe? Mountains to climb, superb scenery, but he knew it was an escapists dream. His climbing days were over and scenery needed someone to enjoy it with. He'd cut the meeting short. He could plead jet lag. It would all keep until tomorrow. He drained the glass and walked down to the staff room.

At his desk early the next morning he surveyed a list of problems requiring his attention. Before he could make a start there was a knock on his door.

'Have you a minute, Mr Forbes Martin.' The school cook looked flustered and there were little beads of perspiration on her face.

'Of course. Come in and sit down.'

'No, no, I'll stand. This won't take a minute. I've come to

give you my resignation. I can't be expected to run the kitchen with only two ladies.'

His heart sank. Like an army, the school marched on its stomach, and she was a very good cook.

'Oh dear, oh dear. I do understood your position, but I'm afraid I just haven't got the funds for any more staff at the moment. I've already had to let the gardener go and asked the groundsman to take on the gardens, as well as everything else. But listen, I'm confident that in a few months' time, I'll be able to take on more people. Can you possibly manage for now?'

He knew he was pleading and clasped his hands in front of him as if in prayer. She looked unconvinced. He didn't blame her. He tried again.

'Please, hang on a bit longer. I promise I'll see what I can do.'

There had, as yet, only been a trickle of applicants from new overseas students. Worse still, the latest examination results were less than spectacular and five of his students had failed to reach the grades required by their chosen university. News like that got around and he could expect to lose pupils from his GCSE year next summer whose parents would choose to send them elsewhere for the all-important 'A' level years. It was a vicious circle. If the level of teaching and the standard of facilities dropped, then there would be fewer pupils, which would mean less money to maintain staffing and upkeep of the facilities and so on, in a downward spiral.

He would have to chase up those contacts in the Far East. The governors would have to be updated as to the increasing gravity of the situation and he made notes for that eventuality. The trouble was they were mostly businessmen and only saw things in terms of profit and loss. What if they decided it was time to cut their losses?

Later that week, he sat in Rachel's kitchen, allowing the mug of freshly brewed coffee in front of him to cool, distractedly folding and unfolding a tea towel.

'It's getting worse,' he told her. 'Several parents have

withdrawn their children from school. Some of the new intake are not coming now and, worse still, the governors have had an eye-watering offer from a leisure company for the building and grounds. It would seem to be an offer they can't refuse, given that the coffers are empty. I tried to be upbeat with our cook who wanted to resign, but actually, I think this is the beginning of the end.'

He looked at her. She was chewing on a thumbnail, her eyes fixed on his face. Was she thinking what a loser he was? He recalled his mother's last words to him on the subject of Rachel, 'Marry her, Chris. She'll make you happy.' He pushed the thought away.

'I'm tempted not to go for another headship. When I got this one, I envisaged giving it about fifteen years then retiring. But now, thanks to Mother, if they close the school, I can afford to take a very early retirement, do some travelling, and then, who knows? There are loads of things I've promised myself I would do once I'd got the opportunity. I've got my painting and I might even try to write a book.'

Rachel tried to smile. Was any place for her in all this, she wondered. Too proud to ask, she was mentally preparing herself for Christopher to depart her life as unexpectedly as he had come into it.

Her resolve broke. She asked;

'When you were away, did you miss me?'

'You aren't supposed to ask that.'

'Why not?'

'It implies a dependence, a permanence. I told you not to become involved.'

She swallowed hard. She was not going to cry.

He was silent for a moment. Then he said,

'If you meant did I think about you while I was away, the answer is yes.

If you meant did I want to see you when I got back, the answer is yes.

If you meant did I miss you, with the dependence and need that that implies, then yes, I missed you'.

55

Rachel sat in her kitchen surveying the detritus of breakfast. There were blobs of marmalade on the table, a coffee mug ring threatened where a mat should have been and a variety of plastic pots containing her vitamins and minerals mocked her feeble attempt to lead a healthy life. She got to her feet and tightened the belt of her blue dressing gown. She'd have to make a start.

An hour passed. She came in from the garden with a bunch of honesty in her hand. As with so many of the things she planted it was a throwback to her childhood. One of the rituals, at the end of summer, was the rubbing off of the papery skins of the seed heads so that the seed fell back down to the ground to grow next year, then bringing in the stems dripping with silvery, translucent coins and putting them in a vase.

On a whim she decided to go back out and get a bunch for Victoria. She didn't have any in her garden and it might cheer her up.

'Come on Bertie. Let's go and see your Auntie Victoria.'

Bertie was excited. There was usually a dish of cat food on the floor by the fridge as well as a real live cat to play chase with.

'Oh God, you've brought the dog. Keep hold of him while I pick up the cat's bowl. You look nice.'

'Thank you. Did you get any replies to the cat advert you put in the post office?'

'Not a single one. Unfortunately this cat's got a reputation round here.'

Rachel sat down at Victoria's kitchen table. There were no

cup rings or toast crumbs on this one, and it glowed with a coating of beeswax. Victoria looked harassed.

'I think the cat's got something under the table. I can't see what it is. Can you?'

She chased the cat out of the back door with a very loud voice. Rachel stifled a grin as it came straight back in through the cat flap. Victoria swore and blocked the cat flap.

'Hold onto Bertie's collar while I get a proper look'.

She shuddered. 'Ugh, it's not a dead bird, it looks like a frog or a toad. I'm not sure which.'

'I think it's a frog. Toads are browner.' Rachel was proud of her knowledge. It wasn't often Victoria admitted to ignorance.

'Whichever it is, I can't pick it up. It might hop off and I'm not chasing it round and round my kitchen.'

Was she to be saddled with this cat forever?

Rachel calmly dropped a tea towel over the motionless frog and captured it. She carried it out of the front door, away from where the cat was lurking, and deposited it on a flower bed.

'There you are. Job done. How fortunate I came round. Who'd have thought a small frog would reduce you to a quivering jelly.'

Victoria looked sulky. 'I like frogs, but not in my kitchen.'

She filled the kettle and Rachel went and stood in the doorway looking out onto the garden. Should she tell Victoria what Christopher had said about missing her? She'd written his little speech down in her diary. It was almost lyrical. And she never wanted to forget it.

No. Too personal. She turned.

'What a dreadful year this is turning out to be. It all started with Diana and Alistair, didn't it?'

'You can't blame them for the school failing,' reasoned Victoria. 'Coffee or tea?'

'Coffee please. What will you do if they have to close the school?'

'Well, I'd given up work, hadn't I, before all this started? I'd be happy to be able to do more with the boys, although

322

Nathan is talking about going away to board. He fancies Marlborough for the sixth form. James left plenty of money for their education. He's had enough of living in a village and I can't say I blame him. Luke doesn't want to go so I'll have more time for him. I'll find something to keep me busy.'

With the memory of the drugs debacle still fresh in her mind, she fervently hoped James wasn't looking down on her, seeing her struggle with his sons' lives.

Rachel raised her mug to her lips and pulled a face; her coffee had no sugar in it.

'Sorry, I forgot you still take sugar. You ought to have given it up by now. What about you and Christopher then? Is he still being negative?'

'He's lovely, most of the time. It's only when I hint in any way that a life together might be nice that he gets prickly. That's apparently what Claudia did. So I have to be careful.'

Victoria spooned a miniscule amount of sugar into Rachel's mug.

'Perhaps if you stopped seeing him, he might think twice about what he's got to lose.'

'No, that would just confirm to him that he's not a nice, normal man and deserves to be dumped.'

'Oh Rachel, did you have to fall in love with a head case?'

'The only thing I can do is carry on being Miss Sweetness and Light, and hope to wear him down. The trouble is I'm not sure how long I can keep it up. Sometimes his negativity is really depressing and I think, I don't need this. I'm off to find a happy man.'

'What he wants is friends with benefits.' Victoria nodded with that self -assurance Rachel found so irritating.

'What do you mean?' She hated having to ask.

'You must have come across the phrase before. It means friends with sex thrown in, but you're still free to see or sleep with other people because you're only friends not a couple.'

'That's horrible. I'm going. I need to give this poor dog a run. You've ruined my day saying that.'

As she marched Bertie down the lane Victoria's phrase resonated in her head. Is that what she was – a friend with benefits? Could she settle for that? If she were to compare Christopher with the unfortunates she'd met when internet dating, then the answer was yes.

It started to rain and the track was muddy. Soon, keeping herself upright became uppermost in her mind and anyone meeting her would have been hard pressed to distinguish the raindrops from the teardrops on her cheeks.

56

Alistair decided he should take the extra time to push his new choir a little harder.

He sat on the bench down by the village pond deep in thought, jiggling the pushchair with one hand, hoping that Grace wouldn't wake. It had been a sleepless night. He was spotted by Victoria.

'Do you mind if I join you?' She clucked and cooed over the sleeping baby.

'Don't wake her up.'

'Spoilsport.' She sat down beside him. 'Are you feeling grumpy?'

'No, I'm thinking about the way forward for the choir after the summer break. It's so easy to lose momentum and if I'm to ask a lot in terms of hard work and commitment, I need to make sure there is some payback for the singers. I've put out feelers and spoken to some of my contacts and I've come up with a proposition.'

'Sounds exciting. Are you going to tell me what it is?'

'No. You'll have to wait till Tuesday.'

He walked down to the church hall. It was raining and leaving his fireside had been a wrench. He knew, though, that once he stepped into the hall he would go into performance mode and all would be well. He stood before them, rocking back on his heels and eyeing them speculatively.

He was going to enjoy this. Challenging his choir to raise their game was one of the most rewarding things he did, not least because, so far, they had always risen to it.

'I'm going to shake you all up a bit. You've got too

comfortable. Complacency isn't allowed.'

A couple of people bridled at this. He ignored them.

'Put down your folders.'

He watched as some, for whom their folders were akin to a comfort blanket, did so with reluctance and that one or two rebels disobeyed.

'Right, we'll sing something you all should know without the music; The Eriskay Love Lilt.'

The tenors laughed nervously. A bass muttered under his breath, 'No chance.'

'You'll remember singing this beautiful song at our last concert, so it should be still relatively fresh in your minds. With your heads up and watching me, the sound will be infinitely better. Come on, think musical thoughts and I'll mouth the words, you read my lips.'

To everyone surprise, except Alistair's, it did indeed sound rather fine.

'You see! You underestimate yourselves. All the notes are there, just not necessarily in the right order. Of course the practice CDs will help. Don't worry. We won't sing without the music all the time, as apart from anything else, it would severely limit the number of songs we are able to get to concert standard. Now we'll have a tea break and when we restart I'll reveal my latest idea. I want to do something we've never done before.'

Ten minutes later, he put them out of their misery.

'I think we ought to make a CD. I've spoken to a chap in the business and he would come here on a Tuesday night and we should be able to put down twelve or so songs in the session. You'll be able to give me one as a leaving present at Christmas.'

He looked around. 'What do you think?'

It didn't really matter what they thought of course. This was something he felt they were ready to do and they were going to have to do it. But the buzz of excitement that ran round the room was comforting all the same.

57

Victoria lay awake in her bed. The darkness outside told her that dawn was still some way away. She tried to empty her mind of all its chatter but that was easier said than done. An hour later, she swung her legs over the edge of the bed and reached for her dressing gown. The birds were silent. She'd make some tea and take it back to bed.

Her thoughts turned to Keith. She'd had an email from him saying he and Isobel were coming back to the area to see his daughters. Perhaps she could have a supper party for them? It would be an opportunity for him to catch up with Alistair and Helen, Rachel and Christopher and she could ask Marcus, just to make up the numbers.

She didn't want to go down the road of cut glass and best silver, besides, her mother's damask tablecloth had long ago mildewed and been thrown out. A simple but wickedly delicious meal at the kitchen table, some good wine and sparkling conversation was what she had in mind.

But the doubts soon started to crowd in. No wonder she so rarely entertained like this. The potential for disaster was huge. Marcus might fall off the wagon and be offensive; the meal could be inedible; Christopher, still mourning his mother, might be depressed and miserable and Helen might insist on bringing the baby and breastfeeding it in front of everyone. It wasn't that she had any objections to breastfeeding, but that Helen invariably made such a performance of it. It seemed to Victoria she expected a medal for doing what, after all, should just come naturally.

She was gratified when her suggestion of a get together was met with enthusiasm from everyone. Marcus promised to be on his best behaviour and Keith said it would be the highlight of their stay back in the area.

Walking down the lane with Rachel and Bertie, Victoria confided her ideas for the menu.

'I wondered whether to do a Seventies style meal. You know the sort of thing - melon boats, fondue and Black Forest gateau, I'm sure I've still got that old fondue set somewhere.'

Rachel wrinkled up her nose.

'Sounds very calorific to me.'

She paused to pull the dog away from the rotting carcass of an unidentifiable mammal.

'Bertie, leave it alone. It smells disgusting. You know I had no idea dogs were such hard work, or so demanding. I'm forever jumping up and down to let him out or let him in, or removing slippers from his jaws. Yesterday he ate a freshly baked coconut cake I'd left out to cool. He's supposed to be company for me, not a damn nuisance.'

Victoria had had her doubts about Rachel's idea to give a home to an abandoned dog in the first place, especially a gaunt grey whippet, and had done her best to dissuade her friend. Having had dogs in the past, she knew only too well how they can scratch your doors, drive you mad by barking at every passing person and deposit turds all over the garden.

Rachel, however, had been adamant.

'I need to lose some weight and I feel stupid walking around on my own. With a dog I'm guaranteed two good walks a day and then I won't be ashamed to get undressed in front of Christopher.'

Victoria thought that giving up her weekend chocolate habit would probably do the job just as well, and be considerably less trouble. But once Rachel had made up her mind to do something, it would be done and hang the consequences.

'Anyway, back to our discussion....' Victoria knew some things were better left unsaid.

They had reached the bench by the far end of the village pond. It bore an inscription to an elderly resident, now deceased, stating; 'He loved this place.' Victoria didn't know why this phrase always irritated her, but she sat down gratefully enough on his bench. The usual ducks and moorhens were conspicuous by their absence. Perhaps they had all gone to Slimbridge for their winter holiday.

She continued, 'At least there are no vegetarians to bother about, thank goodness. Christopher isn't...?'

Rachel reassured her.

'No, no, he's a normal hearty eater. I couldn't be doing with a man who lived on nuts and seeds. Imagine, no delicious bacon sandwiches or juicy steaks allowed in the house.' She hesitated, then turned to face Victoria.

'Look, I have to say this, and I know you'll think this is sour grapes, but you are taking a risk inviting Marcus to your little 'do'.'

Victoria raised her eyebrows.

Rachel ploughed on. 'Don't pull that face at me. You're getting the best of Marcus now. I've told you this before. He's got this new relationship with you and it's different and stimulating for him. When we used to go to friends' houses for meals, all too often the evening ended with him drinking too much, engineering arguments and upsetting people. Eventually, of course, they stopped asking us. I'm just warning you. He's a man who will make anything bad, worse and if something is good then he'll spoil it.'

'Great. Thanks a lot. You've given me something more to worry about. It's too late for me to un-invite him now.'

'Sorry. Maybe it was just me. Perhaps he'll be different with you.'

'Perhaps.'

Victoria watched Rachel as she got up and wandered down to the edge of the pond. She should have known better then allow herself to become involved with Marcus. Having a man in her life after so long alone was tricky enough without him being, if Rachel was to be believed, something of a control freak.

Rachel came back. 'You know, thinking about it – he didn't

really like me very much in the end. The side of me that I claimed was the charming impetuosity of a free spirit, he saw as carelessness and an inability to commit completely to a task or project. He used to say I was slapdash.'

Victoria got to her feet. 'Alright, point taken, but ...'

Suddenly Bertie slipped his collar and set off after a cat. Victoria, grateful for the opportunity to stop discussing Marcus, joined her in pursuit of Bertie, who could out run both of them with ease, and treated it as a fun new game of chase.

Back in her kitchen, Victoria made a heap on the kitchen table of her assorted cookery books. Nigella, Delia and Hugh rubbed shoulders with Jamie and Elizabeth David. Purchased over the years, she'd enjoyed reading them but rarely used them. In the end she gave up leafing through and simply visualised what she would like to see on her plate were she to be invited out to eat with friends.

She considered Rachel's dire warning about Marcus then put it to the back of her mind. That was then. This is now.

She turned her attention to the next thing on her list of worries. The cobwebs, magically only visible when visitors came to the house, would have to be found and removed; the boys' dirty fingerprints, which adorned every door, wiped away and the bathroom must be rendered pristine. She sighed and looked around at her kitchen. It was messy enough to be comfortable, she felt, but not so messy you worried about hygiene. Her friends weren't the type of people to judge anyone on the depth of the dust on the dresser anyway. Victoria chuckled to herself as she looked at the faded chintz covers on the old sofa. She had been so rude to her mother both about her chintz and her love of bone china. It was true what they said, she had turned into her mother.

'And none the worse for that,' she said aloud as she got up, washed her coffee mug out and unloaded the washing machine.

She took the basket full of clean rugby kit down the garden

to peg out. It was cold but maybe the weak sunshine would do some good. By the time she'd hung out the washing; walked down the path to her brand new hen run; checked the nest boxes to see if there were any more eggs; filled up their drinking trough with water and paused to admire her Virginia creeper, reaching its reddening arms up the back wall of the cottage, she'd decided what she would cook.

She finished work at lunchtime on Fridays and a chicken casserole, slippery with minced onion, spinach and lemons was soon in the oven simmering away.

There was nothing to prepare for the dessert as she was just putting together her own favourite of crunchy meringues, piled high with crimson and purple berries from the garden and topped with cream.

By six o'clock she was standing with her back to the sink surveying her beamed kitchen with its quarry tiled floor, her assortment of pretty wine glasses and plates, most of them junk shop finds, and enjoying the delicious smells wafting out of the Aga. A Vivaldi concerto was playing in the background.

The preparation for an event was so often the most enjoyable part of the enterprise, whether it be as a teenager getting made up and dressed for a party, or as a more mature soul having a few friends round. She had consciously tried not to look forward to this evening because, in her experience, she often had the best times at things she'd hadn't wanted to go to. Looking forward to something with pleasurable anticipation so often doomed it to disappointment or even disaster.

Her reverie was interrupted by the jangling of the doorbell.

'Hello! Anyone in?'

Rachel and Christopher stood beaming on the door step, clutching a bottle and some expensive looking chocolates.

'Are we the first?'

Alistair and Helen followed closely behind, bearing a bottle of South African wine and a sleeping baby. Alistair whispered,

'Can I put her upstairs in a bedroom? She shouldn't wake up, honestly.'

Helen added, 'but if she does then I can just give her a quick feed and she'll go off again.'

Victoria managed a smile of happy compliance, but couldn't help hoping that neither the baby nor Helen's breasts would be putting in an appearance that night. She ushered them through into the kitchen which was unusually tidy – the heaps of papers and useful catalogues having been stuffed into a drawer. There were late roses on the table and on the dresser and they filled the room with their musky fragrance.

She was just wondering where Marcus, who had offered to be in charge of the drinks, was when he arrived, full of apologies.

'Sorry, sweetheart, I was held up by Mormons at the front door. I couldn't resist trying a bit of role reversal and try to convince them of the error of their ways. I was just beginning to get somewhere when I saw the time and had to make my apologies. Their loss – now they'll never find out how misguided they are.'

He put two bottles of wine on the table. One, Victoria noticed, was half empty. Following her glance, Marcus said hastily,

'Don't look like that. I had it left over after next door called round last night. He drank it, not me. I haven't touched it.'

Victoria said nothing.

Marcus made generous gin and tonics for everyone, except himself and Helen, who asked for fruit juice. He raised his eyes to the ceiling and said,

'Darling, the gin will go into your stomach not your tits.'

Helen giggled nervously and Victoria felt obliged to frown at him, but she knew she'd rather missed his crass sense of humour.

'I don't know where Keith and Isobel are. I'm sure I said six thirty because he specifically asked to eat early.' As she spoke, the doorbell rang and there they stood, bearing flowers.

'I hope we aren't late.' He spread his arms and hugged Victoria with enthusiasm.

'Victoria, lovely to see you. Something smells wonderful.

Hello everybody. Christopher, you look well. Have you settled in at school?'

Victoria wondered if she was the only one to see Christopher's hesitation before he replied, 'Fine, thanks Keith. The usual problems, the usual suspects,' and he attempted a laugh.

As Victoria served out the casserole, Rachel turned to Alistair beside her.

'Tell us about this new job in South Africa.'

Alistair, always happy to talk about himself, spoke about the school, one of the top private schools in Capetown.

'They've put together a package for us. Flights out there and a house to rent. It's close to the school so I don't have a long commute. I've heard the traffic there is even worse than London.'

'What about you, Helen?' Keith tried to involve her in the conversation. She sat with her head down studying her plate. 'Are you looking forward to having a nanny, a cook and a gardener and a life of leisure?'

'I...I don't know what to expect. It all seems to have happened very suddenly.' She looked at Alistair for rescue.

'We don't know yet. It could be the reality is very different now, Keith. We know the house will be in a gated community and there's been talk of help in the home, but it's up to us to say what we want when we get there and settle in.'

The atmosphere in the room was tense and a rumble of thunder came from outside. Victoria pressed on with serving up the main course.

'Sounds like there's a storm on the way. I hope you've all brought your umbrellas.'

To her consternation, Marcus had poured himself a glass of wine. There were certain trigger topics that would incite him to wade in, drunk or sober, and inwardly she prayed that no one would introduce them into the conversation. She might have guessed it would be Helen who would prove to be the innocent catalyst for his invective.

She was telling everyone that, in the latest overpriced,

pretentious coffee shop to open in South Heath, there was a poster proclaiming their breastfeeding charter, welcoming women to feed their babies whilst drinking their expensive cappuccinos.

'I wouldn't do it myself of course but it's real progress. We've got the divine Germaine to thank for it. Do you remember her? I was watching a programme about her standing up for women's rights against the dominance of the patriarchy.'

She looked around the table for support. 'She wrote this amazing book called The Female Eunuch, I found a copy in the charity shop. Has anyone read it?'

As the thunder crashed again, Victoria jumped up trying desperately to head off the conversation into less stormy waters.

'Marcus, could you open the French windows and let some fresh air in, while I get the dessert.'

But Marcus remained in his seat and fixed Helen with a gimlet eye.

'Are you really that stupid?' he demanded. 'Yes, I believe you are. Your Germaine Greer, with her loony, left wing pronouncements, was responsible for hundreds of thousands of marriage break ups because she persuaded silly women like you that they'd be better off without their husbands. I tell you, you won't find the South Africans having much truck with her nonsense.'

Keith and Isobel looked horrified. 'I say, old chap…' began Keith.

He was interrupted by Rachel, who, like Victoria, knew from experience that once on the subject of Germaine Greer, Marcus was unstoppable. She took drastic action and knocked over a glass of wine which spilt in Marcus' lap, and put a temporary halt to his peroration. Helen fled the room, looking upset, saying she needed to check on the baby.

Christopher attempted to introduce a topic about which, he was fairly sure, Marcus knew little and asked the others if they thought the school had changed since Keith's day. Victoria joined in with the reminiscences, while Alistair related anecdotes from Keith's rule at South Heath. Keith glowed and nodded as stories were told of his glory days.

Marcus leaned back in his chair, a smile of delight on his face. Rachel groaned inwardly. He would enjoy this one. Education was just as much a trigger as Germaine where Marcus was concerned.

'You bloody teachers are all the same. You only work thirty eight weeks of the year; you start at nine and finish at three - small wonder half the population can't read, write or spell. Your unions are full of left wing loonies, calling strikes willy-nilly and demanding more money for doing less and less.'

He paused for breath and Rachel, with the courage she would not have believed she possessed until now, and fuelled by the desire to protect Christopher, leaned forward.

'Sadly Marcus, like so many people, you think that having been to school once yourself, you have a unique insight into all matters educational and, despite the fact you haven't set foot in any educational establishment for many years, you believe you know all about how they are run nowadays. Well, let me tell you that you jolly well don't.'

She stopped, conscious that her voice was betraying her emotions.

Christopher said smoothly, 'I'd like to point out that I work in private education where things are not quite the same as they are in the state sector. But I still feel we should support all our teachers striving to do their best for our children.'

Victoria could see that he was furious. Was it because Rachel had been upset? Whatever the reason, she could see that he was determined to get the better of this argumentative man, especially in his own area of expertise. They parried back and forth and Christopher managed, with a supreme effort, to stay calm and polite, while Marcus, delighting in the cut and thrust of verbal aggression, goaded him remorselessly.

Rachel stood up. 'Can I help you with the dessert Victoria?'

She started to clear away the plates. Marcus sat back in his chair. His eyes resting on each one of them in turn. Victoria squirmed. This was a disaster. Should she ask Marcus to leave? She went to warm up the berries for dessert. Finish the meal, then they could all go. Helen re-joined them and gave Alistair an imploring look. He ignored her and revealed arrangements in hand for the choir to participate in the music festival coming up in Bath later in the year. There was a competition to find the best choir in the South West and to take part in a mass performance of Handel's Messiah in Longleat House at Christmas.

'Of course, at the time I planned to do all this, I had no idea I wouldn't be here, it'll be a real baptism of fire for my successor. We should be able to get the CD done though before I go.'

'I must say I'm surprised at you choosing to go to South Africa,' remarked Marcus, going round with the wine. Place is run by blacks now – if they don't like you they'll be getting the witch doctor in and then you'll be in trouble.'

Jaws dropped and a grinning Marcus took advantage of the silence to continue. 'Mind you, I've heard you've got plenty of blacks at your school already, so you'll be used to dealing with their criminal tendencies. Wasn't there a problem with drugs a while back? I'll bet your coloured friends were behind that.'

Nobody spoke. Victoria, wanting the whole evening to end right now, cried, 'Listen, is that the baby?'

Helen leapt to her feet and came back downstairs, a red-faced, wailing baby in her arms. 'Alistair, we really have to go.'

Victoria accepted everybody's thanks for her hospitality as they took the opportunity to leave. Rachel hugged her and whispered in her ear, 'Don't feel too bad. Even I didn't expect him to be quite so vile. The meal was lovely. I'll speak to you tomorrow.'

Shutting the door on the last of them, Victoria swore to herself that she never wanted to see Marcus again as long as she lived.

58

There was a knock on the door. 'Oh go away. I can't do two things at once.' Victoria scowled at the laptop. She had been struggling for half an hour to book train tickets before she had to leave for work. The knocking grew more insistent. She looked at her clock. It was only 8am but whoever it was clearly wasn't going to give up. She pushed the laptop aside and stamped to the door. It was Rachel's next door neighbour.

'I'm sorry to bother you Victoria, but is Rachel with you?'

'No, she isn't. Why?'

'It's just that Bertie has been barking and barking for the past two hours. It's been driving me mad. In the end I went round to complain but there was no answer.'

Victoria thought she was probably at Christopher's.

'Leave it with me. I'll see if I can track her down.'

Christopher was no help. 'She wouldn't be here on a school day. Have you tried her mobile?'

'Not yet. But don't worry. I've got a spare key. I'll pop round and take Bertie out. She might be having a lie-in.'

She reached for her coat. It wasn't like Rachel not to tell her if she was going away. And if she had, she wouldn't leave Bertie on his own. Victoria was quite used to having the dog for her when required.

There was no answer to her knocking, but Bertie flung himself against the door quite beside himself. Victoria put her key in the lock. 'Shut up, you stupid dog….. Oh God.'

Rachel lay on the hall floor, silent and still. Victoria knelt beside her. She was cold but breathing. Her hair was matted with blood. Bertie nuzzled her face and whimpered. Victoria elbowed him away. She draped a coat over the recumbent figure, shut the dog in the kitchen and pulled her phone out of her pocket.

'I need an ambulance, quickly.' Then she rang Christopher. He was there within minutes, his kind face creased with concern. He knelt on the floor and spoke softly to Rachel, then looked up at Victoria.

'How long do you think she's been here? It could have been all night. I take it you've already called an ambulance?'

'Of course I have. They're on their way.'

The neighbour appeared at the front door, peering anxiously past Victoria. She wrung her hands.

'Oh no, what's happened? I should have done something sooner.'

Victoria told her to go and make some tea. It felt like the right thing to do. Christopher stayed beside Rachel stroking her hair and talking quietly to her. Victoria paced up and down the hall. How did Rachel come to fall? Did she trip over the dog, have a funny turn or had she perhaps been drinking? Surely not. Hadn't she said something a few weeks ago about her blood pressure being very low? Someone hammered on the door.

'Here they are. Let them get past.'

Victoria gently pushed the neighbour aside and told the paramedics what little she knew. They worked swiftly, making checks. As they loaded Rachel into the ambulance, Victoria looked at Christopher. 'I'm going with her. What about you?'

'I'll call school to tell them I won't be in until later. I'll follow you in my car.'

Victoria chafed at the slowness of the journey. The rush hour traffic into Bristol was nose to tail and the ambulance struggled to weave in and out, despite the blaring siren and the flashing lights. She could just about reach Rachel's hand and she stroked and squeezed it intermittently, hating the feeling of helplessness. On arrival at A&E, Rachel was borne away and Victoria subsided onto a chair in the waiting area. She was soon joined by Christopher. 'Any news?'

'Not yet.'

He leaned forward and dropped his head into his hands. Victoria patted him awkwardly on the shoulder. 'I'm sure she'll be fine. She's as tough as old boots.'

She was surprised at what appeared to be genuine grief. It would seem his feelings for Rachel were deeper than she thought. An hour passed. She leafed through magazines. He kept getting up and going outside. She could see him through the windows pacing up and down.

A nurse came out and spoke to the person on reception. She pointed over to where they sat. They jumped to their feet.

She asked, 'Are you with Rachel Williamson?'

Victoria answered, 'Yes we are. How is she?'

'Are you her family?'

'No, there is no family. We're both close friends,' answered Victoria as she heard Christopher tut in impatience.

'Well, she's had a nasty knock on the head and is severely concussed. She's gone down for a scan to check for any bleeding on the brain. We may take her up to ICU if she doesn't regain full consciousness soon. It's a matter of waiting now. Have you any idea what happened?'

Victoria shook her head. 'No. We found her like that on the hall floor....'

Christopher interrupted, 'Can we see her?'

'No, not at the moment. Later, when she's back from the scan and we've stabilised her.'

The nurse turned away and left them standing there. Victoria sat down and pulled on Christopher's sleeve to sit beside her. He shrugged off her hand and strode back outside and resumed his pacing.

Half an hour passed. She went outside and said,

'Come on. We may as well go to the coffee shop. My treat.'

'No, I'd rather not. They might not be able to find us.'

'Oh Christopher, why don't you go back to school? I can stay here.'

'I don't think so. You go back yourself.'

'Well, there just seems to be no need for both of us to wait here. I can let you know as soon as there's any change. You're the Head. The school needs you more than it needs me. And, to be honest, I think Rachel would rather see me than you, when she comes round.'

As soon as she said that she knew it probably wasn't true.

He glowered at her. 'This is ridiculous – squabbling over who should go and who should stay. I'll find someone to speak to and see how she's doing.'

Victoria watched as he stopped a nurse. She went into the room where Rachel lay and came out almost immediately. He returned to Victoria and sat down.

'She said there's no knowing how long it will be before she recovers consciousness, and it's unlikely they'll allow us to see her for quite a while. She suggested I go, and ring up at lunchtime.'

'Perhaps we should both go. We're no use to anyone here. Keeping busy will make the time pass more quickly. We can be back quickly enough when she comes round.'

'OK. Let me just make sure they've got my number.' He fumbled for his phone with a shaking hand and pushed his hair back with the other. He looked up at Victoria with frightened eyes.

'Victoria, do you really think she's going to be alright? She looked so fragile lying there.'

'She'll be thrilled to hear you said that. She's always wanted to look fragile.'

He managed a smile. 'Come on. Let's go and find your car.'

Victoria had only been back at her desk for an hour when she saw Christopher striding past and out of school. She knew where he was going. She allowed herself a small smile. What was it they said about unintended consequences?

He rang her when she got home from work and told her Rachel was conscious and comfortable. She could come in at visiting time for a few minutes.

Later that evening, she sat down by Rachel's bed. There were flowers in a vase on the side table, a glossy magazine and a large bunch of grapes in a bag resting on the bed.

Christopher followed Victoria's gaze. 'I know it's all a bit naff but it's all I could think of in a rush.'

Victoria proffered her tub of brownies.

'I hope they'll allow you to eat these. They're still warm.'

Rachel shifted in her bed and winced. 'No thanks. Later perhaps. They're saying I'll have to stay in a couple of days for a few tests and then I should be able to come home, as long as there's someone there to keep an eye on me.'

Victoria reached for a grape. 'Don't worry about that. If the past twenty four hours is anything to go by, we'll be fighting over you. Have they any idea why you passed out?'

'Not really. I probably just fell over the dog and hit my head. My blood pressure is a bit low so I might have had a dizzy spell. They're going to monitor it. Stop eating my grapes – both of you.

59

'You look done in. Let's go out to lunch. My treat.' Rachel was back to her old self, although very conscious of the bald patch on her head where several stitches had been put in. She had put on her old straw sun hat, the one that Victoria had told her made her look like Worzel Gummidge, to cover the damage.

She'd seen how hard Christopher was working, once the announcement that South Heath was to close at Christmas had finally been made. He was dealing with the press, helping parents find places for their children in other schools, and providing generous references for the many staff who would be having to apply for other jobs.

'Lunch would be lovely. Where shall we go?'

'Relax. It's a surprise. I'll tell you where to drive.'

She directed him to a village near Bath where the pub looked out over the river. They sat in armchairs by the fire and waited for their table. Rachel inspected her fingernails which as always when she was on edge, were bitten down to the quick. She folded her arms to hide them. 'Have you much more still to do?'

He stretched out his legs and inspected his perfectly polished shoes.

'I've still got to do a press release. Thank goodness the letters to pupils' families have gone off already. I've been warned to expect reporters and TV crews from the local news programme to descend in the next few days. No doubt they'll be milking the situation for all its worth.'

Although she could see he was pale and drawn from stress and long hours, she sensed an excitement, and a hope that over the horizon was a new life that he couldn't wait to begin.

'It'll feel like an anti-climax after all the consultations, the petitions, the meetings and the airing of arguments for and against. The end of my career.'

He sat up and beamed at her. 'But the beginning of the rest of my life. How exciting is that?'

He bent over his venison sausages. Stress hadn't had any effect on his appetite she thought as she picked at her ploughman's, grateful it was on a plate, and not a slice of tree.

'I thought I might invite people from the village to the final assembly at the school. So many of them have been involved with the school in one way or another over the years. What do you think?'

'I think that's a lovely idea. Can I come?'

'Of course. I've asked Keith and Isobel too.'

When they got back to South Heath, he thanked her and said, 'Here's hoping for many more lunches like this.'

That wasn't a statement from someone planning to ride off into the sunset alone, was it? Rachel took heart.

She sat at the back of the hall as he led the final assembly on the last day of term. There was a gratifying number of past pupils paying their respects and local dignitaries made speeches recalling the school's successes and bemoaning the financial climate, which they felt had wrecked its future.

Christopher was pale but perfectly composed and her heart went out to him. It was all a far cry from when he first came to South Heath to take up the Headship, not so very long ago.

After singing for the last time the traditional 'Lord, Dismiss us with thy blessing,' everyone filed out of the hall. She watched Christopher bidding goodbye to the various luminaries and then turning to speak to a group of his pupils gathered round him. Finally they were alone standing in the entrance hall looking at the board which listed all the past Heads.

'Right. Thank God that's all over. Come into my office. I have something for you.' He reached into his desk drawer and handed her a small package in a dark blue velvet bag.

What was this this little pantomime about? Was he planning on moving out of the village sooner rather than later and this was by way of a leaving present. She turned it over and over in her hand. He gestured impatiently.

'Just open it.'

Inside the bag she found a small box and, inside that, a ring. It was an emerald surrounded by tiny diamonds, which she recognised had belonged to Eleanor. As she gasped and looked at him in hope and disbelief, he knelt on one knee and said 'Rachel, will you do me the honour of becoming my wife?' A wave of joy and relief crashed over her.

'Are you sure?'

Then, in a rush, before he could answer, she said, 'Yes, of course. Oh yes.'

He took her in his arms. Over his shoulder, she saw the caretaker, passing the open office door pushing a hoover. He swiftly reversed before the Headmaster spotted him and Rachel suppressed a giggle.

That night though, lying next to him, she had to ask. 'What's changed? Ever since I've known you, you've been adamantly against love and marriage. You've never once said I love you. Is this really happening?'

'Rachel, I love you. Now go to sleep.' He slipped his arm underneath her and pulled her closer.

'How can I sleep? You've made me so unhappy with your pronouncements in the past. I really believed you.'

She sat up in the bed. 'I'm scared. You might change your mind.'

He sighed. 'Rachel, if you know me at all, you will know I don't say these things without a lot of thought. While I was away, despite the worry about the school, you were uppermost in my mind – almost all the time.'

His fingers traced her cheek and his voice was thick with emotion. 'And then when I saw you lying in that hospital bed, I was frightened. I tried to imagine my life without you. I realised then that I loved you and wanted to take care of you.'

He put his arms around her and pulled her head down onto

his chest. 'It's taken me so long because I've never felt like this about someone before. I thought these feelings were the prerogative of the young. You mustn't be cross with me for failing to realise that it doesn't matter how old you are, you can still fall in love.'

He dropped a kiss on the top of her head, and continued.

'You have mellowed me and I've lost myself with you. You are the dearest woman I have ever met. Somehow you manage both to soothe me and energise me. I honestly never expected to feel like this again. I've already lost the two women I loved in my life. I'm damned if I'm going to lose you as well. And, most of all, I want to make you happy.'

He kissed the top of her head.

'Now, speech over. Can I please go to sleep?'

Smiling, 'Yes, my love.' She turned onto her side and nestled her head into the crook of his shoulder, encircling his waist with her arm. His breathing soon settled into the rhythm and peacefulness of sleep, but she lay awake long into the night, hearing his honeyed words over and over again.

In the morning she rang Victoria but there was no answer, so she apologised to Bertie for having left him alone all night and took him up for a long walk on the hills. Once up there she spotted Victoria in the distance and rushed to catch up with her.

'Good morning. Isn't it a beautiful day? I've been trying to ring you.' She bent down with her hands on her knees to catch her breath. Victoria looked at her curiously when she straightened up. 'You look like the cat that got the cream. Spill the beans.'

Rachel unfurled her left hand under Victoria's nose with the sparkling emerald on her ring finger.

Victoria cried out with delight. She flung her arms round Rachel and hugged her close.

'Oh Rachel. That's wonderful. I'm so happy for you.'

'I did, of course, say yes.'

'I should think so too. Come on, let's make for home. I want all the details. Start at the very beginning.'

The news rapidly spread around South Heath. Helen suggested Grace could be a flower girl, an offer which was politely declined. Rachel already knew what sort of wedding she wanted and it didn't include bridesmaids.

Alistair offered the services of the choir for the ceremony, on behalf of whoever replaced him.

The local paper said, 'Head of Failed School to Wed.'

Alistair's choir had no intention of letting him go without marking the occasion. He tried hard to convince Victoria that, with the school closing down, a celebration would hardly be appropriate.

'I hate speeches and presentations – all that insincerity. Spare me that, please. Tell them I don't want any fuss.'

Victoria sought out Rachel to see what she thought.

'It's hard to say. Maybe we could all do with a jolly. It's been a difficult few months. Perhaps, in spite of all the disturbing things that have happened, it would help us to remember that without Alistair the choir, as it is now, would not exist. We've all had such fun. Remember Bruges, the concerts and all the wonderful songs we've learnt. Things happen and people move on. That's life. We owe a lot to Alistair.'

'You're right. It's not up to him. It's for us.' Victoria agreed and started a list.

One of Alistair's last acts before his departure was to call up an old friend who led a small elderly singing group in Bristol.

'You need a fresh challenge, Simon. Come and listen to my lot, I'll introduce you to a few people and you can see what you think. I don't want to leave them without a conductor and it'll take the committee months to find a replacement. You'll easily be able to run it alongside your old ladies.'

Simon objected, 'I'm not sure. My schedule's pretty full and from what I've heard of South Heath, it might not be the right place for me. And for your information, my 'old ladies' have just won Best Small Choir in the South West.'

'Congratulations. Just think what you could do with a big choir! Listen. Initially, I'd suggest that you just came as a stand- in to tide them over, as the committee are sure to want to advertise and interview. They do like to do things properly. If you don't like it you can gracefully bow out at that point.'

'I'll think about it. How's Helen? I heard you'd had a baby.'

The party was in full swing. The chairman's house was packed and, in the drawing room, someone was playing songs from the choir's repertoire on the grand piano. Everyone had eaten well and some had drunk too much. Victoria, noticing the tall, swarthy stranger standing at the bar with his back turned to them, whispered in Helen's ear,

'Who's the hunk over there? The one who's just come in.'

'Hunk? That would make him laugh. I always used to call him Woolly Bear, 'cos that's what he always reminded me of. He's a friend of Alistair's. He's a lovely man. I think he's divorced but he might have been snapped up again by now. Alistair's asked him to take on the choir. They'll announce it tonight. He's come to have a chat with the committee. His name is Simon.'

'You must introduce me.'

Fortified by an overlarge glass of wine, Helen wove a path across the room, followed by Victoria, and putting her hand on Simon's arm to steady herself, she said,

'Simon, good to see you again.'

He swivelled round, his face lighting up when he saw Helen. He kissed her enthusiastically on both cheeks.

'Helen! Hello - as lovely as ever.'

She giggled.

'The same old charmer. Can I introduce my friend Victoria? She'll be one of your more stalwart sopranos.'

Simon turned to Victoria. She gasped. She recognised him instantly. How long had it been?

They looked at each other. He swallowed hard, but spoke first.

'Victoria. This is a surprise.'

She didn't know what to do. Her instinct was to hug him, but would he want that?

Stay calm. Just smile.

'Simon, I can't believe it's you. You've hardly changed.'

He ran a hand through his hair. 'Rather less of this than there used to be I'm afraid.'

Helen looked from one to another. 'I take it you have met already?'

'We have, but more years ago than I care to remember.'

Simon turned his back on Helen, 'Excuse us please.' He took Victoria's arm and guided her to a table.

'I expect you're married now.'

'I was, but Robin died twelve years ago.' She felt warm and knew her cheeks were going pink.

'Oh, I'm sorry.'

'That's OK. What about you?'

'I was, but she left me.' He put his glass of beer down.

'Let me get you a drink. We've got some catching up to do. Is it still white wine?'

'Red please.'

Her eyes followed him as he crossed the room. So much water under the bridge. They'd both been too young. How was she going to play this? The twinkle in his eye was still there. Wishing she'd eaten fewer chocolates over the years, she watched him flirting with the barmaid. She wiped the silly grin off her face and replaced it with an expression, she hoped, of pleasant, interested friendliness.

Simon carefully put down the glass of wine and eased his length onto a chair.

'Cheers Victoria.' He raised his glass. 'How did you find your way to South Heath?'

Where should she start? The memory of that wet night in the bus station, thirty years ago flashed before her. There was a lump in her throat.

'Has anyone seen Victoria?' Alistair's voice rang out. He sounded exasperated. She jumped to her feet, grateful for a momentary diversion.

'I'm over here.'

'I need you for a minute.'

'Will you excuse me Simon? I'll be right back.'

He nodded and she made her way to where Alistair stood scowling.

She sorted him out and turned back towards the table where she'd left Simon. He wasn't there. She scanned the room.

Simon wasn't prepared to sit around waiting. He'd done enough of that in the past. He'd learnt a few things about women in the last thirty years, one of which was not to appear too keen. Besides, he needed some time to allow his heart to stop pounding. Time to think about what he wanted for the future. He thought he knew, but he'd been wrong before.

Lucy leaving him, for a banker with a manor house in Surrey had shaken his faith in women and in himself. He'd felt such a fool.

He picked up his glass and walked across to Helen, who was examining her mobile. Perhaps she could fill him in on a few facts.

'I must say you're looking splendid tonight. I bet you're really excited about your move.'

'I suppose so. It all seems to have happened very quickly. Excuse me.'

Simon caught her arm as she went to move away through the crowd.

'You aren't going home, are you?'

She gave him a wan smile and said, 'Yes, I have a teething baby shrieking the house down and an unwilling babysitter. She's just texted me. I need to get my coat and I'll be off.'

He was waiting for her in the hall. An aggressive looking stag's head glared at him from high up on the wall.

'Please let me see you home. If I remember rightly, it's not far away is it? I could do with some fresh air.'

Ignoring her protestations, he walked beside her, tucking her arm in his, aware of her unsteadiness.

Helen found his bulk reassuring. There was ice on the puddles shining in the light from the street lamp.

'I hear the choir's all yours now then. Do you have any plans?'

'Oh yes, lots.' He was smiling.

'Alistair was always having plans. What are you thinking of doing?'

'Well, with all due respect to your husband, I think he might have lost something when he re-formed the choir and introduced auditions. We've been discussing it. I used to come to those early concerts and there was a vitality and an enthusiasm that over-rode the lack of expertise. I would want to recapture that.'

'What, the lack of expertise?'

'Very funny. No, my ideas, and I'm still very much thinking them through, will involve ditching the auditions altogether, ditto those depressing black dresses and trying for a more informal, less precious vibe.'

They reached her gate. He stopped and thrust his hands in his pockets. He looked up and down the deserted village street and hesitated.

'OK. I'll let you into my secret, Helen. I don't want this getting around until Alistair has gone, but I want to make quite a few changes actually. We'll bring the fun and enthusiasm back into performing. We'll wear whatever we like and we might even dance and clap and wave our arms in the air! I've already got a choir I drill mercilessly, aiming at excellence. This one's going to be like a breath of fresh air. What do you think? How will that go down?'

He looked at her with raised eyebrows, his earnestness almost comical. As if she really cared about the damn choir.

'I've no idea, but I expect a lot of folk will be delighted. I know some people hate wearing black. Not so sure about the dancing though.'

'Well, it's only a temporary appointment. If they don't like me they can look for another conductor.'

She opened her gate. He stopped her, his hand on her arm.

351

'Hang on a minute Helen. Tell me a bit about your friend, Victoria.'

'Is that why you walked me home?'

'No, not at all, but it's shaken me a bit, bumping into her again like that, and I could do with getting a few things clear.'

'Such as?'

'She said her husband had died. Is she still on her own? I don't want to step on any toes.'

Helen studied his face. Why was he in such a hurry? He'd always been so laid back and relaxed. Now he seemed positively intense, his eyes fixed on hers, waiting for her answer.

She chose her words carefully. 'She lives alone, but she gets quite involved with other people's lives. I wouldn't have thought she was actively looking for someone. She was very fond of Robin.'

It was clear to him that she was reluctant to say any more, and he wondered why not. While there wasn't actual dislike in her voice, neither was there any warmth.

Still, the coast was clear then. It was up to him. That's all he needed to know. He smiled at her.

'Look, I'd better get back. It's been nice talking to you, Helen. Enjoy South Africa and keep in touch, won't you.'

Helen swallowed hard. 'I will.'

She let herself back into the house and paid the babysitter. Fancy Simon and Victoria knowing each other. They should get on well together. She needed a new friend after that awful Marcus. Helen had been hurt by the rumours of Victoria's support for Diana – and had done her best to ignore them. She had needed her female friends over this past year and had tried to understand how difficult it could be for those with split loyalties.

Back at the party, Alistair took Simon's arm.

'There you are. I've been looking all over for you.' He raised his voice above the hubbub.

'Listen everyone.' He waited for silence. 'I'd like to introduce you all to an old friend of mine – Simon. He's an accomplished musician and conductor and has agreed to take on the choir for a six month trial period. I know you'll make him welcome and, I can promise you, he'll be every bit as hard on you as I have been.' There was an ironic cheer from someone.

He turned to Simon, 'Do you want to say a few words?'

Simon shook his head. 'No, this is your night. I'll see you all in the New Year to start work on the wedding songs. We'll get to know each other then.'

He avoided the well-wishers and slipped away. He was being a coward, but seeing Victoria again had unsettled him. He needed time to think.

The village was quiet as he walked back to find his car. When he turned the corner into Church Lane he almost bumped into someone standing, her head uplifted, looking up into the night sky.

'Oops, sorry.'

Victoria looked embarrassed. 'No, it's my fault. I stopped to look at the stars.'

'I don't blame you. They are pretty spectacular tonight. It would seem we both had the same idea.'

'You mean we're both running away.'

There was a silence. What could he say? There was still something about her that attracted him. Hard to put a finger on it. Possibly her air of amused detachment? She had kept that aura of bohemian artistry which set her apart from the other women - some of whom could be said to be trying too hard, and others who didn't seem to be trying at all.

He said, 'Let me walk you home. It's the least I can do. It wouldn't do for you to be set upon by vagabonds.'

'I think that's exceedingly unlikely, but thank you.'

She took his arm when they came across a particularly pot-holed section of the lane and, when they got to her front door, she asked if he would like to come in.

'I could make us a coffee. Or you could have something stronger?' He hesitated. There was a conversation to be had. Surely tonight was as good as any?

'Both, please.'

She poured him a small glass of her best cognac, and while the coffee brewed they sipped reflectively.

'You broke my heart, you know, not coming to London with me.' His eyes were sad.

She held his gaze.

'I broke my own heart too Simon. It was a mistake. It wasn't the last one I made, far from it, but it's something I've always regretted.'

'I never believed your story, you know.'

Victoria shook her head sadly. 'It was all true. I just lost my nerve. My mother insisted that all young men were fickle and faithless, and that I would find myself alone and abandoned in the capital – and, quite probably, pregnant. She said that you obviously had no intention of marrying me, and that I mustn't ever think I could come running back to them when it all fell apart, because they would wash their hands of me.'

'Why didn't you answer my letters?'

'I never got any letters.' She stared at him. 'God in Heaven, did she intercept them?'

'I only wrote a couple.' He drained his glass.

Victoria admitted, 'I cried myself to sleep every night for weeks. I loved you so much. You have no idea how much I hated her for what she did. And how much I hated myself for giving in to her. Things were never the same between us after that. She tried the same trick when I met Robin, but it was never going to work a second time.'

He reached across and took both her hands in his.

'I don't know why I didn't try harder to make you change your mind. I suppose it was a combination of settling into my first job and the promise of a new life. I was young and didn't know how hard it was to find a real soul mate. I hardened my heart and accustomed myself to life without you.'

His face softened as he looked at her.

'But I've never forgotten you. Now, I must go. If I drink any more I shall forget how to be a gentleman and I won't be able to drive home afterwards.'

'After what?'

She looked back at him, both aware of the challenge in her eyes.

He swallowed hard. 'No, not tonight.' He leaned forward and kissed her chastely on both cheeks.

'We've got plenty of time to get to know each other again.'

She stood in her doorway and watched him walk away. She offered up a silent prayer. He was a good man, or used to be, and she knew she'd treated him badly. It was a hopeful sign that he didn't appear to carry a grudge. She locked the door and turned towards the stairs. Her head was throbbing and her feet hurt. It would all be clearer in the morning. Damn, she hadn't thought to give him her number.

Still at the party, Alistair shifted uncomfortably from foot to foot, aware that Helen should have been at his side while the Chairman payed tribute to his hard work and creative musicianship over the past few years and presented him with an expensive set of suitcases for their journey and a large, framed photograph of the choir.

Does he really think that was going to South Africa with him? God, this whole thing is ghastly.

He loosened his tie. He'd make this snappy. For once he didn't want to be the centre of attention. Diana was never far from his thoughts and the sentimental bonhomie of the send-off, the happy little family flying off to their new life, grated horribly. He tried to smile.

'I'm sorry Helen has had to go home, a teething baby demanded her presence. The suitcases are the perfect replacement for our current shabby luggage - thank you so much. We have seen the emergence of this choir from a keen but inexperienced group of singers to what we have today, which is, indisputably, a wonderful choir with an extensive repertoire, and one which has entertained the local community for the past five years. I have enjoyed it all enormously and I'm sure that with Simon leading you, the choir will go on to greater things. We will both miss you all.

Do please keep in touch.'

He sat down to loud applause and cheers, while Rachel looked at Christopher with her eyebrows raised and whispered, 'I've heard more impressive farewell speeches, haven't you?'

The pianist started to play favourite songs from their concerts and everyone joined in. Alistair, for once happy for the spotlight to move away from him, left the assembled throng to reprise their greatest hits until well past midnight.

61

Rachel confided to Christopher, 'I'd like a spring wedding so I can have lots of daffodils.'

He looked at her fondly. 'I'm happy with that. I've still a mountain of work to do and I said I'd help with the final arrangements for the clearing of the school and the disposal of the contents.

'Is that in your job description?'

'Not really. But I've offered to lend a hand.' He had to keep busy to stave off the sense of failure.

Rachel said, 'I feel sorry for the all the ancillary staff. I bet the teachers will find new jobs more easily than they will.'

'Well, we've managed to secure a promise from the boss of the leisure company that bought the buildings that he will prioritise appointing local people. There should be more jobs going there than there ever were when it was a school.'

Victoria and Rachel were helping Christopher finally bag up his mother's clothes and fill boxes with books and ornaments he didn't want to keep and were destined for the charity shop. It was a job he'd put off for months, feeling unable to face it until now.

'Have you thought about what sort of wedding you want?' Victoria tied a knot in another black bag.

Rachel waited until Christopher left the room, with several armfuls to put in the boot of the car.

'At first,' she confided,' I wanted the works. You know, bridesmaids, ushers, wall to wall flowers, big reception, even a marquee perhaps. But these last few months, I've gone completely in the opposite direction.'

'What do you mean, 'this last few months'? He only proposed a few weeks ago.'

Had she been the blushing type, Rachel would have been as red as a beetroot.

'I have to confess, I've fantasised about marrying Christopher almost since I first met him. Obviously, I never expected anything to come of it, but I've actually been planning this wedding for months.'

'What's so funny?' enquired Christopher, returning suddenly. The two women looked at him with laughing eyes and shook their heads. When he had reloaded and driven off, promising to return in an hour or so, Rachel continued.

'Now I just want it to be very small and understated - no conspicuous extravagance at all. Just the two of us, a few close friends and lots of daffodils. He would like it to be in the parish church and that's fine by me.' Victoria put on a face of mock disappointment, 'What no meringue and tiara?'

'No,' said Rachel firmly.

'And aren't you going to ask me to be matron of honour, Grace an adorable bridesmaid and have Luke and Nathan as ushers?'

'Sorry, no. This will be a minimalist wedding.' She peered at Victoria's face trying to read what her genuine feeling was behind the teasing.

'Do you think I'll regret it?'

'Absolutely not. The simpler the better as far as I'm concerned.' Victoria had no doubts and added, 'When I go to one of those 'over the top' weddings, I spend my time wondering if the length of the marriage is directly proportionate to the amount of money they've spent.'

Rachel ripped another black bag off the roll. 'I hope we've got enough of these. What's that face for?'

'I was just thinking you are one of those women who have a very sweet manner but underneath are absolutely determined to have your own way every time.'

Rachel looked at her astonished. 'What a horrible thing to say.'

'No, not at all. It's a jolly good way to be if you think about it. It won you the lovely Christopher didn't it?'

Rachel scowled. She was going to have to think about this one. Sometimes she never knew quite what Victoria was getting at and whether she should be insulted or pleased.

They continued sorting the clothing into three piles; charity shop, recycling and rubbish.

Suddenly Victoria had a sneezing fit.

'God, these clothes are so dusty.' She wiped her streaming eyes. 'I need a break. I'm going to have to go outside for a bit.'

'OK. You walk round the garden and I'll make us some tea. We'll have it in here though. It's too cold to sit out there.'

Once they were settled with mugs of Eleanor's finest Darjeeling, Rachel dared to raise the topic that had been on her mind all day.

'I've heard on the grapevine that a certain new choirmaster was seen visiting you at the weekend.'

Victoria tried to look cross, but the smile that was on her face fought her frown and won.

'Oh, he only wanted some background on the choir, the sort of things we sang, how long we'd been going and so on.'

'Really?'

'Yes. Really.'

'Oh come on Victoria. That won't wash with me.'

Victoria dunked her biscuit. 'Well, I'm sorry about that. That's all you're getting.'

'That's so unfair. I tell you everything. Well almost everything.'

Victoria shrugged. 'Who said life was fair?'

She picked up the mugs and went back into the kitchen. Her embryonic relationship with Simon felt very special, but she wasn't ready to share it, even with Rachel.

The two returned to the bedroom.

'It's clear Eleanor never threw anything out,' commented Rachel in despair, when Victoria suddenly exclaimed,

'Oh, Rachel, just come here and look at this?'

She had pulled out a dress from Eleanor's wardrobe.

Smelling faintly of mothballs, it was an exquisite gown of oyster satin, embroidered in the same colour with swirls of orchids. Tiny pearls dotted the bodice and ran down the sleeves which came to a point at the wrist. The label said 'Christian Dior, Paris.'

'Wow.' Rachel touched it gently, feeling the rich slipperiness of the folds under her hand.

Victoria slipped it off the hanger and held it against her.

'Couldn't you wear this on your wedding day? The colour is much more flattering than white. Vintage is very fashionable now. What do you think?'

'I don't know if it'll fit me. It looks tiny – something I've never been, even in my wildest dreams.'

'Try it on now. I'll watch out in case Christopher comes back.' Rachel divested herself of her jeans and woolly jumper and slipped into another era.

'Oh, it's no good. Look how tight it is across my bust.'

'They didn't have busts in those days. Let me look. Maybe some cunning corsetry would help? Look how beautifully it hangs and swirls out at the bottom. It really is gorgeous.'

Rachel was despairing. 'It'll take more than cunning corsetry to conceal my assets.'

'OK. Let's think again. I know someone who used to be a dressmaker. I wonder if she could let it out discreetly. I'll give her a ring and see if we can go and see her next week.'

Rachel shook her head despondently. 'It's out of my league. I was going to look in M&S for something sensible that I'll be able to wear again.'

'For heaven's sake, stop being so negative. Think how thrilled Eleanor would have been. I wonder if she wore it for her own wedding.' Victoria folded up the silk gown and found a carrier bag for it. She burst out laughing.

'What?'

'I'm putting a Dior creation in a Tesco carrier bag. How bizarre is that?'

Rachel looked thoughtful. 'I bet there's a wedding photo somewhere amongst Eleanor's things. I'll have a look when

Christopher is safely out of the way.'

The little old woman with long skinny fingers and black button eyes, reverently laid the dress out on her dining room table and inspected it closely.

'It's a long time since I saw something like this.'

Victoria explained how they had found it and how they had wondered if it could be adapted to fit Rachel's curves for her wedding day. The old lady sucked her teeth in time honoured fashion and shook her head.

'I don't know about that. Let's take some measurements. These couture gowns didn't skimp on the seams so there's more available fabric than you'd think. My eyes aren't what they were, but come back at the end of the month. I won't make any promises.'

Three weeks later, Rachel was summoned for a fitting. Those weeks of no cake, no biscuits and zero carbs had had an effect. The dress was perfect. Speechless, but with the widest of smiles on her face, she rotated slowly in front of the full length mirror.

'Keep it on while I find you something to keep your shoulders warm.' The old lady hobbled out of the room and returned with a cape of white fur. It had clearly seen better days but still retained an air of elegance and chic.

'I believe this is not politically correct nowadays. Don't be afraid to say if it offends you.'

Draping the fur around her Rachel gulped. She felt utterly transformed and almost tearful. 'You are an absolute miracle worker. Did I tell you we found out the last owner, the mother of my husband-to be, wore it to her own wedding?'

'She must have had a bob or two then,' said the old lady. 'Times were hard then - in the years after the war.'

Victoria turned away, dabbing at her eyes with a tissue.

'Sorry, I really wasn't expecting this to be all so emotional.' They drove home in almost complete silence. Each deep in her own thoughts.

62

Victoria struggled up the path laden with bags of shopping. Her neighbour was waiting for her. Why did he always look so miserable?

'Hello, Brian. What's with the long face?'

'I've got some bad news,' he pronounced with lugubrious relish.

Her stomach dipped. 'Not the boys?'

'No, no. I'm afraid it's your little cat. I found her body at the side of the road, not long after you went out. She's dead. Someone must have run her over.'

'Oh dear. Where is she now?'

'I wrapped her in a towel and left her by your back door. I thought you might want to bury her.'

'Thank you. I'll go and see to her now. I'll see you get your towel back.'

Victoria first checked that the cat was indeed dead, then she tipped the body into the wheelie bin and rejoiced. She rejoiced for all the birds who would escape a gruesome death. She rejoiced for the frogs and toads and mice who would be able to enjoy her garden in safety. She didn't share her delight with anyone. Not one of them would understand. Her pretence at grief when Nathan and Luke came home was entirely convincing.

The next day she sat nibbling nervously on her fingernails, waiting for the post. The letter box rattled. At last. She was hoping for word that Nathan had got a place in the 6th form at Marlborough. Impatiently she sorted through the leaflets offering cheap printer ink and window blinds. Among them was a white envelope. Ripping it open she heaved a sigh of relief. Thank goodness. About time something went to plan. She shouted up the stairs. 'Nathan, the letter from Marlborough has come.' If that didn't get him out of bed, nothing would.

She made a celebratory lunch in his honour. After they'd eaten, a delighted Nathan went upstairs to share his news with his online friends. Luke sat by the fire with Victoria.

'You're very quiet Luke. Are you worried you're going to miss him? You'll see him at weekends you know.'

'No, it's not that.'

'What is it then?'

She saw him swallow hard. His words came out in a rush.

'You won't send me away too will you? I want to stay here. I'm happy with you.'

She held out her arms. 'Come and sit by me.' He came over to her on the sofa. He looked vulnerable and younger than his thirteen years.

'It's like it's happening again. First my Mum, then my Dad, and now Nathan is going. Everyone leaves me.'

Her first instinct was to make light of his distress and tell him she intended to train him to push her around in her bath chair and spoon gruel into her toothless mouth, but decided that he needed right now was strength and reassurance. The jokes could come later. Stroking his back, she could feel the knobbly bones of his spine. He smelt of biscuits.

'Do you remember me once telling you that there was a home here for you both, as long as you needed it? That will never, ever change. One day you will want to move on, I can guarantee it, but until then we'll muddle along together. OK?'

'Thank you...and Victoria....you know how sometimes I call you Mum by mistake?'

She tousled his hair, anticipating his question. 'Shall we make it official?'

He jumped up. 'Yes, we'll do that. Can I have a yoghurt?'

It was an oddly low key Christmas. Lives were being wound

up, Alistair and Helen were deep in boxes, crates and constant arguments. The closure of the school and his sense of failure haunted Christopher. The wedding plans occupied Victoria and Rachel, as did the celebration of Grace's first Christmas. But even that paled for Victoria when she thought of Diana and little Theo.

They all went through the motions. The Christmas concert was downgraded to an evening of carols and mulled wine held outside round the village Christmas tree. Simon arranged for the town band to join them. It was such a success that Simon told Victoria they should make it an annual event.

'You can't have too much of this sort of thing at Christmas time.'

63

Victoria offered to drive Alistair, Helen and the baby to Heathrow. It was what a friend would do. Who would have expected it all to end like this? She'd done her best. From now on she'd keep her nose out of other people's business.

Helen sabotaged her planned early start, pleading a stomach upset and Alistair added to her irritation by forgetting to install Grace's car seat in Victoria's car the night before.

Her mood improved when a small group of villagers was spotted outside the shop waving goodbye and shouting good luck as she drove out of South Heath towards the motorway.

'Isn't that nice,' she said glancing over her shoulder at Helen. 'You wouldn't get a send-off like that in the city.' Helen nodded.

As she sped along the M4, she could sense Alistair, beside her, electric with barely suppressed excitement, but all the while in her rear view mirror, there was Helen, white and trembling, her upper lip beaded with perspiration, taking frequent sips from her bottle of water. A watery winter sun came out as they took the approach road to Heathrow. Victoria headed for the drop-off zone for Terminal 5. As Alistair unloaded their smart new cases from the boot, she turned to Helen. 'It's quite a walk from here I'm afraid. I'll say goodbye now.'

Helen grabbed her arm, swaying slightly. 'No, please don't go just yet. I need you. Look at Alistair rushing on. He's always going to be half a mile ahead of me.'

Victoria could see what she meant, he had already disappeared through the door marked Departures.

'Really? I shall have to park in a multi storey then.'

She reached for the buggy and unfolded it, then strapped in a protesting Grace.

'Take her and go and get in the check-in queue. I'll be as quick as I can.' Helen shook her head. 'No, I'll wait for you at that door over there.'

It seemed to take an age but eventually Victoria got back and surrounded by glass and steel, they joined a long snake of people pulling suitcases on wheels or pushing trolleys laden with baggage. When they reached Alistair he was almost at the front of the queue. He looked at his watch. Victoria tried to convey to him with her sternest glare, that he needed to show a little more compassion and patience. He either didn't understand or chose to ignore her. Their bags disappeared along the conveyor belt. Helen's heart sank – now there was no going back.

'Come on, we haven't got much time.' Alistair strode off and Helen called weakly after him,

'Wait a minute. I can't walk as fast as you.'

Alistair stopped and looked heavenwards.

'Please, Alistair.' Victoria stepped forward and put her arm round Helen's shoulders.

'What is it? Don't you feel very well?'

'It's everything.' She looked at Alistair for comfort. He was scanning the departures display boards. Oblivious to her distress he said, 'There's ours, we need to go through security now. Down here, I think,' and he set off again.

Victoria was beginning to wish that Alistair and Helen had done as he'd initially suggested and gone by train. She took Helen's arm. 'I'm sorry. It's my fault it's all such a rush. We should have started out much earlier. I didn't realise the M4 would be so busy.' She didn't add that both Helen and Alistair had also contributed to their delayed start. Helen bent over and retched. 'I feel sick.' Her face was tinged with green and her hair clung wetly in strands to her head.

'Are you a nervous flyer? Is that what's upsetting you?' Victoria looked around for something Helen could vomit into. Alistair was nowhere to be seen.

'Yes, I've always hated flying. It's so claustrophobic – sitting in a metal tube and unable to get out. I got some Valium from Dr Wright, but it hasn't kicked in yet. Look, can you just hold Grace while I nip to the loo? I'll splash some cold water on my face and possibly be sick as well.'

Victoria tried to reassure her. 'It'll be a huge plane with lots of space. It's not Ryanair.'

As Helen disappeared back down the concourse, looking for a Ladies, Victoria turned and ran to catch up with Alistair.

'For God's sake Alistair, will you stop dashing off? I'm really worried about Helen. I wasn't expecting her to be in such a state, and you're not helping at all.' She put both hands on his arm to hold him back. He shook her off impatiently.

'What? Oh, Helen. I'm sure she'll be fine once we're aboard – if we ever get that far. Where the hell is she now?'

Victoria scanned the multitude. 'Oh, I think I can see her coming. Thank goodness.'

But it wasn't her. The minutes ticked by. The queue for security grew shorter.

'Don't move an inch from here. I'll go and find her, hurry her up.' The baby was heavy, clinging painfully onto Victoria's hair as she tried to run through the crowds. She cursed her lack of forethought. She should have left Grace with him. People turned and looked at this wild woman, hair unpinned and flying loose, red faced and panting with a wailing child in her arms.

There were women of all colours and sizes in the Ladies, but no sign of Helen. The air was heavy with rank perfume and it was unbearably hot. Victoria felt nauseous. She put the baby down and bent over, her hands on her knees, trying to get her breath back.

The Tannoy boomed.

'This is an urgent message for Victoria Dunn. Will she please make her way to the British Airways Information desk? I repeat…'

Victoria straightened up. That was her! The British Airways desk. Where the hell was that? She picked up the baby again.

Fearing her legs were going to give way beneath her, she saw a sign pointing away into the distance. She set off again. She reached the desk and gasped,

'I'm Victoria Dunn. You put out a call for me? Is Helen here?' The woman behind the desk nodded curtly. She gestured Victoria to follow her into a side room where Helen sat, red eyed but perfectly composed.

'I'm sorry Victoria. I can't do it.' She thrust her hands in her pockets and crossed her legs as if to say she wasn't moving from her chair.

'I'm not going.'

'What do you mean you're not going?' Victoria was conscious of her voice sounding shrill. She couldn't take much more of this pair of idiots.

Helen repeated, 'I'm not going.'

Victoria glared at her. 'Dear God, Helen, you don't mean that.'

'Yes, I absolutely do.'

For a fleeting second Victoria wanted to have a three year old's tantrum. The urge to throw herself onto the floor kicking and screaming with frustration was overwhelming. She took a deep breath.

'No Helen. That's just the nerves talking. Take another Valium. Let's go and find Alistair. He's worried about you.' She mentally crossed her fingers. That was half the trouble. It was quite obvious he wasn't.

Helen shook her head. She was quite calm. She repeated, 'I'm not going.'

'Right. You'd better come back with me and tell Alistair that yourself then.'

This was becoming a nightmare. She thrust Helen's baby back into her arms and stood waiting. Was this really happening? Whatever, it wasn't her problem, let Alistair deal with it.

Alistair waiting, his face creased with annoyance, saw Helen stride towards him, Grace on her hip.

'For Christ's sake, Helen, what are you playing at?'

'I'm sorry but I'm not coming. You know I never wanted to. You all pushed me into it.'

Her voice was steady. He took a deep breath striving to stay calm.

'Oh, come on. This is just pre-flight nerves. You'll be fine once you're on the plane.' He reached for Grace. 'Come on.'

'You're not listening to me. You never did. I'm not coming. Give Grace a kiss goodbye.'

He stared at her, lost for words. She couldn't mean this. Helen turned away. He made a grab for Grace and held her close, covering her with kisses. Grace struggled to get free. She stretched her arms out to Helen, 'Mama.'

Should he take her with him? Then Helen would have to come.

'Give her to me.' It was not an option. He handed the baby back. He tried again.

'Don't do this Helen. You'll be fine once we're on our way. It's all arranged. Your baggage will already be on the plane for God's sake. Where will you live? What will you do for money?'

'I'll manage.'

What more could he say?

'Victoria, could you give us a minute?'

Victoria reached for Grace. 'Come on my lovely. Let's go and watch the aeroplanes.'

Alistair turned back to Helen. She braced herself.

'Now you listen to me. I finished it with Diana and found us a new life and a fresh start. We agreed to stay together for Grace's sake – if nothing else. Now you're throwing it all back in my face. Why, Helen - and why now of all the times to choose?'

Helen looked at him steadily. He didn't want her. All he needed was a mother for his daughter, a cook, cleaner and bottle washer. She felt the worm turn.

'Alistair, I don't think I love you anymore. These last two years have been, apart from having Grace, the unhappiest of my life. I've had enough. I'm not going to a strange country with you when you make me feel so insecure.'

It was like talking to a stranger. She called to Victoria, who hurried back towards them, looking anxiously from one to another.

'Will you take us home, please?'

Alistair stood helpless as Helen took her baby from Victoria and walked away. Grace's little face looked back from over her mother's shoulder, her eyes fixed on his face. She seemed puzzled and raised her hand. Was that a wave?

He returned to the queue which had been watching the exchange with interest. In a daze he went through security and wandered round the airside concourse. People scowled and muttered when he bumped into them unseeing. There was the bar, it was calling to him. Although he'd thought he was in control at last – of his life and his marriage – in truth Helen now held the whip hand. He ordered a double whisky and sank onto a seat. The table in front of him was sticky with the rings of drinks from others before him. He wondered if they were people like him, leaving everything they knew for another life and fearful they'd made a terrible mistake.

He made a sudden decision, downed his drink in one and pulled out his phone, stabbing out the familiar number.

'Diana? It's me. Listen my darling. I've got to be quick because I'm at Heathrow, but Helen's pulled out. She's not coming with me after all. We can be together now: you, me and Theo. I'm about to fly, but you can join me, as soon as we can arrange it. I'll send you the tickets.'

There was no answering gasp of surprise and delight.

'Diana. Are you there? Can you hear me? It's going to be OK after all.'

He heard a long intake of breath. She spoke.

'I'm sorry Alistair. I don't want to join you.'

'Oh come on, you don't mean that. I know it's a shock but it's all come good now...' His voice trailed off.

'No. I'm seeing somebody else. I'm sorry.'

'What?'

'Someone who hasn't already got a wife and child to prioritise over me. As I said, I'm sorry.'

Click. She had disconnected.

'Fuck!' He thrust the phone back in his pocket and slumped back in the chair.

How could she have met someone so quickly? Had she been two-timing him? He'd call her again when he'd settled in. By then she'd see that she'd overreacted. He shouldn't have dropped it on her like that. He cursed his impetuosity. He'd had another chance to fulfil his dream of a new life with the woman who made him happier than he'd been in years, and he'd blown it. His head dropped forward and he screwed his eyes shut to block out the pictures of her in his head laughing, tender - naked.

Diana looked at the phone in her hand. She really had loved him. He made her feel joyous and alive. But he'd made the wrong choice – to stay in a sexless marriage. It was the flaw in his character. He'd wanted to preserve the status quo whilst indulging himself on the side. Thoughts clamoured in her head. Was she being unfair? He'd rung her from the airport as soon as Helen backed out. His first thought had been for her. She'd been given a second chance. Why hadn't she leapt at it? Was she letting pride get in the way of their future together? She went and picked up her son. Alistair's dark eyes looked at her accusingly.

'I'm sorry, baby. I had to do it. I daren't take the risk.'

She put Theo down in his cot for a nap and went over to the window. In the sky a faraway aeroplane headed south leaving a jet trail. Seeking justification for what she'd done, she allowed anger to take hold.

Being second choice wasn't for her. It would have been better if she really had met someone else, but no matter. There'd be someone, someday. Someone who would put her first without a single thought – her and Theo. Her confidence grew with her righteous anger. And if he didn't materialise, then they'd be just fine on their own. She went into the little bedroom and sat by his cot. Was he too warm? His cheeks were flushed and his dark curls clung to his forehead.

What did the future hold for him? She didn't care if he grew up to be musical or not. She'd settle for a decent human being who didn't exploit his friends and betray those who loved him. Or was she being cruel? Alistair had been in an impossible position.

Theo stirred. 'Mummy?'

'Go back to sleep, darling, everything's going to be alright.'

His duvet with its racing car cover was pushed aside and the fishy mobile swung slightly in the breeze from the open window. Outside she could hear a dog barking. She pulled the duvet back across his little body and tiptoed out of the room.

The plane thundered down the runway, rose into the air and levelled out. Below him, Alistair could see everything he knew, everything he held dear, receding far below. Soon it was covered by cloud.

He undid his seat belt.

'Can I get you anything, Sir?' Her voice was soft and friendly. The love of his life would be nice. But he settled for a large whisky and soda.

He sensed that his emotional state on boarding had aroused some sort of maternal instinct in the air hostess, and he managed to put on his wry, injured smile, the one that caused his eyes to crinkle at the corners in a way that he'd found elicited instant sympathy.

'My name is Donna. I'll be looking after you on your flight.'

'Hello Donna. I'm Alistair. Thank you. I can see things are beginning to look up already.'

He watched her walk away from him down the aisle. She moved well. He reclined his seat a little and began to relax. It was out of his hands now. There was nothing he could do.

As the plane soared up way above the clouds heading south, he faced his future with the realisation that everything from his old life was behind him now. What was that unaccustomed feeling? Liberation? Freedom?

He began to feel vindicated. He recalled how a few months ago he had taken Helen to Dorset for a romantic weekend. He'd booked a room in a small hotel which boasted a four poster bed and even left her in the bar while he slipped upstairs to scatter rose petals across it.

But even then she'd insisted Grace slept between them, citing the fact it was an unfamiliar cot and the child wouldn't settle. It was hardly his fault, he told himself, that, dragged down by repeated rejection, he'd gone back to Diana.

Was it any wonder he'd got so involved with the choir as well? He'd compensated for the lack of attention from his wife, with the adoration of forty other women. One in particular.

His lips curved into a smile as he thought again of Diana. He only had to give it time. She'd come round eventually. They had something special. He'd tried to do the right thing by Helen, in spite of his doubts, and she had chosen not to accept. Right. Now he was free to follow his heart.

'Donna, another of your excellent whisky and sodas please, and maybe some cashews.'

64

Victoria drove without speaking until they joined a busy M4 for the journey back to Somerset.

Eventually she broke the silence.

'There'll be an awful lot to do when we get home. The first thing will be shopping for knickers and things to tide you over until you get your luggage back. I'll ring them about that. They'll have had to delay the departure to get it off the plane. At least it won't be winging its way to Johannesburg which is something to be grateful for. If I'd been thinking clearly we could have waited and picked it up ourselves. We should call the letting agent as well to cancel the deal and get you your house keys returned.'

She looked sideways at Helen. 'Are you alright?'

Helen was sitting upright and rigid, her face white, hugging herself with her folded arms. She slid a glance across at Victoria and nodded.

'I soon will be.'

'We'll need to get the boxes of stuff Alistair sent to storage back as well. I wonder if Christopher would give us a hand.' Victoria was worrying about the logistics of this drastic change of plan.

A white van suddenly pulled out in front of them. She swore and leaned on her horn.

'Idiot.'

The noise woke Grace, pinioned in her car seat behind them, and she began to wail. That was all Victoria needed. She cursed the day she ever got involved with Alistair and his floundering marriage. She would have to offer Helen a bed for a night or two while everything was sorted. Whoever would have expected this to happen? Was this Diana's chance?

They pulled into South Heath. Curtains twitched.

'It'll have to be fish and chips for tea. I'm too exhausted to cook. You feed that baby and I'll make up the spare bed. She'll have to come in with you.'

'I don't want anything to eat. Oh God, Victoria, I can't believe I've really done it.'

Helen flopped down into Victoria's comfiest chair. She wrapped her arms around herself and looked across at Victoria, who was prying Grace away from the log basket.

'I can't thank you enough for this.'

'What's done is done. I just hope you don't regret it.'

The next day Helen undid all the arrangements that had been made for her departure. She found her spare house keys. She wanted to go home. She strapped Grace into her buggy and set off down the village. Even though it had only been a couple of days, the house already looked neglected and unloved. Maybe it was just that the front lawn that needed mowing plus a reflection of her own mood.

She put the key into the lock, not forgetting to lift as she turned, it always had been sticky, and opened the door. The air was damp and cold inside and there was an indefinable smell. Grace started to cry. She should have left her with Victoria. What must the child be thinking? This was her home and yet it wasn't. Where were her toys and where was Daddy? Tomorrow the Man with a Van would be delivering the boxes from the storage place. For now all she could usefully do was wipe down the surfaces and put the heating on low. The life she had so nearly thrown away was coming back to her in cartons labelled kitchen, bedroom, bedding and books.

In the morning she begged Rachel to have Grace for a couple of hours and was at the house early. She mopped floors and opened a few windows to let some fresh air in. In her head Alistair complained that she was heating the village. Another

375

of his complaints she'd never hear again.

From the bedroom window she saw the van pull up outside.

'Didn't expect to be doing this so soon,' said the man, his eyes bright with curiosity. Helen ignored that and showed him where the boxes needed to go.

When he'd driven off, she suddenly felt very lonely. Get on with it girl, she told herself, you'll have it spick and span in no time.

She began by unpacking bedding and towels; made the bed, then reassembled Grace's cot which had been stored in the garage. A knock on the door revealed Victoria, bearing two cartons of coffee from the coffee shop. 'I didn't think you'd have any milk.'

'Thanks. Just what I need right now. I'm off to Waitrose when I've got a bit straighter here. Once the fridge is filled it'll feel more like home.'

She pushed her trolley up and down the aisles. It was the supermarket where she'd bumped into Rachel all those months ago, after she'd told Alistair to leave until he'd sorted himself out. Well, he'd certainly done that now, hadn't he? Good luck to him. She'd been strong and chosen the life she wanted. She speeded up. She couldn't wait to get home.

In no time, tins, jars and packets were placed on their shelves with their labels facing outwards and her best saucepans were hung on the rack in strict order of size. She toyed with the idea of lining up the herbs and spices alphabetically, but decided that was a job for another day.

So far, she had not felt the slightest twinge of regret for what she had done. There was a real joy in placing everything exactly where she wanted it, which included banishing the boxes containing Alistair's books, pictures and musical equipment to the garage. She determined to find some work, maybe even have a lodger. She'd get by. He'd have to set up some maintenance payments. It was all his fault after all.

Without the shadow of Diana hanging over her, she was

happier than she had been for a long time, and she picked up her phone to order an extravagant bunch of flowers to be delivered to Victoria, her unlikely saviour.

65

Victoria was thinking about Diana. Since the poor girl had fled on hearing that Helen was going to South Africa after all, Victoria had managed to keep in touch. They'd bonded somehow despite the age difference, and Victoria didn't want her to make the same mistakes that she had all those years ago. Also she had news of her own. News that she didn't want to share just yet with Helen or Rachel.

Diana's new home was nearer than the previous flat and it wasn't long before she opened the door, a smiling Theo on her hip. He loved his Auntie Victoria, who always came with a little treat for him concealed in her pocket. He held out his arms to her. She took him from Diana, who turned towards the kitchen. 'Tea, coffee or something stronger?'

'I've driven, so it had better be coffee please.'

She settled herself on the sofa and gave Theo his sugar mouse. She called through to the kitchen,

'Every time I come this place looks more and more homely. I love all those house plants. You'll have to tell me your secret.'

'Thank you. Until the day when I have a garden of my own instead of a small yard, I make do with these.' Diana came back in with the coffee and the biscuit tin and sat down.

'You said you had some news for me.'

Victoria went pink. 'It will probably come to nothing, but I'd like to share it with someone, who won't think I'm being silly.'

'Silly is the last thing I'd accuse you of being. But I have something to tell you too.' She dipped her custard cream in her coffee and said, 'Who's going first?'

Victoria put Theo down on the floor. 'You go first. As I said, mine is something and nothing.'

Diana cupped her hands around her mug. 'I haven't told you this, but Alistair rang me from Heathrow and said that Helen had refused to board the plane at the last minute.'

Victoria nodded. 'I know that. I was there. I took them – more fool me. The whole thing was dreadful. But I didn't know he'd rung you.'

'Well, he did. He said that Helen had just pulled out and now we could be together. He wanted me to fly out with Theo as soon as I could. He said he'd send the tickets.'

'Did he indeed? He didn't waste any time. What did you say to him?'

'I told him to get lost, basically. I lied and said I'd met someone else and anyway I wasn't prepared to be his stand-in love interest.'

'Oh Diana! You didn't. And now, are you regretting it?'

Diana went to pick up Theo who was starting to grizzle. She retrieved the half gnawed sugar mouse from where he'd dropped it and turned back to Victoria.

'I lie in bed every night wondering if I did the right thing. Was it just hurt pride?'

'And, what conclusion have you come to?'

'I haven't, yet. That's why I'm telling you. You're a wise old bird. What do you think I should have done?'

'Well, after the 'wise old bird' crack, I might just shut up.'

Diana's face crumpled.

'Oh, don't be silly. I was only joking. Is there any more coffee?' 'Diana sniffed and rubbed her eyes. 'Yes, of course. I'm sorry. I'm not handling this very well.'

She picked up Victoria's mug and took it into the kitchen.

Victoria got up and went over to the window. Rows and rows of terraced houses stretched into the distance. The little yard contained nothing but a wheelie bin and a washing line. She could hear the muffled roar of traffic from the main road. Not an ideal place to bring up a child, unless you had no other option. But Diana did have an option.

When she came back with the coffee, Victoria asked, 'How's the new job?'

Diana pulled a face. 'I've had worse.'

'And Theo, has he settled at the nursery?'

'As far as I can tell. But it's very expensive. Hardly worth it for what I'm earning.'

Victoria cradled her mug in her hands.

'OK. I'm going to be practical here. There are two paths ahead of you. One leads to a life on your own, struggling for money in a less than salubrious area. The other leads to the chance of a new life, with the man you love, in the sunshine. Since you've asked me, I have to say it's a no-brainer.'

Diana stared at her. 'But I wasn't his first choice.'

'No, you weren't. But only because he was trying to do the right thing by the woman he'd married. I've known Alistair a lot longer than you and I know he's been struggling for months – torn between his genuine love for you and the pull of morality and respectability. Don't forget the very reason he looked for jobs abroad in the first place was so you could be together and make a fresh start. Remember it was Helen who scuppered that plan.'

'Sometimes I think you'd like to have gone with him yourself.' Diana had intended it as a throwaway remark, but the silence with which it was greeted caused her to turn around and look at Victoria who was still at the window.

Victoria ignored that and turned her back on the shabby view. Her relationship with Alistair was not up for discussion. She regarded Diana steadily.

'Helen has bravely decided to stay, and I admire her for that. It wasn't easy for her. I know it isn't easy for you either. It's a risk. But, in my experience, if you can find a man, who understands and adores you, who makes you laugh and delights you in bed, you've got the best chance of happiness you could have.'

She stood up to go.

'I hope I haven't overstepped the mark. You asked me what I thought, but I've a feeling you don't like what I've said. I've had some experience of missing opportunities due to lack of courage to make the leap.' She picked up her bag and took out her car keys.

'I've got things to do now that won't wait. It's not long 'till the wedding. If you need to talk some more, give me a ring.'

She kissed Diana warmly on both cheeks and left, hoping she hadn't left her in even greater confusion than before.

On the way home she remembered her intention to tell Diana about meeting Simon again. But, in the face of Diana's dilemma, to discuss her own fledgling relationship, based solely on memories from long ago, felt somehow inappropriate.

That night sleep eluded her. How much notice would Diana take of what she'd said? She was no relationship expert. If she examined Diana's options, whilst leaving aside her own romantic notions of soul mates and destinies, she could see other scenarios unfolding which she'd hadn't even considered.

One thing she did know though, Alistair was never going to be alone for long, wherever he was living. The wavy black hair, the laughing eyes, the sexual magnetism and the music. He was a performer. There'd be no shortage of women up for such an enjoyable challenge. But he wasn't faithful or honest – with himself or those he purported to love. And he'd left behind two fatherless children.

Of course Diana could do better. Indeed, she deserved better. Someone less selfish, less conceited. She was intelligent and pretty, some nice man was bound to come along soon. Should she go back and tell her so? She mentally checked herself. She was doing it again. Interfering as well as giving conflicting advice. What did she know?

In the gap between the curtains she could see dawn was breaking. She got up and made a pot of strong coffee. She would drink it, then go for a long walk. By the time she got back she had decided that enough was enough. Her part in that drama was over. She had her own drama to concentrate on now.

66

The wedding was every bit as off- beat and low key as Rachel had wished. Fewer than thirty guests gathered on a chilly Saturday in March.

An emissary from the choir had called round to see her.

'Some of us want to wear hats. Others say you want an informal wedding. Can we have from the horse's mouth? Oh, sorry, that sounds rude.'

'Wear whatever you like. I just want everyone to feel happy and comfortable.'

Victoria stood in the church yard, amongst the grave stones, waiting for the bride to arrive. She had a sudden vision of all those skeletons lying there, their teeth clacking obscenely as they mocked yet another foolish woman imagining she was walking towards eternal happiness.

'Stop it,' she chided herself. Today was a day for optimism and positivity.

She admired the swathes of yellow daffodils in the church yard around, providing a boost to the pale spring sunshine. She knew Rachel would love them as much as she did. Inside, there were many, many more, as she'd spent the evening before with Helen filling vases and tying little nosegays on the ends of the pews.

Christopher came up behind her.

'Come on, best woman. Let's go in and do the deed. Take my arm.' They went into the church together and walked up the aisle to the front pew and sat down. Christopher seemed calm and composed.

She waved at Simon who was chivvying his choir into their places, then turned back to Christopher.

'Nervous? You certainly don't appear to be.'

'Yes, horribly nervous. Have you got the ring?'

'What ring?'

She was instantly sorry to have teased him. The ring, an intricately plaited circlet of Welsh gold, was safe in her pocket. She closed her fingers around it and made a wish.

The choir looked wonderful as they sang Irish Blessings to the waiting congregation. No hats. Victoria thought how nice it was to see the women in colourful outfits. Rachel had asked Simon if they could ditch the funereal black and he was happy to concur. She envied them. Their view from the choir stalls, of the couple as they made their vows would be perfect, and she'd have liked to sing. They'd sung at funerals before but never a wedding and this was certainly rather a special one. She'd floated the idea to Christopher that she might leave his side to sing with the others.

'I'll need your calming presence, Victoria, please don't desert me.'

A whisper ran round the church. 'She's here.'

The organ thundered out and Wagner's Bridal Chorus rang forth, thrillingly dramatic, and the congregation stood, turning to see the bride.

Nathan blushed and grinned sideways at his brother as he processed up the aisle with Rachel on his arm. Everyone smiled when Grace broke free from Helen's grip and toddled down to the bride for a hug.

Rachel glowed with timeless elegance in her Dior gown and, at the back of the church, an elderly dressmaker nodded with satisfaction.

Christopher watched his bride-to-be approach, his face radiating love and affection.

Victoria enjoyed the peerless language of the marriage service and felt her customary frisson of fear at the 'any just cause or impediment why these two should not be joined together in holy matrimony' bit. She thought the vicar extended his pause unnecessarily.

She produced the ring without dropping it and it slid easily onto Rachel's finger. Now she could relax. There was nothing else to go wrong unless the choir's final contribution, while the register was being signed, came adrift. Simon looked across at her and they smiled at each other. The organ began the melodious introduction and Jesu, Joy of Man's Desiring echoed faultlessly around the old church.

As she emerged following the newly-weds, out of the stone porch into the sunlight, she saw a group of villagers gathered at the church gate to look at Rachel's dress, about which there had been so much speculation. She watched as a few photographs were taken and then Christopher and Rachel left for the Royal Oak, where the wedding breakfast awaited.

She grabbed Helen's arm. 'I don't know about you, but I need a large glass of wine. I wasn't expecting to feel so nervous in there. I had nightmares about dropping the ring and it rolling away and disappearing down a grating into the crypt. Oh look, you've got a damp tissue in your hand as well. Aren't we silly? Come on, let's beat the rush.'

The village pub was warm and welcoming. The new husband and wife stood by the log fire holding hands.

Victoria had heard with some relief that although Marcus had been invited, he had declined, pleading a previous commitment.

She saw Simon across the room. He raised his glass to her and winked. She'd thought long and hard since meeting him again. Life had brought her courage, and this time she would dance to his rhythm, but of her own volition and free from outside interference.

67

In Capetown Alistair stared at his phone in disbelief. She wasn't coming – her final decision. He couldn't believe it. Dumped by text – as if he was sixteen.

How could things have gone so very wrong for him? He threw the phone down on the bed. As he showered and shaved, his anger grew. Diana was borderline bonkers anyway. And Helen was a neurotic prude who only needed a Dyson and a duster to keep her happy. He pitied his children, stuck with those two, without him to lighten their lives. He would find a kindred spirit, someone lithe and tanned and uninhibited, a thousand miles away from British hang ups and colluding gossips.

He hadn't time to dwell on it now. He didn't want to be late for the first practice of his new choir. Anxious to make a good impression in the first few weeks of term, he'd told one or two people of his previous successes. They had begged him to set up an informal group of singers comprised of staff and parents. Flattered by their admiration and excited by their enthusiasm, he'd gone ahead and recruited thirty or so people, eager to perform.

He strode into the hall. The doors at either end were open and a warm breeze rolled through the room. There was a hum of conversation which died away as he walked up to the music stand in front of them all and gripped it with both hands. His eyes ranged across the rows. Most were smiling at him. In the altos, he saw a blonde woman lean back in her seat and cross her legs. She pushed back a lock of blonde hair and eyed him speculatively. He looked away and took a deep breath.

'Good evening everyone. Thank you all for coming. I look

forward to getting to know you all. But first, let's see what you are made of. Can I have a C major chord please?'

The End

Acknowledgements

Thank you to those of my family and friends who offered supportive friendship, editorial insight and good humoured encouragement while I was writing this book.

Especially Tom Davies, Jane Dunn, Kate Seymour, Penni Ravenhill, Nic Robinson, John Hill, Val Shelton, Shirley Mann and Judith Baron.

Also to Alex Davies and the members of the Creative Writing group at Derby Quad for constructive feedback and helpful discussions.

Stephanie Hill is a writer and an artist. She lives in Melbourne, Derbyshire where, eight years ago she founded a community choir. She has written for magazines and newspapers but this is her first novel. Prior to retirement she had a career in teaching and latterly was the Literacy co-ordinator in a team working with children who had special educational needs.

20584724R00219

Printed in Poland
by Amazon Fulfillment
Poland Sp. z o.o., Wrocław